PAYOFF PITCH

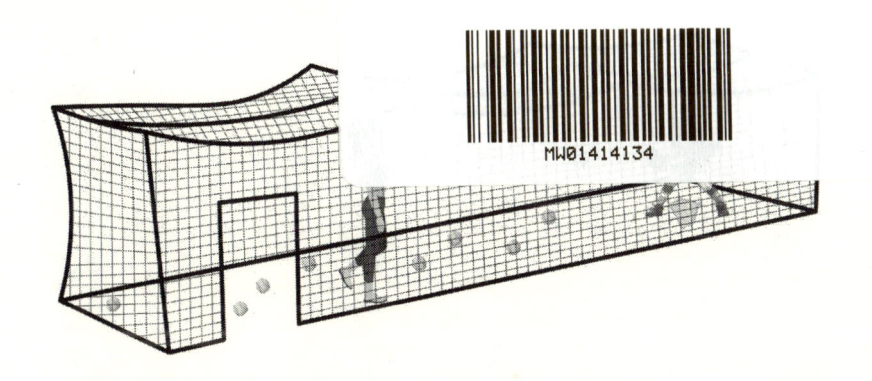

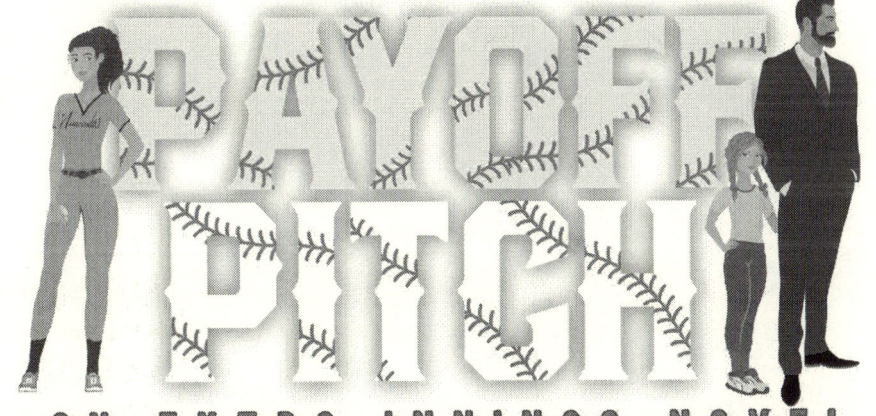

AN EXTRA INNINGS NOVEL

AK LANDOW AUTHOR

PAYOFF PITCH: An Extra Innings Novel

Copyright © 2025 by AK Landow

All rights reserved.

No part of this book may be reproduced in any form or by any electronic or mechanical means, including information storage and retrieval systems, without written permission from the author, except for the use of brief quotations in a book review.

Published by Author AK Landow, LLC

ISBN: 978-1-962575-22-5

Edited and Proofread By: Chrisandra's Corrections

Cover Design & Illustration By: K.B. Designs

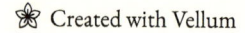

❀ Created with Vellum

DEDICATION

*To those with a daddy fetish. You're seen. You're heard. You're loved.
You're a good girl.*

*"A woman is like a tea bag; you never know how strong she
is until she's in hot water."
— Eleanor Roosevelt*

BASEBALL/SOFTBALL GLOSSARY

WORD/PHRASE	DEFINITION
The Slot	Throwing at a lower arm angle allowing for quicker release
Free Ride	When the pitcher walks the batter
Bang-Bang Play	A play hard to determine the outcome with the naked eye
Sacrifice Bunt	Deliberately bunting the ball, before 2 outs, to advance baserunner
Bases Loaded	Offensive players on first, second, & third bases all at once
The Zone	Area of space the pitch must pass to be considered a strike
Pinch the Middle	The shortstop & second baseman playing toward second base
Beat it Out	To reach a base slightly ahead of the fielded ball thrown to that baseman
Gassed	Nothing left in the tank. When a pitcher is spent.
Playing Shallow	A fielder playing closer to home plate than is normal for that position

payoff pitch

[pā-ôf pich] • noun

This is the name of the pitch that occurs when there is a full count on the batter. The next pitch will either "payoff" for the hitter (hit or walk) or the pitcher (strikeout or fielding out). Also known as the ultimate decision maker.

PROLOGUE

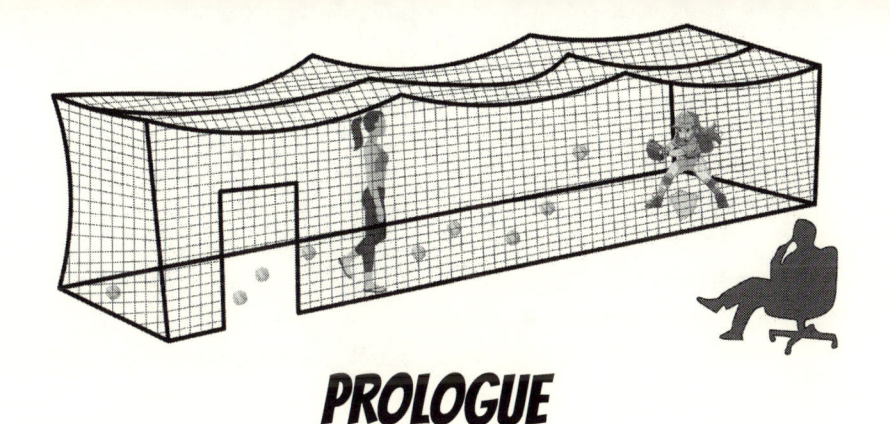

TANNER

"Are you having fun at Dylan's house, bug?"

I hear her sigh through the phone. My daughter is only eight years old, and the attitude has already begun. "Yes, Dad. I've slept here a million times before. Don't worry."

"Humor me, Harper. Whether you're eight or eighty, I will always worry about you."

Another sigh. When did this start?

"We just had dinner. We're in the playroom. Her mommy and daddy are sitting by the fireplace with drinks." Then she adds in a whisper, "They're very cuddly."

I smirk. Cassandra and Trevor Knight are certainly not shy about their love. She's much older than him and they simply don't care. I wish I had half of their gusto.

I hate that my daughter sees a cuddly couple as abnormal. This is where I've damaged her.

"Please thank them for me. I'll pick you up at about nine in the morning."

"No, Dad, tomorrow starts my time with Mom. She's picking me up."

My face falls as I realize she's right. We've been divorced for well over five years, and I still struggle with the fact that I only have Harper half the time.

I rub my dark beard, one that is a little grayer than it used to be. "Oh, right. Have fun with Mommy."

"Thanks. Does Arizona look pretty? She's probably the prettiest bride ever."

"The ceremony hasn't started yet. I haven't seen her, but I'm sure she does." She's a gorgeous woman.

"Does Bailey look pretty?"

"She's a bridesmaid. I haven't seen her yet either." She undoubtedly looks exquisite. No woman is more beautiful or sexier than Bailey Hart. Unfortunately for me, she's fifteen years my junior and is my daughter's nanny. Well, she's actually a professional softball player, but in the off-season, and during the season when her schedule permits, she doubles as our nanny.

"Okay, Dad. I gotta go. Tell Uncle Layton that I said congratulations."

"I will. Love you, bug."

She grits out, "Don't call me that. It's embarrassing. I'm not a baby anymore."

"Love you, Harper Jayne Montgomery."

"Love you too, Dad."

I mimic her sass. "Don't call me that."

"Love you too, *Daddy*."

I smile as I end the call and slip back into the groom's dressing room. Calling Layton the groom is a bit of a stretch since they've been married for roughly ten months, but they did so quickly and secretly without any friends or family around. They're finally having their big day in front of all of us today.

Layton is a retired professional baseball player, and

Arizona is a professional softball player. I'm both of their agents. Her season just ended, so they can finally celebrate their union. I'm a groomsman who's had a front-row view to witness their incredible love story. What began as a PR stunt blossomed into something truly special.

I smile as I watch the rest of Layton's groom's party huddled around him doing shots. It's comprised of Layton's foster brother, Henry, his former teammates, Cruz "Cheetah" Gonzales, Trey DePaul, Ezra Decker, and Quincy Abbott. Quincy is Arizona's brother and Layton's best man.

Cheetah smiles. "Lancaster, are you sure you want to do this? When you say *I do*, it will be the last decision you ever get to make for the rest of your life."

I chuckle but otherwise keep my mouth shut. I know nothing about marriage. Mine was an epic failure.

Trey places his hand on Layton's shoulder. "Don't listen to him. He doesn't know his ass from his head. When you find the right woman, it's the greatest ride of your life. Marrying Gemma is the best decision I've ever made."

I know he means that. Trey and Gemma have a perfect marriage. I'm equal parts happy for him and envious of what they share. The same goes for Layton and Arizona. They're the real deal too. Madly in love.

Cheetah shrugs as he slaps Trey's back. "It's the greatest ride because you married a smart woman with a smokin' body who writes about sex and asks you to act out the scenes. She's a unicorn."

Gemma DePaul is an attorney by day and romance author by night. She's all the things Cheetah mentioned.

Trey smiles with pride while Cheetah refills the shot glasses and encourages everyone to hold theirs in the air. "Lancaster, you found a unicorn too. May all your ups and downs only occur in the bedroom."

Everyone laughs and clinks glasses except Quincy, who

simply shakes his head and grumbles, "Can we please not talk about my sister in the bedroom?"

Cheetah winks. He and Layton both say things like that in front of Quincy all the time just to mess with him.

After one last round of shots, it's showtime.

The music starts playing and the planner is gradually connecting each of us with our bridesmaid counterpart to walk down the aisle. That's when Bailey comes into view for the first time tonight. She's in a tight royal-blue strapless dress. It's ankle length with a slit up the side, showing a hint of her long, toned legs. The same ones that were wrapped around my face just a few days ago.

Her normally straight hair is wavy and pinned back on one side. Her makeup is professionally done. She's a vision.

As we come together and I offer her my arm, I whisper, "You're beautiful."

A shy smile finds her lips as she looks me up and down and takes my arm. "You're not so bad yourself."

"You're coming home with me tonight so I can tear that dress off you."

"What about—"

"She's sleeping out."

We walk down the aisle. I couldn't even tell you what music is playing. I'm completely besotted with the woman on my arm.

We watch on as Layton and Arizona tearfully vow to love each other forever. I did that once. Fallon and I promised forever. It turns out that forever was a little over four years. At least we produced Harper. That's the only silver lining.

I stare at Bailey, who's crying tears of joy as the vows are read. Could I ever do this again? If I did, it would be for Bailey. I told her we could only be casual, and she accepted that. She's so much younger than me. She doesn't even turn thirty until next year. She's got too much life to live. I don't want to hold her back, but I can't seem to let her go. I don't think I want to.

Layton just recited his vows. His sentence, "You're everything I never knew I always needed," resonates as I continue to stare at the beautiful brunette on the other side of the aisle.

The officiant eventually announces, "You may kiss the bride."

Layton dips Arizona and kisses her in a manner that I'm happy Harper isn't here to witness. Cheetah shouts, "Save it for tonight, big guy."

Layton stands upright as he and Arizona smile blissfully into each other's mouths. I love seeing my friend so happy. He's had a hard life and deserves this.

"May I present Mr. and Mrs. Layton and Arizona Lancaster."

Layton holds their joined hands in the air as a sea of applause erupts, and they work their way back up the aisle.

The reception immediately kicks into high gear with the music blaring and bodies on the dance floor. I watch from the wings as Bailey happily dances with her friends—Arizona, Ripley, and Gemma—as well as her twin sister, Kamryn. All of them except Gemma play on the professional softball team the Philly Anacondas.

Bailey and Kamryn are considered identical twins with their long dark hair, big chocolate-brown eyes, and stunning figures, but the two couldn't be more different. Kamryn is brash and promiscuous. Bailey is neither of those things. She's shy and introspective. She's classy and kind, without a bad bone in her body. In other words, she's perfect. Too perfect.

The faster song ends, and a slow one begins. All the couples pair off, leaving Bailey alone. She's close friends with Ezra. I know he'll rescue her, but I can't stomach the thought of his hands on her gorgeous body, one I've spent hours worshiping.

I see him step toward her but then stop when he sees me doing the same. Despite his best efforts, he knows she prefers me to him.

I approach her from behind and run my hand down her arm. Goosebumps immediately erupt on her soft skin.

She turns in my arms and smiles. "People will talk."

"What people? No one else is here."

She pinches her eyebrows together. It's unusual for me to talk like this to her.

I grab her waist and pull her body to mine. She happily wraps her arms around my neck, leans her body into mine, and we move to the sultry beat of the music.

I bend and kiss her neck.

"What's gotten into you tonight?"

"It's me who will be getting into you. In fact, let's get out of here and start that process now."

She giggles. "I'm not leaving. It's too early. She's one of my best friends."

"And what am I?"

"My fuck buddy." She painfully uses my words against me. "You're supposed to be my *secret* fuck buddy, but you're not doing a good job of hiding it tonight."

"Half the people here know anyway."

"And the other half?"

"I don't care."

She pulls her head back and gives me a questioning look. I can't blame her. I've given her mixed signals since the day I met her over a year ago.

A FEW HOURS LATER, the bride and groom finally wave goodbye to leave for their honeymoon on the other side of the world. I grab Bailey's hand. "Let's get out of here."

She pulls away. "Seriously, what's gotten into you tonight? You're acting weird. Have you been drinking?" She gives me an accusatory look.

"Not in hours. I'm just anxious to get you alone. It's been a while. Is it so terrible that I miss you?"

She gives me an incredulous look. "It's been four days."

I look around. Not seeing anyone, I grab her face and smash my lips to hers. She yelps at first, until my tongue slips into her mouth. Giving in, she relaxes her body. Her tongue meets mine before sweeping through my mouth. I love her sweet taste.

A noise causes us to pull apart. Her chest rises and falls rapidly as she breathes, "Okay, let's go. Now."

I take in her appearance. Her hair is messy from my hands, and her sensual lips are swollen from our kiss. Her face is a bit red from my beard. So beautiful.

As if on cue, she licks those full lips. I imagine them wrapped around my cock. There's nothing better than those lips wrapped around me with her innocent eyes staring up at me.

She notices my line of sight and narrows her eyes at me. "You're thinking about me sucking your duck, aren't you?"

Yes, she calls it a duck, not a dick, because she's trained herself not to curse in front of Harper. She has substitute words for every dirty word in the dictionary.

I chuckle. "Why do you know that?"

"Because you're a filthy man, *Mr. Montgomery*."

Her calling me that has my half chub growing to full chub.

Her eyes find my pants and one of her eyebrows raises. "Told ya so. Let's get out of here. I'll see what I can do for you, *Mr. Montgomery*."

I close my eyes, willing myself to not pull her into a closet, lift that sexy dress, and fuck her right here. I have to remove my jacket and drape it in front of me to cover the bulge in my pants.

A few minutes later, the valet pulls around in my brand-new Maserati MC20. He's got a big shit-eating grin on his face as he exits the vehicle. "I kept her in a special place, sir, just like you asked. I've never been in a nicer car. This baby must have set you back a pretty penny."

Yep, about a quarter of a million dollars.

I nod as I hand him a hundred-dollar bill. "Thanks for taking care of her."

He smiles in gratitude before his eyes find Bailey and take every inch of her in. If I thought he was drooling over the car a moment ago, it doesn't compare to what he's doing while staring at my girl. I think the saliva is dripping from his mouth.

I clear my throat. He snaps his head to me, and I give him a nasty look.

He realizes what he's done, drops his head, and mumbles, "Sorry," as he walks away.

Bailey rolls her eyes as I open the passenger door for her. "Was that necessary?"

"Yes, it was. I didn't like the way he was looking at you."

"And how was that?"

"Like he wants to fuck you."

She smiles playfully. "You look at me like that all the time."

"And I want to fuck you all the time."

She laughs as I close the door, walk around to the driver's side, get in, set the car in gear, and peel out of there. She leans back and closes her eyes. "Hmm. I love this car. It's such a turn-on."

"I thought the wetness I smell pooling between your legs was because of me, not my car."

She squirms a bit. "Nope. It's the car that does it for me. It's brand new. You're old," she jokes.

I reach over to tickle her side, and she giggles. I love that sound.

"You're not being very nice to me, sweet girl."

Her eyes meet mine. "Maybe I don't feel like being so sweet tonight."

She's had a few drinks, but not so many that she's drunk. This is unusually aggressive for her though.

She reaches over and runs her hand up my thigh before rubbing it over my straining cock. After unbuckling her seatbelt, she leans over and kisses my dick through my pants. Just feeling her hot breath on me makes it leak.

Before I realize what's happening, she unzips my pants, reaches in, and pulls out my cock. "W...what are you doing?"

"My filthy man said he wants his duck sucked." She strokes me a few times and then licks across my tip. "I'm here to service you, *Mr. Montgomery*."

While doing this in a car is a little crazy, I'm still a red-blooded man. I'm not looking a gift horse in the mouth.

She takes her time licking around the bulging head of my cock. The slow seduction is everything. It takes every ounce of willpower I have to not close my eyes and to fully give myself over to the ecstasy.

She sucks the tip past her lips and into the warm, wet confines of her mouth. I lean my head back. "Oh fuck."

I have one hand on the wheel, and I gather her hair to watch the show with the other. I'm trying to keep one eye on the road and one on her as she bobs up and down on me.

She lets out a series of moans around me as I hit the back of her throat with every methodical, meaningful pass. I love the way she sucks my dick. It's never rushed, like she's just doing it to achieve the end result. She savors it and, in turn, helps me to savor it.

The car swerves a little before I straighten it out. Oh shit. Keep your eyes on the road, Montgomery, not on the sexy piece of ass with her lips wrapped around you.

Given that I've been hard for her all night, it doesn't take long for that tingling sensation to shoot down my back and straight to my balls.

She clearly senses it and hastens the pace of her mouth on me. "I'm going to come in your hot little mouth, sweet girl."

She increases the suction, and my vision temporarily blackens as I come long and hard down her throat.

After swallowing every last drop, she tucks me in and lifts her head. I turn to smile at her when she screams, "Watch out!"

My eyes take in the car stopped in front of me, but I'm going too fast. I'm going to hit it if I don't do something. I slam on the brakes and swerve to avoid the car, but we're headed toward a pole. I hold out my arm to attempt to protect Bailey against the inevitable crash.

I hear a crunch, and she's thrown forward, not having her seatbelt on. I hold her as best I can, but there's only so much I can do.

I think I must black out for a few seconds because I blink my eyes open to the sounds of sirens. I turn to Bailey who's unconscious and slumped over.

I immediately remove my seatbelt and reach for her. "Bailey, baby, are you okay? Wake up."

Nothing.

I lift her face and hold it in my hands. I'm frantic. "Wake up. Oh god. Please wake up."

Pulling her lifeless body onto my lap, I continue to gently shake her. Eventually, her eyes blink a few times. She breathes, "What happened?"

I quickly scan her body with my hands and eyes. I don't see any blood. "We crashed. Are you okay?"

Still lifeless, she croaks out, "My head hurts, but I think I'm okay." As if realizing why we crashed, she sucks in a breath and tears find her eyes. "I'm so sorry, Tanner. This is my fault."

I hold her close to me. "No, it's not."

"Oh god, your new car."

"I don't care about the car. Just you. Are you sure you're okay?"

Before she can answer, a police officer knocks on the window. "Sir, is anyone hurt?"

I lower the window. "I'm not sure. I think she hit her head. She needs to go to the hospital to get checked out."

"Okay. Stay where you are. An ambulance will be here in a few minutes."

I nod.

"How did this happen?"

I can't help the small smirk as I look at Bailey and whisper, "Do you want to show him?"

She narrows her eyes at me.

I chuckle as I look back at the officer. "I swerved to avoid a car, but I couldn't manage to avoid this pole." I motion toward the pole now sitting in the engine of my car.

He nods in understanding. "Can you turn off the ignition, sir? The car is still running and it's likely unsafe."

"Let me try."

Despite my efforts, I can't reach it because of the damage to the car and Bailey cradled in my lap.

I look at her. "Can you reach it?"

She nods as she attempts to shift her body, but her eyes quickly widen in horror.

I look at her with concern. "What's wrong? Are you hurt?"

"Tanner, I...I can't feel my legs."

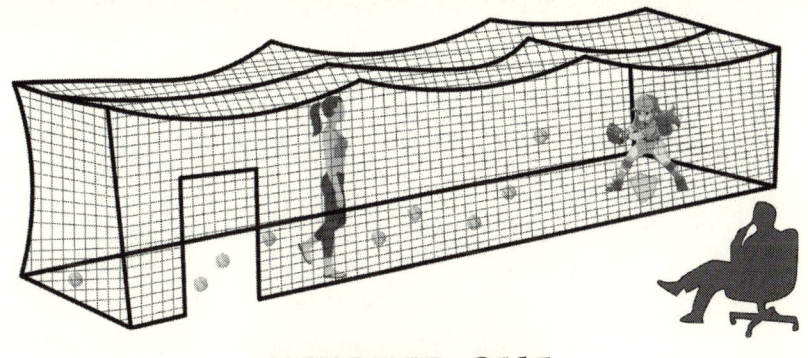

CHAPTER ONE

SIXTEEN MONTHS AGO

BAILEY

"Ma'am, for the last time, please sit down. We can't take off unless you're in your seat and buckled up."

I give the flight attendant an apologetic smile. "Sorry, my sister is a nervous flyer. She likes to pace before takeoff. I'll make sure she's seated and fastened in right away."

I pull Kam's arm, and she plops down next to me sighing. "Cheez, who lit the fuse on her tampon string?"

The flight attendant pretends not to hear her even though Kam purposefully said it loud enough for anyone within ten rows to hear.

I buckle her seatbelt for her and then tighten it as though she's a small child. "They can't push away from the gate until everyone has their seatbelt on. We've been through this a thousand times before."

She leans her head back and blows out a breath. "I guess. Fuck, I hate flying."

I take her hand, as I have on every single flight we've been on in our twenty-eight years. "I've got you. Don't worry."

She narrows her eyes at me. "If we go barreling down toward the earth from forty thousand feet, will you have me then?"

I smirk. "You jump, I jump."

She intertwines her fingers through mine and nods, silently acknowledging our often-used *Titanic* reference. "Always. Love you, big sis."

I lean over and kiss her head. "Love you too, little sis."

We both smile at our big and little sis comments. I'm only nine minutes older than my twin, but it might as well be nine years. I'm the mature, sensible sister, while she's the playful, fun sister. People gravitate toward her. She's larger than life, while I happily remain in the background.

I know her well enough to realize I need to distract her through takeoff. After that, she'll be fine.

I ask, "Do you swear you didn't put pressure on the Anacondas to sign me too?"

My sister refuses to go anywhere or do anything without me. I was a star basketball player, considering playing in college, while she shined at softball. I was fine with that dynamic until she begged and pleaded with me to start playing softball in high school so we could be on the same team. She was one of the best players in the country and almost every top college wanted her. She wouldn't consider offers unless they offered me a softball scholarship too. That's how we ended up at UCLA. She was the shortstop, and I was the second baseman. Always side by side, even in softball.

After college, she was the third overall pick in the professional softball draft. She made it clear to the team that she wouldn't sign a contract with them unless they picked me as well. In fairness, I've turned into a damn good softball player in my own right and deserved to be drafted, but I wasn't sure I wanted to continue playing ball. I enjoy working with kids. I always saw myself as a teacher or something along those lines. But my sister needed me, so I've been playing professional softball with her for the past six years for a team out of Chicago.

Our contracts expired last month. The team was happily ready to re-sign us both when a new team formed in Philadelphia, the Philly Anacondas. Their first order of business was to sign our close college friend, teammate, and catcher, Arizona Abbott, who was playing for a team in Southern California. Their second order of business was to sign our close college friend, teammate, and pitcher, Ripley St. James, who was playing for a team in Houston, Texas. Then they called my sister, Kamryn. She claims they wanted both of us, not just her, but I'm not convinced. Regardless, they're paying us both double the salaries we were earning in Chicago, and it's a chance to be reunited with our friends. The Olympics are four years away, and they want to train together. The three of them have been talking about the Olympics since the first day we met them at freshman-year orientation. It's not my dream, it's theirs. I've just been going along for the ride.

Kam rolls her eyes at me. "No, they want both of us. Stop being insecure. It's a lot of money and we get to be reunited with Arizona and Ripley. It will be like college all over again."

I mumble, "I hope you sleep with fewer people than you did in college."

Sharing a dorm room with her has forever scarred me.

She gives me her special Kam smile. "You're only young once, Bails. I don't want to have any regrets. Would you rather I be like our mother?"

I scrunch my nose. "Ugh. No."

Our parents started dating in high school. Our father was a star basketball player who was recruited to play in college. She followed him there like a groupie and then became pregnant with us during their senior year. He had to give up playing to get married and get a job. They don't have a marriage that either of us envy. Just the opposite. The fact that we're twenty-eight and unmarried is a sore spot for our mother, who we do our best never to see. We only talk to him, not her, on the phone. Our only contact with her over the past ten years has been when she walks in on a FaceTime call with him and grumbles about our life choices.

She modeled before she had us and then channeled all her missed aspirations onto us by forcing us to model and act for years. She spiraled after we quit. We don't know why our father stays with her. She's a complete disaster. I don't share the same disdain for her that Kam has, but unfortunately, we have no relationship with her.

Kam nods and gives me a knowing look. "Exactly. A fresh start will be good for you too."

I can't deny that. I was dating a man a few years older than me who I recently discovered had a fiancée. I broke things off as soon as I found out, but he kept showing up at our apartment, begging me to take him back. To the point where Kam called the police to get him to back off. Kam also paid his fiancée a visit. She said it was our obligation under the parameters of girl code to let that woman know who she was going to marry. Kam really did it to mess with him on my behalf. That's my sister. Always protecting me.

"You're right. This will be fun. You signed the lease on the apartment, right?"

She answers, "I did. And..." She bites her lip. She's about to say something crazy. "I ordered myself a waterbed."

I can't help but smile. My sister has wanted a waterbed since we were little kids. She asked for that and a puppy for her birthday every single year. Our parents never gave her the bed. It's silly, but I'm happy for her.

"Oh god, with all the sex you have, the sucker is definitely going to burst."

She giggles. "I hope I burst before it does."

I deadpan, "Can't wait to hear it. Every night. Those walls better be thick. You're very loud when you orgasm."

"And you're not loud enough. You need to be fucked properly

for once." She looks out the window and gasps. "Oh my god, we're above the clouds." She turns back and narrows her eyes at me. "You distracted me on purpose."

I simply smile before she lays her head on my shoulder. "What would I ever do without you, Bails?"

"Probably become a prostitute."

"Nothing wrong with that. It's the oldest profession in the world for a reason."

WE LAND, gather our luggage from baggage claim, and are about to walk outside to catch an Uber when we see Arizona and Ripley standing there with big smiles. Arizona is holding a huge sign that reads *Porn Queens Welcome Kamryn and Bailey Hart*, while Ripley holds one that reads *Casting Call for Good Will Humping*.

We burst out laughing, though my face burns red with embarrassment. Kam will probably proudly prance around town with the signs.

Even though it's only been a few months since we last saw Arizona and Ripley, the four of us embrace like long-lost sisters. I'm so happy we're here.

TANNER

"Here comes the wicked witch of the west."

I roll my eyes. "Dad, cut it out. Fallon isn't a wicked witch, and you know it."

My ex-wife smiles at me as she makes her way up the metal bleachers to sit next to me. All eyes in the stands turn to her. Not because we're exes who support our daughter and sit together, but because she's a stunning woman, with blonde hair and turquoise blue eyes. A killer body only contributes to the allure of her overall physical beauty. It doesn't matter that she's in scrubs, her hair is in a ponytail, and she's not wearing an ounce of makeup. People take notice when Fallon Montgomery enters a room. They always have.

He grumbles, "The floozy broke up your happy family."

"Floozy? Who uses that term?"

"At my community in Florida, we have several of them. They're always knocking on my door. I'm quite the commodity, you know." He pats his own head. "I still have all my hair. It gives me an edge. And I manscape. Women like that."

I close my eyes. "Don't ever talk to me about your manscaping again. And for the record, Fallon and I *both* broke up our family, not just Fallon. We certainly weren't happy. Neither of us. We weren't right for each other. Four years has given me that perspective." Before she's in earshot, I instruct, "Be nice to her. I mean it. No matter what your feelings are, she's Harper's mother and always will be."

He growls, but I know he'll behave. He'll put Harper's needs above his own personal feelings of resentment toward Fallon. Ones I don't share.

I offer my hand and help her up the last few steps before she plops down next to me. She blows out a long breath. "Thanks. I didn't miss anything, did I? My last patient had a few issues, and I couldn't leave."

I shake my head. "Nope, they're taking the field now."

She leans her head forward and waves her hand at my father. "Hi, Dad."

She gives me a playful smile, knowing she's ruffling his feathers. I bite back my own smile.

He nods his head at her. "Fallon. You look...rested."

"Thank you, Dad. I'm always aiming for that well-rested

look. How long is your visit? We should have lunch and catch up."

She's messing with him. She knows that will never happen.

He fumbles. "Umm, only a few days. I'm booked solid though."

She giggles to herself.

I ask, "Are your parents coming?"

She shakes her head. "They just left for a month-long Mediterranean cruise. I'm happy they're finally doing this. They've been talking about it since I was a little kid."

Dad mumbles in my ear, "You're probably paying for the damn cruise."

I elbow him and give him a stern look.

Fortunately, Fallon's attention turns toward Beckett Windsor and his fiancée, Amanda Tremaine, walking up into the stands. He's helping her, as she's about six months pregnant and looks like she's nine months along. That's going to be a big baby. I don't remember Fallon being that big, even at full term.

Beckett is extremely well known, being a billionaire entrepreneur who famously sold his business seven years ago when his first wife died during childbirth. He wanted to stay home with his daughter, Andie, who's Harper's best friend, classmate, and teammate.

Once he ensures that Amanda is comfortable in the seat in front of us, he turns and holds out his hand for me to shake. "Tanner, good to see you."

I shake his hand. "You as well."

He leans toward me and quietly whispers, "I may be entering the world of professional sports team ownership in the very near future. Our paths will start to cross more often."

This is news to me. I haven't heard anything along these lines, and I'm usually in the know, being one of the biggest sports agents in the country. "What sport? What team?"

He shakes his head. "I can't say, but you'll probably know within a week or so. We're heading to Italy later this month, but let's have lunch when I get back."

I pretend to be patient and nod, muttering, "Sounds good," as I quickly pull out my phone and shoot out a few texts to my contacts to figure out which team he's buying.

I notice Fallon place her hands on Amanda's shoulders. "How are you feeling, beautiful? You look great."

Amanda shakes her head in exasperation. "Like a whale. There's a reason women don't normally do this at forty-five. It was much easier my first time around at twenty-two."

Fallon giggles. "It wasn't easy at thirty either, I promise. Certainly worth it in the end though."

I look out to the field at my sensational daughter, taking her place as the shortstop, and think, *more than worth it.*

Harper is a true combination of both Fallon and me. Her hair is light brown, the perfect mix between my darker brown hair and Fallon's blonde hair. She's got my darker complexion but Fallon's beautiful eyes. She has her mother's pretty smile but my fuller lips. I could stare at my daughter all day long. She's the best thing to ever happen to me, and I'll never take her for granted again.

Amanda nods. "Andie is so excited to have a sibling after all these years being an only child."

I turn to Dad. "Speaking of much younger siblings, how's Linc?"

My brother, Lincoln, lives a transient life. He spends a lot of time in California, but I don't think he lives anywhere in particular.

He's over a decade younger than me and a bit of a free spirit. He bounced in and out of at least three colleges that I know of. I'm not sure he ever graduated. He equally bounces in and out of jobs. He saves money for a few months and then quits the job and travels. He also manages to find women to support his lavish lifestyle. Enabling him was always a sore spot for my parents until Mom passed a few years ago from cancer. Linc didn't bother to fly in for the funeral. I don't even remember the last time I saw him.

Dad blows out a breath. "I don't know. I think he's surfing in Tahiti and plans to stay to watch the Olympic surfing events there. I'm sure he's sponging off some older woman he's charmed."

I roll my eyes. My brother is good-looking and manages to find sugar mamas wherever he goes.

"He needs one. He doesn't have Mom funneling him cash anymore. I certainly don't give him any."

Dad nods. "Me neither. Better some sugar mama than us. I keep thinking he'll grow up, but no such luck. I don't know how my kids could possibly be so different from one another."

I can't disagree with that.

I hear Fallon mutter under her breath, "Such an asshole." She hates my brother with a vengeance. I don't blame her. I don't think he ever had a conversation with her that didn't revolve around him ogling her body.

After a great game by both Harper and Andie, the coach has the team huddled. He's kind of a douche, and the girls all hate him. It looks like he's yelling at them. They won by eight runs. We're playing the worst team in the league. What in the world could he have to yell at seven-year-olds about?

After a twenty-minute post-game speech, they run off the field to us. Andie heads straight for Amanda's waiting arms. "Did you see my hit, Mommy? It went all the way to the outfield. It's the furthest ball I ever hit."

I glance at Beckett, and he leans over. "Amanda is adopting her, and Andie chose to start calling her Mommy. Amanda is thrilled."

I nod as Amanda warmly embraces Andie and lovingly fixes one of her dark, curly strands of hair. "Of course I did. You were fantastic."

I'm happy to see Beckett like this. He was a lonely widower for a very long time, raising Andie all on his own.

Harper looks up at me. "Did you see my hit?"

I smile. "We all saw it. Your hard work is paying off." She asks me to take her to the batting cages every single day that I have her. Frankly, I'm contemplating having a batting cage built for her at my house. Her work ethic at such a young age is remarkable.

Fallon wraps an arm around her and squeezes her lovingly. "You were great. I'm so proud of you."

My father gives her a playful jab to the shoulder. "You look just like your dad used to at your age. He wasn't only a pitcher. He played shortstop too."

Harper has a huge grin on her adorable face. "I know. That's why I like to play shortstop. I get to be like Daddy." She looks up at me with hopeful eyes. "Can we get ice cream with Andie? She said her mommy needs two scoops every day."

Beckett lets out a laugh while Amanda elbows him in the gut and scrunches her nose. "Not *every* day."

Andie lifts an eyebrow and then giggles. "It's every day, Mommy. Sometimes twice a day."

Beckett pulls Amanda close. "I'll buy you ten gallons a day if it puts a smile on your beautiful face. The place near here has cherry ice cream, your favorite." He wiggles his eyebrows at her.

She gives him a dreamy look as she nestles into his much bigger body. Their love practically radiates. Even better, Andie is grinning from ear to ear at their interaction.

My poor kid will never see that. At least not from me. I hope Fallon finds someone just so Harper can see a loving relationship.

I interrupt their moment. "I could go for some ice cream."

I immediately notice Fallon shuffle uncomfortably. "Umm, okay, it's your night with Harper. I guess I'll head out. You guys have fun."

I shake my head. "Nonsense. You're more than welcome. I know the place nearby has excellent rum raisin, your favorite."

She breaks out into a huge smile and rubs my arm. "Thank you."

Amanda moans, "Ooh. Yum. Now I need two scoops of rum raisin...on top of the cherry ice cream."

Beckett lifts Andie over his shoulder as she squeals in delight. "Double scoops for everyone. My treat."

CHAPTER TWO

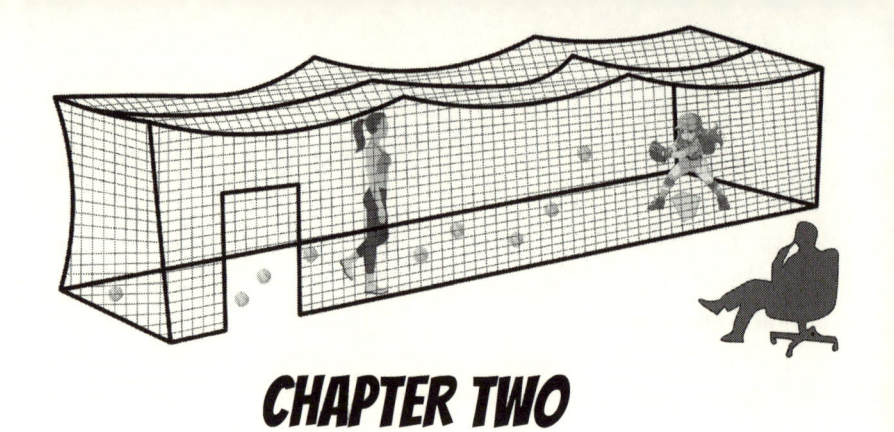

BAILEY

We've been in Philly for a few weeks now. I'm enjoying this town and being reunited with our friends. Our new team seems great. We're contenders for the league title this year.

Kam and I hit back-to-back home runs at our game tonight. The press in Philly have dubbed us the slugger sisters. Despite the Anacondas being a new team, the city has already warmed to us. Attendance rises every single game. In part due to some of the local baseball players being regulars.

Arizona's brother, Quincy, plays for the local professional baseball team, the Philly Cougars. Somehow Arizona is already dating one of the biggest baseball players on the planet, Layton Lancaster. It's not that surprising. Arizona has model-worthy good looks and is one of the best people I know. When they don't have a game of their own, they come to ours, along with their teammates Cruz "Cheetah" Gonzales, Ezra Decker, and occasionally Trey DePaul joins them too.

If both teams have home games, we all usually go out late at night when we're all done playing. Tonight we're going to Screwballs with the guys. It's a local bar that has a chill vibe with good drinks, good food, and local bands. The owner treats us like celebrities, and we end up going there at least a few times a week.

I don't know if Trey's wife, Gemma, will be there since they have a baby at home. We've only met her once, but we all like her a lot. She's different from us in that she's an impeccably dressed lawyer, but she's very down-to-earth and funny. All the guys on the team seem to have a sisterly bond with her.

I'm in Ripley's bedroom with her while she applies a little makeup even though none of us dressed up for the evening.

I sigh. "I still can't believe Arizona is dating Layton Lancaster. She didn't seem impressed when she met him right after we moved here. In fact, she was kind of rude to him."

He hit on her, and she rejected him in glorious fashion.

Ripley shrugs. "They had to go to that PR event, and I guess they hit it off. They decided to make a go of things. Wouldn't you date Layton Lancaster if you had the chance?"

I nod enthusiastically. "Hell yes. Leave it to Arizona to bag the hottest guy in town within a week of moving here. What about you, Rip, have you been dating?"

She shrugs. "A little bit. I'm open to meeting someone. There was a guy at the gym who asked for my number and then texted me. I think I'll text back. What about you? I assume you're not with that older guy anymore, are you?"

"No way. He ended up being a dick. I guess I'm open to meeting someone too."

Kam walks in and says, "Damn straight you are. Me too. I'm hoping to find a hottie willing to give my waterbed a little wave action tonight. He or she is in for the ride of their life."

Kam is bisexual. She'll happily spend time with both men and women, not remotely favoring one over the other. She's also all about casual sex, bringing home new people all the time. I'm the exact opposite. I need an emotional connection with a man before I consider something physical.

I roll my eyes. "Your waterbed has already gotten plenty of

action in just a few weeks. The splashing noises from your room are making me have to pee every five minutes."

She winks. "Those splashing sounds aren't the bed."

I scrunch my face. "Ugh. You're gross. I truly don't know how you sleep with so many strangers."

She scoffs. "You're so uptight. You gotta live a little. Remember, life is like a pussy. Sometimes it's tight and restrictive, and other times it's loose and accommodating. Regardless, it's always there waiting to be explored and experienced."

Ripley bursts out laughing. I can't help but smile and shake my head at my ridiculous sister. "Where do you come up with this shit?"

She grins. "It's a common proverb."

I let out a laugh. "Oh, yes, I think I read it in Bible class when we were kids."

She gives me a knowing look. Our mother made us go to Bible class when we were in elementary school. Kam got kicked out almost immediately due to her foul mouth. At six. After a few months, our modeling schedule interfered and, fortunately, Bible class fizzled out.

Ripley turns to me. "What about Ezra? He seems into you. And he's hot."

I exhale a breath. "It's true. He's good-looking and so damn sweet. He's made it clear to me that he's interested, he just doesn't stir anything in me that way. He's a friend. I don't see it ever being anything more."

Ezra Decker is the star second baseman for the Cougars. He always asks me out, and I always say no, but we end up sitting together when we're out in a group, and I enjoy his company as a friend.

Kam rolls her eyes. "Why don't you fuck him and find out? You could certainly use a little sour cream in your burrito."

Ripley giggles. "Kam, I'm constantly learning from you, master."

PAYOFF PITCH

Kam bows as she unwraps and then licks some kind of mini-ice cream cone. I look at it. "What's that?"

"Just The Tip."

"Huh?"

"It's ice cream called Just The Tip. It's a cone filled with ice cream, but it doesn't go above the rim. Just the tip of the cone is filled, hence the name."

I scrunch my face. "You're fucking with me, right?"

She turns, walks out, and returns a minute later with a box that indeed reads Just The Tip.

Holding it out, she says, "See. Told ya so. Sometimes all you need is the tip."

Ripley shakes her head. "Not me. I like it three scoops deep. At least."

Kam nods. "I know. That's why your vibrator is so damn long, Rip. It probably busts through your uterus."

She narrows her eyes at Kam. "I won't say this again. Stay away from my vibrator. It's a hard boundary line that you're clearly crossing. Why would you even want to go near another woman's vibrator?"

Before Kam can answer, Arizona walks into the room. Even dressed down with her hair in a messy bun, she's stunning. "Layton and the boys are heading over there now. Are you guys ready?"

Kam asks, "You gonna seal the deal with Layton tonight?"

My chin drops. "You're still not sleeping with him?"

She nervously bites her lip and shakes her head.

Hmm. That's odd. I wonder why.

WE WALK into the bar and toward the booth permanently roped off for us. Well, it's roped off for the guys, since they're famous, but it's become just as much ours in the short period of time we've lived here.

The patrons, who didn't know us a few weeks ago, all cheer when we walk in. I do love how much the people in this city have become softball fans in such a short time.

My eyes immediately find Ezra Decker's handsome, comforting face. He's got wavy dark hair that would likely be curly if he let it grow and the warmest hazel eyes. I wish I felt something more than friendship for him. I just don't feel that spark. He's so sweet, but it's not there for me. He's only two years older than me. For some reason, I've always gravitated toward older, more mature men.

He gives me a big smile when I walk in and motions for me to sit in the booth next to him. I see my favorite beer already there waiting for me. He's so thoughtful. I sit down and smile. "Is this for me?"

He nods. "It is. I know you guys had a long game in the heat today. I thought you could use it. I ordered your favorite apps too. I figured that you're probably hungry."

Like I said, thoughtful.

"You didn't have to do that."

He kisses my cheek. "I wanted to. I like taking care of you."

I rub his leg. "Thank you. You're very sweet." *Too sweet.*

Cheetah smiles at my sister. He's been trying to get into her pants since the second they met. She's been toying with him, stringing him along. Every single time we come here, the two of them make bets as to who can score with a random woman. Kam always wins.

I'm not sure what the holdup is. He's her type. He's a sexy, blue-eyed Latino man and is very funny. He's right up her alley.

"Kam bam," that's what he calls her, "you were the last to arrive."

Arizona and Quincy's mother started a game when they were kids and Quincy brought it to the Cougars. Whoever is last to arrive has to give a random fact. It happens to be interesting, and

I've learned a lot from it. We all always have random facts on hand in case we're the last to arrive.

Kam smirks. "I've got one for you, kitten." That's what she calls Cheetah. "The impulse to ejaculate comes from the spinal cord. No brain is needed. It explains why men ejaculate so easily, doesn't it?"

Cheetah slowly nods. "That makes a lot of sense. I do get a little tingling in my spine right before I release my sweet vanilla cream into a woman's warm coffee."

Kam gives him her playful smile. "I guess it's a good thing that I'm not lactose intolerant." She licks her lips suggestively. "I enjoy drinking sweet vanilla cream all night long. From both the pink and blue bottles."

"I prefer pink bottles with sexy brunettes on the other end of them." Cheetah over-enthusiastically wipes his face with his napkin and then winks at Kam. "Am I clearing you a place to sit down, Kam bam, or are you planning to bump donuts like you always do?"

Kam rolls her eyes. "I don't *always* bump donuts, kitten. I'm bi. If you weren't so clueless, you'd know that all women are bi."

I raise my hand. "I'm not."

She nods. "We all are. We're either bi-polar, bi-lingual, bi-sexual, or bi-tch."

The things that come out of my sister's mouth would make a prostitute blush.

Cheetah and Kam keep going at it punch for punch until Gemma interrupts the madness by asking Arizona, "Are you excited for your *Sports Illustrated* shoot this week?"

Arizona and Layton are being featured in the *Sports Illustrated* couple's body image issue. They're going to look amazing, though I know Arizona is a little uncomfortable with it. I don't know why; she has a beautiful body, and she and Layton have undeniable chemistry.

Arizona shrugs nervously. "I guess."

Gemma fans her face. "It's going to be hot as hell. I would do that in a millisecond. Trey's hands all over my nearly naked body all day? Him standing in his underwear all day? Yes please."

Trey pulls her onto his lap and rubs his hands all over her body. "I don't want anyone else seeing your body, baby. It's only for me. If you want my hands all over you, no problem."

She smiles as she turns her head and kisses him, uncaring that they have a huge audience.

Ezra leans over and whispers, "You'll get used to it. That's how they are." He then visibly swallows. "Have you umm... changed your mind about me yet? Will you let me take you out? There are a lot of really good restaurants in Philly. I'd love to show you some of them."

I take his hand in mine. "Ezra, I adore you. You're kind and so handsome. I'm sure there are women lined up for you. I just don't see it being more for us, and I don't want to give you any false hope. I really like you. Can't we stay friends?"

He pinches his lips together and nods. "Sure. I...umm...just thought it would be cool if the two second basemen in town were together."

"It would, but I'm not there right now."

Kam mouths to me, "Just fuck him."

Nope, not happening.

THE NEXT NIGHT, we're all at a Cougars game. Because of Arizona's status as Layton's girlfriend, we have season passes for the seats right behind the Cougars' dugout. We're all wearing Cougars jerseys given to us by the owners. The same group that owns the baseball team owns the Anacondas, and they like to cross-promote. The guys wear our jerseys to our games too.

In fact, one of the owners, Reagan Daulton, is walking toward us now. She seems to be the ringleader, which is incredible because she can't be more than a few years older than us. While we're in jean shorts and baseball jerseys with our hair in ponytails, she's in a high-end pantsuit and heels with her blonde hair and makeup looking like they were professionally done.

She smiles when she sees us. "If it isn't my favorite softball players. I love seeing you ladies here. The fans do too. Great win yesterday."

Arizona shakes her hand. "Thank you. Everything is clicking for us."

Reagan nods. "Glad to hear it. It's my understanding that sponsorship opportunities are starting to trickle in. You're making your mark. More will come. If you need help managing it all, don't hesitate to reach out. We'll connect you with lawyers and agents as needed." She smiles at Kam and me. "I remember you two in a Doublemint commercial when I was a preteen." She sings the famous line, "Double your delightment...with the right mint."

Kam giggles. "Double your pleasure. Double your fun..."

Everyone except me joins in and sing-screams, "That's the statement of the great mint in Doublemint gum!"

They all laugh. I do my best to fake a smile. Those memories aren't good ones for me. They symbolize the end of our relationship with our mother.

Kam simply shakes her head. "We had to chew that fucking gum all day every day for weeks. I still can't smell it without getting sick to my stomach. I'm a Hubba Bubba kind of girl now."

Kam chews grape bubblegum during every game. She always has. At this point, it's a superstition.

Reagan tilts her head to the side. "Hmm. My sister, Skylar, went to business school with the head of marketing at Hubba Bubba. Maybe we can pitch them something."

Kam's eyes widen in excitement. "That would be great. Thank you."

Reagan turns her head to me in question. "I'm not a Hubba Bubba enthusiast like my sister. I'll leave that one to her."

I can hear Kam sigh in frustration.

Reagan slowly nods. "Gotcha. Well, I have my whole big family up in the owner's suite tonight. I should get back. I just wanted to say hello and thank you for all you're doing for the team. Have a good night."

When she walks away, Kam elbows me. "What's your problem? That could be a big deal for us. The twin thing is always a differentiator."

"I told you; I'm never modeling again."

"What are you going to do all off-season?"

"I want to search for a nannying job. You know how much I like that."

I worked for two families in Chicago for the six years we were there. They were both upset I was leaving the city. It was so hard to leave the kids.

Kam doesn't get it. She never has. Working with kids makes me happy.

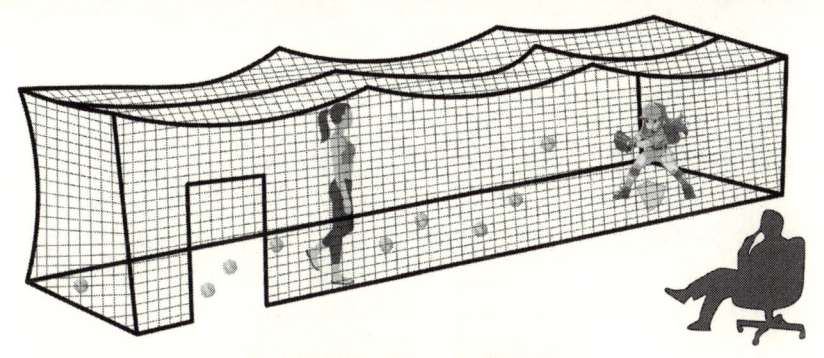

CHAPTER THREE

TANNER

> Hildy: Please accept this text as my resignation.

Oh shit. I don't need this today.

> Me: Why? Did Harper misbehave?

> Hildy: Harper is an angel.

> Me: Then what is it?

> Hildy: I don't think I have the energy for it anymore, and I have some things going on in my personal life. I'm very sorry to not give you proper notice, but I won't be in anymore.

She's not wrong that she was struggling to keep up with my energetic daughter, but a little notice would have been nice. Her timing couldn't be worse.

I immediately click on Fallon's contact information and

press the call button. She answers right away. "Hey, Tan. I'm walking into my continuing education class. What's up?"

Double shit. I forgot she's been in New York City for a few days. Can this day get any worse? And it's not even eight in the morning. Is it too early for a glass of whiskey?

"Hildy suddenly quit. No notice. She's gone."

I hear her blow out a long breath. "Oh no. Can you drop her at the Windsors' house?"

"They're in Italy for a few more days."

"What about the Knights?"

"They both work. Dylan and Brandon go to camp during the day."

Harper didn't want to go to camp this summer because she's playing competitive softball and said she needed the extra practice time. Seven-year-old competitive softball. I love her passion, but having her home necessitates constant coverage on the weekdays I have her.

"Right. My parents are still away. You'll have to take her into your office."

I feel my jaw tighten. "I have meetings all day today. Any chance you can come back early? I'll pay for the car service to grab you right now."

"Tan, it's hard enough without her going to camp. I've crammed all my work commitments into the days you have her so I can be with her on my days. I have to get these hours in to maintain my certification. I'll barely be home in time for her game tonight, and that's only if I don't hit traffic. I'm sorry."

I'm silent, doing my best not to show my agitation. Not entirely at her, at the situation.

She sighs. "I know what you're thinking. You make a lot more money than I do, you pay me alimony, and I'm not relieving you to get to your *super* important meetings. Well, maybe being a physical therapist isn't as big a deal as being the famous sports agent, Tanner Montgomery, but it's important to me."

My shoulders fall. I'm an asshole. "I'm sorry. You're right. Don't worry about it. She'll come to work with me and Shannon will take over when I'm in meetings. It's my responsibility. I'll manage it." It's not ideal, but she can hang out with my secretary for a few hours today.

Her tone softens. "Okay. I'll see if I can sign in and then sneak out after lunch to come to your office to get her. I'll take her to an early dinner before her game tonight if I can."

"That would be super helpful. Thank you. I'll meet you guys at her game. And this way I don't have to leave early to get her there in time for the warm-ups."

"No promises. I'll do my best. I'll text you later and let you know."

"Perfect."

I end the call and yell upstairs, "Harper, pack a few books. We're going to my office."

She walks downstairs with a scowl on her face. "Where's Humpback Hildy?"

I chuckle. "She's not that bad."

Harper scowls. "She's a hundred years old, only likes to sit inside, moves like a turtle, and has breath that smells like egg. Rotten egg."

I smile at my daughter. "Hildy isn't going to be here anymore. She has some family obligations. Until I find a replacement, you're going to have to come to my office."

Her face falls. "Ugh. So boring."

I wiggle my eyebrows as the subject of my first meeting occurs to me. "Not today. I have a meeting with Arizona Abbott. You'll get to meet her in person, bug."

Her eyes widen. "For real? *The* Arizona Abbott?"

I nod. "The one and only. She's looking for representation. She might be my client."

"Wow! Arizona might sign with you?"

I inwardly laugh. I represent most of the biggest stars in sports and she's never been impressed. It's Arizona Abbott who finally impresses my daughter. Perhaps I need to add more women to my list of clients. It will be good for Harper.

"Yes. That's what the meeting is about. Bring your jersey. Maybe she'll sign it."

"Awesome."

She runs upstairs to grab her Abbott jersey. When she returns, she asks, "Daddy, can I get a new sleeping bag for the camping trip next weekend?"

Harper's class at her school is having a huge family camping trip next weekend. It's a welcome-to-second-grade tradition at the school. A bit of a rite-of-passage bonding activity, and Harper has been looking forward to it all summer.

"What's wrong with the one you have?"

Her adorable face scrunches in disgust. "It's for babies. It has Bluey on it."

"Did you ask Mommy?"

Her face falls. That means she asked Fallon, and she didn't say yes. "Umm...well..."

"Harper, you only got it last year. It's practically new."

"But it's for six-year-olds. I'm seven and a half."

"I'll talk to Mommy about it."

She mumbles under her breath, "Now I'll never get a new one."

I cross my arms. "Don't be a brat. Did you go to the bathroom this morning?"

Her frown turns into a smile. "I did."

"And?"

"Echt."

I twist my lips. "Hmm. That's a hard one."

For Christmas last year, one of Harper's stocking

stuffers was word of the day toilet paper. For some reason, Harper used to refuse to go to the bathroom in the mornings. She'd be ready to burst in the car on the way to school, often having accidents. I thought this might incentivize her to sit on the potty in the morning. We've made a bit of a game to see if she can stump me with unusual words.

It's been a massive success. She loves it so much that she begged me to stock her bathroom with rolls of it. It's hard to constantly find new ones, but it's working, so I do my best. I happen to have a high vocabulary, but I'm sure the day is coming when she finally stumps me. It started as a way to get her to use the bathroom, but increasing her vocabulary has quickly become an added bonus. Now and then I'll hear her work one of the words into casual conversation. The looks on people's faces are priceless.

"Do you know it?"

"Only that Mommy is an echt Philadelphian. It means true or genuine."

Her face falls. "Why do you know so many words? Your brain must be huge."

I wink. "I guess I'm an echt smart person."

BAILEY

Coach Billie motions for our hands to meet in the middle. "Great practice today, ladies. No one beats the snakes."

Kam raises an eyebrow and whispers to me, "I don't mind beating certain snakes."

Even though they didn't hear her, Arizona and Ripley smile knowing what likely just came out of Kam's mouth. Coach Billie has a knack for making all Anacondas' cheers unintentionally sound sexual.

Coach Billie is about fifteen years older than us. She was an outfielder in the Olympics twenty years ago. She's got a ton of energy, and we all adore her, though she's a little naïve at times.

Kam smirks at me before yelling. "Hell yeah, Coach Billie, no one will drain these snakes."

Coach Billie's dimpled smile grows. "That's the spirit, Kam."

Everyone on the team giggles.

Coach Billie continues, "Let's get showered and onto the bus. No one likes a dirty snake. We've got an important road trip coming up."

Kam turns and wiggles her ass at me. "I prefer to dirty them up myself."

I scrunch my face. "I always wanted a disgusting teenage brother. The good news is, I feel like I have one."

A little while later, as we step out of the showers, Arizona asks me, "Did Tanner Montgomery ever call you?"

She told me that, when she met with him this week, he mentioned needing a nanny and she recommended me. She seemed to think he was very interested.

Apparently, he's divorced with a seven-year-old daughter. I know that he's a huge sports agent, but I know nothing else about him.

"Not yet. I hope he calls and that he can work within my schedule."

After we get dressed, we board the bus. I'm sitting with Kam while Ripley and Arizona sit in the seats directly across from us.

Kam brought a giant cooler. I hope it's not booze. The coach won't like that.

I peek inside and stare in disbelief. "Kam, why do we have seven containers of chopped-up pineapples in here?"

She simply smirks. It's the official signal that something ridiculous is about to come out of her mouth.

"I recently read an article about what certain foods do to your system. It said that pineapples make your pussy taste good. Some shit about the pH balance. I'd offer you a container or two, but I'm not overly optimistic that anyone will be tasting your pussy anytime soon. It feels wasted on you."

Before I can consider a reply, Arizona and Ripley look into the cooler. Arizona pinches her eyebrows together. "Why the fuck do you guys have so many pineapples?"

I roll my eyes. "My sister thinks it will make her vagina taste better."

Ripley nods. "I've heard that too. Along with cranberries and cinnamon."

My sister types away on her phone and mumbles, "Adding cranberries and cinnamon to our grocery list."

Arizona shrugs. "I've heard that caffeine and red meat have the opposite effect."

Kam's eyes widen. "And…I just became a vegetarian and decaf drinker."

Arizona and Ripley giggle at my crazy sister before Arizona asks her, "You're the only one of the four of us who has tasted pussy. Have you noticed a difference based on diet?"

Kam twists her lips. "I'm not sure I've ever thought about what they eat, but the pineapple thing is science. That's real."

Ripley shakes her head. "I don't think I could ever wrap my head around the notion of licking pussy. I guess I'm fully straight."

Kam rolls her eyes. "Did you grow up fantasizing about sucking cock?"

Arizona mumbles, "A little."

We all laugh and then make not-so-subtle grabs for a few sliced pineapples…just in case. I have a feeling we're all about to single-handedly boost the pineapple industry.

Just then, my phone starts ringing. After noticing it's an unknown number, I move to an empty seat in the back of the bus to answer it. "Hello?"

In a smooth as silk, deep voice, I hear, "Bailey Hart?"

"Yes?"

"This is Tanner Montgomery. I got your name and number from Arizona Abbott."

I'm practically bouncing off the seat with excitement. "Oh, yes. She mentioned that you might reach out. You need help with your daughter, right?"

"Yes. She's not in camp this summer and my nanny unexpectedly quit."

"I'm sorry to hear that. As you may know, I'm in season right now. My free time is subject to my softball schedule. When the season is over, I'll have much more availability."

"I understand. I'd love to figure out a way to make this work. Harper is freaking out at the prospect of having you here. She's a huge fan of the Anacondas. I'll take whatever free time you can give me until your season is over, and then we can figure out something more consistent for your off-season. She'll be in school by then. Why don't you come by tomorrow to meet with both of us? I'm hopeful we can discuss logistics and find a way to make this happen."

A big smile finds my lips. I love working with kids and miss it. "We're on our way out of town for a short road trip. Can we meet when I get back?"

"No problem."

We set up a time for me to come by on the afternoon of a day off we have later this week. Arizona has her big *Sports Illustrated* photo shoot all day, and I think Kam mentioned that she has plans that day. I'll be free.

We get to the airport and I'm on cloud nine. I hated saying goodbye to the families I worked for in Chicago. I miss the kids. This is exactly what I need to feel fulfilled.

I'm in a bit of a dreamy state as I begin to go through airport security. My carry-on bag gets flagged, and I'm pulled aside. The TSA agent, a young burly man, says, "Ma'am, according to our x-ray machines, you have a water bottle in your bag. I'm going to have to open the bag and remove it."

PAYOFF PITCH

A water bottle? That's odd. Maybe he's mistaken. I shrug. "Umm, okay. I don't remember putting one in there, but maybe it was left in there by accident."

I hear Kam giggling as she pulls out her phone to start recording. I narrow my eyes at her. "What did you do?"

She gives me her mischievous smile. "I was a good little sister and helped you pack. You can thank me later."

The TSA agent unzips my bag, lifts the flap, and sucks in a breath. Everyone on the team starts laughing. They're obviously in on whatever my sister is doing to me.

I begrudgingly peek over the flap. Oh. My. God.

Right next to a big water bottle, clearly planted by my sister, is a giant, and I mean giant, brand-new vibrator in a box, also clearly planted by my sister.

I can feel my face turning red with embarrassment. I close my eyes and grit out, "Kamryn Sarah Hart, I'm going to kill you."

I can hear her hyperventilating in laughter.

I reopen them to see her still smiling and still recording this. "But the TikTok I'm making will go viral."

I ball my fists at my sides. "Do *not* post this."

Arizona throws her arm around me and smiles. "That's a giant vibrator. You like the big boys, don't you, Bails?"

I grit out, "It's not mine."

Kam nods. "It is now, sis. You're welcome."

Ripley makes a sound of disgust. "Ugh, I'm Bailey's roommate for this trip. Wait until I'm in the shower before you use it."

She winks. She's messing with me.

I shake my head. "How are you all my best friends?"

They're all still laughing. I feel like everyone in the airport is staring at me.

My sister is officially a lunatic.

LATER THAT NIGHT, Ripley and I are in our hotel room, about to go to bed, when I see her on her phone, typing away like she's in a text conversation. She's smiling goofily.

"Who are you texting with the big ol' smile on your face, Rip?"

She looks up like she's been caught doing something bad. "Oh, sorry. Just this guy I met at the gym. The one I mentioned to you before. He's been asking me out and I finally said yes. We're going to dinner later this week after we get back. I'm kind of excited about it."

"That's great. Tell me about him."

She smiles. "He's in finance but played football in college. He's really cute, with a beard. I love a guy with a beard. And he's a big man. You know I need that."

Ripley is tall, about six feet, and curvier than the rest of us. She only likes to be with bigger men.

When we were in college, she didn't have the highest self-esteem because of her body. She was always a bit uncomfortable in her own skin. I hate that for her. Just because she's a little bigger than society deems acceptable doesn't make her any less beautiful. She happens to be a gorgeous woman with her red curly hair, blue eyes, and porcelain skin. None of us are stick-thin. We're athletes. We have muscle mass, though Ripley is bigger than the rest of us.

Whoever she was dating in Houston changed that for her. She's always been tight-lipped about whoever it was. While it's still a work in progress, she definitely feels more comfortable about her body. She's even doing a plus-sized lingerie ad in the next few weeks.

"That's exciting. Where are you going?"

"I'm not sure. He said to dress nicely, so I'm guessing a fancy restaurant."

"Good for you, Rip."

"What about you? Any prospects?"

"My new vibrator is the only action I'll be getting in the near future. I can't imagine any man living up to that monster."

She giggles. "It's a big boy, for sure. What about Ezra? You won't consider giving him a chance? He's hot and clearly into you."

I blow out a breath. "He just doesn't give me *that* feeling. You know the one I'm talking about."

She scoffs. "I do. Trust me, I do. Maybe it will grow in time though. You two would be so cute together."

I sigh. "I don't believe that. Either you're immediately attracted to someone or you're not. I've never had a situation where I felt nothing and it eventually turned into something. Have you?"

She shakes her head. "No, I suppose you're right."

"When you want someone, it hits you right away."

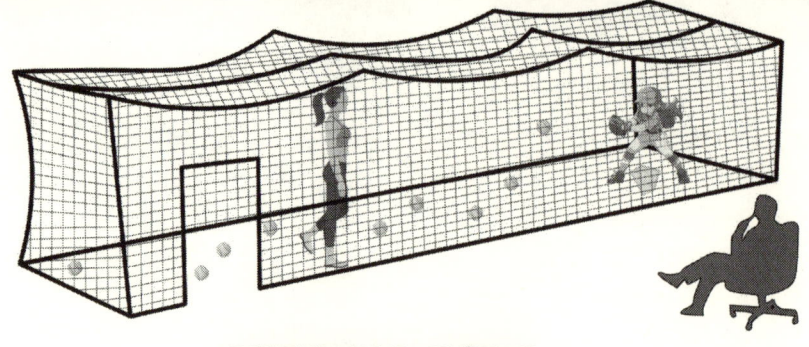

CHAPTER FOUR

BAILEY

The Uber drops me at the address Mr. Montgomery gave me. I look up at what can only be described as the biggest mansion I've ever seen. I mumble to myself, "Being a sports agent must pay well."

I look down at my wardrobe, suddenly feeling underdressed in black leggings and a small Anacondas sweatshirt. Do rich people dress fancy all the time? Will he need me to dress fancy when I babysit his daughter? I have a few nice things, but not enough to wear every day.

I also notice a few contractors' pickup trucks parked in the driveway. What else could he possibly be doing to his house? How much space do a single man and his daughter need? Maybe Arizona was mistaken and he's not single. Or maybe like forty people live here. They'd certainly fit.

I thank the driver and walk toward the front door. Before I have the chance to knock, the door swings open and the most adorable little girl appears, jumping up and down. Her hair is in messy braids, and she's wearing athletic shorts and an Anacondas T-shirt, immediately putting me at ease.

She screeches, "Bailey Hart is at my house! Omigod, wait until I tell my friends."

I crouch down and smile. "You must be Harper." I hold out my hand. "It's nice to meet you. I hear you're a softball player too. A really good one."

Her eyes widen as she takes my hand. "You've heard of me?"

So precious.

I nod. "Arizona Abbott told me all about you. She said you might be on the Anacondas in a few years."

She gasps as I hear footsteps making their way toward the door. I look up as the imposing figure approaches, and my mouth immediately goes dry. The man is tall and shockingly well-built, apparent even in a business suit. He has dark hair with a hint of gray, golden brown eyes, and a trim beard my sister would describe as *sitworthy*. I'm starting to understand the term.

His navy-blue dress pants do little to hide his thick legs. He's wearing a white button-down shirt with rolled sleeves and a vest that matches his pants. I'm speechless. He's unquestionably the sexiest man I've ever seen in my life.

This right here is what I was describing to Ripley the other night. This *holy fuck he's hot* feeling.

He holds out his hand and smiles with full lips. "Thank you for coming. I'm Tanner Montgomery."

Silence. Awkward deafening silence.

Say something, Bailey. Anything.

He smirks before turning his attention to Harper, "Bug, let Bailey inside. I think we're scaring her."

While Harper steps back, I finally get my shit together enough to hold out my hand, which he shakes and then uses to gently pull me up. His hand is big and warm, and I'm suddenly thinking about what it would feel like on my body.

He maintains his hold on my hand and nods. "It's nice to meet you, Bailey."

"You too...Mr. Montgomery."

His face twitches a bit. I don't know why. We stare at each

other, still holding hands, for a few long beats until Harper interrupts us. "Bailey, want to see my new batting cage? They're almost done. Daddy said it will be ready to use today."

Our hands release, and I turn toward her. I take a deep breath to calm myself and answer, "I'd love to."

She takes my hand and quickly pulls me through the house. I look around and take in the incredible beauty of this home. It's a huge, open floorplan with high ceilings and windows everywhere. The wood floors are dark and wide-planked. Most everything is in various shades of black, gray, or white, with small splashes of color scattered throughout. It's masculine and modern. It's tasteful yet homey. High-end yet comfortable. I've never seen anything like it.

We reach the back of the house and look out to a huge backyard with a pool and land as far as the eye can see. Sure enough, about five guys are seemingly putting the final touches on a brand-new batting cage. A *big* batting cage right next to a full-length basketball court. Wow, this place is like Disney World for athletes.

Tanner joins us. "They're just setting up the machine now, bug."

Harper jumps up and down with excitement. "Maybe Bailey and I can hit today."

Tanner shakes his head and smiles. "She's here to meet us. She's not on the clock just yet."

I shrug. "I don't mind. I'd love to see your new batting cage, Harper. You're lucky to have one at your house."

He nods. "Wonderful. Thank you. Why don't we sit and chat for a bit, and then we'll see if they're done and make sure everything is in working order before I let my most precious commodity in there." He winks.

He's so hot. And I can smell his aftershave. It's making my head spin.

We walk over to a living room area with a huge, comfy-looking cream-colored couch, a matching loveseat, and three complementary chairs. Tanner and Harper sit together on the couch. She immediately cuddles her little body into his big one and he wraps his arm around her. It's obvious that they're close.

I sit in a chair across from them while noticing Harper pop a few Skittles into her mouth.

Tanner breaks the silence. "Bailey, why don't you tell us a little about yourself? Harper and I go to a lot of your games, so we know you play a fantastic second base and are a great hitter. I mean beyond that."

I smile. "Of course. I grew up in a small town in Southern Florida. My parents still live down there in the same house we grew up in. I'm sure you know that Kamryn is my identical twin sister. She's my only sibling. We went to UCLA together. That's where we met Arizona and Ripley. Together we won two national championships. We've all been playing pro ball since, though not together. Kam and I were in Chicago until a month or so ago. At UCLA, I majored in early childhood education. I was leaning toward teaching when my sister talked me into playing ball for a few more years. I've always nannied in the off-season to make ends meet and because I love working with kids. I've worked with them as young as two and as old as twelve. I emailed you the references you asked for right after we spoke on the phone."

He nods. "Yes. I've spoken with them all. You have a lot of Chicago families who wish you still lived there. Do you have your driver's license? Driving will be involved."

"I have my license, but we don't have a car here. We saw no need for one while living in downtown Chicago, and the same goes for living in Philly. If this works out, I'm going to have to figure out public transportation to get myself between your house and my apartment. Taking Ubers will get expensive."

Tanner waves his hand dismissively. "I have several cars. If this works out, you'll just take one of mine."

"I...don't know if I can do that."

"I need Harper driven around. Once the school year begins, I'll need you to pick her up and, on the odd occasion of an early morning meeting, drive her to school. Frankly, I'd rather it be in one of my SUVs. It's safer for her."

I run my bottom lip through my teeth. "Okay. What about my schedule through the season? It's demanding. I don't want to leave you disappointed and without coverage when you need it."

"Harper isn't a baby. She can come to my office now and then, or I can arrange playdates. I imagine you know in advance when your practices and games take place so I can work around them. My ex-wife has her half the time, so it's mostly during working hours on the days I have her until school starts back up again. My afternoons are a little more flexible. Barring a work commitment, I'm with Harper in the evenings when I have her. I don't like to miss that time. Fallon, Harper's mom, is a physical therapist. She loads her schedule on the days I have Harper, but it's fluid, and we help each other out when we can. Neither of us miss Harper's games or anything along those lines."

So different from my family. Our mother didn't work, and our father worked like a dog. He tried to make it to as many games as he could, but it was hard for him. Our mother rarely came to games even though she had nothing else to do. She would have preferred we did something more *girly* than sports.

He continues, "Her close girlfriends, Andie and Dylan, are usually around. You may have met Andie. Her father, Beckett Windsor, is one of the new owners of the Cougars and Anacondas."

"Yes, I've seen them around. They come to just about every game. I suppose most of our games are in the afternoons. I can be here in the mornings unless we're on the road. Harper can even come to the ballpark with me when you're in a pinch. No one will mind. One of the girls on the team is a mom and her baby comes now and then when her husband is busy."

Harper's face lights up. "In the locker room? With the team?"

I smile. "Of course."

She seems giddy, and Tanner smiles down at her before looking back at me. "During the school year, I need her picked up from school and cared for until dinnertime. On odd occasions, a little later, but I try to avoid that as much as possible."

"Once the season is over, sometime in October, that won't be a problem at all. I'm wide open."

He nods. "Great. Given Harper's level of excitement and your references, I don't see why this can't work out. I just want my ex-wife, Fallon, to meet you. She needs to approve anyone who's around Harper."

"I understand completely."

"We'll figure out a time to make that happen."

Harper scrunches her nose. "Tell Mommy to come over after work today to meet Bailey. I want her to start right away. My summer season is almost over, and I want to hit with Bailey. Coach says I should be getting more power in my swing."

Tanner blows out a breath. "Her coach acts like they're adults. They're seven. It should be fun for them, don't you think?"

I nod. "Of course. I know a few fun drills." I turn to Harper. "If it's okay with your daddy, maybe I can show you a few this afternoon."

Harper looks hopefully at Tanner and he nods.

TANNER

I'm sitting on the deck, smoking a cigar, watching the sexiest woman I've ever seen in my life play softball with my daughter. When she walked in, something passed between us. She felt it too. I could tell.

She bends over to retrieve a ball, giving me a direct view of her perfect ass. At least a portion of her body was covered when she was wearing the sweatshirt. Now she's in a fitted tank top with those tight leggings, and I'm finding myself constantly in need of...adjustment.

Just a regular middle-aged man, drinking whiskey, smoking a cigar on his deck, getting hard from simply watching his kid's potential nanny play with his daughter. Totally normal.

I run my fingers through my hair. How did I get here?

Hiring Bailey might be the biggest mistake of my life. I'm half-hoping that Fallon rejects her as a candidate, though I can't imagine she will.

As if I manifested her, Fallon walks outside. My friends and family think it strange that she has a key to my house and is free to come and go as she pleases, but at the end of the day, she's Harper's mother. I have keys to her house too, though I don't use them as liberally as Fallon does mine.

She plops down next to me. "Hey. Sorry I'm late. Crazy day at work. Is she still here?"

I point toward the batting cage where Harper and Bailey have been for the past two hours. "The two of them are breaking in the new batting cage. The contractors finished it today, and Harper was anxious to get in there."

She smiles. "I bet she was. It's incredible, Tan. She's a lucky little girl."

I nod. "I think she wants to live in that sucker."

Fallon looks more closely and lets out a laugh. "Oh cheez, Tan. Your new nanny is a far cry from Hildy, who could have doubled for Mrs. Doubtfire. Is she a model?"

I shake my head and blow out a ring of smoke. "Much better. She's a professional softball player. She plays for the Anacondas."

"Ahh. I thought she looked familiar. Harper must be over the moon."

"She was bouncing off the walls with excitement. She's been watching Bailey play all season. Now she gets to possibly hang out with one of her idols, but if you don't like her, I'll try to find someone else." I mumble, "Though I don't think it gets more perfect."

She continues to watch them happily interact before turning to me. "If you hire her, you can't sleep with her."

I straighten my shoulders, immediately feeling defensive. "For god's sake, Fallon, she's a kid herself."

She's no kid. She's a woman. *All* woman, down to each and every perfect curve. Her eyes may scream innocence, but her body certainly doesn't.

Fallon gives me a skeptical look. "Don't bullshit me. Who you sleep with is your business, not mine, but it can't be our kid's nanny. That could lead to heartache for Harper."

"I don't plan to sleep with her, Fallon. She's not even my type."

She rolls her eyes. "She's everyone's type. Look at her. *I* want to freakin' sleep with her."

I chuckle, and she smiles playfully. "Seriously, how old is she?"

I shrug. "I don't know. She graduated a few years ago. Late twenties, I guess." Twenty-eight and a few months. I may have looked it up while sitting out here, hoping she was at least thirty and I wasn't a pervert. "She loves kids. Her references are impeccable. She wants to eventually be a teacher, even majoring in childhood education. She nannies during every off-season and always has. That's as far as I got until the guys said they finished the cage and Harper begged to break it in with Bailey."

She shrugs. "It's your call. I trust you. I certainly know you wouldn't put Harper in harm's way."

"Of course not."

"If she's the best person for the job, then you have my blessing."

I nod. "Okay. I'll let them know. You've certainly made Harper a happy little girl. I mentioned to Bailey that you might need her now and then when you're in a bind and your parents aren't around. It makes sense to have one nanny for consistency. I'll take care of it whenever you need her."

"Thank you. That's very generous of you." She bites her lip nervously. "Speaking of my parents, I got a call on my way here. My father tripped on a cobblestone street in Spain and broke his foot."

"Oh shit. Is he okay?"

"He'll eventually be fine, but physically getting him home is too much for Mom. Between the luggage and him in a wheelchair, she just can't manage it all. Fortunately, it was the last stop on their cruise. I told them not to get back on the ship. To stay put. I need to fly over and help them get home. I'm slammed at work for the next few days. He won't be able to fly before then anyway, but I'll be there through the weekend and into next week. Can you handle Harper, or should I bring her with me?"

I think for a moment. "She'd miss a few games. She'll freak out. I'll keep her." My eyes widen in realization. "Shit. You're going to miss the team's family camping trip."

Without me noticing it, Harper and Bailey had stepped up onto the deck as the words trickled out of my mouth.

Harper's face falls and she screeches out, "You're missing the trip, Mommy? We've been planning it all summer."

Fallon's eyes fill with tears. "I know. I'm so sorry, baby. I hate to miss your special night. Poppy got injured. I have to go help him. He needs me. You'd help Daddy if he were hurt, right?"

Her lip trembles and her head falls. Tears spill over her long eyelashes. "Y...yes."

I stand and pull Harper into my arms. "It's not Mommy's fault. She wants to be with you more than anything, but she's being a good daughter. Poppy needs her. I'll do the mommy and daddy activities. You won't miss anything. I promise. You can decorate my hair and beard with all the girly stuff you want."

She shakes her head as the tears begin to fall heavily. She sobs, "You can't do the mommy activities. It's girls only."

I ask, "What about Michelle? She has two daddies."

"Her aunt is coming."

Bailey asks, "If you don't mind me asking, when is this trip?"

I look at her. "Saturday night."

"We have a Saturday morning practice and no practice on Sunday since we leave for a short road trip on Monday. I don't want to overstep, but I can go if you'd like."

Harper lifts her head and she gasps, the tears immediately stop. "Bailey Hart coming on our trip? Everyone will be so jealous. Please, Daddy, can she? Can she?"

"Umm...umm..." I look at Fallon. It's up to her.

I can tell it hurts, but she doesn't want to disappoint Harper more than she already has. "Thank you, Bailey. It's a very generous offer. Why don't we chat for a bit and get to know each other before deciding?"

Bailey smiles innocently, completely unaware that Fallon is hurting. "Anything to help."

I point to the chairs at the table on the deck. "Let's sit for a minute."

Everyone takes a seat, including Harper. I turn to Bailey. "I want Fallon to get to know you, Bailey. We're a unified front when it comes to parenting our angel. I know I mentioned you possibly helping when she's at Fallon's from time to time. Her parents are extremely helpful in that regard, but her father is injured, and it may be a trying few months for them. We may need you more than I thought."

Bailey nods. "Of course."

Fallon squeezes my arm in appreciation. "Thank you." She turns to Bailey. "Tanner said you play softball and that you may want to teach someday?"

Bailey's face lights up. "Yes, I do. I enjoy softball, but

working with kids is my passion. I've even tinkered around with writing a few children's books. I have two *very* rough drafts sitting on my laptop. I work on them when I can, but I've been neglecting them for a long time now. I hope to dive back into them one day."

Fallon asks, "What are they about?"

Bailey looks over at Harper and winks. "Young female athletes, of course. There's so much evidence of the positive effects of athletics on young girls. They're more physically fit, mentally healthier, and they perform better in the classroom. It helps with both verbal and non-verbal communication, increased self-esteem, and overall leadership skills. My sister and my teammates are among the strongest women I know. They've all overcome adversity on varying levels. Sports are a big part of that."

Fallon nods. "I was an athlete back in the day. I get it. I'm a physical therapist now and certainly agree with everything you said. It's part of the reason we're so supportive of Harper's passion."

Bailey asks, "What was your sport?"

"Basketball."

Bailey lets out a laugh. "That was my main sport until Kam begged me to spend more time with her playing softball."

I sit back and smoke my cigar while the two of them trade a few basketball war stories. They're getting on like old friends. I think it's official. The sexy Bailey Hart is now my daughter's nanny, and I'll be looking at her gorgeous face several times a week.

At some point, Harper stands, walks over to me, removes the cigar from my mouth, and, without an ounce of remorse, extinguishes the flame in my ashtray. "Smoking is bad for you, Daddy." She turns to Fallon. "Right, Mommy?"

Fallon and Bailey both laugh as Fallon pulls Harper onto

her lap. "It sure is. Don't let him smoke. I tried for years to get him to stop. You need to succeed where I failed."

I turn to Bailey, pleading for help, but she shrugs. "They're right, Mr. Montgomery. Smoking is terrible for you."

My face falls. "Oh my god, it was bad enough when it was two against one, now there are three of you. How did that happen? At least I don't pump my body full of sugar like you two." I look at Bailey. "Fallon and Harper each have quite the sweet tooth."

All three of them smile but Bailey's is a bit more conspiratorial. "Harper, I have a fun little game we can play to make your daddy stop smoking. Are you in?"

Harper's face lights up. "Yes! What is it?"

She motions for Harper to come to her, which she does. Bailey then whispers in her ear. Whatever she says leaves Harper in a fit of giggles.

Fallon looks at me, nods, and gives me the thumbs up.

Oh boy. This should be interesting.

CHAPTER FIVE

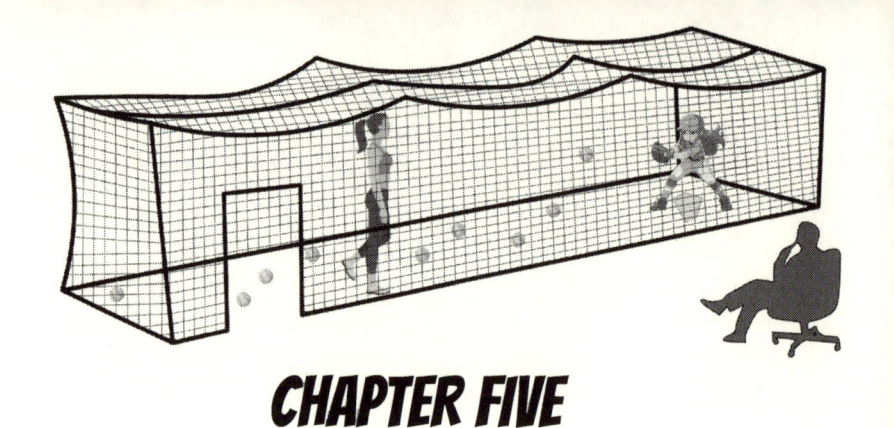

BAILEY

"Are you two sure you want to learn to throw from the slot? It's an advanced throwing technique. Even some professional players don't know how to do it properly."

Harper and her best friend Andie look at each other wide-eyed and nod enthusiastically. "Yes. We want you to teach us."

"You both have good overhand throwing mechanics. If you didn't, I wouldn't teach you this. Never stop practicing good mechanics. It's so important to learn them while you're young. How about your stomach muscles? You need a strong core to throw from the slot."

They both lift their shirts enough to reveal their little bellies, looking at each other to try to figure out if they have strong muscles. I nod and inwardly giggle. "Okay, you guys look *very* muscular to me."

They smile at each other and high-five. Andie says, "My daddy has a boxing ring at our house and sometimes I practice. I think that's why I'm so strong." She flexes her biceps.

A boxing ring? Oh right, he's a billionaire. Andie is the

sweetest, most humble kid. You'd never know that her father is one of the wealthiest men in America.

She returned home from a family trip to Italy this morning and the first thing she wanted to do was come see Harper. Their other best friend, Dylan, is at camp. Apparently, she doesn't play softball. They want to practice before she comes over to swim later this afternoon. Tanner said he'd be home in time to give the girls dinner.

Andie has wild, dark curly hair that we wrangled into a messy bun. Harper is wearing her light brown hair in braided pigtails, as she was when I met her. They're adorable together and I love hanging out with them.

"Alright, girls, throwing from the slot should only be used when you're in a rush or on the move. You can't throw it quite as hard or as far as a regular overhand throw, but it's a quicker release and sometimes necessary. I use it at second base a lot because I don't need to throw as far, but I do often need to get rid of the ball quickly."

Harper toggles her head back and forth in contemplation. "Maybe I should play second base, like you. My daddy played shortstop when he stopped pitching. That's why I do it, but I think I might want to try second."

I cross my arms and lift an eyebrow. "When a coach asks you what position you play, what's the right answer?"

Andie yells out, "Third base."

Harper looks at me skeptically. I've learned in my short time with her that she's very smart and very contemplative. Her wheels are always turning. She knows there's a reason I'm asking the question. I see it in her face the moment she knows the right answer. "I think I'd tell them wherever they need me."

I smile at her. "Correct. Always be a team player. You'll play wherever the coach wants you to play. You should learn as many positions as you can while you're young. You never know where you'll be needed, and if you've learned every position, coaches will love having you on their teams."

We spend the next thirty minutes doing drills as they attempt to learn the advanced throwing technique. They fail miserably, but by the end there are a handful of good throws. It's not easy to learn, but they're determined.

At some point, we hear a voice from the balcony. "Softball time is over. The fun queen is here."

I look up and see another little girl with dark hair holding her hands in the air doing a little twirl. Even from down below, I can see her piercing ice-blue eyes. Standing next to her is an exceedingly attractive man with dark hair and a huge smile. He's in a business suit. He looks a little young to be her father, but who knows? Maybe he's her older brother.

He shouts out, "Are you two going pro yet?"

They giggle as Harper waves to him. "Hi, Trevor. Is Cassandra with you?"

He shakes his head. "No, she's at work. Sorry to disappoint."

Andie smiles conspiratorially at Harper before shouting, "Where's Brandon?"

Harper whispers to me, "Dylan's twin brother, Brandon, is super cute. Andie has a crush on him."

Trevor smirks. He knows why they're asking. "I dropped him at a friend's house. Sorry, Andie."

He looks down at me. "Hildy, you look better than the last time I saw you. Have you lost weight? And the hump on your back is gone. Congratulations."

The girls all start giggling uncontrollably, and he winks before he waves at me. "I'm Trevor Knight. You must be new. I'm Dylan's dad."

I wave back. "Hi. I'm Bailey Hart. Nice to meet you."

Am I living in a sexy dad factory? Tanner, Trevor, and Andie's father, Beckett, are all gorgeous men. I think I'm developing a daddy fetish. *I know I am.*

He gives a genuine smile. "I need to get back to the office. Thanks for having her. Andie's dad will give her a ride home later."

"No problem." I turn to Andie and Harper. "Do you two want to keep playing or do you want to swim?"

Harper begins to pick up the balls. "We need to swim. Dylan is super smart, but she hates sports."

I place my hand on my hips. "You can be both. You're smart. I think I'm pretty smart, and my sister is probably the smartest person I've ever met. She got straight A's her whole life." I whisper, "Don't tell her I told you. She likes to keep it a secret."

Harper laughs. "Her secret is safe with me. Let's go swimming. I'm hot."

The four of us change into our bathing suits and head into the gorgeous pool, complete with a slide and waterfall. The three girls are so much fun. They're all smart and a little sassy, but Dylan is the sassiest. Not in a disrespectful way. She's very witty and confident. I wonder what her mother is like.

I ask her, "How old is your dad? He looks so young."

"He just turned thirty-four. We had a big party for him. Our family is huge, and everyone wanted to celebrate him and his twin brother."

"Only thirty-four? Your parents had you fairly young."

She shakes her head. "My mom isn't young. She's old. Even older than Andie's dad. She said she's a cougar."

I can't help but laugh. "Can't wait to meet her."

As dinnertime nears, Tanner isn't home and the girls are all hungry. I find a few frozen burgers in the freezer and fire up the grill. With the way the house is set up, I'm able to flip burgers from the deck and still keep an eye on them in the pool.

At some point, I hear a noise behind me. I turn to see Tanner practically drinking me in. I'm suddenly feeling exposed in my bikini, though his lingering gaze fills my body with tingles.

He's in a business suit, looking sexy as sin. I've never been with a man who dresses like him. It's so mature and manly. It's like I'm being taunted to find out what's underneath the suit.

I blink my eyes to break myself out of the daydreaming and

smile. "Hey. The girls were getting hungry. I hope you don't mind."

"I was going to order them pizza."

"Harper said she had pizza with you last night. She should eat healthier. I have some peppers on the grill too."

He smirks. "Schooling me on day one?"

"I'm sor—"

"I like it." He licks his bottom lip. "You're right. I should do a better job with her diet. I'm a terrible cook. I do have some ingredients for a salad. Why don't I go make that? You've got your eyes on the girls, right? Or do you need to leave? I know I said I'd be home by now. Sorry I was running a little late."

I shake my head. "My friends are at the Cougars' game tonight. I'm in no rush. I'll meet them out after the game."

"Do you guys go to Screwballs?"

I nod. "Most nights."

"You must get hit on all the time." His eyes widen. "Sorry, that's none of my business."

I smile. "It's okay." Though I don't answer the question.

It's awkwardly silent for a minute before I say, "I'm more than happy to do some grocery shopping if you want. Harper and I can go tomorrow. I love to cook. Your kitchen is fantastic. I could make some healthy meals and leave them in the fridge for you both."

He nods. "That would be great. I'll leave a credit card with your keys on the kitchen counter. You're always more than welcome to join us for those dinners."

"Perfect." I look through the windows into the house. "What are those paddles I saw in the kitchen? I've never seen anything like them."

"They're pickleball paddles. Have you ever played?"

I shake my head. "No. What's pickleball?"

"It's to tennis what softball was to baseball. It was invented to be played in smaller spaces than tennis. It's a marriage between tennis and ping pong. You're obviously a natural athlete. You'd be good at it. I'll take you to play sometime. I taped out the court on my basketball court so I can teach Harper how to play, but I play at a local club. It's a nice way for an old man like me to keep competitive."

"You're not that old, are you?"

He gives me a sexy smile. "Older than I'd like."

I resist the urge to ask him exactly how old by looking down and flipping the burgers. I manage to shout back toward him, "They'll be ready soon," without making any more eye contact.

"Right. I'll be back in a few with the salad."

He returns ten minutes later without his suit jacket and with his sleeves rolled up. So sexy.

He places a salad bowl on the table, sits, and lights up a cigar. I'm about to say something about it but bite back a snarky response. I already gave him one tonight.

I yell down to the pool, "Girls, dinnertime."

They get out of the pool and wrap themselves in towels. Harper looks up at me, and I silently motion that her dad is smoking a cigar. She smiles and nods conspiratorially.

I turn and look at him. He leans back in his chair and smokes as if in deep thought. I can't help but drink him in. He oozes sex appeal. The way he crosses his legs, the way he holds the cigar, the way he fills out the chair. Every single thing he does.

I've never been around a man who smokes a cigar. As unhealthy as I know it is, it's so hot when he does it. His dark beard has a few gray hairs at the bottom. His big red lips wrap around the cigar. I'm jealous of the damn cigar.

He's lost in thought when I see the girls slowly tiptoe up the stairs. I motion for them to spread out, which they manage to do quietly.

Holding up my fist, I slowly lift one finger at a time until I reach three. When I do, they all run toward him and squirt his cigar with the water guns I bought.

Tanner chuckles as he wipes his face and looks at me. "This was your plan all along, wasn't it?"

I shrug as I unsuccessfully bite back my smile. "Don't do the crime if you can't do the time."

The corners of his mouth raise in amusement. "You're a bit of a brat, aren't you?"

My whole body flushes at the comment as I imagine all the ways I want him to punish me. *Wait, what? Where did that come from?*

Before I can respond, he quickly grabs a giggling Harper, takes her water gun, and then starts squirting it at me. "Get her, girls!"

They all turn on me and squirt me until I can only stand there and cover my face. I inadvertently yell out, "Oh shit," and all the girls freeze.

I cover my mouth. My damn sister and her potty mouth are rubbing off on me. "I'm so sorry. No more cursing. I promise."

Harper shakes her head. "That's ten dollars in the swear jar."

My mouth opens in shock. "What? That's an expensive swear jar."

"Daddy says inflation is a bit—"

"Harper," Tanner warns, "you don't want to give up your entire allowance, do you?"

She does a big, exaggerated zipping of her lips and shakes her head.

He turns back to me. "Since Bailey didn't know the rule, we'll let this be her one warning."

I do the same exaggerated zipping of my lips that Harper did.

He smirks and mouths, "Brat."

Maybe it's just me, but everything he says to me feels sexual. And I like it.

We're finally seated for dinner. Tanner looks at Harper. "What were you and Bailey up to today?"

She smiles. "Bailey taught us how to throw from the slot."

He chokes on his whiskey. "Wow. That's advanced stuff. I don't think I learned how to do that until I was fourteen or fifteen."

I nod. "It's a work in progress, but they wanted to learn. I think they were better by the end. Harper said you were a shortstop. Did you play in college?"

He nods. "I played at a small division three school. My dream was to play in the big leagues. At some point, I realized it wasn't going to happen for me, so I focused on getting into law school in hopes of being a sports agent."

"I guess it worked. You're one of the biggest agents around. You probably have athletes lined up to sign with you."

"It took time. I worked for a big sports management agency in New York City for years, building my reputation and client base. That's why Layton, Cheetah, and Trey are special clients to me. They all signed with me out of high school. They're among the first few clients I signed myself. When I left the big company and went out on my own, they were my first three calls. All said yes without asking a single question. They blindly followed me. They're more than clients. They're friends. Hell, they're family. Harper calls all three of them uncle."

I smile as the girls happily chat quietly among themselves. "That's nice. When did you move here from New York?"

"When we got divorced. Fallon is originally from Philly. Her parents live here, and they help her with Harper when she works. Frankly, they help both of us. I wasn't thrilled about the move at first, but I'm happy we did it. It's best for Harper to be near family."

"Where does your family live?"

"Dad is in Florida. Mom passed a few years ago. My brother is kind of a drifter. I'm never sure where he's living, and we rarely see him. Harper doesn't know him at all."

I want to ask more questions, but I don't. I'm not sure why I want to know more about him. Nonetheless, I switch gears.

"Arizona said you've been helpful to her. She's excited to have signed with you."

"I'm sure she's in shock over the number of sponsorship offers she's had. I feel like it exploded overnight. She's one of the most popular female athletes in the world at this point."

I nod. "Yep, we've all had an increase in offers, but she's certainly got the most. By far."

He steeples his fingers. "I see. Well, better you ladies get the offers than reality stars. You're the ones we want our daughters to look up to. Not people famous for S-E-X tapes."

Dylan giggles. "We can spell. We're not two. You just said sex tapes. What are those?"

Tanner's lips twist and he mumbles, "Ask your mom." He looks back at me. "What offers have you had?" His jaw tics. "Let me know if you need help."

"Thanks, but no thanks. I'll never model again. Our mom had Kam and me modeling at a young age. Apparently there's a big demand for twins."

"Gorgeous twins. That's the demand," he grumbles.

Harper giggles. "You just called Bailey gorgeous, Daddy. Do you want to K-I-S-S her?"

He playfully narrows his eyes at her. "Watch it, Harper."

All the girls giggle while I imagine what it would be like to kiss him.

Yep, I officially have a crush on my boss.

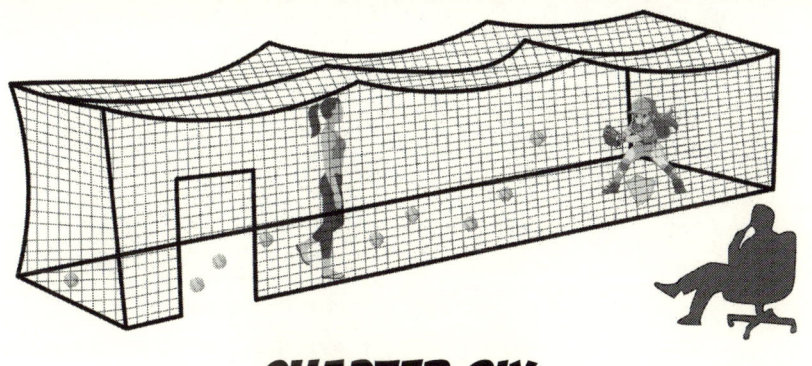

CHAPTER SIX

BAILEY

I smile at my computer screen. "Yes, Daddy, she's behaving."

Kam stands behind my computer out of his line of vision, shakes her head, and mouths, "No, I'm not."

I can't help but let out a laugh, and my father smiles. "She's behind your computer and she's not behaving, is she?"

I shrug and Kam dives onto my bed in front of the screen. "I always behave, Daddy. I'm an angel."

She bats her eyelashes while he raises an eyebrow. "Kamryn Sarah Hart, you haven't behaved a single day since you were born. Your sister came flying out with ease and then the doctors had to reach into your mother to pull you out kicking and screaming."

Kam twists her lips. "I certainly can't imagine why I'd want to stay in Beverly. Even her uterus is probably hostile."

Dad sighs. "You know she hates when you call her by her first name."

"The title of mother is an earned one, Daddy, and she most definitely hasn't earned it."

He shakes his head. "Stop vilifying her. She's not a bad person."

Kam scoffs. "Did you throw up a little in your mouth when you said that?"

I better break this up. "As fun as Mom-bashing is, let's change the topic. Daddy, have you seen many of our games?"

He smiles widely. "I watch all of them. You two are killing it. The announcers said Philly is loving you all and attendance grows every single day."

I nod. "Yes. I'm sure you've heard that Arizona is dating Layton Lancaster. He comes to the games and brings other Cougars players. It's been a huge draw."

He shakes his head disapprovingly. "No, Bailey, it's because of you and your teammates. You all are showing them how great you are. You've had three games where you two have gone back-to-back in home runs. With the way you two, Arizona, and Ripley are playing, that's why the fans are attracted to you."

Kam nods enthusiastically. "Fuck yeah, it is!"

Dad scolds, "Kamryn. Watch your mouth."

I nod in agreement. "Speaking of which, I just got a job nannying and found myself cursing in front of the kids. I need to censor my Kam-inspired potty mouth."

His face falls. "I thought you two were making more money in Philly. Are you okay? Why do you need a second job during your season?"

Kam answers, "We're making decent money, and we have a lot of modeling offers, but Bails doesn't want to do any of them. I'm doing ads for a skincare line. Bailey would rather work for pennies compared to what we can get for a few hours in front of a camera."

I place my hands on my hips. "I enjoy working with kids. It's so fulfilling. Why is this a foreign concept to you?"

"Maybe because I had a shit mother and therefore I don't have a maternal bone in my body."

We hear a nasty, froggy female voice yell out, "Stop your whining. And stop with the silly ball playing. You two should be married by now."

My head snaps to Kam, and I mouth, "Don't start."

We never FaceTime with our mother. He should know better than to call us when she's around. And holy shit, her voice has gotten bad.

Before we can continue, I hear the front door of our apartment open. I get a glimpse of Ripley's red hair, and I don't want Kam and our father to get into things. I quickly mumble, "Daddy, Ripley is here to go to our game. We'll talk to you soon."

He blows out a breath. He knows I'm playing peacemaker. "Okay. Maybe during our next call you'll chat with Mom for a bit," he says hopefully.

Kam scrunches her face. "Ooh, I think I have a proctology appointment that day. That sounds more appealing."

He shakes his head and sighs. "Love you both."

In unison, we respond, "Love you too, Daddy."

I end the call and look up at Kam. "Why do you start with the mom shit?"

She rolls her eyes. "Because she sucks. Thank god I've had you to mother me my whole life. Otherwise I'd probably be in jail."

I NOTICE LAYTON, Cheetah, Quincy, and Ezra all in the stands at our game this afternoon. Ezra waves at me and turns around, showing me that he's wearing an Anacondas jersey with my name on the back.

I look over into the next section as something catches my eye. It's Harper and Tanner. She's waving like crazy at me and gets excited when she catches my attention. She turns around to show me that she's wearing my jersey too. So cute.

Tanner smiles down at her. He's such a loving father. He reminds me of my own in that regard.

This is the first time I've seen him in casual clothes. He's in what appears to be golfing shorts, and an Anacondas T-shirt is spread across his broad chest. He's just so hot.

When the game is over, I see Harper being hugged by all the Cougars. How exciting for her that she gets to be around so many superstars.

Kam, Ripley, Arizona, and I walk over to them. Arizona kisses Layton while Harper jumps into my waiting arms. I love how comfortable she is with me already.

I tug on her jersey. "I like your new shirt, sweet girl. Want me to take it to the locker room and have everyone sign it?"

She grins. "That would be awesome. Thank you."

Cheetah nods. "That's very charitable of you, Bails."

Kam crosses her arms. "Are you not charitable, kitten?"

He winks at her. "I'll have you know that I give about fifty percent of my money to Charity." I smile at the sweetness but then he continues, "And when she's not working, I give it to Destiny."

The guys all chuckle. Fortunately, Harper has no idea what he just meant. Tanner and I look at each other and shake our heads.

He pulls Harper to him. "Ignore Uncle Cheetah. He's a neanderthal."

"Is he pompous, Daddy?"

Everyone looks shocked by her use of the word. I know her toilet paper is the reason for her enormous vocabulary, but they don't.

Tanner smirks while he nods at her. "He most definitely is pompous."

Layton, sensing a topic change is needed, says to Harper, "I heard a good joke. Want to hear it?"

She nods.

He turns to Cheetah. "Start dancing. Shake your booty."

Without hesitation, Cheetah does as instructed. Harper is already grinning from ear to ear while watching his over-the-top moves.

"Faster."

PAYOFF PITCH

Cheetah complies.

Layton smiles as he looks back to Harper. "What do you call a cow who twerks?"

Naturally, Cheetah begins twerking.

Harper giggles and asks, "What?"

"A milkshake."

Harper's giggles get louder. "That's silly, Uncle Layton."

Arizona looks at Layton practically with hearts in her eyes. She fell hard and fast.

TANNER

Even though it's my night with Harper, I allowed Fallon to take her tonight before she leaves tomorrow to travel to her father. I texted my poker group about putting together a last-minute game.

Monthly poker games with several of my favorite local clients have been something I've always done. When Fallon and I were married and we lived in New York City, I hosted them there. Since I moved to Philly a few years ago, I've continued the tradition, though most of the faces have changed. Layton and Cheetah are now regulars. Trey comes sporadically. I think Gemma forces him to socialize with the guys now and then, though he prefers to spend all his free time with her. Vance McCaffrey and Daylen Humblecut from the local professional football team, the Philly Camels, are regulars too.

We drink high-end whiskey, eat good food, smoke Cuban cigars, lose money, and have a lot of laughs. I value this time with my clients who I consider my closest five friends.

I called my regular caterer to see if she could put

together a few last-minute snacks for us, but she couldn't do so on such short notice, so I just ordered a few pizzas. These guys don't care. I prefer for it to be classier for my clients, but it doesn't faze them.

I have a fantastic bar and game room in my house. Some might call it a mancave, but I think it's a bit nicer than that. It does have a large, fully stocked bar, along with professional-grade poker and billiards tables.

Layton and Cheetah are pouring their drinks when Vance and Daylen arrive. They have a friendly rivalry. Cheetah holds up his fist for Daylen to bump. "How's it going, Bumblebutt?"

Daylen lets out a loud, bellowing laugh from his enormous tight end's body. "It's Humblecut, *Cheetah*. Did you know that cheetahs can't even roar? They're the only big *pussy* cats who can't. They only meow. So pathetic."

Layton chuckles. "That's a great fact. I'm using it with our team."

Cheetah elbows him and mumbles, "Says the man who's pussy whipped."

Layton licks his lips and wiggles his eyebrows. "Sure am." He looks at his watch. "In fact, you've got about two hours until my girl is back and then I'm outta here to go be with her."

Cheetah turns his attention to Vance. "What about you, camel-toe QB, are you seeing anyone?"

Vance and Daylen are night and day, yet somehow, they're the best of friends. Vance, with his dark, nicely brushed, and slightly overgrown hair, shows the world a grumpy exterior, even though I know the heart of a lion exists inside him. Daylen and I are the only people privy to just how big that heart is.

Daylen has blond hair that seems to have a new style each week. It toggles between longer and messy to a damn mohawk. He messes with his facial hair just as much. He's goofy and lights up every room he enters with his larger-than-life personality.

Vance narrows his green eyes at Cheetah. "I might have my eye on someone from the Anacondas that you all like to hang out with. You know Kamryn Hart, right? She's smokin' hot. I met her at a club recently and we hit it off."

I see Cheetah's jaw tighten, and I turn to Layton with an unmistakable expression of surprise. He mouths, "He has a thing for Kam."

Interesting. In all my years of knowing him, Cheetah has never been serious about anyone. I clear my throat. "I met her twin sister this week. She's Harper's new nanny."

Vance asks, "Are they identical? I don't think I met her."

I nod, desperate to maintain a cool demeanor. "They are."

Daylen wiggles his eyebrows. "Are you going to tap your nanny?"

Before I can answer, Layton does. "Hell no. Ezra has a thing for her. He's super into her."

I nearly break my glass I'm gripping it so hard. I bite back the unexpected surge of rage and casually ask, "Are they together?"

He shakes his head. "No. She keeps shooting him down, but he's not giving up. He follows her around like a puppy dog."

Cheetah nods in agreement. "I told him to play it cool, but he has no chill when it comes to her. She's shy. I can't imagine she goes to clubs at all. Bailey and Kam are total opposites. Kam is outgoing. She's the funniest chick I've ever met."

Vance winks at me. He knows about Cheetah's crush on Kamryn and is messing with him. He looks back at the guys. "Kamryn told me they're from southern Florida. I love it down there. The weather is amazing. For ten months of the year, it's *bend her over the balcony and lift up her sundress* weather." He bites his lip and mock shivers. "And Kam's ass is quite a sight. When I had my hands on it—"

Cheetah stands and grabs Vance by the shirt, but Vance just starts laughing. "I'm just fucking with you, man. It's clear you're into her. I didn't lay a finger on her."

Cheetah releases him and mumbles, "Asshole."

Vance nods. "Yes, I wear the asshole tag proudly. I did meet her. She's a cool chick, though I thought she was into girls. I think she went home with one the night I met her."

Cheetah smiles. "She's into both. So fucking hot."

Daylen smirks. "I have a lesbian friend, Bella. She gave me a Rolex watch for my birthday last year. I think she was confused about what I meant when she asked me what I wanted for my birthday. I said I wanted *to* watch, not *a* watch."

We all burst out laughing. Daylen may be an even bigger goofball than Cheetah. The two of them together bring epic levels of madness.

Cheetah shakes his head before turning it to Daylen. "Bumblebutt, she's bi, not a lesbian. There's a difference."

"Ooh, nice. What do you call a lesbian with braces?"

Cheetah thinks for a moment before a huge grin finds his face. "A box cutter."

Daylen lets out a laugh. "You got it, pussy cat."

Cheetah nods toward the pizza. "While you're busy laughing at your own joke, hand me a slice."

Daylen grabs one for Cheetah and one for himself and then snarfs down his slice in two bites. I swear the man must be half giant. I'm six feet, two inches and he's at least four or five inches taller than me. He smiles when he notices me staring, and asks, "Did you ever wonder why pizza, which is circular, is put into a square box? And the biggest kicker of it all? We cut it into triangles. It's one of the greatest geometrical mysteries in the world."

I shake my head. "You're a weird dude."

PAYOFF PITCH

"Thank you."

"It wasn't a compliment."

He gives me his big, goofy smile.

We have a great night of drinks, poker, and ball-busting. These nights always lift my spirits. I love this group of guys.

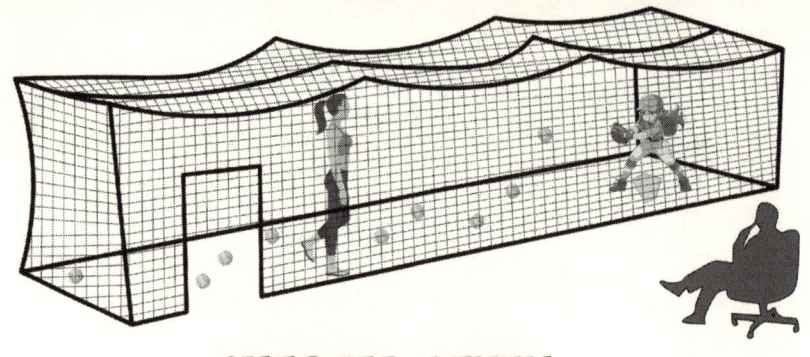

CHAPTER SEVEN

TANNER

I'm driving the two-hour trip to the campsite with Bailey and Harper sitting in the backseat. I can't stop staring at Bailey in the rearview mirror. She's effortlessly gorgeous. It's not just physical beauty. She has an inner glow about her. Her genuine, happy interactions with Harper are so endearing.

I take in her profile. She really should model. Her body and face are perfect for it. I can't pinpoint the reason I'm happy she doesn't want to do so. I hate the thought of people looking at her. I know exactly what those horny fuckers will be thinking.

The same thing you're thinking, Montgomery.

Bailey is touching the new space in Harper's teeth. "I can't believe I missed your tooth falling out. We were wiggling that sucker all day the other day."

Harper giggles. "Daddy told me to bite an apple. As soon as I did, it came out."

"Ahh. Your daddy is a pro. I wouldn't have thought of that. What did the tooth fairy bring you?"

Harper's face lights up. "A hundred-dollar bill. The most she's ever given me. I can't wait to buy candy with it."

Bailey's chin drops as her eyes meet mine in the mirror. "Wow. Your tooth fairy is way more generous than mine ever was. Maybe I should pull a tooth out."

I grumble, "The tooth fairy may have had a little too much to drink that night and thought the hundred-dollar bill was a ten-dollar bill."

Bailey giggles. "I guess drinking and tooth fairying don't mix."

I shake my head. "They certainly don't."

I notice Harper squirming. "Bug, did you go to the bathroom before we left?"

I can see her toothless grin in the rearview mirror. "Oh, yes. I forgot to ask you about the word of the day. It's a hard one though so I had to write it down." She reaches into her pocket and hands a piece of paper to Bailey.

Bailey reads it. "Abibliophobia. Hmm. I feel like I can figure this one out." Her lips twist. "Phobia is fear and biblio has to do with books and reading. Is it a fear of books?"

I smile. "Close. It's someone who's afraid of running out of things to read."

She harrumphs. She's been enjoying the word of the day game as much as Harper has. "I never get them right. I take them home to Kam every day and she always knows." She looks at Harper. "How about we add to your softball vocabulary today? Those are the words I know."

Harper's face lights up. "Yes! Maybe that can be my tradition on the days you're with me."

Bailey nods. "I like it." She thinks for a moment. "Do you know what the payoff pitch is?"

Harper shakes her head. "No. Do you know, Daddy?"

"I do."

"What is it?"

I answer, "It's the pitch that's thrown when you have a full count, three balls and two strikes. It's the payoff because unless it's a foul ball, it's the big decision pitch. Will the batter strike out, get a hit, walk, or simply get out in the field of play?"

Bailey nods in agreement. "Yep. It's the most exciting pitch. So many different ways things can go."

I see the wheels turning in Harper's head as she absorbs the phrase. I love the way her mind works.

We arrive at the campsite. Fallon was in charge of pre-ordering tents through the school. They're supposedly set up for us already. We just have to bring everything that goes inside the tents.

I open the trunk to unpack and notice that Harper has a new sleeping bag. Bailey and Harper packed the car while I was on a business call this morning, so I didn't notice it then.

I look down at her. "Did Mommy get you a new sleeping bag?"

Her face falls. "Umm...well..."

Bailey interrupts, "We bought it the other day when we went shopping for snacks. On the way, she said she needed a new sleeping bag, so we stopped at Target to get one." Her eyes toggle between Harper and me. "I'm now thinking that I should have asked you first."

I turn to Harper, not happy with my little girl right now. "That's going to cost you a month of allowance."

"But, Daddy—"

"Don't argue, bug. You're lucky it's not worse. I know exactly what happened. Mommy and Daddy said no, so you took advantage of Bailey. That wasn't nice. You owe her an apology."

She drops her head. "Sorry, Bailey."

"And?"

"My mommy and daddy told me I couldn't get a new bag. I knew you'd say yes. I was wrong."

Bailey mouths to me, "Sorry."

I shake my head, letting her know not to worry about it. It's the principle that bothers me, not the cost of the bag.

A big black Suburban pulls up next to us in the gravel parking lot. Beckett, Amanda, and Andie all emerge from the backseat. A giant, slightly older, bald man in a black suit steps out of the driver's seat and immediately begins unpacking the trunk.

Harper yells, "Nico," as she runs over and hugs the big man.

With one hand, he picks her up by the ankle. In a militant, deep voice, he asks, "Are you carrying any contraband, Miss Montgomery?"

She giggles, "What's contraband?"

"For you, it's candy."

She shakes her head. "No."

"So, there are no Skittles in your back pocket? If I were to shake you right now, none would fall out?"

I smile. Harper always has Skittles in her pockets. He clearly knows her well.

"Well...umm...maybe."

Maintaining his serious demeanor, he says, "If you give it to Andie, she'll be up all night. If she's up all night, Amanda won't get her sleep. If she doesn't sleep, Beckett will be grumpy. No one likes a grumpy Beckett Windsor."

Amanda and Andie both giggle along with Harper. Harper promises, "I won't give her any Skittles. I swear. Put me down."

He gently places her on the ground and holds out his pinky. Harper takes it in hers. "I promise. No Skittles for Andie." She loudly whispers, "I have other candy too, Andie."

Nico shakes his head. "Monsters. All of you."

Beckett chuckles as he shakes my hand hello. "Don't mind, Nico. He adores the girls."

I nod. "And he clearly knows them well. My daughter is an endless supply of candy."

Andie tugs on his leg. "Daddy, you didn't tell me my joke today."

Amanda smiles as she looks at me. "He tells her the corniest dad jokes every morning. It's kind of their tradition."

It's like our word of the day. It's sweet.

Beckett scratches his face. "Hmm. How many tickles does it take to make an octopus laugh?"

Andie tilts her head in contemplation for a moment. "How many?"

"Ten-tickles."

Andie and Harper start hysterically laughing, and Beckett winks at me. I can only shake my head. "Wonders never cease to amaze. Beckett Windsor, brilliant mind filled with a bevy of corny dad jokes."

He smirks and then notices Bailey. "Bailey Hart. Andie mentioned that you're Harper's new nanny. I didn't realize we'd see you here."

She smiles warmly. "Fallon had a family emergency. When Harper was worried about some of the girl activities, Fallon was kind enough to allow me to come in her place."

Just then, another SUV pulls up. Trevor, Cassandra, Dylan, and Brandon emerge. Even dressed down, they're always dressed up. They're a *designer family*, as Fallon has named them.

Cassandra is much older than Trevor. At least twenty years older. I don't know all the details, but Fallon mentioned that Cassandra is best friends with Trevor's stepmother and it was a bit scandalous when it all went down. They had the twins via gestational host, given Cassandra's age. However, if you see them together, you know they happen to be a perfect match. They both have a great sense of humor, always cracking jokes. They're clearly in love, so I pass no judgment.

Cassandra is a well-known, high-powered attorney in Philly. She's stunning, with shoulder-length dark hair and ice-blue eyes. Dylan is her mini-me in both looks and attitude.

I mumble to Bailey. "Warning, Cassandra has no filter."

She whispers, "Dylan mentioned that her mom is a cougar. It looks like she's much older than Trevor."

I whisper back, "In age only. She might actually be younger in maturity."

Bailey silently laughs as they approach us.

The three girls immediately huddle into their own private conversation while Brandon walks over to a group of boys.

Trevor shakes mine and Beckett's hands while he kisses Amanda on the cheek. He winks at Bailey. "Nice to see you again, Hildy."

Bailey lets out a laugh. "You as well." She holds out her hand for Cassandra. "I'm Bailey. You must be Dylan's mom. She told me all about you. I adore her so much. She's a riot."

Cassandra takes her hand and looks her up and down before turning to me. "Did you bring yourself a little snack, Tanner? I didn't realize it's *that* kind of sleepover."

I chuckle as I kiss her cheek. "Tactful as always. Good to see you. This is Bailey Hart. She's a professional softball player and Harper's new nanny."

She gives her mischievous smile. "Hmm. Why don't you boys deal with our stuff while Bailey and I get to know each other?"

I look down at Bailey and she nods that she's fine. She has no idea what's in store for her.

As I'm about to walk away, Cassandra says to me, "Funny thing. My daughter came home the other day and said that Harper's dad mentioned that she should ask me about sex tapes. That was a fun conversation." She winks. "I owe you one for that."

Oh boy. I'm in for it.

BAILEY

It seems as though Fallon only ordered one tent for the family. I'm sure it slipped her mind to order me an extra with all she had going on this week. Tanner felt terrible and begged a few families to give up a tent, but it was to no avail. I assured him that I'm fine sharing a tent with the two of them. The tents are huge. We have three sleeping bags and Harper will be in the middle. It's not a big deal.

We did a few activities on the lake this morning, which were fun. We're now split into groups. The kids had the opportunity to sign up for different activities. Harper and her two best friends chose crafts. I wouldn't define this as a purely "girlie activity," but there are fifteen girls and only two boys in it. There are no fathers. I suppose I understand why Harper felt like she needed a female with her.

We're making friendship bracelets. The girls are all gathered together while I'm with Cassandra and Amanda. Amanda is sketching.

I look over her shoulder and see a near-perfect sketch of the three girls laughing together. "Oh my god. That's amazing."

She looks up and smiles. "I love to draw."

Cassandra scoffs. "Don't let her downplay it. She's a professional artist. Her paintings are amazing."

Amanda scrunches her face. "It's more of my passion than anything."

I shake my head in disbelief. "Wow. I could never do something like that. I wish I had that kind of talent."

Amanda deadpans, "You're a freakin' professional athlete. I'd say that's a talent too."

I twist my lips. "Hmm. I suppose. I wouldn't say it's my passion though."

Cassandra asks, "What's your passion?"

"Working with kids. I like writing too."

She nods. "Take it from someone who's been around the block a few times. Life is too short not to do what and who you love."

I'm not sure how to answer that with regard to love and she notices. She continues, "It's not like I don't know what people say and think about me and Trevor. At some point, I just stopped giving a fuck. We make each other happy."

"I'm not judging. I think it's great. You're probably a hero to most women."

She lets out a laugh. "Damn straight. I've got a young, hot stud of a husband who thinks the sun rises and sets in my pants. Luckiest woman ever. Speaking of getting into someone's pants, is there anything going on with you and Tanner?"

Amanda rolls her eyes. "Leave her alone, Cassandra."

Cassandra shrugs, "What? When she was in her little bikini on the paddleboard, Tanner was salivating."

Amanda sighs. "She's twenty-eight, gorgeous, and has a sexpot figure. Every single man was salivating, not just Tanner. The piles of drool were bigger than the lake."

I let out a laugh. "You two know that I'm sitting here, right?"

They giggle. Amanda has a sheepish look. "Sorry." She rubs her big belly. "I'm just jealous."

Cassandra appears unapologetic. "Nah. I have a keen sense about this kind of stuff. Tanner was staring at you like he wanted to eat you. The tents at the campsite weren't the only ones being pitched today."

I shake my head. "It's not like that at all. He's my boss. That's it."

"A sexy, single boss. There's chemistry. It's obvious."

"He's much older than me."

She smiles. It reminds me of Kam's. "Have you seen my husband? Age is just a number. When you fight natural passion, it only leads to more passion."

TANNER

After a few activities as a larger group, we split, and the girls are off doing their own thing, leaving those of us without a son a few minutes alone.

I'm sitting in an Adirondack chair overlooking the lake next to Beckett as we enjoy cigars. Trevor is with his son, Brandon.

He blows out a plume of smoke. "How is Fallon's father?"

"She's on her way there now. He's been discharged from the hospital. I guess he'll be immobile for a bit. He's in good shape though. He'll bounce back."

"She must have been upset to miss this trip. I know it means a lot to the girls. I didn't want Amanda sleeping out here in her condition, but she didn't want to disappoint Andie."

I lift an eyebrow. "I saw the setup in your tent. I think she'll be more than comfortable."

He had real beds brought in.

He smiles. "Anything for the woman I love."

"When are you two getting married?"

He sighs. "She wants to wait until after the baby comes and she gets her figure back. Frankly, I was in the doghouse for a while and am still working my way out. We didn't plan to get pregnant at fifty and forty-five, but it's a blessing in disguise. Amanda coming into our lives has been a blessing for both me and Andie."

"I'm happy for you. All of you. How's team ownership going?"

He smiles. "Fantastic. Reagan does most of the work. I don't know when that woman sleeps. Between you and me, she's talking about expanding. She wants to dabble in football too, and, with the success of the Anacondas, she wants to bring more professional women's sports to Philly. She's looking into the costs of starting a basketball franchise."

"Good for her. I think it's great for our girls to see professional female athletes. They're fantastic role models. Harper worships the ground Bailey walks on."

He nods. "Andie likes her too."

"Bailey is a good kid."

He chuckles. "Kid? She's no kid. There's not a red-blooded man who wasn't looking at her in the water earlier. Anything going between the two of you?"

"Of course not. She's young. She's got her whole life ahead of her."

"You're forty-three, not eighty-three. I didn't even have Andie until I was your age, and now I've got another on the way."

I shake my head. "I can't imagine. Harper is it for me. Getting married again and having more kids isn't in my future."

He gives me a knowing smile. "Yep, I said the same thing, and look where I am now."

HARPER PASSES out after a long day of activities, including a cornhole tournament that we easily won thanks to Bailey. Harper was on cloud nine. It's fun to watch her in her element with her classmates. I have a pang of sadness for Fallon that she's missing it. I sent her a bunch of pictures of Harper having fun, hoping it sets her mind at ease.

I see Bailey in her sleeping bag reading on her Kindle. I whisper, "What are you reading?"

She whispers back, "I'm reading Gemma's first book. Have you read it?"

I shake my head. "No. Is it any good?"

She clutches her heart. "It's amazing. She's so talented. Cheetah made it seem so lascivious, but—"

"It's not?" That surprises me. I thought they were sex books.

"It has those parts too, but it's actually a love story. Funny too, but ultimately a beautiful, complicated love story. She's such a romantic."

"I guess she married the right guy then. Trey lives for her. The story of how they got together would probably make a great romance novel."

"What did he do?"

I smile at the four-year-old memory of how crazily Trey behaved when he was trying to get Gemma's attention. "Let's just say that it was love at first sight for him and he was more than determined to do whatever it took to win her heart. They had a few bumps in the road, but their love is the real deal. I've never known a couple like them who click so perfectly and are always in sync. It's enviable."

Harper stirs, and I glance down at her. She's still asleep but I don't want to wake her. I look back at Bailey. "Do you want to walk down to the lake? There's a full moon tonight. It should be beautiful. And I brought whiskey. I thought I'd drink with Beckett, but he's fawning all over Amanda, afraid to leave her for a second. Trevor and Cassandra are probably off having sex somewhere in the woods. They're known for that."

She silently laughs. "They're an...interesting couple."

"They sure are. What did she say to you earlier?"

Bailey gives a shy smile. "Let's just say that she has no problem asking probing questions."

I chuckle. "That's for sure."

She scrunches her face. "Are we okay to leave Harper alone? What if she wakes up and we're gone?"

"There are thirty families around, and we'll only be up the road."

She bites her lip. "Okay. Let's leave her a note just in case she wakes up. I don't want her to be scared."

I smile at her thoughtfulness. "That's a good idea."

We leave her my cell phone along with a note letting her know to call Bailey's phone if she needs us.

As we exit the tent, I notice that the campsite is unusually quiet. I guess the parents are as exhausted as the kids.

With a blanket, two plastic cups, and a bottle of whiskey in tow, we silently walk through the trees until we reach the lake. Her eyes widen as we approach the glass-like still water sparkling in the bright light of the moon. "Wow. It's beautiful out here. Is it safe?"

"Why wouldn't it be safe?" I ask as I lay down the blanket right next to the shoreline.

"We could never do this on a lake in Florida at night. Too many gators."

I let out a laugh. "No gators up here. You're safe. I promise."

I sit on the blanket, but she remains standing and picks up a few stones, expertly throwing them. They skip across the lake dozens of times, leaving a trail of ripples in their wake.

"Wow. You're pretty good at that."

She smiles. "It's basically throwing from the slot, right?"

I nod. "I suppose it is."

"It's how our dad taught us to throw from the slot. I was thinking about it when I was teaching Harper and Andie this week. He used to take Kam and me to a nearby lake. Only during the day though, and never too close to the water where a gator could pop out and surprise us."

"It sounds like you're close with your father." Her affection for him is clear.

She smiles warmly. "Very. He's the best."

"Do you visit him in Florida much?"

She scrunches her face before blowing out a breath. "We don't get home very often. Unfortunately, we don't have a great relationship with our mother. We struggle to be around her. Kam hates her. I don't hate her, but I understand Kam's contempt. We're both very close with our father and do our best to encourage his visits. I suppose I'd be willing to go home for holidays and the like, but Kam is very dependent on me. She doesn't like to be apart, and she won't go down there. We've never even flown separately. She's a terrible flyer and I need to soothe her just so the plane can take off."

"I guess that explains your maternal nature. Aren't twins supposed to be close?"

"Yes, but she's overboard. She wouldn't accept college scholarships unless they gave me one too. That's kind of how I ended up playing softball. I really did prefer basketball."

I'm surprised to hear this. "You're a phenomenal player. Just as good as her."

"It's nice of you to say. She's the star though, and I'm okay with that. Honestly, I'm better now than I was then. I didn't deserve the scholarship at the time I was given it, but I was determined to prove myself worthy and worked my ass off to get there. I just started much later than the rest.

PAYOFF PITCH

Softball is more important to my sister and friends than it is to me. I could leave the sport tomorrow and be fine. Kam, Arizona, and Ripley won't accept anything less than making the Olympic team in four years."

"You don't want to be an Olympian?"

"If it happens, great. If it doesn't, that's fine too. I wouldn't lose a wink of sleep if my life took a different direction."

She tosses me a stone that I easily catch. "Let's see what you've got, old man."

I love when she gets a little bratty with me. I smile. "I'd resent the title, except if I throw this without warming up, my whole arm will be sore in the morning."

She giggles as she reaches for my arm and pulls me up. "You're not that old."

I lightly toss the stone into the lake. "I'm old enough to know warming up and stretching are mandatory."

"One throw." She hands me another stone.

Feeling my manhood challenged, I throw it and grimace. It does skip a few times, but it hurts.

Her mouth opens. "Did that one throw really bother you?"

I nod. "Did I tell you that I suffered an arm injury as a teen?"

She winces. "Ugh. Sorry. I didn't know. Sit and I'll show you an old trick my high school coach taught us."

I sit on the blanket and she begins massaging my arm. My dick starts to harden. I look down at my gray sweatpants. Shit, I should have worn black. I have to pull my sweatshirt out a bit to cover the evidence of what she does to me. Little does she know, I've been jerking off to her pictures online every night since she started with us.

She sits next to me. I can smell her heavenly scent. She reaches for me. "Give me your hand."

I do.

She pinches the fleshy skin between my thumb and forefinger. "It's a nerve ending. If you pinch it hard, it helps with pain. Something about redirecting the stimulation."

It definitely doesn't redirect the stimulation I've got going on in my pants. It only adds to it.

I need distance. Pulling away, I mumble, "Feeling all better. Thanks."

She smiles innocently. "Told ya so."

"Any other pearls of medical wisdom from your high school coach?"

She giggles. "Just the one time Kam had a bloody nose. We didn't have any gauze in the medical kit, and she refused to come out of the game. Our coach stuck a tampon up her nose."

I let out a laugh. "A tampon?"

She nods with a huge grin on her gorgeous face. "Yep. She played an entire game with a tampon dangling from her nose. She truly doesn't give a shitake."

I raise an eyebrow at her. "Shitake?"

"I'm working on not cursing in front of Harper. I'm substituting all curse words, even when Harper isn't around. I have to retrain my brain. My sister has a filthy mouth, and it rubs off on me."

She's so adorable.

I smile. "Good thinking. I might try that myself."

I pour us two cups of whiskey. She appreciatively takes a cup from me. We each take a sip before I ask, "You mentioned before my stone-throwing old-man injury that Kam is dependent on you. Why is that?"

"I'm not a shrink, but if I had to guess, I'd say it's because we weren't mothered properly. Like it or not, I've become her mother. We're very different. Kam is a true wild child. She's always needed me to be the *adult*," she air-quotes adult, "in our relationship."

"That's a lot of pressure on you."

She shrugs. "I guess. It's all I know. We bicker at times, but I love my sister more than anyone in the world. There's nothing I wouldn't do for her, and I know she feels the same for me."

I take another long sip. "If you don't mind my asking, what made your mother so terrible?"

She twists her lips for a moment before admitting, "A lot of things, but mostly because she's an alcoholic."

I place my hand on hers. "I'm so sorry. I didn't know."

"Why would you? I don't let it keep me down anymore. She wasn't always that way, at least when we were little. She channeled her addictive personality differently. Back then she was obsessed, I mean *obsessed*, with us becoming models and actresses. She modeled when she was a teen and supposedly passed on several modeling opportunities so that she could stay with my father. They had us very young and it ended her career. Back then there weren't many models who were moms. I think she decided to live vicariously through us. You've heard the term momager, right?"

I chuckle as I nod. "Of course."

"That's her. She made Kris Kardashian look laid back. She pushed and pushed. Kam and I would be in tears, begging to just be normal kids. We hated it so much. We didn't want long days on sets being manipulated into every pose imaginable. We wanted to play with our friends and go to school like normal kids. Imagine two very obvious tomboys having to spend their days in hair and makeup, pretending to peddle products we knew nothing about. We were homeschooled until junior high so that we'd have time to model. We pleaded with her to let us go to regular school, but she never listened to a word we said. Kam started acting out. She's stubborn as hell and was heading toward a bad place. Finally, when we were twelve and my sister had been busted shoplifting for the hundredth time, our father stepped in and pushed for us to go to a regular school. He's a good man with a good heart, but he has no backbone and rarely stands up to our mother. Even if he was a little late, that was the one time he did. We're thankful for that, but in the absence of momaging us, she turned to the bottle even harder than she had before. It was always there, but it hit a new level once she lost her purpose."

"That's a shame. It's commendable how the two of you persevered."

"It was really bad. She'd show up to school events trashed. She'd swerve into parking lots picking us up from places. Kam was arrested at thirteen for driving without a license. It was that or allow our barely conscious mother to drive us." She lets out a small laugh. "Kam ended up driving all the time. That's just the only time she got busted. She'd never let me do it, only her. She didn't want me to get into trouble."

"Wow. That's hard to believe. I assume your parents are divorced now?"

She shakes her head. "Nope. I'll never understand it, but no, they're not. I think he feels guilty. They were high school sweethearts, and she followed him to college where he was a star basketball player. He was about to sign a contract to play overseas after graduation when she became pregnant with us. Kam and I have no doubt that she purposefully became pregnant to keep him around. It's something she would do. She's very manipulative. We honestly assumed he'd divorce her when we left for college, but he stayed. Kam and I have reacted differently to it. I want the exact opposite relationship of my parents, but I do want a relationship. Kam doesn't ever want to get married."

"Never?"

"That's what she says. She hops around from bed to bed, both men and women, but she hasn't had a serious relationship since high school, over ten years ago."

"Are you into both men and women too?"

She smiles and shakes her head. "People ask me that all the time because of Kam. Nope. Just men for me. And I'm not comfortable being as...casual as she is. She's relationship phobic. I think seeing our parents' shitty marriage made her afraid of something real."

"That's my fear with Harper. That our divorce will damage her future relationships. She won't know what a healthy relationship looks like."

Bailey tilts her head. "I completely disagree. She sees a healthy relationship every single day."

"But we're not—"

"Healthy doesn't have to mean married parents. Families come in all shapes and sizes. You and Fallon both prioritize Harper's needs. You very obviously care for and respect each other. Look at how you reacted when Fallon had to miss tonight. You defended her to Harper. My parents are married, and my mother would have blasted my father's parenting skills if we encountered this situation. She would have shamed him into staying. Married doesn't mean healthy. Maybe you two aren't in love with each other anymore, but you love each other on some level. Harper picks up on that. Trust me. As a kid who saw nothing but games and manipulation growing up, your way is much better, and Harper will be more than fine. She's an amazing kid. I've worked with a lot of children and have seen it all. She's a wonderful, happy little girl."

I sip my whiskey as I let her words sink in. Maybe she's right. "You're wise beyond your years, Bailey Hart."

She lets out a laugh. "I've had to be the female adult in my house since I turned three."

My brows furrow. "That's not fair to you. I'm sure you need someone to take care of you sometimes."

She gives me a bit of a mischievous smile. "Don't worry. Kam takes care of me in her unique way." She lets out a small giggle. "I had a messy breakup before we left Chicago. The man wasn't who I thought he was."

"In what way?"

She hesitates briefly before admitting, "Well, I thought we were exclusive, and it turns out, he had a fiancée. I was completely in the dark and a total mess when I found out. I immediately broke things off and told him I never wanted to see him again. That wasn't good enough for Kam though. She wanted him to pay."

I chuckle. "Oh boy. What did she do?"

"In simple terms, she blew up his shitake. Big time. Pretending to be me, she showed up at his fiancée's apartment when she knew they'd both be there. How did she know they'd both be there? She hacked into his texts. Needless to say, they're no longer engaged." She scoffs. "You know what bothered me the most?"

"What?"

"He thought she was me the whole time she was there. We dated for months, and he couldn't tell the difference between us? I know we're identical, and it takes a lot of time for people to see the subtle differences, but anyone who knows us well can tell us apart. He was my boyfriend, had seen me in every way imaginable, and yet he still thought Kam was me. On some weird level, that hurt more than his lies."

"I can certainly understand that. I've only known you for a week and I can't imagine I wouldn't know who was who."

"It takes time. It took Arizona and Ripley a while before they could tell the difference." She wiggles her eyebrows. "Maybe Kam and I will *Parent Trap* you one day and test that theory."

I let out a laugh. "I'm guessing you two did that to a lot of people."

She giggles. "All the freakin' time."

"Did you take her tests for her in school?"

She shakes her head. "The opposite. Kam is freakishly smart. Off-the-charts, perfect SAT scores, never had to study, Mensa-level-IQ smart."

"Really?"

"Yep. People underestimate her all the time because she's silly and has a dirty sense of humor. People don't see past her exterior. She's the smart one, not me."

"You seem smart to me."

"Maybe I'm normal-smart. She's special-smart. Trust me. She has a photographic memory. She could read one of your legal books and recite the laws word for word when she was done. *All* of them."

"Wow. Does she enjoy working with kids too?"

She lets out a laugh. "Definitely not. She's horrible with kids. Doesn't know what to do with them. Treats them like adults. She's happy to continue to do a little modeling though. Always on her terms, but she'll do it. I have offers but I have no interest. Those scars still run deep for me."

I truly don't know why it makes me happy that millions of people won't be objectifying her, but it does.

I begin to refill our glasses, which are already empty. She holds up her hand. "I'm such a lightweight. I shouldn't. I usually nurse a beer or two, not whiskey."

I fill her cup nonetheless. "You'll need it to sleep out here. The crickets are like a frat house symphony."

She nods as she takes another sip while looking up at the moon. It illuminates her face. She's so breathtakingly beautiful.

She drops her chin back down and looks at me. "Do you mind me asking why you and Fallon got divorced? You get along so well."

I lean back on one of my elbows, cross my legs in front of me, and blow out a long breath. "That's a loaded question. Will this stay between us? I don't like to speak ill of her to anyone. No matter what, she's Harper's mother and I'll always be protective of her because of that."

"Of course. I understand completely."

I can't believe I'm going to admit this to her. "Only my father knows this. Not even my closest friends know. Fallon was unfaithful to me. It was one night, and she wasn't herself, but it happened."

Bailey's eyes widen. "She cheated on *you*? Who the hell would ever cheat on a man who looks like you?"

She gasps and covers her mouth. "Oh my god. I'm so sorry." She mumbles, "Damn whiskey. It's like truth serum for me."

I chuckle. "It's fine. Don't worry about it. My father faults Fallon for breaking up our marriage, but she cheated because I wasn't a good husband. I don't blame her in the slightest. She was lonely. I was more married to my job than I was to my wife. I neglected her and her needs. It took a little time and perspective for me, but I see that now."

She pinches her eyebrows together. "But you're always there for Harper. I can't imagine you being neglectful."

"I was a terrible father at the time too. For years I was building a reputation. Around the time Harper was born, I went out on my own. I worked hard to grow my business. I was never home. It sounds crazy, but the divorce made me a better father. I'm thankful to Fallon for forcing me to open my eyes. I would have ignorantly missed most of Harper's childhood if Fallon hadn't come home in tears telling me what had happened."

"And you didn't think about working things out after that?"

"Unfortunately, we were too far gone. Both of us. Neither of us was happy. We're a better divorced couple than we were a married couple. I didn't put up much of a fight when she requested to move Harper down to Philly from New York. While I was busy working, she was alone in

New York for years and always missed her family. And she wanted Harper to have family around her. I didn't want Harper to have to travel back and forth from Philly to New York. My company was in a good spot, so I decided to move our headquarters down here. I'm relatively happy in Philly. Harper is exceedingly happy in Philly. I'm okay with how everything went down. I needed it to get my head straight about what's important. Harper is more important than anything to me. Sometimes good things come from bad situations."

She lays down and looks up at the sky again. Her sweatshirt lifts a bit, revealing her belly. She's so fucking sexy and so fucking unaware of it.

Sighing, she says, "That's a good way to look at it. I think it's sort of how Kam and I differ about motherhood. We had a selfish mother. I want to be the opposite kind of mother as her. I want a ton of kids, and I want to be there for them in all the ways she was never there for us. I will shower them with love. Kam, on the other hand, doesn't want kids."

Just then we hear moaning. It gets a little louder and we very clearly hear, "Ah, Trevor. Harder."

We turn our heads and smile at each other. I scrunch my nose. "Maybe it's time to go."

She giggles. "I think you're right."

I stand first and offer her my hand to help her stand up. She does so but stumbles a bit and falls into me.

Our eyes meet as I catch her. Hers are a little glassy, and her breath smells like a mixture of sweetness and whiskey. I think she's drunk.

Neither of us moves. We simply continue to stare. I want to run my finger over her soft face. I've never seen a woman with more perfect features and skin than Bailey Hart.

"Mr. Montgomery?"

Hearing her call me that should douse my libido, but it only seems to make it burn deeper for her.

I tuck a loose piece of hair behind her ear. "Hmm?"

She adorably hiccups. "I'm a little drunk."

"I know."

"Can you help me get back to the tent?"

I nod before helping her back to the tent and into her sleeping bag.

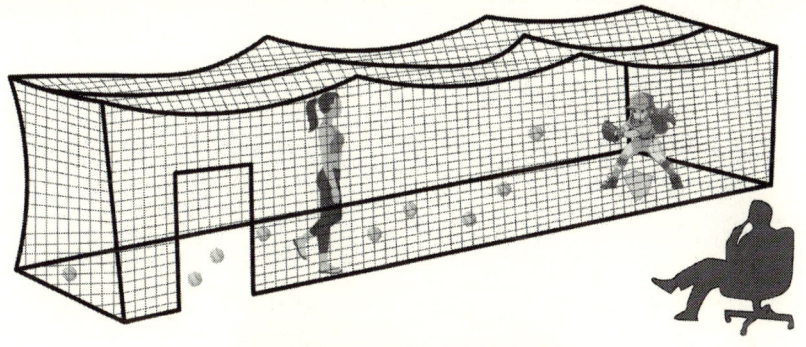

CHAPTER EIGHT

BAILEY

I'm brushing Harper's hair in her bathroom. She's in a towel, just having gotten out of the shower. We were practicing softball all afternoon, both in the batting cage hitting and defensive drills. Tanner should be home any minute to pick her up and take her to the Cougars game tonight. I'm going to the same game with my friends.

My eyes meet hers in the mirror. "Are you excited for the game? I think Quincy Abbott is pitching tonight. He's one of my friends."

"How cool. He's so cute. I love his curly hair. Dylan has a crush on Uncle Layton though."

I smile. "He's very taken."

She nods. "I know. He loooooves Arizona. Daddy says Layton is whipped. I don't know what that means."

I giggle at her innocence. "It just means he's *super* into her. And I think your daddy is right about that."

"Daddy said I can have cotton candy tonight. Andie and her parents are coming too. We're sitting in their box."

"Does your mommy ever go to games?"

She scrunches her freckled nose. "Not really. Maybe one or two times." Harper puffs out her chest and proudly announces, "She prefers my games."

I nod in agreement. "I prefer your games too." I went to her game this week. It was so cute to see them play. I nearly forgot what it was like at that age.

I continue, "You know, it's great that you're working so hard. I barely played at your age. Kam played, and I tagged along sometimes. You're going to be a huge superstar."

She smiles. "Do you really think so?"

"I do. Just make sure you love it."

"Do you love it, Bailey?"

I think for a moment. "Sometimes. I love my teammates, and I love that I get to live and play with my sister. She's my best friend."

Harper's face falls. "I wish I had a sister like you do."

"Maybe you will one day."

She shakes her head. "Daddy says he's not having any more kids, and Mommy says she's getting too old."

"How old is your mommy?"

"Thirty-seven. She'll be thirty-eight on Christmas Eve."

"Ooh, that must be a fun day for her. Lots of presents."

"Yep. Daddy and I always get her two presents. One for Christmas and one for her birthday. She said growing up, her family always gave her one present for both, so Daddy says we *always* have to get her two. He told me that when I'm a grownup, I have to make sure to keep doing that for her."

So sweet.

I finish her braids and tie them with a rubber band. "All done."

She inspects my handy work. "I need a hat. Can you get one for me, please?"

"Sure. Where are they? I haven't seen any in your closet."

"Just grab one of my daddy's. He has them all in his room."

"Okay. You get dressed, and I'll find you a hat."

PAYOFF PITCH

I walk down the long, wide, bright hallway toward Tanner's room. I haven't been in there yet.

I slowly open the door and peek inside. It's not what I expected. The rest of the house is modern, but this is more traditional. Almost regal. The bed has four huge posts with round metal handles coming out of them. There's a large chest at the foot of the bed. It looks like an oversized treasure chest.

I inhale. Yum. It smells like him in here. It's a manly aftershave and cologne combo that I swear my body involuntarily reacts to. Especially when we were in that tent last week. I felt enveloped in it.

I notice two picture frames on his night table and walk over to look at them. One must have been a few years ago with him and Harper at a ball game. So cute. The other is a family of four. I look closely and realize one of them is Tanner in a baseball uniform. This must have been him in college. He was hot then, and I more than love seeing him in his uniform, but it's nothing compared to his more mature sex appeal now.

Both of his parents are in the picture, along with a little boy. I know he has a younger brother, but I didn't realize the age difference. He's at least ten years younger than Tanner. Maybe more. They're an attractive family.

Looking around the room, I don't notice any hats.

I walk inside his closet. Holy shit. It's bigger than my bedroom. How does one man have so many clothes? And everything is lined up perfectly in color order. It's like being in a high-end department store. Wow.

I look around, but I still don't see any hats. Maybe they're in the big chest near his bed.

I walk over. It has a combination padlock, but it's unlocked. It's odd that it would have a lock.

I lift the heavy lid to open it. My eyes almost bug out of my head. The chest is full of ropes, cuffs, chains, whips, paddles, and all kinds of items that I've never seen before.

What the fudge? What is Tanner Montgomery into?

Suddenly, I hear the front door open and Tanner's voice yells out, "Bug, where are you?"

She responds. "Getting dressed, Daddy."

I quickly close the chest and quietly run back to Harper's room. "Sorry, I didn't see any hats."

She's now dressed and takes my hands. "Come on, silly. I'll show you where he keeps them."

"You get the hat. I'll be downstairs."

I walk downstairs and see Tanner on the phone. He looks stressed as he barks out, "I agree, Jerry. There's no *I* in team, but there is one in dickhead, and that's what you're being. He deserves every cent I'm asking for. In fact, he deserves more. You have until noon tomorrow to come to your senses. After that, his price tag is going up. We both know what he'll garner on the open market. Good luck fielding a team next year without him."

He aggressively presses the end button on the call without any further word and mutters, "Asshole," under his breath.

Seeing him in his element, being commanding, just took his sexiness up another notch. I'm going to have to change my panties before the game.

I think I let out a moan or some other noise because he whips his head around to me. "Hey. Sorry if you heard that. I didn't see you standing there." He runs his fingers through his hair. "Some people are such short-sighted assholes."

I take a few calming breaths, resisting the urge to fan my face. "Honestly, I think it's great that you advocate so hard for your clients. Don't apologize for doing your job. I didn't realize how antagonistic it can be." *And how freaking hot it is.*

"Not every negotiation is like that. I've always had amicable negotiations with the Cougars. I think it will be even stronger with the new ownership. Reagan Daulton is smart and understands value."

"She's been more than fair to us. Honestly, she's overpaying all of us."

He smirks. "Investing, not overpaying. You guys are putting

butts in the seats with your play. You're the best in the country. There's something special about your group that Reagan identified before this team even came to fruition. She did her homework. The Anacondas will win the league in the team's first year of existence. That's practically unheard of in professional sports. Trust me, if anything, you're underpaid. Value yourself or others won't value you."

I simply contemplate his words as he continues, "Honestly, I've never worked much with female athletes. A few tennis players here and there, but nothing more. I see the way my daughter idolizes you all. I think I want to find more female agents, probably former athletes, and start a division in my company devoted solely to representing people exactly like you who aren't paid enough. Look at your male counterpart on the Cougars."

"Ezra?"

"Yes."

"He's a great ballplayer."

"He's a solid defensive second baseman and a mediocre hitter. You're better in your sport than he is in his."

"But the Cougars draw more fans. It's dollars and cents."

"Perhaps, but they don't come to see Ezra Decker. They come because the Cougars have been a staple in this town for a century and because of stars like Layton Lancaster, Trey DePaul, and Quincy Abbott. Even Cheetah is a draw, not only for his play, but his larger-than-life personality. It's not Ezra, and he makes probably forty times what you make. That's not right. I get more indignant every time I think about it."

We hear Harper's voice as she enters the kitchen. "Indignant. Anger toward something unfair. What's unfair, Daddy?"

"That women aren't paid as much as men for doing the same damn job. When you're a professional softball player, I want you to make as much money as the boys."

She crosses her arms and emphatically nods. "I won't charge you for the bad word since you think I'll be a professional softball player."

I can't help but smile at the confidence he's instilling in her. *And me.*

I'M at the Cougars game with Kam, Arizona, and Ripley. Quincy is pitching a gem.

Now that Arizona and Layton are the *it couple* of Philadelphia, the cameras constantly find us in our seats directly behind the Cougars' dugout. Kam loves the spotlight and is always dancing for the cameras, often to a sea of applause. We're staples on the big screen at the stadium at this point.

When we were recently shopping for the upcoming *Sports Illustrated* reveal party, I made the mistake of asking Arizona if Tanner was coming. My sister latched onto it and has been cracking jokes about me and Tanner for the past few days.

While Arizona and Ripley are busy chatting away, Kam leans over. "Seriously, is something going on with you and Tanner Montgomery?"

I shake my head. "No. I swear."

"Are you into him? I know you like more mature men."

I bite my lip. "I have a little crush. It's harmless though. He's a lot older than me. I think he sees me as a kid."

She raises an eyebrow. "We're a lot of things, Bails, but kids isn't one of them. No man sees us that way and you know it. Just because you choose not to use your assets to your advantage doesn't mean they're not there."

"*He* doesn't see me any other way. I'm simply the nanny to him, that's it." I swear there was a moment at the campsite where he wanted to kiss me, but I think it might have been the whiskey in me seeing things. Hoping for them.

"Whatever you say. If you're not careful, soon you'll be going from dancing clubs to Sam's Club. Phrases like *bulk buy* will turn you on."

I let out a laugh. "Cut it out, freak."

I hear my name being shouted. Looking around, I notice Harper and Tanner up in the owner's box. They're both waving at me.

I wave back and smile. Harper looks so darn cute in her oversized Layton Lancaster jersey and Cougars hat. Tanner is in jeans, a Cougars sweatshirt, and a Cougars hat. He looks hot.

Kam catches my line of sight. "Look at that, it's Harper and Tanner. Right on cue." She lets out a whistle. "He's fucking sexy. He better keep that hat facing forward."

"Why?"

"When a man's hat goes backward, he goes from dad to daddy."

I giggle. "Seriously, where do you come up with this shitake?"

She smiles as we see Gemma walking down the aisle toward us. She rarely makes it to games with a little one at home. That and she's a successful attorney. I learned a few weeks ago that she writes romance novels under a pen name. The other girls don't know yet. It slipped when she and I were talking, and she asked me to keep it quiet for now.

She sits next to me. "Sorry, it took me a while to get out of the office tonight. It looks like we're doing great."

I nod. "We are." I lean over and whisper. "I finished your first two books. I'm obsessed with them."

She smiles. "Really? Thanks. I have so few of my real-life friends who read my books. I appreciate that you made the time."

That's kind of shocking. She needs better friends. "I can't imagine why. I love them. I've already ordered the rest. The love stories are amazing."

"Thank you. I'm so sick of people calling them porn books. They're love stories."

"I agree. I told Tanner the same thing."

"You discussed my books with Tanner?"

"Yes, I was reading one at Harper's retreat last week after she went to sleep."

She smiles. "You were at the retreat? Is something going on with you two?"

I shake my head. "Of course not. He's my much older boss."

She lifts an eyebrow. "Do you have any idea how popular age-gap romance books are?" She winks. "Get back to me after you read my ninth book. Add in a little single dad and nanny aspect, and we've got ourselves a best seller."

AFTER QUINCY GAVE up a few runs late in the game, Layton hit a huge home run to lift the Cougars to victory. We're all at Screwballs celebrating. Kam and Cheetah have been trading sexually charged jabs all night. I wish those two would just do it and get it over with. It's so unlike Kam to drag someone along like this. I wonder if she genuinely likes him.

Gemma leans over and asks me, "Do you guys know what you're wearing to the *Sports Illustrated* reveal party?"

I nod. "Yes, we all got new dresses. You should join us for hair and makeup that day. Reagan hired us professionals. They're coming to Arizona and Ripley's apartment that afternoon. Do you have your dress yet?"

"I'd love to come, thanks, and yes, I just bought something. My grandmother is in town and she's my best shopping partner."

Cheetah interrupts, "Grammy Jane is in town? I miss her brand of crazy."

Gemma smiles. "Yep. She's here with her *lover*. They're home with Fletcher tonight."

Cheetah chuckles. "I love that Grammy Jane is in a reverse age-gap romance. She's the coolest grandma ever."

Gemma nods in agreement. "Yep. She's definitely not the kind of old-school grandmother who has plastic on her sofas, though I don't think people have plastic-covered sofas anymore."

Kam and I look at each other and smile. I admit, "Our

grandparents totally had plastic on their sofa when we were growing up. They lived in fear of us spilling grape juice on it."

Cheetah shakes his head. "It had nothing to do with your spilling. If your grandparents had plastic on their couch, it's because your grandmother was a squirter and your grandfather knew what he was doing."

I burst out laughing. "Oh my god. That's a horrific image that will now haunt me."

He nods with his trademark smirk and sparkling blue eyes. "But it's true." He winks at Kam. "Right, lickalotapus?"

Kam starts laughing hysterically. "That's a good one, kitten. I haven't heard it before."

He smiles at her. "I love your laugh, but I'd love to hear your moan even more."

I lean over to Kam and whisper, "I think Cheetah is your soul mate. You two come up with the most random stuff."

She whispers back, "I think I might finally sleep with him tonight. I'll fuck with him for another hour or so, but then I'm taking him home. I've been with all women recently. Time to play a little hide the sausage in my fun factory."

"Finally. I was starting to feel bad for him. Go sooner rather than later so I don't have to hear it. It's almost closing time here and I can't deal with your loud ass."

She narrows her eyes at me. "I feel like you've never been fucked properly. Is this a cry for orgasm help? Blink twice if you're in danger."

I roll my eyes, and she sighs. "Fine. We'll leave soon. You'll be okay to get home without me?"

"I'm good. I'll walk home with Arizona or Ripley."

"Why don't you go home with Ezra? He looks like he wants to give you orgasms."

I look over at him and he winks at me. I mumble to her, "I'm not into it. I will never be with him. Don't push me. You know I can't do the random hookup thing, and even if I was, I wouldn't do that to Ezra."

"That's because you want Daddy Tanner and his dry beard."

I pinch my eyebrows together. "What makes you think his beard is dry?"

"Just assuming. Why don't you sit on it and condition it?"

I can only smile at my ridiculous sister.

She winks at me. After some more back-and-forth between her and Cheetah, she finally tells him it's game on, and he immediately throws her over his shoulder and sprints out the door in excitement.

After another round of drinks, the only people left are Trey, Gemma, and Ezra. I'm not sure where everyone else went. Ezra and I were chatting about his family when they all disappeared.

He's homesick. He's from a small town and has a huge family. I think being in a big city is hard for him. I wish he would find someone. He'd be happier if he did.

With the bar beginning to empty out, the sound of the door opening draws my attention. Tanner walks in. I've never seen him here before. I smile as he approaches. "Hey. What are you doing here? It's late. Where's Harper?"

"She's sleeping at the Windsors'. Layton invited me to come but I got hung up talking to Reagan. Where is he?"

Trey chuckles. "He and Arizona couldn't keep their hands off each other. They left a while ago."

His eyes toggle between me and Ezra. "Am I...interrupting? I can leave."

I shake my head. "Not at all. Please sit. It's last call anyway. Have one drink with us."

Could I be more obvious in my excitement to see him outside of work?

I slide down in the booth, and he sits next to me. I only then realize how awkward it is. Trey and Gemma are on one side all over each other. I'm on the other side now sandwiched between Ezra and Tanner. I wish I were more like Kam right now. She'd be in heaven sandwiched between two hot guys. She'd probably give both hand jobs under the table without breaking a sweat.

After the waitress brings us another round, Tanner smiles at Trey and Gemma. "Gem, Trey said he's taking you on a trip for your anniversary after the season. Are you excited?"

Trey's eyes widen. He grits out. "That was supposed to be a surprise, big mouth."

Gemma lovingly rubs Trey's scruff with her fingers. "A surprise trip? I'm so excited. Where are you taking me?"

He licks his lips. "Hopefully from behind, but that's all the info you're getting from me right now."

Gemma giggles as she covers his mouth. "I can accommodate that request."

She brings her lips to his and kisses him. Deeply.

Did I say it was awkward a few moments ago? It just got a lot more awkward.

Suddenly the manager, a middle-aged woman from south Philly shouts, "Last call! If yas don't work here, sleep here, or fuck somebody that works here, pay yas tab and go home."

Gemma breaks the kiss and spits in laughter. "Holy shit. That's funny. I'm using it in a book."

I look at her. "You should. That's in line with the humor of your books. By the way, we don't have practice until the afternoon tomorrow. We're having brunch. Do you want to join us?"

"Sure. Having my grandmother in town frees up my time, but can't we just say we're gonna day drink? Is there any reason to bring eggs into this?"

I giggle. I really like Gemma.

Trey pays our tab, and we all walk out the door. Ezra lives near Trey and Gemma, so he shares an Uber with them. They offer to drop me home first, but Tanner has his car and says he'll drive me.

We get into his red McLaren. I've seen the car at his house, but I've never been in it since there's no backseat and I've never spent real time with Tanner without Harper.

"Wow, this car is beautiful."

He smiles, looking sexy as sin getting into the driver's seat. "I love it. I've got my eye on another sports car that will be out next year. A Maserati."

"Have you always been a car guy?"

"I guess so. When I was growing up, my father restored old cars as a hobby. I used to work on them with him. Even my little brother helped now and then."

"Where is he now?"

Tanner lets out a laugh. "Who knows? We're total opposites. He's a free spirit. Last I heard, he was surfing on the other side of the world. He's a good-looking fucker and always gets slightly older, wealthy women to bankroll his goal to never work an honest day in his life. Maybe one day he'll grow up."

"Wow, you two are different."

"Night and day. My mother coddled him. He was a later-in-life whoops for them. She was forty and Dad was fifty when he was born. I think she felt guilty and let him get away with murder. It made him lazy and a bit of an asshole."

"Do you ever see him?"

"He randomly shows up on my doorstep every few years. I won't give him money, but I usually let him stick around for a bit. We're not close like you and Kamryn."

"I can't imagine another sibling. Kam is about all I can handle."

He chuckles as he pulls up in front of my building. "This is you, right?"

"Yes, thanks for the ride."

He places the car in park. "It's late. I'll walk you up."

"You don't have to."

"I insist."

We walk inside and into the elevator. As soon as the elevator opens on my floor, I hear Kam's moans. Our apartment is right near the elevator bank.

Tanner looks at me in question, but I shrug. "My sister is a screamer. I've been dealing with it for years." I reach into my purse for my AirPods and hold them up. "These help. I have noise-canceling headphones in my bedroom."

He smiles. "You came prepared."

"My sister has a lot of...suitors. She's a busy girl."

He tilts his head to the side. "I imagine you have plenty of *suitors* too. Honestly, you're one of the most beautiful women I've ever seen in my life."

He's staring at my lips.

I hold my breath. Is he going to kiss me? I'm wondering if this is a fantasy, but it's not. This is real. Tanner Montgomery's lips are moving toward mine. His hand tentatively touches my waist.

I inhale his distinguishable scent. My nipples immediately harden. There's no denying it. I want him. Badly.

I close my eyes as his mouth moves closer to mine, but before our lips can meet, we hear a deep voice yelling something in Spanish.

The warmth of Tanner's hand and body withdraws. I open my eyes and see a look of shock on his face. "Is that Cheetah?"

I nod. "It is. They left together just before you arrived."

He steps further away from me. "I should...umm...go. Have a good night."

I blow out a breath as he steps into the elevator and the doors close.

So close. Even if only for a moment, he wanted me.

I slip in my AirPods and turn on my playlist before entering my apartment. Without even bothering to glance at her den of sin, I walk straight into my room, past the pile of clearly discarded clothes on the floor, and close my door.

With music blaring in my ears, I slip into my pajamas, brush my teeth, and get into bed. I toss and turn for a few minutes before bringing my hand to my lips. Tanner was so close to kissing me. I wanted it. *Really* wanted it.

I reach over into my drawer and grab my vibrator. My real vibrator, not the massive porn dick that Kam bought me.

Pulling down my shorts and panties, I run the vibrator

through me. I'm already wet. Spending time with him seems to have that effect on me. There's something about the way he controls things. His conversation on the phone earlier today. His car. All of it is so attractive to me.

I slide it in and close my eyes, trying to imagine it's him. Seeing the contents of that wooden chest today has my mind reeling as to what he's into. I've never done anything that kinky but find myself wanting to experience it with him. I can only imagine the way he must dominate a bedroom. He dominates everything in his life. I want to be dominated by him.

Would he tie me up? Would he spank me with that paddle? Being at Tanner Montgomery's mercy sounds like just about the best thing I can imagine.

I pump the vibrator in deep. Tanner is a big man. I bet he's big everywhere.

And his lips. They're plump for a man. Women pay thousands of dollars for lips like those. I almost felt them tonight. Tracing my fingers over my nipples, I imagine they're his mouth moving all over my body.

What would that sexy beard feel like on my face? Between my legs? What would it look like covered in me?

That's my tipping point. I come with images of his face buried between my legs, my juices dripping from his beard after he makes me come.

Just as I finish, I hear a screeching so damn loud that I know it's not from sex.

I quickly slip back into my panties and shorts before running out of my room. I'm definitely not prepared for what I see. Cheetah is naked, running around like a madman. There's water literally pouring out of Kam's room, immediately saturating our living room carpeting. She walks out, completely nonchalantly, as naked as the day she was born as if it's not Niagara Falls in our apartment.

She smiles at me. "He fucked me so hard that my waterbed

burst." She scrunches her nose. "Damn, I was seconds away from another orgasm. Such a bummer."

"*That's* the bummer? That you didn't have *another* orgasm? Not the flood happening in our apartment or the one below?"

Cheetah is throwing towels at her room as if it makes any difference. It's like trying to drain a swimming pool with a sand bucket.

I look closely at him and turn to Kam. "Why are his balls absurdly large?" I've honestly never seen balls that big in my life.

She nods. "I know, right? And he likes them tickled. I might have a G-spot, but he has a B-spot. I think he could come from it."

"If he tea-bagged you, you'd probably suffocate and die."

She smiles. "Did you know that the female equivalent of tea-bagging is a flappachino?"

I sigh. "No, I suppose I didn't." I sarcastically add, "What a useful piece of information, especially given what we're dealing with right now in our apartment."

She giggles.

I motion toward her state of undress and take in her hickey-covered breasts. "Do you want to cover yourself so we can deal with this nightmare?"

She points to Cheetah, still running around like a lunatic, and shrugs. "I think he's got it completely under control."

Not even close.

We both laugh before I quickly grab Kam the sheet from my bed to cover up and then call the emergency maintenance number we were given when we moved in. They say they'll send a maintenance crew right up.

Cheetah is still screaming in Spanish when Ripley bursts through the door. She takes in the whole crazy scene and then smiles. "The waterbed popped?"

Kam nods and proudly announces, "We fucked it to death."

CHAPTER NINE

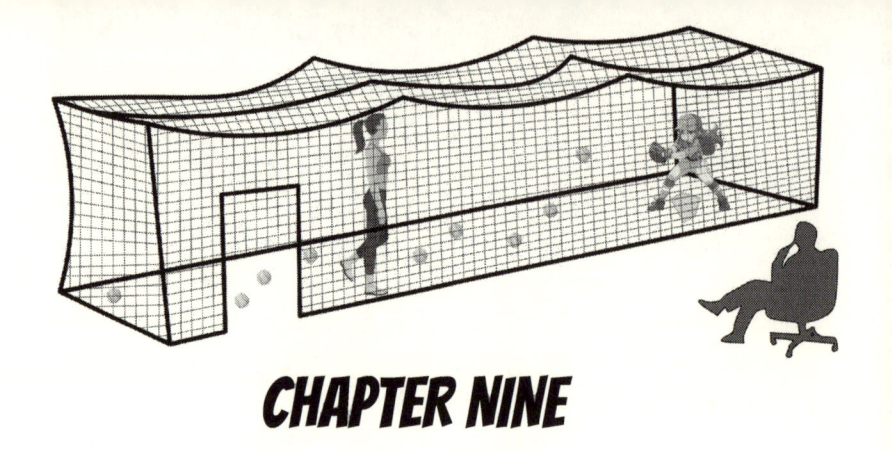

BAILEY

The past few days have been crazy. Our apartment and those on the two floors directly below it are in need of major repairs. Fortunately, insurance is covering all of it but it's still a huge hassle. We apologized profusely to those living under us, but they're rightfully pissed as hell.

Arizona offered to stay at Layton's so Kam and I could share her bed. I had to make my sister promise not to bring anyone home.

I forgot how much I hate sharing a bed with her. She doesn't stop talking. I swear, she never sleeps. Her mind is always moving. When she's not talking, she's on her laptop. Even at three in the morning, she's on her laptop. I have no idea what she does or how she functions with only an hour or two of sleep.

After yet another night of me not getting enough sleep, I asked Tanner if I could stay in one of his many guestrooms, even offering extra free babysitting. He briefly hesitated before agreeing. I told him it's only three nights and he has Harper all of those nights. When she goes to Fallon's, we have a road trip. After that, we should be able to get back into our apartment.

PAYOFF PITCH

I'm at Tanner's house getting settled in when Harper arrives home from her stay at Fallon's house. I make my way toward the foyer to greet them. As always, Harper runs into my arms.

I hug her close. I miss her when she's at Fallon's. "Did you have fun at Mommy's, sweet girl?"

She scrunches her nose. "We were at Nanny and Poppy's a lot. Poppy is very grumpy right now."

I look up at Fallon. "He's still recovering?"

Her shoulders fall. "Worst. Patient. Ever." She looks at her watch. "I should probably go make them dinner. My father whines that he hasn't had a home-cooked meal since they've been home from their cruise, but at the same time won't give my mother two seconds to herself to make anything. I think he's stir-crazy. And I'm a terrible cook, so I'm sure he'll complain tonight too."

She looks exhausted and defeated.

"I was just about to cook dinner for Harper and me. Tanner has a meeting. Why don't you stay and I'll make extra. Then you can bring it to them. You look like you could use a glass of wine. Relax. I'll take care of it."

Her face looks hopeful. "That sounds amazing. You don't mind?"

I shake my head. "I honestly love to cook. It relaxes me. And this kitchen is a dream."

She visibly relaxes her shoulders. "You're an angel."

I let out a laugh. "It's just dinner." I look at Harper. "If you take your shower now and eat all your veggies at dinner, I'll let you hit two full buckets of balls in the cage and then we'll make popcorn and watch a movie. I want to introduce you to my favorite childhood movie tonight."

Her face lights up, and she says, "Deal," as she quickly makes her way to the stairs.

I yell after her, "Don't try to brush your hair. I'll do it."

"Gotcha, Bails."

"And no Skittles before dinner."

"Ugh. Fine."

Fallon smiles. "You're so good with her." She grabs her own ponytail. "Harper got my not straight yet not curly, pain in the ass hair."

"It's worth the hassle to get your eyes. They're so gorgeous. I've never seen anyone with the same shade as the two of you."

"Thank you. What can I do to help?"

I start taking things out of the refrigerator and cabinets. "You can sit on your behind and open a bottle of wine. Tanner said it's been hard for you since your parents got back. It's okay to take a minute for you."

She nods in gratitude as she makes her way into the wine cellar just off the kitchen. She yells out, "Are we drinking red or white?"

I yell back, "I'll be alone with Harper. I'm not drinking."

"It's one glass, Bailey. I won't tell your boss. And he can't judge. He's single-handedly keeping the whiskey industry in business."

I let out a laugh. "True. Whatever you want. I don't care. Just a half a glass though."

She walks back out with a big smile. "Let's all thank Tanner for this thousand-dollar bottle of cabernet."

My chin nearly drops to the floor. "A thousand dollars? For one bottle? That's nuts."

She nods. "I agree." Her eyelids flutter. "But it's *damn* good."

"It better be good. It should give you an orgasm for that amount." I cover my mouth. "Sorry."

She giggles. "It's fine. I'm not sure I remember orgasms, but the fading memories are fond ones."

I look at her in surprise as I cut up the vegetables. "You don't date? You're gorgeous, funny, accomplished, and all-around amazing. Men must be lined up for you."

Fallon is one of those women who don't need an ounce of makeup or fancy clothes to appear sexy. It's effortless. Her body looks like she spends hours in the gym, even though I know she doesn't.

She pours two *full* glasses, hands me mine, plops down in a chair, and then lets out a long breath. "I think divorce hits men and women differently. Men can more easily remove emotion when getting back out there. It's been a little harder for me. Plus, I've been working longer hours since the divorce. I either work or am with Harper. And now I have to help my parents. It doesn't leave a lot of time for me."

"You're a physical therapist, right?"

She nods. "Yes, I work in the rehab center at Philly Hospital. The major injuries department. I load the days I don't have Harper so I can be with her when I have her. It's hard only having her half the time. I don't like to miss a minute of it."

The veggies are sizzling, and the chicken is cooking. I allow myself my first sip. Wow, it's good. Not a thousand dollars good, but certainly the best I've ever had.

I look at her. "You should get out there, Fallon. You have so much to offer."

"Maybe I'll think about putting myself out there when Harper is back in school. Do you date?"

"Not as much as I'd like. Remember, I'm new to the area and we're in season. Maybe when the season is over."

She smirks and echoes my words to her. "You should get out there, Bailey. You have so much to offer."

I smile. "Touché."

"What do you do for fun? Twenty-eight and unattached sounds both magical and like it was a hundred years ago, even though it was only ten."

"In addition to heavy workouts given my profession, I do normal things. I hang out with my sister and my friends, listen to music, eat, drink, and all that kind of stuff."

"Music? Now you're speaking my language. Who's your favorite band?"

Without hesitation, I answer, "Coldplay. I know it dates me a little bit, but I love them."

"Have you ever seen them in concert?"

"No. Have you?"

"Yep. About fifteen years ago. They're phenomenal."

"I bet. I'm so jealous."

Thirty minutes later we're seated at the table. Fallon takes her first bite and lets out a moan. "Oh my god. I think I just had my first O in forever. This is so good."

I giggle but Harper questions, "What's an O?"

Fallon's eyes widen. I answer, "What was the word of the day last week that began with an O?"

Harper thinks for a moment. "Oh, I remember. Omnipotent."

I nod. "Right. And do you remember what it means?"

"Having lots of power."

"Right. Your mommy is eating her veggies like a good girl, so she's feeling powerful. That was her O."

Harper tilts her head in contemplation. "Hmm."

Fallon holds back a laugh and mouths, "Thank you."

A FEW HOURS LATER, Harper and I are watching the movie. Tanner called to say that his dinner meeting was running late. I told him not to rush. I don't have plans tonight, and I'm staying here anyway.

He arrives home just before Harper's bedtime. Her head is in my lap and I'm running my fingers through her hair, subtly working out the knots.

He walks into the family room and smiles at us. "There are my two favorite girls."

Harper turns her head but doesn't lift it. "Hi, Daddy. Bails and I are watching *The Goonies*. She said it's a classic."

He nods. "I can't argue with that. It was one of my favorite movies when I was a little kid. Have you taken a shower yet?"

"Yes, and I ate all my veggies tonight. I'm feeling omnipotent.

Mommy is too. She said eating them made her feel like she had her first O in forever."

Tanner's eyes widen and he looks at me. I mouth, "I'll explain later."

He nods.

I point to the other sofa. "Come watch with us. There are about forty-five minutes left. I told Harper she could stay up a little late to finish it."

"I think I might grab a quick jog before the rain comes." He pats his completely flat stomach. "I had a lot to eat tonight. Bug, is the pitching machine under cover, and are all the balls picked up in the cage? I don't want any of it getting ruined in the storm that's rolling in."

Harper scrunches her nose. "There may be a few still out. I'll run down when the movie is over."

He lifts one of his sexy, thick, dark eyebrows. "You won't fall asleep?"

She shakes her head. "Nope. Wide awake."

I can't help but bite back a smile. She's definitely going to fall asleep.

Forty-five minutes later, Harper is fast asleep on my lap while the credits scroll. Tanner walks in wearing running shorts and nothing else. Holy shit, his body is ripped. He's got a smattering of dark hair across his broad chest. Every man my age waxes their chest. I love that he doesn't. And he's sweaty. God, he's sexy.

Once I swallow down all the saliva pooling in my mouth, I whisper, "Shh, she's asleep."

He shakes his head. "Wake her up. She needs to clean the cage."

"You carry her to bed. I'll clean up out back."

"You're spoiling her, Bailey."

"You had a batting cage installed along with a several-thousand-dollar pitching machine. I'm the one spoiling her?"

"Hmm. Fair point."

He walks over and reaches down to pick her up. I can't help

but take a deep inhale. He smells so manly. I want to lick the sweat off his body.

I hear him inhale too. Was he smelling me? It was probably Harper. She always smells like her baby shampoo. I love it.

As he lifts her, a bag of Skittles falls from her pocket. We both smile at each other.

As I'm walking down to the cage, I hear the first crackle of thunder. Oh shit. I better hurry.

I run down and am picking up the balls when it starts to downpour. Hard. I'm running around to get everything under cover while my hair and clothes are getting completely soaked.

There's a sudden bolt of lightning, illuminating the sky enough for me to see Tanner run into the cage.

He shouts, "You shouldn't be in here with the lightning. It's not safe. I'll do it."

He's quickly grabbing balls on the other side, trying to get them out of harm's way. The rain is pummeling both of us.

I see him making his way toward home plate. I yell out that it will be slippery, but he doesn't stray from his path, steps on home plate, slips, and falls hard onto his back.

He lets out a grunt as I run over to him and fall to my knees next to him. "Are you okay?"

He grumbles, "Give me a second. That hurt."

He lets out a few moans of pain.

After a few moments of him lying in what is now a puddle, I grab his hand and pull him into a seated position. "We should get you inside. Maybe take some Ibuprofen before bed."

He subtly nods but doesn't otherwise move. We stare at each other, both uncaring that the rain is pouring down on us.

He's gorgeous, topless, drenched, and so damn sexy. The raindrops falling down his bare body only add to the appeal. I've never in my life wanted a man the way I want him.

Rain catches on both of our thick eyelashes as we continue to silently stare. The intensity of the mutual attraction is palpable. I know he must feel it too.

Heat is radiating off his body. He's staring at me like he wants to devour me. I *want* him to devour me.

His face is almost pained as he reaches out to move my hair off my face. His thumb runs along my lips. He breathes, "You're so beautiful."

I can't help but reach out and run my fingertips over his beard. Something I've been dying to do since I met him. He's the one who's beautiful.

It finally becomes too much for both of us. We slowly move our lips toward the other's until they meet for the first time.

The kiss is tentative, as if he's savoring it. It starts off soft and sweet. Almost like his lips are brushing over mine, testing the waters.

In mere seconds, he grabs the hair on the back of my head and pulls me closer. The kiss deepens as his tongue slides into my mouth.

His taste is so Tanner. It's masculine and minty with a hint of sophisticated cigar and whiskey. I'm immediately lost in it, wanting to explore all of him.

He easily lifts me and maneuvers my hips until I'm straddling his lap and then grabs my ass pulling my center to his hardness. His *long*, thick hardness. I grab his hair and moan into his mouth, unable to help myself.

His grip on my hair tightens, which drives me wild. I can't help but grind my hips over him. He lets out a groan into my mouth.

I'm desperately turned on. I want him to take me right here. I don't care about the storm. In fact, the whole scene is hot as hell.

My nipples harden to a near-painful point. They're poking through my flimsy top, rubbing against his hard chest. The throb between my legs is relentless, begging for him to touch me. To fill me.

The rain pours down on us, but neither of us pays it any attention. We're both giving into the passion that's been building between us.

Just then, a huge bolt of thunder strikes, startling both of us into breaking the kiss.

Tanner briefly closes his eyes and breathlessly says, "Shit. We can't do this."

I breathe back, "We can. I want you."

He grabs my face. "I want you too, Bailey. I truly do. But I can't do this to you. I can't do it to Harper either. She loves you. This isn't right."

I'm silent. I won't beg him. If he doesn't want me, I certainly won't force it.

I silently nod as I lift my body off his and turn my face toward the house before he sees the tears brewing in my eyes.

He stands and holds me in his arms while I bury my head in his chest and hold back the sobs. Rubbing my hair gently, he says, "I promise, this is for the best." He pulls back. "Let's get you into a hot shower before you get sick."

I momentarily hold out hope that he'll get into that shower with me, but he doesn't. He merely drops me at the door of the guestroom and wishes me a good night.

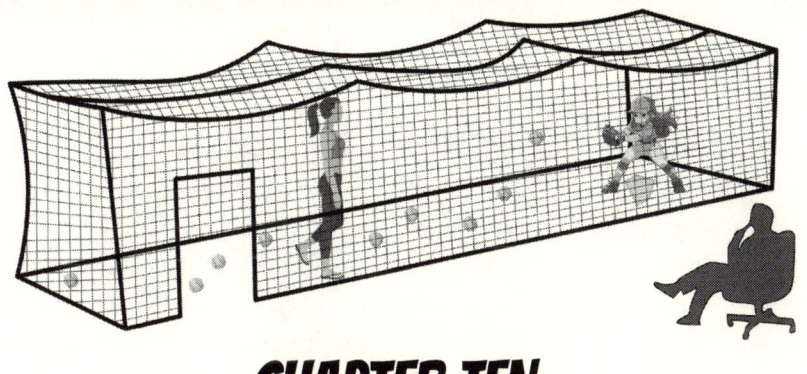

CHAPTER TEN

TANNER

It's been an awkward week since that night in the batting cage. She lived with us those first few days but wouldn't make eye contact with me and barely said two words to me. She left her room just in time for me to head out and went back to her room as soon as I arrived home. That's never been the case before that night. She never acted like she was on the clock. She would always arrive early and always stick around when I'd get home for dinner or to finish a movie. I hate this strain in our relationship.

I haven't seen her for the past few days. Harper was with Fallon, and Bailey had a road trip. But I'll see her tonight at the *Sports Illustrated* reveal party.

Even though it's my night with Harper, I need to be at this party. Fallon is taking her for the evening. She should be here shortly to pick her up on her way home from work.

I'm attempting to tie the bowtie on my tuxedo when Harper walks into my room and gives me a huge smile. "Wow, Daddy, you look like a movie star."

I smile at my princess. "Thanks, bug. I can't get this tie done right though. Any chance you know how to do it?"

She shrugs. "I can try."

She makes several attempts but fails adorably.

We eventually hear the front door open and close. Fallon's voice carries through the house. "Hello? Anyone here?"

Harper yells, "In Daddy's room, Mommy."

We hear her make her way up the steps and then she walks in. Her eyes take in my outfit, and she lets out a whistle. "Damn, Tanner, you look good. *Really* good."

"Mommy, that's ten dollars."

"*Damn* is a bad word? Since when?"

"Daddy says it's a lazy word."

Fallon smiles. "Hmm. I don't want to be lazy." She wiggles her eyebrows. "Hot diggity dog, you look good, Tanner. Is that better?"

Harper giggles. "Yes."

Fallon takes notice of my tie situation. "Do you need some help?"

"Please. Harper, take note. Your mommy is a pro at this."

Fallon walks over and expertly works the tie, as she's done many times for me in the past. I smile down at her. "This reminds me of that time I had to stop at your office in New York on my way to the big ESPN event in Connecticut." I look at Harper. "I was going to the biggest sports awards ceremony in the country each year. Mommy was the only one who could make my tie look good. I had the car service stop at her office on the way just to fix my tie for me. It was before you were born."

Harper shakes her head in amusement. "That's so silly. Why didn't Mommy go with you? She loves sports too."

I pinch my eyebrows together. I don't remember why.

PAYOFF PITCH

Fallon steps back and gives a forced smile. "I had another hour of work. Daddy couldn't wait that long."

My shoulders fall. It's not that I *couldn't* wait that long. I *wouldn't* wait that long. I now remember the fight, but I was so caught up in appearances, I refused to wait for my wife like any decent husband would have.

I nod at the memory. "I should have waited. It was wrong of me. I'm sorry."

She visibly swallows, gives me a small smile, and says something I've said to her several times throughout the past few years. "Water under the bridge."

I take in her nicer-than-normal appearance. She's usually dressed for work when I see her. "You look pretty. What are you ladies up to tonight?"

Her face lights up. "We've got a girls' night. We're doing hibachi with Dylan, Cassandra, Andie, and Amanda."

Harper gasps. "We are?"

Fallon nods. "Yep."

"Yay. Thanks, Mommy. I'm going to catch the shrimp in my mouth on the first attempt this time. Bailey and I were practicing."

Fallon lets out a laugh. "I bet you were. Only you would practice for something like that. Will Bailey be at the *Sports Illustrated* event tonight?"

I answer, "She will. Arizona is one of her closest friends. A bunch of the Anacondas and Cougars are going. The crew is taking a party bus up to New York City for the event, but I declined their invitation. I'll take my own car service and make some business calls on the way."

And I don't want to make Bailey uncomfortable. Things are a little weird between us right now.

A FEW HOURS later I'm at the party, sipping whiskey, chatting with Reagan Lawrence-Daulton and her husband, Carter. They're a remarkably attractive couple, both in their thirties. She's tall with blonde hair, blue eyes, and a stunning figure. He's huge, built like a linebacker, with dark hair and a beard. Aside from Beckett Windsor, they're probably the most famous people in Philly and easily the most photographed couple. Though Arizona and Layton might be giving them a run for their money lately.

When Reagan first bought the Cougars and then brought the Anacondas to Philly, she proposed that Layton and Arizona enter into a public relations relationship. Her reasons seemed a little far-fetched at the time, but I have to admit that she's achieved everything she wanted to. Both teams are thriving.

She didn't want them to actually date, and I don't think she knows they're the real deal yet, but they're definitely real and the public is loving every minute of it. They're nothing short of a PR dream.

Reagan smiles. "So, Tanner, Layton and Arizona aren't looking so fake anymore."

I inwardly laugh. Reagan is very perceptive. I guess there's not much she misses.

I smirk as I give her a bit of a tongue-in-cheek response. "My lips are sealed. I'm afraid I'm bound by attorney-client privilege."

She lets out a laugh. "What a bunch of bullshit. Hopefully it plays out well and they hold it together for a few more months. My internal spies told me that their photo session was hot as hell, and they might be the cover couple."

My eyebrows raise. "That would be incredible. I guess we'll find out within the hour. It would be great for both teams and for each of them individually. My phone will be ringing off the hook if that happens. Sponsorship opportunities will flow like champagne."

She nods. "I agree. I can't wait to find out for sure, but I'm feeling confident."

She already knows the answer. I can tell. Reagan Daulton has eyes and ears everywhere. She's a force to be reckoned with.

An attractive, slightly older couple approaches. They both have dark hair and green eyes and look familiar, though I can't place them.

The woman wraps her arm around Reagan in a warm, familiar way. "Thanks for inviting us, doll face. It's all so exciting."

She kisses the woman's cheek. "Of course, Mom."

Mom? The woman doesn't look more than a few years older than me.

"Mom, Jackson, this is Tanner Montgomery. Tanner, this is my mother, Darian Knight, and her husband, Jackson Knight."

Ah, that's why they're familiar. Jackson is a well-known developer in Philly, and he happens to be Trevor's father.

I take Darian's hand. "It's nice to meet you."

She smiles warmly. "You too. Trey DePaul's wife, Gemma, works for me. She has for years. Well before she started dating Trey."

And that's why she looks familiar. I must have seen her at their wedding.

I shake Jackson's hand as well. "It's nice to finally meet you. My daughter is very close with your granddaughter, Dylan."

He smirks. "She's a ball of fire like her mom, isn't she?"

I chuckle. "She sure is."

Jackson whispers something in Darian's ear, causing her to grin widely and nod. They excuse themselves and leave the room.

Carter attempts to bite back a smile, and Reagan shakes her head. "They're definitely finding a closet right now to have sex in."

My jaw widens. "Are you serious?"

Carter chuckles. "Reagan's mom is like a horny teenager. They do this all the time." He winks at Reagan. "We should go give them a run for their money."

And...that's my cue to walk away.

I mingle for a bit before making my way toward the bar for a refill. As I approach, I see Bailey with her back to me. She's in a gold dress that is extremely short and tight. I'm surprised she's wearing such a revealing dress. It seems unlike her.

I place my hand on her lower back and whisper in her ear, "You look stunning."

She turns around, and I immediately realize my mistake. Pulling my hand away like she's on fire, I say, "I'm sorry. I thought you were Bailey. You must be Kamryn." I hold out my hand. "It's nice to officially meet you. I'm Tanner Montgomery. I know we stood together in a group a few weeks ago, but I don't think we were introduced."

She smiles. It's a completely different smile from Bailey's. It's more playful and full of mischief. I briefly think of the ex-boyfriend that Bailey mentioned. How the hell could he not tell the difference? Yes, they're identical, but the contrast is blatantly obvious to me.

She takes my hand in hers. Her touch is different too. "Sorry to disappoint, though I'm impressed you knew the difference. You must know my sister *very* well. It's nice to meet you too."

Her tone is laced with innuendo.

Before I can respond, Cheetah approaches. "Oh look, it's two of my favorite people, together."

Kam turns to him. "Oh look, it's my eighth favorite feline."

Cheetah lets out a laugh as he rubs her back. "You know cheetahs are your favorite animal. Don't deny it, Kam bam."

"I'm not sure about that, kitten." She turns to me. "Though I know my sister's favorite animal. Silver foxes."

Everything Bailey has mentioned about her sister is becoming clear as day to me. This girl is trouble with a capital T.

The lights dim, mercifully ending the conversation. After remarks by the editor-in-chief of *Sports Illustrated*, they lower a screen where the contents of the issue are revealed. Arizona and Layton's interior photo is nice, but when they're revealed to be the cover couple, there's a collective gasp.

It's extremely provocative. I can't believe they're publishing it. They're half-dressed in each other's jerseys with their undergarments showing. Her legs are wrapped around him while he has her pinned to a scoreboard with his face buried in her neck. She looks like she's mid-orgasm. Wow. This will catapult both their modeling and sponsorship careers into the stratosphere. I better prepare my office for the onslaught coming when this issue hits the stands.

As the buzz fills the room, Bailey approaches and gives me a forced smile. "Hello, Mr. Montgomery. You look nice."

I take in her appearance. Her dress is a bit more demure than her sister's, though still sexy. Everything about her is sexy. She oozes class in a way Kamryn doesn't. I rub her arm. "You look exquisite." She's a vision in white. It contrasts beautifully with her olive-toned skin.

"Thank you. Can I introduce you to my sister and one of my friends? Both Kamryn and Ripley have a bunch of sponsorship offers. I know they're too small for you to take on as clients, but maybe you can offer them some advice?"

"I'd be happy to."

After offering to provide my services to an elated and

surprised Kamryn and Ripley, I pull Bailey aside. "Can we talk?"

She exhales a breath. "Sure. What's up?"

"I want to apologize for the other night."

She shakes her head. "No need."

"There is a need. I shouldn't have let it get that far. I was wrong."

Her face falls. That's clearly not what she was hoping for.

I take her hand in mine. "You're everything a man could ever want in a woman. We're just in different places in life, and you're Harper's nanny. She adores you. I don't want to do anything to jeopardize your relationship with her."

She looks up at me with sincerity written all over her gorgeous face. "I love Harper."

"I know you do. Can we go back to how we were before that night? I like it when you come early to chat and when you stay for dinner. Dinners you usually prepare. I consider you a friend and I don't want to lose that because of a moment of indiscretion."

Pain slices through her face but this needed to be said. I can't give in to the temptation that is Bailey Hart.

She eventually nods. "I'd like that too."

BAILEY

We're on the bus on the way back from the party. Arizona is on Layton's lap, and his hand is up her dress. Trey and Gemma are in a dark corner practically having sex. They're marriage goals. I would give anything for a man to look at me the way Trey looks at her.

And then my eyes find Ezra across the bus, and he's drinking me in with his heated gaze. He's looking at me *that* way. Why have I been denying myself this? Tanner doesn't want me. Ezra does. He's handsome, kind, sweet, loving, and age appropriate. Why haven't I truly considered it before? Maybe it's time I give things a chance with him.

I stand, walk over to him, and sit down. He leans over and whispers, "Are you okay? You seem a little off tonight."

The way he can read me and the genuine concern in his eyes flick some sort of switch in me. The sides of our bodies are pressed together. The comfort of his body suddenly feels like a warm blanket on a cold day.

I look into his eyes and nod as I thread my fingers through his and quietly respond, "I want to go home with you tonight."

He visibly swallows. "You do? Are you sure?"

"Yes. I want to...I want to give things a go with you. You and me. Together."

His look of concern morphs into a huge smile. He squeezes my hand. "I'd like that. I think I can make you happy."

I think so too.

He spends the remaining bus ride with his thumb rubbing soothing circles on the back of my hand. Regardless of who we're each talking to, his hand is always on mine.

By virtue of geography, we arrive at his place first. I imagine everyone on the bus is in shock when I stand with Ezra and walk with him toward the exit door.

I catch my sister's look of concern, but I hold up my hand and shake my head. I don't need Kam trampling this. It's my decision. I need to do this. I need to stop fantasizing about a man I can't have and start spending time with a wonderful man I can. One I know for a fact cares deeply for me. One who would never reject me.

Her lips tighten into a line, but she respects my wishes and doesn't get involved. Instead, she mouths, "Call me," and I nod that I will.

Everyone else is whistling and catcalling, but I ignore them and stay the course. Ezra wraps his arm around my shoulders, his way of shielding me from the onslaught.

The rest of the unmarried guys on the team have apartments and condos in the city, but Ezra has a house in the suburbs. It's not as big as one would anticipate from a professional baseball player, but as soon as I walk in, I understand why he chose it. It's homey. It's warm. It's Ezra.

I can't help but smile, especially at the wraparound porch with rocking chairs. "I love this place. It's so you."

He gives me a shy smile in return. "It reminded me of the house I grew up in. The guys give me a lot of shit for not living in a bachelor pad in the city, but when you grow up in a small town, city living is a shock to the system. I'm not too far from them, and I prefer the peace and quiet."

I rub his arm as we walk into the house. "It's perfect, just like you."

He nervously chews on his lip. "Can I get you a drink? Are you hungry? I can make you something to eat."

I shake my head. "No thanks."

I walk over to the wall of pictures that appear to be of Ezra and his family. Looking at the big family picture, I immediately identify the sister he's mentioned to me. I point to her. "This must be Leigh. You two look alike. She's beautiful."

I suddenly feel the warmth of his body pressed to the back of mine. He pulls my hair to the side and runs his lips along my neck. "It's you who is beautiful." His fingers run up and down my arms. "You have no idea how long I've dreamed of having you here. Touching you. Feeling you. Kissing you. Making love to you."

His hands move to the zipper on the back of my dress. "Is this okay?"

I nod, and he slowly slides the zipper down my back. I can feel his hands shaking as he does so. It's sweet how nervous he is.

My dress eventually falls to the floor. I step out of it and turn around. I'm in white satin panties and a matching strapless bra. It's in stark contrast to my sun-kissed, naturally darker skin.

His hazel eyes drink in my entire body while the bulge in his pants pushes against his zipper. His jacket is gone. He must have removed it when I was looking at the photos. Ezra Decker is imposingly handsome.

I can now see his hands shaking and he notices my line of sight. "I'm sorry. I've fantasized about this so many times. I'm having a hard time believing it's real."

I wish I could say the same, but I can't. My fantasies are full of a certain bearded, older man.

I hate that I'm thinking about Tanner right now. Ezra deserves all my attention. I shake off my thoughts and do my best to return them to the wonderful man standing in front of me, dying to touch me.

I grab his hand and bring it to my face. "It's real, Ezra."

The backs of his fingers stroke my cheek before he moves his lips toward mine. I welcome them with my own and slide my tongue into his mouth.

His taste is like him. Sweet. Comforting.

Before I know what's happening, I'm pinned to the wall and his hands lift the backs of my thighs until my legs are wrapped around him. I lock my ankles and try to match the intensity of his kiss.

His hardness presses between my legs while his hands roam my body. It feels good, but I don't feel the same fire I felt with Tanner.

Stop it, Bailey.

I'm committed to pushing Tanner out of my mind. Ezra is here and wants me. Desperately wants me.

His hands squeeze my ass, and he mumbles into my mouth, "You taste even better than I thought you would."

He kisses down my neck, which is a big erogenous zone for me. I love having my neck kissed. I finally relax and begin to truly give in to the pleasure, relishing in what he's doing to my body.

His hardness rubbing me and lips on my neck finally have me where I need to be. In the moment, enjoying this.

Ezra's face is clean-shaven and is rubbing against the area between my shoulder and neck. I can't help but start to imagine what Tanner's bearded face would feel like on my neck. I bet it's rough. I bet he's rough. Everything about him is just so domineering.

I moan, "Tanner."

Ezra freezes. At first, I don't know why. It takes me a moment to realize what I've done.

Oh my god.

He slowly drops my legs and takes a step back. His face is pained while the guilt fully sinks in for me. I'm a horrible person.

Tears fill my eyes, and I cup my mouth with my hand. "I'm so sorry, Ezra."

He runs his fingers through his wavy hair. "It's Tanner? I knew it was someone, I just didn't expect it to be him."

Leaning against the wall, I close my eyes and let the tears spill over. "I don't want it to be."

"But it is."

I nod.

"Why did you come home with me?"

"Because I want it to be you."

"But it's not."

I shake my head and croak out, "No. I'm so sorry. I don't deserve you."

Without another word, he turns and walks upstairs. I take a few long, deep breaths. I should get dressed and call an Uber, but I slide down the wall and let the tears continue to fall. I'm so ashamed of myself. I've hurt an innocent man.

He returns a few minutes later with an oversized sweatshirt and enormous shorts. "I've had too much to drink to drive you home, and I don't want to put you in an Uber alone at this time of night. If you're comfortable staying here, I'll make up my guestroom for you and drive you home in the morning."

I reach for him, "Ezra—"

He steps back. "It's fine. I get it. You're not into me." He drops his head. "You never will be."

"I want to explain."

He shakes his head. "No need. It only makes this worse."

He hands me the clothes, and I quietly and quickly slip into them. I have to roll the shorts ten times to get them to stay up. "Thank you. I understand if you don't want to talk. Can we watch a movie or something? I don't want to say goodnight to you yet."

It seems that much colder to simply go to bed. I want to spend time with him. He's still my friend. I can't lose that.

He sighs. "Sure. What do you want to watch?"

"It doesn't matter to me."

He turns on a movie, and we silently sit down on the couch together. I barely remember any of it before I pass out.

I WAKE in the morning enveloped in warmth with something very hard poking my ass.

Blinking my eyes a few times, I realize that I'm on Ezra's sofa, he's wrapped around me, and he doesn't have a shirt on.

This feels nice. Why can't it be enough for me?

I'm contemplating falling back asleep in the security of his arms when I hear music blaring and the song "I Just Had Sex" by The Lonely Island begins playing. I giggle as I lift my head to see Cheetah standing there with a big smile, holding his phone up, singing and dancing along with the lyrics.

Without having to open his eyes to see who it is, Ezra groans. "Go away, Cheetah."

Cheetah chuckles. "I'm just glad your dick still works. Though sex is easier when you're naked in the bedroom, not clothed on the couch. Has it been so long since you had playtime at the farm that you forgot how the hokey pokey works?"

Ezra starts to answer, "We didn't—"

I cover his mouth with my hand and interrupt, "We didn't even make it to the bedroom before we tore each other's clothes off and went at it." I nod toward my dress on the floor. "And the only farm analogy appropriate here is that Ezra is an animal in the best way possible. I got cold during the night and grabbed a sweatshirt that smells like him." I inhale it deeply. "Hmm. So good."

Cheetah lifts an eyebrow. "Ezra Decker an animal in the sack?"

I nod and Ezra sighs. "I forgot that we had plans for this morning. We need to run Bailey home. Go wait outside. We'll get dressed and meet you in your car."

"Fine, party pooper."

He walks out and I turn around in his arms. I look up at him and run my fingers over his handsome face. "I'm really sorry about last night, Ezra."

"It's okay. You didn't have to lie to Cheetah."

"Yes, I did. You can tell the guys whatever you want about last night. I'll go along with it."

"Does it really seem like my personality to brag about my sexcapades like Cheetah does and Layton used to before Arizona?"

I twist my lips. "I suppose not."

He begins to stand, but I hold him close and sink my nose into his chest. "I don't want to lose our friendship. You mean a lot to me, Ezra."

He relaxes and hugs me back. "You won't. You mean a lot to me too. Tanner is a lucky man."

"I'm not with him and don't think I ever will be."

He gently caresses my hair. "He'd be crazy not to fall for you. I did the first night I met you. You're everything a man could possibly want in a woman. You're kind, smart, and so damn beautiful that sometimes I find it hard to breathe around you."

I tilt my head up and softly kiss his lips. "You're going to make some lucky woman incredibly happy one day."

I GET HOME and see Kam asleep in her bed. That's a rare sight.

I need to confide in someone though, and I don't want it to be her. She can be overbearing.

I let myself into Arizona and Ripley's apartment. Arizona's door is open, and her bed is made. She must have slept at Layton's. I open Ripley's door. "Rip, I need to talk to—"

Shock isn't a big enough word for what I see. Ripley is naked with Quincy equally naked. His face and hands are on her breasts. "Holy Red Wedding! What the fudge is this?"

Quincy quickly covers their bodies. I had no idea that they were sleeping together. Oh my god. I wonder if Arizona knows that her best friend and brother are doing it.

She mentions that it was a one-time thing, but Quincy looks annoyed by the comment, and I'm not sure I believe her. Nonetheless, I leave them to it and tell Ripley to let me know when she's free to talk.

About fifteen minutes later, she texts me to come back, and I do. I walk in and she pours me a cup of coffee. I look up at her. "What the freak is going on?"

She sighs. "Don't make a big deal of it. Quincy and I fool around sometimes." Her eyes fill with tears. "It's meaningless, which is why we don't want anyone to know."

"Arizona?"

She shakes her head. "No. No one."

"Rip, why are you crying? Maybe you care more than you'd like to admit."

"It doesn't matter. He'll never want more than casual. In

what world does a man who looks like Quincy Abbott end up with a woman who looks like me?"

"Because...beautiful men and beautiful women don't end up together?"

"Because fit men and fat women don't end up together."

"Don't call yourself fat, Rip. You have curves. Men love curves. You're perfect. You model lingerie for crying out loud."

She mumbles, "Plus sized," and then sighs. "It's not happening. Drop it. I don't want to talk about it."

Wiping her tears, she says, "Enough about me, though I hope you'll keep this between us."

I nod. "Of course."

"Did you sleep with Ezra? I honestly thought you were into Tanner."

I exhale a breath. "Tanner isn't interested in me. I wanted to try things with Ezra. He's so sweet and so into me, but in the end, I couldn't do it. Why can't I have casual sex like my sister does?"

She rubs my back. "There's nothing wrong with needing an emotional connection with someone before the physical."

Tears fill my eyes. "I'm so fudging attracted to Tanner. On all fronts."

"Does he know?"

I nod. "He does. We kissed once but he ended it. He said he can't do it to Harper and that I'm too young for him."

"But not that he wasn't attracted to you?"

I twist my lips and think back. "I suppose he didn't say that."

"Maybe it will happen one day."

"Doubt it. I just want someone to set me on fire the way he does. Hell, I think I'd settle for half as much as he does."

Before we can continue, Kam walks in. She's wearing panties and a crop top with no bra. Her nipples and the bottoms of her breasts are more than visible. She rubs her eyes like she just woke up.

I shake my head. "You can't just walk around the apartment building like that, Kam. We're not in a college dorm anymore."

PAYOFF PITCH

She waves her hand dismissively. "Meh. It's fine. It gives the weird ginger across the hallway something to look at. It's probably as close as he'll ever get to seeing a woman naked."

Ripley narrows her eyes at Kam. "You know his name is Justin, and what's wrong with gingers?"

"Ginger women? Nothing. You're all hot. I've banged a few ginger women in my day. Ginger men? Not so much. What do you call a ginger man in a porn film?"

Ripley contemplates for a moment before asking, "What?"

"The cameraman."

I can't help but giggle. Ripley does her best to swallow hers down.

Kam continues, "What do ginger men miss most at a great party?"

I bite back my smile. "What?"

"The invitation."

Ripley and I can't help but burst into laughter.

I shake my head. "Oh my god. Your mind is truly bottomless. It's one of the great mysteries of life."

Kam curtsies. "Thank you. Speaking of mysterious behavior, you didn't call me. I know you didn't sleep with him. Why did you go home with him?"

"Maybe I did sleep with him."

She rolls her eyes. "You didn't. It's a twin thing. I can feel it when you have sex."

I scrunch my face. "Eww. That's weird. Though I wish I could feel when you did. I'd be much more satisfied. Twin orgasm telepathy would be the best thing to ever happen to me."

Kam wiggles her hips. "You would have been having a *great* time last night if it worked."

"Who were you with?"

"Doesn't matter. I want to know about you."

I blow out a breath. "You're right. I couldn't go through with it. He's so adorable, and I wish I could, but we just hung out."

"It's because you want Daddy Tanner. He wants you too."

I shake my head. "He doesn't."

"Trust me, Bails. He does."

"He's not attracted to me."

She scoffs. "Not to sound like a narcissist because we're twins, but you're hot as hell. Also, I met him last night before you officially introduced us. When my back was to him, he thought I was you and told me how beautiful I looked. The second I turned around, he knew I wasn't you. He sees you, Bails. I'm telling you, he's interested."

I shrug. "I'm not forcing it. It's not my style."

She gives me her unique Kam mischievous smile. "But there are always ways to help things along. Men are simple beings. They're so easy to toy with." She throws her arm around my shoulder. "Ever heard of playing hard to get?"

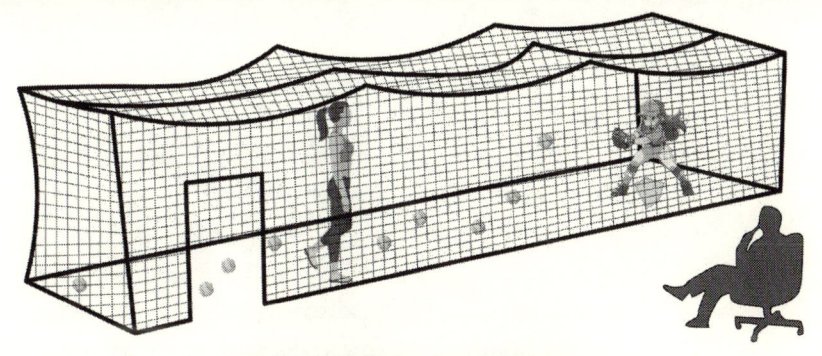

CHAPTER ELEVEN

TANNER

It's been weeks since the *Sports Illustrated* party. Things were a little awkward with Bailey for a bit, but they've gotten much better.

In fact, she's been acting completely unaffected by it all. I'm the one who's pining after her while she's seemingly moving on. She even mentioned leaving for a date the other night. I nearly put a hole in my wall in frustration and jealousy after she left.

We've settled into a routine now that Harper's school year is underway. During the evenings Harper is with me and Bailey doesn't have a game, I come home to dinner in the oven, and Bailey and Harper are either in the batting cage or the pool. I think Bailey's bikinis are getting sexier and sexier each time, but it might be my imagination.

Both the Cougars and the Anacondas are well into the playoffs, so we've unfortunately seen a little less of Bailey for the past two or three weeks. I do my best to schedule my meetings on the small handful of afternoons and early evenings that she's available right now because when she's not, I have to leave work early to get Harper.

Tonight will be the last home game for the Anacondas. They're down two to one in the best-of-five championship series. If they lose tonight, their season is over. If they win, they'll go down to Miami later this week for a decisive game five.

The Cougars won their World Series game this afternoon. They're up two to one in the best-of-seven series. They're off tomorrow but then play in Philly the following two nights.

Harper and I are at the Anacondas' game. The buzz is electric. The stands are overflowing. Ticket prices were through the roof. I love how much the city has embraced this team. Their tough, gritty play has truly ingratiated them to the Philly fans.

Harper is wearing her *B. Hart*, number thirty-four jersey, which Bailey had signed by everyone on the team. Harper probably wears it at least five times a week. I warned her that it might fade, but Bailey promised her a new one if it did and told her to keep wearing it and supporting the team. She's so good to my daughter, which makes me that much more attracted to her, as if I needed any help in that department.

Harper didn't want to sit in the owner's box tonight. She wanted to be in the action, as close to the field as possible. We're sitting with Cheetah, Layton, Quincy, and Ezra. I warned them all to be on their best behavior.

The game hasn't even started, and they've already removed their shirts to reveal a giant anaconda that continues across each of their chests. Naturally, Cheetah has the tongue on his and manages to roll his belly in a way that makes the tongue look like it's moving. Harper was in a fit of giggles when she saw it.

As he always is at Anacondas' games, Cheetah is wearing

PAYOFF PITCH

a cowboy hat. I don't know why he does that because I've never otherwise seen him in one. Perhaps it's because he's from Texas. Regardless, he keeps placing it on Harper's head, and she's having a blast. He's so sweet to her.

The Anacondas take the field. As she does every time he's at a game, Arizona's eyes immediately find Layton and he blows her a kiss.

He's a different man. He was the biggest playboy I'd ever met until she entered the picture. Now he's a complete goner for her.

I've noticed Quincy paying a lot of attention to Ripley lately. I wonder if anything is going on there.

Ripley is the best pitcher I've ever seen, but she must be getting tired after a long season. She hasn't had her best stuff lately. She's still great, maybe the greatest ever, but not as perfect as normal. It's a good thing the team has scored a lot of runs in the playoffs. Kamryn and Bailey have both been on fire lately, leading the offensive charge.

I notice Ezra staring at Bailey as she takes the field. I realize he's wearing her jersey too. Why does that make me insanely jealous? They make perfect sense together while she and I don't. But the thought of another man's hands on her drives me insane.

I glance at Bailey to see if she's looking at him, but she's smiling and waving to Harper, who's in heaven over the attention.

The game is moving along, and we're down a run heading into the bottom of the last inning. Arizona, the leadoff batter, bunts her way on base and then easily steals second. She's probably the fastest baserunner in the league. The second batter lays down a perfect sacrifice bunt, moving Arizona to third base as Bailey steps into the box.

I lean over to Harper. "There's one out. What does Bailey need to do here?"

Harper shouts, "Hit a home run!"

I shake my head. "Nope. That's not what the team needs. The team needs Arizona to score to send this game into extra innings. All Bailey has to do is either hit a ground ball to the right side or hit a sacrifice fly. She shouldn't be swinging for the fences. It's called situational hitting. It's also called being a good teammate."

Harper nods. "Right. That makes sense. You don't want to swing your hardest and risk striking out."

"Exactly."

"Do you think Bailey knows?"

I smile at her naivety. "I'm confident she does."

I notice Bailey choke up on the bat and nudge Harper. "You see that she moved her hands up on the bat. She's just trying to make contact. She's doing the right thing for the team."

Harper watches on with rapt fascination. I love sharing my love of the game with her. The small nuances of this sport make it a thinking person's game. It's so perfect for Harper.

She squeezes my hand. "I'm nervous, Daddy."

I squeeze hers in return. "Me too. I believe in Bailey though."

The first pitch comes in. It's inside, and Bailey leans her front elbow into the pitch and takes a hard fastball to the upper arm. I wince. That's going to leave a big bruise, but she was hit by the pitch and takes first base.

I say to Harper, "That's called taking one for the team. She leaned into it. Did you see how she subtly moved her elbow so the ball would hit her?"

Harper nods. "I saw, but now she won't be the hero."

"Heroes come all in different forms. Kamryn is the best hitter in the league. Bailey did what was best for the team to get the best hitter up in the biggest situation. And now not only is the tying run on base, but the winning run is on base too."

PAYOFF PITCH

Harper nods. "Bailey could be the winning run!" She takes a few deep breaths. "My heart is pounding so fast, Daddy."

I chuckle at how much she cares. "So is mine."

Cheetah takes Harper's other hand and places it over his eyes. "I can't watch. I'm too nervous. Tell me what happens."

Harper laughs and playfully slaps his arm. "Stop it. You do this all the time."

He winks at her and sighs. "I suppose I do, but it's harder when you're in the stands and it's your friends."

All the fans are on their feet clapping and cheering for Kamryn. She watches the first pitch for ball one.

Harper audibly releases the breath she was holding.

The next pitch comes in, Kamryn swings, and crack. It's a line drive to the left-center gap. Everyone is going nuts. That easily scores Arizona to tie the game and should move Bailey over to third base.

Suddenly I see the third base coach waving Bailey around to try to get home. Why the hell is the coach doing that? She's going to be out.

The cheers of Arizona scoring quickly morph into gasps as everyone collectively holds their breath watching Bailey barrel toward home plate.

The throw from the left fielder arrives at the catcher well ahead of Bailey. She fields it cleanly and is about to tag Bailey out when Bailey literally jumps up and over the catcher, somersaulting across home plate.

The crowd is quiet as the umpire signals that she's safe and the game is over. The Anacondas win.

Cheetah looks at me wide-eyed. "What in the pigs flying universe did I just see?"

I'm speechless. I breathe, "She's unbelievable."

The whole stadium erupts in cheers. The Anacondas' dugout empties and piles on top of Kamryn. Yes, she had the game-winning hit, but Bailey is the one who should be celebrated.

KAMRYN'S HIT and Bailey's acrobatics from last night have been playing on repeat on all local stations and all the national sports stations. It's great attention for the sport and team. *#HartHasHeart* is trending all over the place.

Kamryn did a million interviews. She was born to be in front of the camera. She's charming and witty. Her innately outgoing personality shines through, and the reporters are eating it up.

She tried to pull Bailey into a few of the interviews, calling her the true hero of the game, but Bailey was more than happy to let Kamryn have the limelight. It's interesting how much they look alike yet how different they are.

It's been a long day. I'm glad Bailey is off today and was able to help with Harper this afternoon and into the early evening.

I had an unavoidable meeting that lasted way longer than it should have and was wildly unsuccessful. Some people are such assholes. A negotiation by definition is supposed to be a discussion to resolve differences. That's hard to do when one side won't budge at all. It's got me all stressed out.

And I missed dinner with Harper. Damn it. At least I'll be home before she goes to bed. I'm excited to see Bailey and talk to her about the game. Hopefully she'll stick around for a bit tonight.

Or maybe I'm just excited to see Bailey in general.

Layton, Cheetah, Vance, and Daylen all walk into my

office. I look up at them. "What are you all doing here? I'm just about to head out for the day."

Layton answers, "Let's grab a drink. You've seemed stressed lately."

I shake my head. "Not tonight. I need to get home to Harper."

Cheetah turns to him. "Told you he'd say that." Looking back at me, he says, "One drink. Thirty minutes. Tops. You can choose the location."

I run my tongue over my teeth. "Fine. The bar across the street, and only one drink. I really need to get home to my girls."

Cheetah smirks. "Girls?"

"Girl. I meant girl."

"Sure, buddy. Let's go."

Ten minutes later, we're all sitting at a table with a round of drinks. All eyes fall on me.

I look around at my friends and take in their serious faces. "Why do I feel like this is an intervention?"

Cheetah nods. "It is." He swallows. "After the *Sports Illustrated* party a few weeks ago, did you know that Bailey went home with Ezra?"

I can't stop my jaw from ticking. My grip on my glass becomes so tight that I think it might break. The thought of her with him or any other man makes me ill.

Cheetah turns to the guys. "Told ya so. He's into her too."

I lift an eyebrow. "Too?"

He nods. "She's into you."

"Not if she went home with Ezra."

"Nothing happened. He said she couldn't go through with it because she's hung up on you. I now know that you want her too. What's the problem?"

"I'm pretty sure you're hung up on Kamryn. What's your problem?"

He shrugs. "Kam will eventually come around. She'll wise up one of these days."

"According to Bailey, Kamryn is already extremely wise."

With a completely straight face, he declares, "Nearly all women at one point possess highly intelligent DNA. But most eventually spit it out."

I can't help but chuckle before turning to Daylen. "What about you? You were seeing that Linda woman. What's going on with her?"

He scrunches his face. "She asked me to name all my sexual partners."

Everyone grimaces. Layton shakes his head. "Oh no. Never answer that. It's a trap."

Daylen twists his lips. "It's even worse than you think. Note to self, when asked that question, be sure to stop at the name of the woman asking. They don't like when you name people after them."

I sigh. These guys are idiots. Well-intended idiots, but idiots nonetheless.

Cheetah nods at me. "Come on, Montgomery. Spill it. What's the story with you and Bails? What's stopping you?"

I scratch my fingers through my beard. "Where do I begin? She's too young for me. She's too good for me. And she's Harper's nanny, who Harper happens to idolize. It's all a recipe for disaster."

Vance shakes his head. "You're allowed to be happy, Tanner. All you do is work and spend time with Harper. What about you? You need to do something for yourself. Trust me, man, I know."

Vance is one of the most selfless people I know. Because of it, life has been an uphill battle for him.

"Being with Harper makes me happy. I was a shit father for her first three years. I need to make up for it."

Layton sighs. "You weren't a shit father. Maybe a shit husband, but never a shit father."

I give him the finger, even though I know he's right. "Thanks, asshole."

He chuckles. "Sorry, man. It's the truth. You know it is."

I blow out a long breath. "I do, and that's why I can't get involved with anyone, especially someone so important to Harper. And Bailey deserves to be treated right. Look at my track record. I haven't had a real relationship since my divorce. Nothing but meaningless encounters. There's a reason for that."

Layton places his hand on my shoulder. "Look at what's happened in my life over the past few months. I thought I didn't want anyone until I found the right someone. Leave the possibility open. Bailey is an amazing woman. You're one of the best men I know. I think you two could be incredible together."

I shake my head. "No. Not happening. I'm not interested in something real with her or anyone else. Meaningless encounters. That's it for me for the foreseeable future."

He nods toward an attractive woman sitting alone at the bar. "She's gorgeous and she's been staring at you since we sat down. If you're not into Bailey, go talk to her. Go have a little casual fun with her."

He's challenging me. Maybe I need to do this to get over Bailey. To move on from my infatuation.

I stand. "Fine. I will."

I'M FINALLY on my way home. After ultimately being uninterested in an extremely willing and attractive woman, I'm more stressed than ever. The guys were testing me, and I failed. I don't want anyone but Bailey. They know it. I know it. The question is, what am I going to do about it?

I arrive home just after nine, meaning I won't get to say goodnight to Harper. It's rare, and I hate when it happens. My time with her is already cut in half. When I miss one of my nights it feels like double the amount of missed time.

I walk in through the garage and the entire first floor of the house is dark. I wonder where Bailey is. On the few rare occasions I've been late getting home, and Harper is asleep, I always find Bailey in the family room either watching a movie or reading a book.

The only light I see is in the stairwell leading to the second level. I quietly make my way upstairs and hear voices. In her sleepy voice, Harper asks Bailey, "Will you still be my nanny when your season is over? All through the school year?"

"If you'll have me, sweet girl."

I can't help but wince at the nickname she calls Harper. It makes me cringe.

Harper whispers, "I don't ever want you to leave. I love you."

My heart melts for my little girl and how much Bailey has come to mean to her.

I hear Bailey sniffle as if Harper's words clearly made her emotional. "I love you too, Harper. Don't worry. I'm not going anywhere. My season will be over tomorrow. Then we can spend even more time together."

"Will you come to my championship game next week?"

"I sure will. Nothing could keep me away."

"Do you think you'll be the hero again tomorrow night?"

"My sister was the hero last night. Not me."

"Daddy says you're the real hero. Will you teach me that flip thing you did?"

Bailey lets out a laugh. "I'm not sure you can teach that.

I was a little crazy for doing it. I think my adrenaline got the best of me."

Harper giggles. "It was the coolest thing I ever saw in my life. Daddy and I replayed it on his phone a thousand times."

"Throwing from the slot at seven years old is pretty cool too. I think you've finally got it down."

"I've been doing what you told me. I'm visibilizing it."

I hear Bailey giggle. "It's visualize, not visibilize. You've got to close your eyes and imagine yourself doing the things you want to do."

"I will. I'm going to visualize being a hero like you."

"I have no doubt it will happen for you. Do you remember the softball phrase of the day?"

Harper responds, "Ducks on the pond. When two or three runners are on base. You say it to the batter to encourage them to knock in the runners."

"Excellent." I hear her kiss Harper. "It's time for bed. It's past time for bed. You need to rest up and eat well going into your big game next week."

Harper lets out a huge, audible yawn. "Okay. Will you tell my daddy to give me a kiss when he gets home? Even if I'm asleep."

"I sure will."

I quickly tiptoe back downstairs. Without bothering to turn on any lights, I throw my jacket on a kitchen chair and pour myself a glass of Macallan. I swirl the amber fluid a few times before taking a much-needed sip.

It slides down with the smoothness only a fine whiskey can, immediately softening the edges I can't seem to shake. Leaning back on the kitchen counter, I think about how strong my feelings have become for Bailey. Months ago, I never would have turned down what was being offered at the bar tonight. Now, the thought of touching anyone but Bailey disgusts me.

I run my fingers through my hair. What the hell am I going to do? This woman has implanted herself inside me. I can't shake it. I can't shake her.

Are the guys right? Should I go there? It seems like a disaster in the making, but it equally feels out of my control. I'm not sure she even wants me anymore. She doesn't act like it.

A few minutes later, I hear Bailey walking down the stairs. She doesn't notice me. I simply watch her as she walks into the family room and tidies it up. As always, she's in spandex shorts and a tank top, revealing every perfect curve on her body.

She doesn't turn on any lights. The large windows and full moon afford plenty of illumination in the open family room and kitchen spaces.

She bends over and places the now-folded blankets back into the basket next to the couch. Her ass is taunting me.

My cock didn't get the memo I've been trying to send him. He stands at immediate attention.

Seemingly satisfied with the state of the family room, she makes her way to the kitchen. Despite the darkness, she notices me and gasps when she steps in. She clutches her chest. "Oh my god, Mr. Montgomery, you scared me. I didn't realize you were home yet."

"I'm sorry. I didn't want to disturb you and Harper. I could tell she was just about to fall asleep, and if I went in, it would upset the apple cart."

She nods. "I understand. She wants a kiss when you can."

I loosen my tie with my free hand. "I know. I will. Does she have water up there?"

Bailey shakes her head.

"I'll leave her some water too. She gets so thirsty during the night. Did you two have fun?"

She gives me a genuine smile. I have this overwhelming desire to make her smile like that too.

"We did. We hit for hours, as always. She's still working on throwing from the slot. I think she has it down pat." She lets out a laugh. "My sweet girl is a hard worker."

I can't help but wince again at the nickname.

She notices and pinches her eyebrows together. "Does it bother you that I call her sweet girl? I don't mean to overstep. If I've done anything to—"

"It doesn't bother me for the reasons you think it does," I interrupt.

She tilts her head to the side questioningly. "Then why does it bother you?"

I take a long sip of my whiskey. More than a sip. A gulp.

Looking her straight in the eyes, I admit, "Because *I* want to call *you* sweet girl."

She sucks in a breath as her big eyes widen and her nipples immediately harden under the thin, tight material of her shirt. "I...I...I thought we discussed that anything between us would be a bad idea. A mistake. You said you don't want me like that."

I give a small nod. "It's still a bad idea, a mistake, but it doesn't mean I don't want to taste your sweet lips again. It doesn't mean I don't want to know if the rest of you tastes just as sweet. It doesn't mean I don't want to hear your moans as I give your tight little body a pleasure it's never known."

Her breathing picks up and her cheeks redden. I notice that she subtly rubs her thighs together as her eyes find the unmistakable bulge in my pants. One I don't bother attempting to hide.

I see her then eyeball my drink. Holding up my glass, I ask, "Would you like some whiskey? It's the good stuff."

She slowly licks her lower lip. It's not meant to be seductive; it just is. Everything about her seduces me.

She takes a few steps in my direction. I assume she's going to reach for a glass in the cupboard, but she doesn't. She stands directly in front of me. Her soft fingers brush against mine as they find their way around my glass. I release it, assuming she's going to take a sip from it. Again, I assume wrong.

She removes the glass and places it on the counter next to me before standing on her tippytoes and then licking across my lips.

She settles her feet back down and tastes her lips with her delicate pink tongue. "Hmm. That *is* the good stuff." Her eyes meet mine in a lustful look that fantasies are made of. "I think I'd like some more of that."

The last of my restraint snaps as I turn us and use my body to cage her into the corner of the countertop with my face only inches from hers. "You have three seconds to stop me, sweet girl, because if you don't, I won't walk away this time."

She smiles as she runs her hands up my chest. "I don't want you to walk away this time. I didn't want you to walk away last time."

We stare at each other. She wants me every bit as much as I want her. Her cool demeanor of late was an act. I think we're at the point where it's unavoidable. The draw is too strong. And I'm done fighting it.

She grabs my tie and pulls me until our lips smash together. Her sweet taste is everything I remember it to be, but there's nothing sweet about the way she's kissing me back. Her tongue runs along my lower lip before sucking that lip into her mouth. This aggressive kiss is unexpected but more than welcome.

I give it right back as we deepen the kiss and our tongues explore each other's mouths. The passion we're sharing has my mind spinning. Perhaps it's the months of longing. The buildup.

I squeeze her ass and pull her tight to my rock-solid erection. She moans into my mouth, causing my tip to leak like a damn teenager. I'm desperate to be inside her. There's no stopping this now.

Grabbing the bottom of her tank top, I lift it up and off her body. Our lips break as her shirt passes through. I glance down and see her pink nipples just visible through her black lace bra. Her tits are round and perky. Slightly more than a handful. My mouth waters.

She looks up at me with all the confidence of the magnificent woman she is as she removes her shorts, leaving her in a matching lace thong. I run my eyes and fingers down her curves. The pads of my fingers brush against her soft flesh with a reverence I didn't know I was capable of.

Perfect. That's the only word to describe the woman in front of me.

I lift an eyebrow. "You just so happened to have on matching lace undergarments?"

She gives me a sexy smile and breathes, "I've been waiting for you to notice me."

My brow furrows. She doesn't understand. I cup her face with both of my hands. "Sweet girl, you're all I see."

She whimpers, "Tanner. I want you."

She's never called me Tanner. Is it wrong that I think I prefer Mr. Montgomery? There's something dirtier and sexier about it.

I lift her so she's seated in the corner of the countertop. She immediately spreads her legs in invitation.

Still standing tall, I take a deep inhale. "You're wet for me. I can smell it."

She nods as she squirms a bit. "Feel for yourself."

I run my fingertips just under the waistband of her panties. Back and forth. Back and forth. Her skin is so warm and silky.

Tremors work their way through her body. Desire is written all over every inch of her.

I pull my fingers back out and move them down her panty-covered pussy before rubbing them over her covered center a few times. She's soaked.

She wiggles. "Please touch me. I can't wait any longer."

Gently sliding her panties to the side, I slip a finger through and then into her heat. Her eyes flutter and she releases a nearly unrecognizable sound of pleasure. Her body constricts around my finger. She's tight. *Very* tight.

After a few pumps, I pull my finger out and, without breaking eye contact, immediately suck it into my mouth. "Hmm. So damn sweet."

BAILEY

I watch him lick my juices off his finger and nearly combust. I've never seen a man do that before. His eyes practically roll to the back of his head in ecstasy.

I've never wanted a man more than I want him right now. I pray he doesn't stop this again. I don't think I could handle it.

For the past several weeks, I've been playing it as cool as possible, per the advice of my sister. Acting unaffected by him. Acting disinterested when I'm anything but. I may have exaggerated evening plans a few times, making it seem as though I was going on dates. I also borrowed a few of Kam's borderline erotic bikinis to wear in front of him.

Catching Tanner Montgomery staring at me has become my new favorite hobby. I've basked in his very apparent inner struggle. For some reason, tonight it snapped for him. At least I hope it has.

I can't take the slow seduction anymore. I frantically move my hands to unbuckle his belt, but he grabs my wrists to stop me.

Oh no. He's not going to go through with this.

But I'm wrong. *Very* wrong.

With his long fingers still wrapped around my wrists, tightly, he says something that I'll never forget. "You may be used to being with undisciplined boys who fumble with excitement at the possibility of being with a woman like you. They may give you control, but that's not how it is with me. I'm a real man and I like to be in control." He pushes my hand between my legs and applies pressure to my pussy. "When you're with me, you're at my mercy. Tell me you understand."

I'm dumbfounded, but I nod. I think I would promise him anything at this moment to make sure this happens.

In his deep voice, he gives me the approval I didn't know I needed. "Good girl."

For some reason, I'm panting. I haven't moved in minutes, but I feel breathless. My heart is pounding so fast that it feels like it's going to burst out of my chest.

His hands release my wrists and slowly skate up my back as he unclasps my bra. It falls away, freeing my breasts.

Cupping each, he breathes, "So fucking perfect." He briefly tugs and twists each nipple, turning them into hardened peaks. It causes a slow throb to begin a steady pounding between my legs.

His fingers then find the waistband of my panties again. I momentarily bring my legs together and lift my hips as he slides them down my legs with no sense of urgency.

He's so slow and controlled. I want to tear his clothes off, yet he meticulously and unhurriedly discards mine. My body is physically shaking in anticipation. I don't know what he's going to do next, and I'm here for it.

He removes his tie before instructing, "Put your wrists together and hold them out for me."

Holy hell.

I do as I'm told, and he uses his tie to bind my wrists together in some sort of expert fashion. Why does he know how to do this so well?

He asks, "Have you ever been tied up before?"

I shake my head. I haven't, but I've fantasized about it ever since I opened that chest all those weeks ago.

"I'll be gentle tonight, but I still want you to have a safe word."

"A safe word?" I question.

He nods. "If at any point I become too much for you, use your safe word."

"What is it?"

He thinks for a moment before a small smirk finds his big lips. "I think I might like *payoff pitch*. It's the ultimate decision, isn't it?"

I smile at him using the phrase I had mentioned on the way to the camping trip. I whisper, "Okay."

He manages to hook the tie to the handle of the cabinet above my head, leaving my arms suspended in the air. I'm naked and under his control. I've never been more turned on. My pussy is pulsing in anticipation.

His big hands cup the swells of my breasts as he bends and runs his tongue through my mouth. I attempt to deepen the kiss, but he pulls away and slaps my nipple. Hard.

I gasp but it causes a fluid to gush through my pussy.

He shakes his head. "No, no, no. I'm in control tonight. There may be times when I allow you to take some control, but that's not tonight, sweet girl. Do you understand?"

I swallow and nod again.

He smiles at my answer before his tongue traces a line down my neck and chest until he reaches one of my nipples. He bites it, causing more moisture to pool between my legs. How can a person be this turned on?

Sucking my aching flesh into his mouth, he soothes the spot he just bit. I'm confident my nipples have never been this hard before.

His tongue then continues its downward descent. He mumbles into me, "So beautiful."

Every inch he moves has my body thrumming. Throbbing.

Just as he's about to reach the spot where I need him the most, he changes direction and moves back up my body.

He repeats the same down-and-up pattern over and over until I feel like one swipe of his tongue through me will push me over the edge.

I'm trembling, silently begging him to stop the teasing and put me out of my misery.

This time when his mouth meets mine, his fingers move through the drenched flesh between my legs. I can't help but moan into his mouth.

"Is this where you want me, sweet girl? It certainly feels like it."

I beg, "Yes. Please."

He smiles. "It's time for me to feast on you. Don't come too quickly. I want to savor it."

Fat chance of that. I'm already teetering on the edge.

He kisses his way down until he's on his knees staring at the most intimate part of my body. I've never been more grateful to Kam for forcing me to go get groomed with her every few weeks.

He inhales deeply. "Spread your legs as wide as they can go. I want to see all of you bared to me."

They're spread wide but he manages to push them a drop wider. My feet are on the countertop. My arms are tied above my head. I'm truly and completely at his mercy. There's something deeply sensual about it. I've turned over all control to him. And I'm not remotely scared about it. In fact, I think I love it.

He licks through me, and I swear if I wasn't tied up, I'd slip right off this counter into a puddle on the floor. His tongue then sinks inside me while his fingers expertly work over my clit, applying the perfect amount of pressure.

My orgasm is already at the surface. I can feel it about to

explode through me. I moan, "Don't stop. Oh god, please don't stop."

"Shh. No yelling. Not tonight."

I have no control over my body, including the sounds coming out of my mouth.

He pulls his face away from my center. I shout, "No, don't stop!"

"You're loud, bad girl. I might have to take you over my knee and spank you."

"Oh my god." My body is shaking like a leaf. I'm like an addict in need of my next hit. "I'll...I'll try."

His fingers sink inside me while his mouth crashes against mine. His thumb then takes over on my clit.

His tongue in my mouth drowns out my moans of ecstasy. The taste of me on him drives me wild. My orgasm builds back up in seconds. I'm about to come when he withdraws again.

I'm about to scream out when my eyes catch his. He wants to control me. He's showing me who's the boss. As long as he makes me come, he can have whatever he wants.

When he realizes I'm doing what he wanted, his fingers and mouth return to my body in the same fashion until a hurricane swirls around and then crashes through my body. I explode into a million pieces.

My vision has gone dark. My legs are numb. I can't even wiggle my toes. My tied hands and Tanner's weight on my body are the only things keeping me upright. I've never felt more depleted of energy or more satisfied in my life.

When my vision returns, Tanner's shirt is unbuttoned and he's unbuckling his belt. His chest is even sexier than I remember. He's so broad and manly. "Tanner, I need to touch you. Please untie me."

He stops his movements and slides the fingers that were inside my pussy into my mouth. "Who did we decide is in control?"

I mumble around them, "Y...you."

"That's right."

He couldn't possibly move any slower as he finishes unbuckling his pants, then unbuttoning them, then unzipping them.

I whimper. I need him inside me.

"The more you wiggle and whine, the slower I'll go. If you want my cock inside that pretty pink pussy of yours, stay still. Obey me, sweet girl."

I do my best to remain still, though the tremors in my legs give me away. His lips simply curl in amusement when he takes notice. "It's hard to be teased, isn't it?"

He's doing this on purpose. This is payback for my teasing him for the past few months.

I can only nod, unable to form words.

After removing a condom from his wallet, he finally pushes his pants and boxer briefs down enough for his cock to spring free. Calling it a cock isn't really enough for what I'm looking at.

I play for a team called the Anacondas. I bet the person who named the team had no idea that there are men out there hiding them in their pants because that's exactly what I'm looking at. I don't think I can take him inside me. I've never been with anyone nearly that big.

As if reading my mind, he says, "Don't worry, it will fit." He gives himself a few long pumps. "Your tight pussy will take this and love every second of it."

And then be ruined for life.

I watch as he rolls the Magnum condom down his cockasaurus rex. I suddenly have this urge to take him in my mouth, but I'm pretty sure it's not happening right now.

"You're licking your lips. You want to taste him, don't you?"

I nod. "Yes."

"Next time. For now, I need to be inside your pussy. I've dreamed of it every single night since we met."

It gives me a little more confidence knowing that he's wanted me as much as I've wanted him.

"Tell me, do you touch yourself thinking of me?"

I breathe, "Yes."

He smiles before he runs his tip through me. "Still so wet for me."

Wet isn't a big enough word. I'm like a bathtub faucet for him. I can feel it leaking down my inner thighs.

"Are you ready?"

I thrust my hips up. "So ready. Please. Now."

He raises an eyebrow, giving me a chastising look. I quickly still my body.

He nods in approval. "Smart girl."

He moves his hips forward until his tip enters me and, without breaking eye contact, pushes further and further into me.

A shudder works its way through my body. I can't control it. He doesn't stop though. He must know the effect he's having on me.

I feel so full. Fuller than I've ever felt. I glance down and see that he's only about halfway in. How is that possible?

Just as my eyes meet his again, he slams the rest of the way in. His mouth covers mine as I scream into it. Oh god, so deep. So full.

He stills inside me and begins to kiss me, likely allowing me a little time to get used to dino-dick.

After a minute or so, he breaks the kiss long enough to instruct, "Wrap your legs around me."

With every ounce of strength I can muster, I do just that, locking my ankles at the curve of his narrow waist.

His hands grip my ass as he begins his heavenly thrusts inside me. I'm feeling a pleasure I didn't know existed. It's been less than a minute and I'm addicted. He could ask anything of me right now and I'd do it. Anything to keep this euphoric feeling going.

I arch my back and tilt my hips to give him the best angle possible. He lets out a groan. "My sweet girl likes it, doesn't she?"

My mouth seals over his as I mumble, "Uhm-hmm."

He continues plunging into me over and over again. I pull on my arms, still tethered above my head, dying to touch him but equally knowing that if I ask for it, I'll never get what I want.

Without breaking our kiss or any strides of the deep fucking he's giving me, he reaches up and releases my arms. My wrists are still tied together but at least my arms are free.

I'm able to touch his beard, his neck, and his sexy chest, covered with the same-colored dark hair that sits on his head. God, he's sexy. I want to touch and lick every inch of him.

Eventually, I wrap my arms around his neck as the onslaught continues. My belly tightens, knowing another orgasm is closing in.

With each thrust of his hips, my body is lifted off the counter. I'm climbing the ascent with the peak in reach, but part of me doesn't want to get there yet because the journey is so damn good.

As if sensing it, his mouth takes mine again to drown out my noises. The wave begins to crest, and I can't hold back anymore, so I let go. It crashes down as the most intense orgasm of my life washes over me.

His tongue has to suck mine to keep my screams at bay, but as my orgasm recedes, his intensifies and he groans into my mouth. I suck his tongue this time to keep his loud final roar at a lower volume.

His thrusts slow until they eventually stop, though our mouths remain together. We're both breathing loudly. I love his breath on me and in me.

Eventually, our lips peel back and it's just his forehead on mine.

He breaks the silence first. "I knew this would happen."

"You knew we'd have sex tonight?"

He shakes his head. "I knew if I had one little taste, I'd be addicted to you."

I'm about to admit the same when we hear Harper's voice at the top of the stairs. "Daddy? Are you home yet?"

He quickly pulls away from me with a worried look on his face. "Yes, bug. Need some water?"

In a sleepy voice, she croaks out, "Yes."

"Stay upstairs. Get back into bed. I'll bring you some in a minute."

"Okay, Daddy."

He quickly disposes of the condom, pulls up his pants, buttons his shirt, and grabs a bottle of water. "I'll be right back."

I shake my head as I hold out my wrists. "Untie me and then go be with her. She'll want a story to fall back asleep. I'm going to head out."

His brow furrows while he releases my wrists from their confines. "I think we should talk about this. Don't go yet. I want you to stay."

I don't want to come down from this high. What if he tells me that it's a one-time thing? Or worse, a mistake. I couldn't bear it. I want one night to bask in the afterglow of the best sex of my life.

I peck his lips and then begin to gather my clothes. "I'll see you in the morning, Mr. Montgomery."

He hesitates briefly before finally heading toward the stairs.

While he's upstairs, I quietly dress, leave, and drive home. Flashes of what we just did play on repeat in my mind. My body is still pulsating with both excitement and contentment. There's a delicious ache between my legs. The same goes for my lips, nipples, and wrists. That was more than sex, and I want more of it. More of him.

I quietly enter my apartment. Kam is, mercifully, fast asleep on the couch. She was probably waiting for me. She's going to interrogate me in the morning. I'm glad I need to be at the Montgomery's house early. Maybe Kam will still be asleep when I leave.

After laying a blanket on her, I head to my room. I should shower but I can still smell him on me. I'm not ready to let go of that yet. Even though I have to be up early, I decide that I'll shower then. I want to smell him on me all night while I dream of him, though the real Tanner is much better than any fantasy I've ever had.

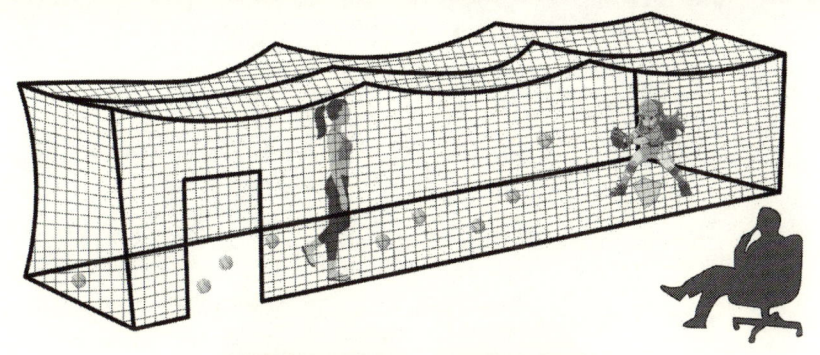

CHAPTER TWELVE

BAILEY

I peel my eyes open to the sounds of my alarm in the early morning. I see a blurry figure I know like the back of my own hand. Kam is standing over me, staring at me. She sniffs. "You had sex last night."

Shit. I don't want her to know. I pull the blankets up on my body. "Ugh, what are you rambling on about at this ungodly hour? Why are you awake? Why are you *always* awake?"

"Don't deflect. You weren't here when I got home. Where were you?"

"Mr. Montgomery was working late. I had to stay with Harper."

She narrows her eyes. "I don't know if I believe you. Something is off. I can sense it." She places her hands together in front of her chest, as if in prayer. "Confess your sins, my child."

"No, Father, there was no penetration."

I sleepily giggle at my own joke, but she grabs my arm. "Let me smell your hands. I bet they have daddy cock cream all over them."

I let out a laugh as I pull my arm away. "No, you freak. Go

away. I need to take Harper to school today. Leave me alone to get ready."

Arizona and Ripley walk in. Kam nods toward me. "Doesn't Bails look like she just had sex?"

Arizona pinches her eyebrows together. "With who, her vibrator?"

I give a bemused Arizona the finger and Kam shakes her head. "No, with a certain sexy older man. In pornos, they call older men daddy instead of dad. Do you know why that is?"

I blow out a breath. "God help me. Why?"

"Because he gives the extra D. Is that what you're getting? A little extra Vitamin D from Daddy Tanner?"

I giggle. "You're nuts."

"Are you getting nuts...on your chin?"

Ripley wraps her arms around Kam's waist and pulls her away, rescuing me. "Leave her alone. Not everyone is as horny as you."

As she pulls Kam away, she mouths to me, "Did you sleep with him?"

I let a small smile find my lips and wink.

She has a huge grin on her face as she drags Kam out of my room.

I take a quick shower, get dressed, walk out, and see them all sitting at our kitchen table eating donuts along with their now daily dose of pineapples.

After last night, I guess I'm happy with my recent uptick in pineapple intake.

We all usually eat healthily except when Kam is PMSing. She goes even more crazy during that time of the month. She eats everything in sight and acts like a lunatic. We all know to go along with it and not poke the bear. At least it explains her behavior this morning.

I look at her. "Getting your period?"

She makes a sound of disgust. "Ugh. Yes." She shoves another donut in her mouth. With a full mouth, she garbles, "I can't stop eating. You know why they call it PMS?"

"Of course I do. It's an acronym."

She smiles as she shakes her head. "Nope. Because Mad Cow Disease was already taken."

We all burst out laughing. I shake my head. "Your mind is an endless supply of useless shitake."

She scowls. "That's useful."

I grab a few pineapple slices and Kam lifts an eyebrow. "I bet I know why you need to taste good. Has Daddy Tanner been tasting your...*pineapple juice*?"

I roll my eyes and sarcastically say, "I truly hate to eat and run, but Tanner asked me to come by this morning to get Harper off to school. He has an early meeting."

She mumbles, "A meeting? I think this meeting is him using his telescope to explore your black hole."

"What does that even mean? And why are you all awake?"

Ripley replies, "Reagan Daulton asked to meet with us about our sponsorship deals. She just wants to make sure everything is on brand with the Anacondas."

I suppose that explains why I didn't know about it. I've turned everything down. "Gotcha. Have fun. I'll see you guys later."

Kam waves her fingers at me. "Have fun wiggling his toothpick."

Oh, Kam, it's no toothpick.

I mercifully head out the door without any further inquisition or euphemisms for sex.

I have no idea what it's going to be like between me and Tanner this morning. I hope it's not awkward. More importantly, I hope he doesn't regret it. I certainly don't.

My question is quickly answered seconds after I arrive.

My key isn't even in the door yet when it opens. In a flash, Tanner walks out, closes the door behind him, and then does some sort of ninja spin move and pins me to it.

Before I can get a word out, his mouth immediately crashes into mine, and his fully formed erection pushes onto my stomach…all the way up to my cleavage. I immediately drop my bag and grab fistfuls of his dress shirt, kissing him back with everything I have.

Unlike last night when his breath was laced with whiskey and cigars, this morning it's minty and fresh. I'm not sure which I like better. They're both sexy because they're his.

His hands slowly explore the curves of my body until he breathlessly breaks the kiss. Without moving away, he says, "I wish you would have stayed last night. I couldn't stop thinking about you. Smelling you on me was driving me nuts. I need more of you."

I can't help but smile as I move my hands up his solid body. "Me too. I could smell you on me all night. I almost didn't shower this morning."

He runs his nose along my cheek. "I need to dirty you up again. Fallon has Harper tonight. I want you to come back. Spend the night with me so we can do all the things we couldn't do last night. So I can make you scream to your heart's content."

I let out a moan. "That sounds amazing, but we leave for Miami this afternoon. You know that."

He tilts his head back and blows out a breath in frustration. "Shit. I forgot." He pulls my hair so I'm forced to look up at him. "I don't know if I can wait three more days to have you again. One taste wasn't nearly enough. I'm about to explode."

I like this version of Tanner. A lot. I'm practically melting into him right now. If he wanted to take me right here, I wouldn't stop him. In fact, I think it sounds like a good plan.

Our intimate moment is broken by Harper's voice yelling from inside the house, "Daddy, where are you? I need you, Daddy."

I don't know what comes over me, likely my sister's craziness, but I smile and coo, "I need you too, *Daddy*."

He lets out a growl from deep in his chest and then grips his cock. "Holy fuck. Is it wrong that my cock nearly exploded when you called me that?"

I bite my lip. "Should I call you Daddy instead of Mr. Montgomery?"

His eyelids flutter. "My cock likes both." He thrusts it onto me so I can feel the truth of his statement. "Every time you've called me Mr. Montgomery over the past few months, all I could imagine was bending you over my lap and spanking you."

Holy crap. Why do I like the sound of that?

We both smile. Our lips are about to meet again when the door opens. I almost fall through, having to catch myself.

Harper grins. "Bailey! I didn't know you were coming today. Yay!" She pinches her eyebrows in confusion. "Why are you outside, Daddy?"

Tanner quickly picks up my bag to cover his unmistakable bulge. "I was outside checking on the rose bushes when Bailey arrived. I'm helping her with her bag."

Rose bushes? It takes everything I have not to laugh. He has a gardener and has never once attended to the massive grounds himself.

He's sweating at the brow, unable to make eye contact with her. He's a terrible liar. I think I like that about him.

She's looking at him skeptically. I need to distract her attention. I rub her hair. "Did you go to the bathroom this morning, sweetie?"

She looks up at me and smiles. "Yes. Daddy won't know this one. It's a funny word."

"Well, what is it?" I ask.

She giggles. "Bumfuzzle."

I shrug. "I have no idea. Is it a hairy butt? It sounds like one."

Harper breaks into hysterics. "No, silly." She looks up at Tanner. "Do you know, Daddy?"

He scratches his chin as he smirks. He definitely knows. Smart bastard. "Let me think. This one has me a little... bumfuzzled."

Harper's face and shoulders fall. "You know the word. I thought today was finally the day."

He turns to me and winks. "It means confused."

I nod in understanding. "I've certainly never heard of it before. I'm bumfuzzled that your father knows every random word ever created. I'd love to see him go at it with Kam over a battle of wits."

Tanner smiles. "Anytime." He sighs. "I need to head out to my meeting. Bailey, can you help me with something in the garage?"

"Sure, Mr. Montgomery." I look at Harper. "Take out the eggs and any veggies you want in your omelet. We'll make you a good breakfast before school. I'll let you flip it today."

Harper's eyes widen with excitement. "Fun! Can we also have pineapples like you always eat?"

"Absolutely."

As soon as she turns toward the kitchen, Tanner grabs my hand and pulls me toward the garage. Once in there, he takes me into his arms.

I wasn't sure whether Tanner would be regretful, awkward, emotionless, or something similar today. But I definitely didn't have *rabid for me* on my bingo card. I couldn't have dreamed up anything better.

He kisses up my neck, and I moan, "Just so you know, my neck has always been my weakness. Your beard on my neck could probably make me come one day."

I feel him silently laugh before he brings his eyes to mine. "I suppose that gives me something to work toward." He rubs my arms. "Good luck tomorrow night. We'll be rooting for you."

"Will you be at the Cougars' game?"

He nods. "Yes. I've got five clients playing in that game. I need to be there. They promised to show updates of your game on the big screen. Everything has clicked for you guys. I don't see them beating you."

"We'll see. The girls are already talking about partying on South Beach when we win."

His brows furrow, "Don't party too hard."

I can't help but smile. "Are you jealous, Mr. Montgomery?"

He adjusts himself. "Ugh. Don't call me that right now. Not when I can't do anything about it."

I giggle.

He tucks my hair behind my ear as his face turns serious. "Are you okay about last night? I know I came on strong and I know how I can be in bed."

"What bed? That was a kitchen counter. The same one I'm about to use to make omelets."

The corners of his mouth raise in amusement. "They'll never taste as good as you. I can promise you that. I wouldn't mind flipping you over like an omelet."

I wouldn't mind that either.

He nods at me. "We're good?"

I run my fingers through his beard. "We're more than good." I smack his ass. "Go get to your meeting. I'll text you from the hotel tonight, and I'll see you when I get back."

He gives me one long, hard kiss, along with an ass squeeze.

I walk back inside in a dreamy state until I see about twenty different vegetables sitting on the counter. "That's a lot of veggies, Harper."

"I want to play just like you in my championship game."

TANNER

I walk into my office building feeling better than I have in weeks. Months. Years.

I smile at my longtime secretary. "Good morning, Shannon."

She eyes me skeptically. Have I really been that grumpy lately? I suppose I know the answer.

"Umm, good morning, Mr. Montgomery. Mr. Lancaster is in your office waiting for you."

"Yep. Can you—"

"Your coffee is in there waiting for you."

"Thanks, Shannon. You're the best."

"Are you...okay, sir?"

I inwardly laugh. I guess I am an asshole. "I'm great. More than great. Why don't you head to Parc for lunch today and use the company card? Invite a friend. It's on me." Parc is the nicest restaurant within walking distance of the office.

Her face lights up. "Oh. Wow. That sounds wonderful. Thank you."

I nod. "You're very welcome."

I walk into my office and see Layton sitting there. He looks me up and down. "Who are you and what have you done with Tanner Montgomery?"

I lift an eyebrow. "What do you mean?"

"Umm, you're smiling. You look like you're about to break into a song." He gasps. "Did you and Bailey finally bruise the beef curtains?"

I avoid eye contact and sit at my desk pretending to look through a file. "You sound like Cheetah. And I'm a grown man. I don't engage in locker room gossip."

He wiggles his eyebrows. "Ahh, but that means there's something to gossip about."

I roll my pen between my thumb and forefinger. "We may have taken our physical relationship to another level last night. That's all you're getting from me."

He has a huge grin on his face. "That's awesome, man. I'm happy for you. Truly."

"Thank you. Let's get to business. I have a crazy day today. What's with the urgent meeting? Though I'm slightly grateful because it meant I needed Bailey to come by this morning to mind Harper, but tell me why you're here."

He winks. "Glad I could help. I want to talk about my contract extension with the Cougars."

The Cougars initially told Layton a few months ago that there would be no talk of an extension until after the season. I felt terrible for him, but I wasn't surprised. He was playing poorly. He's thirty-four, which is old in baseball. I tried to encourage him to consider life after baseball, but he wouldn't hear me at the time.

Then Reagan Daulton and her group bought the team. They struck a deal with Layton. They offered a three-year extension, for considerably less money, if he agreed to date Arizona and promote the Anacondas. Fast forward a few months, and they're in love and their relationship is gold for both the Anacondas and Layton's game. He hasn't played this well in years. She's breathed life into his career.

"You've lived up to your end of the bargain. They'll give you your three years. You'll get to retire as a Cougar like you wanted."

He runs his fingers through his hair and blows out a breath. "For the first time in my life, Tanner, I'm thinking of life after baseball. I held onto this sport because it was all I had. That's not the case anymore. When Arizona and I are on location for the big photo shoot next month, I'm going to ask her to marry me. I already bought the ring."

They're being paid huge dollars by a bathing suit company to travel all over the world for two months in their swimsuits taking photos.

I let the shock of him considering marriage sink in. "It's only been a few months. Don't you want to wait a little longer?"

"When you know, you know. She's it for me. She'll have the Olympics in four years and will need to train hard. I don't want the time apart. And what if we have a baby before then? She'll need me to take care of things at home so she can achieve her dream. I've already achieved mine. I don't want to stress about letting the Cougars down. See how much money you can get me for one more year, and then I want to retire. One more dance. That's all I want to do. I'll get to go out on my terms. Maybe I'll even get to go out on top."

He's actually making a lot of sense. "Okay, buddy. I'll see what I can get you."

He smiles as he stands and holds out his hand. "I know you're only nine years older than me, but you're the closest thing I've ever had to a father. Thank you for everything you've ever done for me. I hope to return the favor one day."

I grab his hand and pull him in for a hug. "It's been an honor and a privilege."

THIRTY-SIX HOURS LATER, Layton broke his leg in a collision at home plate in one of the most horrific sports injuries I've seen in my entire twenty-year career. He'll never play another game of baseball again.

I've been sitting in the hospital with the entire team, waiting for him to get out of surgery. As the hours draw on, most of the guys leave, vowing to return in the morning. It's now just me, Quincy, Cheetah, Ezra, and Trey. I suppose we're Layton's inner circle.

Just before his collision, they played the final out of the Anacondas' game on the big screen at the Cougars' stadium. They won the league in their first year as a program. It's unheard of in professional sports.

I got to watch Bailey pile on top of her teammates in a moment of pure glee. Seconds later, Layton's injury took place, and it's been mayhem ever since. I didn't even get the chance to congratulate her.

For the first time in hours, I pull out my phone. I see

hundreds of missed calls and texts. I scroll down my texts to Bailey and see that she was indeed checking on me. She's called a few times too.

It's the middle of the night. I'm not going to call. I decide to text.

> Me: Sorry. Just seeing your calls and texts. You're probably out partying. Congrats to you guys. You were amazing. So proud of you.

There's no response. I'm sure they're having fun. I don't want to bother her.

I also see a missed text from Fallon.

> Fallon: I hope he's okay. I'm sure you're busy. Thinking of you. Harper was hysterical. It took hours to get her to sleep. Send me a status update when you're able so I can tell her that Uncle Layton will be okay.

> Me: Still in surgery. I'll let you know.

Cheetah looks at me. His always-present smile is nowhere to be found. "He'll be able to rehab and play again, right?"

I slowly shake my head. "His leg broke like a twig. I don't see it. He's a catcher at the end of his career. It's unlikely."

Cheetah's face falls. Tears build in his eyes. It's every athlete's worst nightmare.

Even if it's possible, he'd probably have to sit out a year and then work his ass off to try to get back into things. I doubt he would want to do that. That's not my business to say though.

He eventually gets out of surgery. They think it went well, but only time will tell. We're all in his room with him, half asleep, waiting for him to wake up, when my text tone rings. I see that it's Bailey.

> Bailey: Hey. Sorry. I was on a flight when you texted.

> Me: A flight. Where?

> Bailey: Home.

> Me: Shouldn't you be celebrating?

> Bailey: Once news of Layton's injury broke, the party atmosphere ended. Arizona flew home on Reagan's private jet. She should be at the hospital any minute. I flew home commercial. Just landed.

> Me: Why?

> Bailey: I was worried about you. I know how much Layton means to you. Are you home?

I'm a little choked up with emotion that she did that for me.

> Me: I'm still at the hospital. He's out of surgery. I want to be here when he wakes, and then I'll leave.

> Bailey: Okay. I guess I'll head home.

> Me: Will you go to my place? I want to be with you.

> Bailey: I'll Uber straight there and wait for you.

PAYOFF PITCH

SECONDS LATER, Arizona barges in and nearly loses her shit. We're able to calm her while Layton remains sleeping. Just after he wakes up, she kicks us all out.

I pull into my driveway in the middle of the night. I'm not sure if Bailey will be sleeping, but I don't care. I'm just glad that she's here.

I find her curled up fast asleep on the couch with the television on. She looks so beautiful and innocent.

I grab a quick drink to settle my nerves and then head back to find her still peacefully asleep. I should leave her here, but I'm selfish and want her with me.

I scoop her up into my arms, and her eyes blink open. "I was trying to stay awake."

"Go back to sleep. I've got you."

"I didn't know if I should go into your bedroom."

"That's where I need you."

"I can walk."

I sink my nose into her hair and take in her familiar scent. "I'd rather carry you."

She nuzzles into my chest as I walk us upstairs and into my bedroom. Once there, she pats my chest. "You can put me down."

I do but pull her into a hug. The tears start to flow for me. I've been holding them in for hours.

She squeezes me close. "You don't have to be brave. I know how you feel about him. It was traumatic. Let it out."

And I do. For thirty minutes I cry on the shoulder of my daughter's nanny, who's fifteen years younger than me, and who I only started an intimate relationship with two nights ago. And there's no place else I'd rather be.

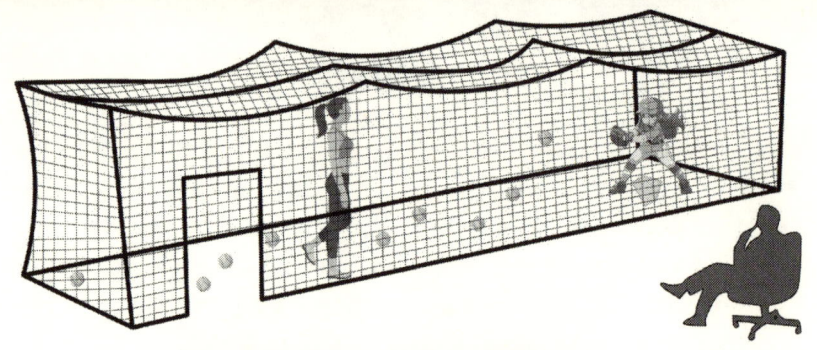

CHAPTER THIRTEEN

TANNER

I wake in the morning wrapped around Bailey. I'm slightly embarrassed by my needy behavior last night. I was tired and emotional. I've never been like that with anyone in my life. So vulnerable. I think I fell asleep in her comforting arms.

I'm in my boxer briefs, and she's in a T-shirt and panties. Pulling away slightly, she sleepily falls onto her back. I lift her shirt and take in the flawless skin surrounding her belly button. She's almost too perfect to be real.

I bring my lips to her soft, feminine stomach and begin kissing my way up her body until I reach her rosy nipple. I suck it into my mouth, and she lets out a moan. Despite her eyes being closed, her lips turn up into a smile and her fingers run through my hair.

"Hmm. I guess you're feeling better."

I mumble into her, "It's time for me to make you feel better."

She spreads her legs. I've just gotten settled in when I

hear the familiar sounds of my front door opening and closing followed shortly thereafter by, "Tan?"

It's Fallon's voice.

I quickly lift my head to see Bailey wide-eyed. I'm sure my look mirrors hers.

I hear her walking up the stairs. "Tanner Montgomery, are you actually still asleep? I never thought I'd see the day."

I scramble out of bed and run out my bedroom door, quickly closing it behind me.

Fallon reaches the top of the steps. "Were you sleeping?"

"Wh...what are you doing here?"

"Harper was worried, and you weren't answering my texts. She demanded to come and make you breakfast."

She looks my body up and down. I'm not fully hard anymore, but I'm not exactly limp either.

It suddenly occurs to her. She sucks in a breath and covers her mouth. "Are you...is there someone with you?"

I nod. "I'm sorry. I didn't know you guys were coming here."

She swallows. "No, it's my fault. I shouldn't pop in with her like this. We'll go."

"No, no. Let me throw on some clothes. I'll come down to see her. Then maybe...you should take her for a bit?"

"Okay." She fidgets nervously. "Umm...this is weird. I'm really sorry, Tan."

I sigh. "I suppose it was inevitable with us having keys to each other's houses. It's amazing we've made it this long without something like this."

"Right. Maybe I'll start knocking instead of walking in."

I shake my head. "No. You're Harper's mother and you're always welcome." I twist my lips. "Maybe keep surprise visits to a minimum though. Or at least a confirmation from me that it's a good time."

She gives me a small smile. "Good idea. I'll be

downstairs. Harper wanted to make you breakfast in bed to cheer you up. I'll keep her busy down there and make sure she doesn't come up."

"Thank you."

She walks back downstairs, and I open my bedroom door. Walking back inside, I see Bailey hiding under the covers and I chuckle. "The coast is clear. They're downstairs."

Her head pops out and she sits up. Her cheeks are flushed. "Holy shitake. That could have been a disaster."

I nod. "I know. Fallon feels terrible."

She gasps. "Does she know it was me?"

I shake my head. "She'd have no reason to suspect you." I reach into my drawers and pull out sweatpants and a sweatshirt. As I put the pants on, I say, "Harper thought I'd be sad about Layton and wanted to come make me breakfast."

Bailey smiles. "She's so thoughtful."

"She is, which is why I can't kick them out."

"Of course not." She looks around. "I'm not sure how to sneak out. I can't exactly climb out the window, and I don't even have a car here."

"Can you stay here until they're gone? Why don't you relax and take a shower? Or go back to sleep. It was a long night for you. Whatever you need."

"Sure." She looks me up and down and bites her lip. "I've never seen you dressed like that."

"In sweatpants?"

She nods and swallows. "*Topless* in gray sweatpants." Her head plops down on the pillow and she fans her face. "So hot."

I look down at myself in bewilderment. I'm in gray sweatpants about to put on an old college sweatshirt. "This is hot?"

She briefly closes her eyes. "Yes. Everything you do is hot, but you in gray sweatpants with your sexy chest..." She blows out a breath. "Any women's toys in that chest of yours?"

I suck in a breath. "What do you know of my chest?"

She smiles. "I may have taken a peek in there once."

I walk over and lean over her. Bringing my mouth to her ear, I whisper, "Then you've seen the paddle, and you know bad girls who snoop get punished."

She lets out a moan. I can see her nipples harden through her T-shirt.

I bring my hand to her panty-covered pussy, feeling how wet she is. "You'd like that, wouldn't you, sweet girl?"

I slide her panties to the side and slip my finger inside her. She's soaked. Her body flutters around me.

"I thought so."

With my finger pushing deep inside her, I run my tongue along her neck, and she whimpers.

I pull my finger out and taste just the pad of that finger. "Hmm. I think I'll take your sweet cream in my coffee this morning. I'll be back soon. Don't you go getting into any more trouble. I'd hate to have to punish you more than I already plan to. I expect you to be waiting with your ass in the air when I get back, ready to take what I'm going to give you."

Her breathing is labored, and she's fisting my sheets. Yep, she and I are going to have a good time.

I MAKE my way downstairs with a goofy grin on my face. I can't help it. Bailey brings it out in me.

Harper's face lights up when she sees me, but she doesn't

break stride from the task at hand, carefully tending to an omelet of my liking.

I smile at her. "Good morning, bug."

"Morning? It's nearly eleven, sleepyhead."

I pinch my eyebrows together and look at the clock on the oven. "Wow. I didn't realize the hour. I was at the hospital with Uncle Layton until very late. I can't believe you came over to make me breakfast. You're so good to me."

She nods. "I'm making it just like Bailey taught me to."

I'm in my head thinking about Bailey upstairs waiting for me when she continues, "Mommy said the television told her that Uncle Layton broke his leg."

I nod. "He did. Arizona is taking good care of him though."

She scrunches her face. "Isn't she in Florida?"

"She came home to be with him."

She nods in understanding. "Did you see the Anacondas win? Have you talked to Bailey?"

"They played the final out on the big screen at the Cougars' stadium. I saw her celebrating with her friends. She texted to check on Layton, but we didn't discuss the game yet."

The good news is that Fallon will assume Bailey is in Miami and won't suspect it's her upstairs in my bed.

Fallon hands me a mug of coffee. "They must have partied their asses off last night in South Beach."

Harper gasps. "That's ten dollars, Mommy."

Fallon winces. "Darn. You're like the fuzz, Harper."

"What's fuzz, Mommy?"

I chuckle. "It's the police, and yes, she is. I imagine there was a big Anacondas celebration. I have no idea." I blow on my cup. "Thanks for the coffee."

She nods. "I'm sure. Let me grab you a spoon."

I shake my head. "No need," I say as I make good on my

promise to Bailey and stir my coffee with the finger that was inside her before sucking it into my mouth.

Yum. I need to eat quickly. I can't wait to get back upstairs.

ABOUT THIRTY MINUTES LATER, I'm taking the steps two at a time, anxious to get to my bedroom. I'm sure Bailey heard the front door close and knows I'm coming for her.

I'm not prepared for what I see when I walk in. She's naked, on all fours, with her ass facing me. She breathes, "I'm ready for my punishment, Sir."

I chuckle. "You watch too much porn. I don't want you to call me Sir."

She turns her head and gives me a sexy smile. "I don't *watch* porn. I *read* my porn like a lady."

I can't help but laugh. "I stand corrected. Still, don't call me Sir."

"Whatever you want, Daddy."

I have to close my eyes and squeeze my dick. Yep, that hit the mark.

I make my way to her and slowly run my finger up her spine. "Have you been a bad girl going through Daddy's private chest?"

She runs her bottom lip through her teeth before nodding. "It's locked right now, but it wasn't a few weeks ago."

When she was here taking care of my daughter.

I exhale heavily. "As much as I want you right now," I look down at my cock tenting my sweatpants, "I think we should talk about us. We didn't get the chance after the other night."

She whines, "Can't we just shelve it for a little while? I want you. I've been waiting forever for this." She wiggles her ass. "I'm ready to take my punishment like a good girl. Give it to me. Please."

What man in their right mind could possibly say no to that?

I rub her ass. "Hmm. I like how willing you are."

Smack.

She gasps at the shock of me spanking her while I run my hand soothingly over the handprint I just left on her.

Smack.

I do it again but this time she moans.

"You like that, sweet girl?"

She nods as I run my fingers through her center. She more than liked it. I wasn't planning on taking things too far today, but maybe she's ready for more than I thought.

After walking over to the chest, I unlock and open it, pulling out a paddle and two rubber restraints. She watches on with a mix of fear and fascination showing on her gorgeous face.

Sitting on the bed, I motion for her to lie across my legs. I then see a moment of hesitation in her eyes. "We don't have to do anything you don't want to do."

She nods. "I want to try it. I trust you."

"You remember your safe words?"

She smiles. "Payoff pitch. The ultimate decision maker."

"That's right. This is all about pleasure. I know what I'm doing, and I like to be in control. I think you like that version of me. When I slapped your nipple the other night, you nearly came. When I just spanked you, I only saw pleasure emanating from your body. This is about pleasure, Bailey. If at some point it's not pleasurable for you, use your words."

She takes a deep breath and lies across my lap with her

ass in the air. I can't help but admire it. "You have the most perfect ass I've ever seen."

"It's good to know my squats are paying off."

With lightning speed, I grab the leather paddle and apply a sharp smack to her ass. "I might like your smart mouth outside of this bedroom, but in here, your bratty behavior has repercussions."

I smack it again before I rub away the sting.

She writhes in my lap, grinding herself against me. "Oh god."

"You'll be calling me that soon enough. Are you going to behave?"

She hesitates and I smack her ass again, quickly followed by soothing circles from my hand.

"Ahh. Y...yes. I'll behave."

"Good girl. Now get on your knees with your hands behind your back."

She adorably stumbles a bit as she stands but then drops to her knees. I begin to pull down my pants and she goes to reach for them.

I lift my eyebrow, and she freezes, immediately placing her hands behind her back. I can tell she wants to say something about it but is holding her tongue. She's learning how to be submissive.

"You keep those hands behind your back or I'll cuff them back there."

Discarding all my clothing while standing right in front of her, I then give my cock a few long pumps right in her face. She watches on with lust-filled eyes, practically licking her chops.

"I'm going to feed my cock into your bratty mouth like I've wanted to do since you came to our door that first day and I first saw you crouched down. I've played the scene of you on your knees in front of me a thousand times since. I've made myself come every day to that image."

Her whole body flushes, and she licks her lips. She shifts her hips and rubs her thighs together.

I begin tracing those lips with my tip. "No hands. I like a woman's mouth to do all the work. I know I'm big. You'll have to learn to relax your throat. It might take a few times." She visibly swallows. "Now stick out your tongue."

She does, and I rub my pre-ejaculate all over it. She shivers and her nipples further pebble. "Is this turning you on, sweet girl?"

She nods as I begin to feed my cock further into her mouth. "I don't think I'll last long. Seeing you on your knees with your hands behind your back and my cock stuffed into your mouth is almost too much to bear."

She smiles around me as she begins to apply suction.

I'm trying to be gentle when all I want to do is grab her by the hair and thrust myself down her throat.

She takes her time, allowing her tongue to pay respect to every vein and ridge of me. I expected sloppy. That's not what I'm getting. I'm getting a woman who knows how to please a man and who's genuinely enjoying this.

After circling the underside of my crown several times, she makes eye contact with me as she pushes her mouth forward, taking in nearly all of me. My tip hits the back of her throat with only a slight gag from her, though she never alters course.

"Very impressive, Ms. Hart. Are you ready for more?"

She nods and I grab the back of her hair, beginning to thrust in and out of the wet, warm confines of her mouth. Long, hard strokes. Her eyes water and saliva drips from her mouth, but she doesn't make any attempt to pull away.

Each time I draw nearly all the way out, she tightens her lips and sucks me back in. Her tongue works magical swirls over my tip.

I'm starting to lose control. "Oh, fuck. That's good."

My grip on her hair tightens as I truly let loose in a way

I haven't in a long time. I'm realizing I haven't wanted a woman as much as I want her in as long as I can remember. Maybe ever.

Her innocent honey-colored eyes haven't left mine. Her gaze is adding to my gratification. My balls begin to tighten, preparing for an extreme detonation.

She lets out a moan of pleasure, causing vibrations all over my dick. I can't take it anymore. "Yes, sweet girl. That's it." I thrust in deep and release myself into her with a loud grunt.

She swallows nearly all of me down. Only a drop drizzles from the corner of her mouth. I scoop it with my thumb. Before I can do anything with it, she turns her head and sucks it into her mouth.

It's going to take me all of thirty seconds to get hard again.

I grab under her arms, lift her, and smash my mouth to hers. I can taste my saltiness in her mouth. There's something primal about tasting myself on Bailey Hart's sweet tongue.

She climbs my body like a spider monkey, sinking her fingers into my hair and wrapping her legs around me. I can feel her wetness against me. She's frantic with need.

I kiss down to her neck, and she tilts it to give me better access. "Oh god, Tanner. I want you." She thrusts her wet pussy over me.

I toss her onto the bed. I like that she's strong and I can be a little rough with her. "Your turn. Lay down and spread your legs wide. Time for me to have another breakfast."

She goes to open her mouth but immediately closes it.

"Tell me what you were going to say."

"I...I..." She sits up and reaches her fingers for my beard. "You may have fantasized about me on my knees, but I've fantasized about sitting on this beard."

I smile as I lay down on the bed. "I aim to please."

Motioning for her, I command, "Get that sweet pussy on Daddy's face."

She eagerly climbs up my body until she's situated with her legs spread open on my lips. I give her what she wants and rub my beard through her juices.

She lets out a loud moan. "Oh my god." Her legs start quivering around me. "This is going to take thirty seconds."

I grab her ass and immediately latch my lips onto her clit. It's swollen and throbbing. Her smell and taste have me instantly hardening again.

The pad of my thumb toys with her entrance but doesn't penetrate. Yet.

Her fingers run through my hair as her hips gyrate over me. She looks down at me with a slack jaw. "You're so hot. Holy sh—"

She interrupts her own words with a loud scream as my thumb sinks inside her. She's so damn wet. I love that she's as hot for me as I am for her.

"Grab your tits. Let me see you play with them."

She immediately does as she's told, teasing and pinching her own nipples. Despite the squirming and rubbing, she never breaks eye contact. I don't know that I've ever seen a woman do that before. It's like she's looking into my soul. It's incredibly erotic.

It takes less than a minute for her to come all over my face with loud screams I no longer have to muffle. I love a good screamer.

After a few long calming breaths, she slides down my body and licks around my lips, all over my beard.

"You like tasting yourself on me."

She lets out a giggle.

"What's so funny?"

She smiles. "Kam. She's been cracking jokes about how much she knows I want you. She made a comment about me offering your beard a conditioning. I think I just did that."

In a fast move, I flip us over so I'm on top of her, rubbing my cock through her wetness. "Let's not talk about your sister when my cock is on your pussy. She's no match for you."

She pinches her eyebrows. "We're twins. Identical twins."

"Maybe physically. Maybe to the outside world. But from my perspective, you're nothing alike. I could tell the difference between you two from a mile away. There's just something special about your shine, Bailey Hart."

She stares into my eyes, undoubtedly seeing the truth of my statement. She then gently takes my face in her hands and brings her lips to mine in a tender way, completely contrasting our earlier kiss and actions.

The kiss doesn't stay soft for long. Her tongue becomes increasingly hungry, ravaging every inch of my mouth. This girl can kiss.

I planned to tie her up, but I don't think I can wait another second to be inside her. I'm usually so measured and controlled, but this woman drives me mad with desire.

I break the kiss, and she whimpers her malcontent. Reaching for a condom, I quickly tear it open and sheath myself.

She whines, "Mr. Montgomery, please. I need you inside me. I can't take another second without you."

I demand, "Spread your legs as wide as they can go."

Without hesitation she does. "Now. Please."

"Grab your ankles."

She does before whining, "I need you inside me."

Fucking hell.

Propping myself up on my hands, I bring my tip to her entrance and thrust straight into her.

She exhales like the wind has been knocked out of her lungs before taking a deep inhale and pulling her legs as far apart as possible. "Oh my god."

I probably should have entered her more slowly, but she drives me crazy. I lose my mind with her.

I remain still inside her as she takes a few moments to regain her breath. She briefly closes her eyes, and I see tears leak out the sides. Am I hurting her?

"Are you okay?"

She nods and mumbles, "So much. So big. So good." I can feel her stomach muscles contracting below me.

Lifting her head to nibble on my lower lip, she releases her ankles, wraps her legs around me, and breathes, "Give it to me, Daddy."

My eyelids flutter as I begin my punishing thrusts. I grit out, "I both love and hate when you call me that."

Our eyes are locked as I give her everything I have. I suppose most women close their eyes during sex, but not Bailey. I've never thought about it before, but the intimacy of it truly adds to the pleasure. She's completely locked in on me. I see both innocence and lust in her eyes at the same time.

Her moans of satisfaction only drive me to go harder and deeper as I rut into her without mercy.

I usually prefer a woman's hands tied, but I don't mind hers moving all over my body. Why is this so different?

She grabs fistfuls of my hair as she thrusts her hips up onto me. We manage to work perfectly in sync with each other.

I want to keep staring into her eyes, but it's too much. It's like she's looking into my soul. I drop down from my hands and sink my face into her neck, inhaling her unique scent. One that has filled my house for months. One that my body always reacts to.

The sounds of our sweaty bodies pounding together fill the room along with our mutual moans of ecstasy.

"You're so fucking sexy. Come for me, sweet girl. Make Daddy happy."

PAYOFF PITCH

Her back arches, and she yells out into her orgasm. Thank fuck because I don't know if I can hold off much longer with her. She's just...everything.

I bite her neck and grunt her name as I come so fucking hard, filling the condom. My body collapses in exhaustion but she grabs my face and kisses me long and hard before mumbling into my lips, "Thank you. That was amazing."

BAILEY

That was unequivocally the best sex of my life. I'm not even sure I can consider what I've done before sex after experiencing the dynamic masculinity of Tanner Montgomery.

He falls down next to me, completely out of breath.

I lift my head and smile at him. "Can't handle it, old man?"

He grabs my ass hard, and I squeal. He practically growls, "Ever been fucked like that, *young lady*?"

I twist my lips, unable to deny the truth. "Can't say that I have. I guess men are like a fine wine."

His brow furrows. "I'm not that old."

"Whatever you say, Daddy."

He tickles me, and I giggle. "You are a brat."

I bite my lip. "Maybe I need to be punished again." I totally got off on it.

He pulls my body close to his. "You liked it, didn't you?"

"I did." I motion toward the untouched items. "What were those bands for? You never used them."

"I planned to tie you up, but I was too ravenous for you and couldn't wait another second to be back inside you. You turn me into a horny teenager unable to control myself."

I plop my head down on his chest. "You seemed very in control to me. When can you go again?"

He chuckles. "I just came twice. Give me a second to catch my breath. Speaking of doing this again, we should talk."

I trace his sexy chest hair with my fingers. "I know what this is, Tanner. Can't we just enjoy it while it lasts? I'm not an immature girl with illusions of forever. I don't need a label."

"I don't want you or Harper getting hurt. I'm not looking for anything long term."

"I've gathered."

"You're so young and have things to experience. Things I'm done experiencing. I will never get married or have any more children."

"Ever?"

"Ever. Sexual encounters are all I'm looking for. All I'll ever want. I need you to understand that if we're going to keep doing this."

"I may be younger than you, but I'm not young. I can handle it and would certainly never want to do anything to harm Harper."

"I know." He's quiet for a brief moment as his fingers run over my body. "Honestly, I haven't begun to scratch this itch for you. I thought if we finally broke the dam, I could get this all-consuming need for you out of my system, but it's not. If anything, I want you more than before."

I can't help but smile. "I feel the same way. It's purely physical. I get it."

"I enjoy spending time with you, but if you want this to continue, it stays behind closed doors. For Harper's sake and for yours."

I can't deny a little bit of disappointment, but the fact is that I don't want anyone but him. This itch hasn't been scratched for me either. If anything, I'm more curious about what he can do to my body. I'll never be my sister where I can have purely meaningless, emotionless sex, but I can channel her enough to spend time with a man with who I know I have no future. He's not some stranger. I care about him and feel connected to him but understand what we are.

"I'm in."

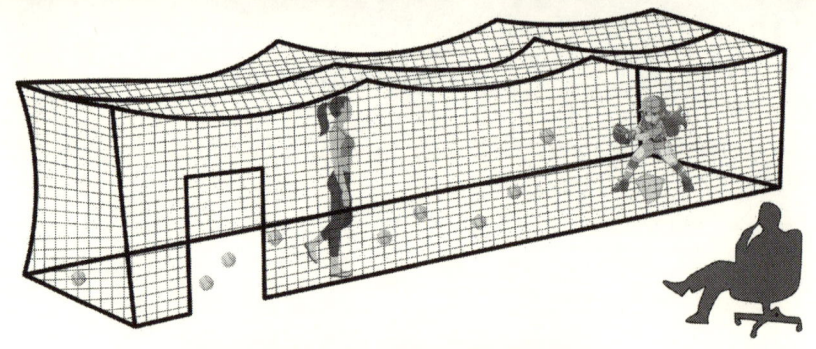

CHAPTER FOURTEEN

BAILEY

Today is our victory parade down Broad Street in Philly. The whole city is shut down to celebrate us. We're all excited about it.

The Cougars lost their steam after Layton's injury and were knocked out of the World Series in game six. All the attention is on us.

Despite the sadness of Layton's injury and their season ending, the guys are all excited for our victory and are coming to celebrate with us. Layton demanded the doctor put on his cast so he could come too. Apparently, they were waiting for the swelling to go down.

The parade is about to start, and we're all in the big float. It's our entire team plus a few of our close Cougars friends.

Ripley seems off. I don't know why. I pull her to the side. "Are you okay?"

She takes a few deep breaths. Worry is written all over her beautiful face. "Today is for celebrating. We'll talk later."

Cheetah throws his arms around us. "Why do you two look so

serious? It's a party day!" He nods toward a table full of shots. "Let's get this party started!"

He hands out shots to several people and lifts his in the air. "To the Anacondas!"

Everyone screams out, "To the Anacondas," as they take the shots.

After ensuring everyone has another shot in hand, he lifts his glass again. "Here's to love. Here's to honor. If you can't come in her, come on her."

Everyone starts laughing as they take another round of shots.

The parade begins down Broad Street. It pauses now and then as Kam, Cheetah, and a few others jump off the float to dance with the crowds. The two of them are nuts, but all the fans are eating it up. I can't help but watch them together. I don't ever remember anyone making my sister smile so much. I hold out hope that he can eventually break down the walls she's so carefully built throughout the years.

I lean over to Arizona. "Are Kam and Cheetah doing a choreographed dance right now?"

She laughs. "They sure are."

After a very bizarre dance routine, we're approaching the cross street where Tanner said he'd be standing with Harper and Andie. My eyes immediately find him as we approach. If there was ever anyone made to stand out in a crowd, it's Tanner Montgomery.

Flashes of what he's done to my body for the past few days play on a loop in my mind. He now has Harper for the next few days, so I know we'll be on pause, but the time I've spent with him recently has been incredible. I've experienced pleasure I'm not sure I ever knew existed. I'll be gagging for it by the time she leaves for Fallon's again.

We make eye contact, and he winks at me. I notice Harper in my jersey and Andie in Arizona's.

I immediately jump off the slow-moving float and run to grab Harper and Andie's hands.

Harper's eyes widen. "What are you doing?"

I smile down at her. "It's time for you to join the parade."

She squeals, "What?"

"Come on. Let's celebrate."

I bring two shocked and excited little girls onto the float with us. Everyone is welcoming. The girls smile as they wave to the crowds lining the streets with pure and total glee. I know it's a moment neither of them will ever forget.

IT'S BEEN a crazy few days of partying. This town knows how to celebrate its champions.

Tonight is about Harper though. It's her league championship game.

I arrive at their house a little before we need to leave. As soon as I step in the door, Tanner pulls me into his arms and kisses me. I wrap my arms around him, immediately losing myself in all things Tanner. His lips suck me right in. Damn, this man can kiss.

I love the way his beard rubs my face. I know my face will be red when we're done and there's something so hot about being marked by him.

He kisses his way down my neck and mumbles into it, "Hi, beautiful. I've missed you."

I can only manage a, "Hmm," as my body melts into his.

When he eventually pulls away, I'm a little unsteady on my feet from the affection. He has to hold me upright for a moment.

When I regain my senses, I drink him in. He's in jeans and a hoodie with a baseball hat for Harper's team. He's so hot. And he's mine...for now.

I eventually breathe out, "Hi."

He winks at me, knowing the effect he has on me, and then adjusts himself before he turns and walks back into the kitchen area. I follow him and notice a big box on the counter. "What's that?"

"The girls are flipping out that you'll be at the big game tonight. I bought your jersey for each of them. If you don't mind, maybe you can sign them."

"They're flipping out for *me*?"

He gives me an incredulous look. "Yes, Bailey. You're a superstar on a championship team. Did you not see the tens of thousands of people at the parade? I hate to break it to you, but you're famous. Arizona may be the face of the team, Ripley may be the backbone, and Kamryn may be the flashy smile, but you, my beautiful girl, are the heart and soul. You must realize that."

Hmm. I've never thought of it that way.

I smile in gratitude for his words. "Thank you. I'm happy to sign them." I look around. "Where's Harper?"

"She said she needed time alone to visualize." He smirks. "Know anything about that?"

I giggle. "I may have talked to her about it." I hold out my hand. "Give me a Sharpie. I've got some jerseys to sign."

He hands one to me. "Great. We'll give them to the girls after the game. A celebratory gift if they win, and something that will make them feel better if they don't. They'll certainly need it if they lose. Their douchebag coach will tear into them. Actually, win or lose he'll probably tear into them."

He's a yeller and screamer coach. I've seen him in action and marvel that he treats seven-year-old girls that way. I marvel more that the parents allow their kids to play for him. I wouldn't.

An hour later we're sitting in the stands with Fallon, Beckett, Amanda, Cassandra, Trevor, and Dylan.

Fallon greets me warmly, congratulating me on our big victory and telling me that she and Harper were glued to the television watching the final game.

I'm seated between Tanner and Cassandra. I lean past Cassandra and smile at Dylan. "It's nice of you to come support your friends."

"Mommy says anchor friends are the most important in your life. She's had her best friend for, like, a hundred years."

Cassandra playfully elbows her. "A hundred? Like fortyish." She winces. "Ugh, that's actually a lot. Now I feel old."

Trevor shakes his head as he reaches over and rubs her leg. "Sexy, you don't look a day over thirty."

She blows him a kiss which he proceeds to catch and then simulates throwing down his pants.

I let out a laugh as my attention turns from Dylan's crazy parents back to Dylan. "I think it's incredibly sweet that you're here. And I've never heard the term anchor friends."

Cassandra nods. "They're the ones you can rely on. The ones you need to keep you in place when you feel adrift. The ones who never let you float away."

"Hmm. I love it. That's how I feel about my closest friends."

She leans over and whispers, "Is that beard rash I see on your neck?"

My hand instinctively moves to my neck, and she silently laughs before mouthing, "I knew it."

Just then, an older bald man approaches the group. He appears nervous. "Ms. Hart. My name is Richard Inner. I'm the league commissioner. Thank you for being here. We would be honored if you threw out the ceremonial first pitch of the game. The girls on the field are all buzzing with excitement that you're in the stands tonight. I know it would mean a lot to them, if it's not too much of an inconvenience for you."

I point to myself. "Me?"

Tanner sighs and whispers, "Famous."

The man nods. "Yes, of course."

"Oh...sure. I'd be happy to."

"Thank you so much. Would you mind posing for a few pictures as well?"

"No problem."

I see Cassandra and Trevor exchange bemused looks. I turn to her and lift an eyebrow. She smiles. "His name is Dick Inner? Were his parents on crack?"

I hear Trevor chuckling. Tanner simply shakes his head. Cassandra and Trevor truly are children. I find their behavior somewhere between shocking and charming.

After throwing out the first pitch to an astonishingly loud sea of applause and a bouncing up and down Harper, I pose for pictures with both teams. I feel like a movie star.

When I return to the stands, I see Tanner and Beckett with their heads together. I narrow my eyes at them. "You two are up to no good."

They both laugh before Tanner nods at Beckett. Beckett then clears his throat. "We've been discussing the spring season. Could we, by chance, convince you to coach the girls? No one wants this coach to return, even if they win. The value of having a woman like you coach them is immeasurable. It's roughly one or two games and one or two practices a week. We'd happily pay you for your time."

I turn to Tanner, and he smiles hopefully. "It would be incredible. The spring season is from early March through May. It ends before your games begin."

"I'd like to do it, but I might have a few conflicts with my team practices toward the end."

Tanner nods. "We know. We'll work everything around your schedule as best we can. I'll help out if there are times you can't be there."

I look out onto the field. I've never considered coaching before, but getting to work with all the girls sounds like heaven.

Beckett interrupts my thoughts. "You can take time to think about it. We know it's a big time commitment."

I shake my head. "I don't need to think about it. I'd love to do it."

Beckett and Tanner high-five, and I inwardly giggle at the notion of two men like them being nervous to approach me about this.

The game has begun when I see a familiar figure approach the stands. It's Kam, wearing a hat that reads *I Heart DILFS*.

As soon as she reaches me, I grab it off her head. "You can't wear that here."

She smiles. "I brought it for you. It's a gift."

I narrow my eyes at her. "What are you doing here?"

"I came for Harper's big championship game. You've been talking about it all week."

"Fine. Thank you. Sit down and be quiet. No shenanigans."

She smirks. "Me? Never."

We slide down and make space for her to sit between me and Cassandra. Cassandra looks Kam up and down. "You two must be in the sexual fantasies of every man in America. The twin thing is a kink."

Kam lets out a laugh. "Right? I can't get her to do porn with me. I told her we'd make a fortune. We only do separate porn. Bailey prefers porn monogamy."

Cassandra smiles, and I elbow Kam. "She's kidding, Cassandra. No porn for either of us."

Kam rolls her eyes. "My sister is no fun. You know the difference between two cocks and a joke? Bailey can't take a joke."

Cassandra bursts into laughter, and I cover Kam's mouth, motioning toward Dylan. Through gritted teeth, I say, "Cut it out. Young ears."

Fortunately, Dylan isn't listening to us.

Kam points to the field. "Lighten up. It's seven-year-old softball. Where's Harper?"

I point to her spot on the field. "She's the shortstop."

Kam wiggles her eyebrows. "Like me. Excellent choice."

The game progresses and happens to be a good one. Harper's team is up by one run in the final inning, but the other team has runners on second and third with two outs.

The batter hits a very slow roller toward Harper. At this level, there's no chance of her being able to field that in time to record the out at first base. It's going to be a hit and the runner from third is going to score, tying the game.

But Harper does something no other seven-year-old little girl or boy has probably ever done. She charges the ball and quickly throws from the slot to get the batter out at first by a hair.

Game over. They win.

I think the chin of every player and parent is on the floor at her executing the advanced technique so perfectly, especially in such a big moment. Even Kam breathes, "What in the fresh fuck did I just see?"

I can only smile in satisfaction. Tears sting my eyes. We've practiced that thousands of times at this point. To see it come to fruition is truly one of the most rewarding things I've ever experienced. I can't wait to coach these girls and have more moments like this.

After the initial shock wears off, every single person stands and erupts into cheers like we just watched the last out of the World Series. The girls on the field are all celebrating Harper.

When she eventually walks off the field, she sprints into my waiting arms. "Did you see me? I did it. I threw from the slot."

I hug her and twirl her around. "I did. It was amazing." I whisper in her ear, "You're better than Kam was when she was seven."

Harper smiles while she looks up at Kam, who high-fives her. "I know Bailey just made some comment about you being better than me when I was a kid. Honestly, I couldn't do that until I was thirteen or fourteen. That was fucking sick."

I smack Kam's hand. "Don't curse in front of her."

Harper nods. "You have to put ten dollars in our swear jar."

"Ten dollars? What the shit? That's insane."

Harper crosses her arms. "Now it's twenty."

"F—fine. You're a real ball-buster, kid."

"Make it thirty."

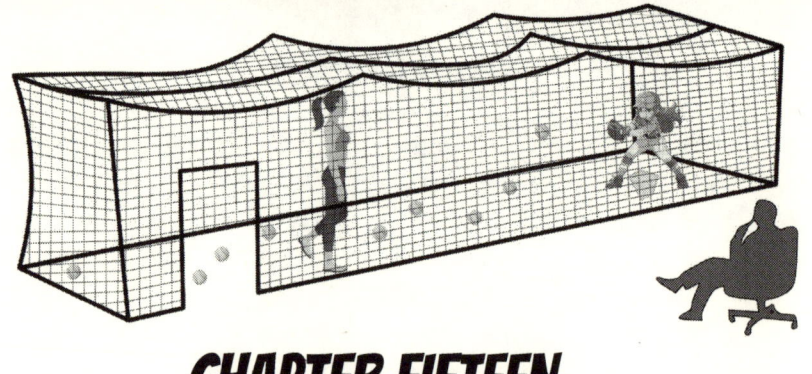

CHAPTER FIFTEEN

BAILEY

The past few weeks have been a little crazy. Arizona is gone on the overseas bathing suit campaign. Ripley is going through some personal struggles. Struggles that truly shocked us to the core. Kam has had a few photoshoots, but she and I have spent a lot of time with Ripley lately helping her nurse a broken heart. I've also been able to help with Harper more consistently as we establish the off-season schedule.

As for Tanner and me, we spend nearly every night he doesn't have Harper together. And even when she's at his house, there are plenty of stolen moments for kissing and touching. We're insatiable for each other and it keeps getting better and better. I've never experienced this level of pure, unquenchable need for a man, and he seems to feel the same about me.

We don't go out in public, but it's not only sex between us. We talk and watch movies. Sometimes I cook for him, and sometimes we get takeout. Our boundary lines have very quickly become blurred. I can't deny that I have real feelings for him.

He mentioned that they rent a cabin in Vail, Colorado to ski every winter. Apparently, they celebrate Christmas Eve and

Christmas morning as a family unit here in Philly, but then he takes Harper to Vail for a week. Fallon flies out on his last night there. He then flies home, and she stays out there with Harper for another week.

He invited me to come with them. With Harper bringing Dylan this year, needing the extra help is an easy excuse for me to join them. I've never skied and am excited at the prospect, but I've never gone that long without Kam. I told him I need to talk to her about it. He mumbled something about codependency being unhealthy. I'm not sure he's wrong, but it's still a conversation I want to have with her before I commit.

Even though she's away, Arizona begged all of us to spend Thanksgiving at Quincy's so that Layton wouldn't be alone. He's been in a state of depression since she left. He was originally supposed to go with her, but his injury threw a wrench into those plans.

We tried to talk my father into flying in, but he won't leave my mother, and she barely leaves the house at this point.

It's the night after Thanksgiving. Ripley packed up and went home to her mother's in California. After some prodding as to what was the matter with her, she dropped a bombshell on us that she's pregnant. She's emotional and said she needs to get out of town for a yet-to-be-determined amount of time. I have no idea what this means for our team, but her mental health is more important right now, and she wants to be with her mother.

It's just Kam and me. I'm nervously fidgeting, knowing I need to talk to her about Colorado. She sighs at me. "Spit out whatever it is you have to say. You're sweating like a cucumber in a convent."

I scrunch my face in disgust. "Ew. That's gross. I'll never look at a cucumber the same again."

She crosses her arms in waiting.

I sigh. "I want to talk to you about Tanner."

"Ooh. Are you ready to give me all the juicy details yet?"

She obviously knows I'm having sex with him at this point since I sleep there all the time, but I haven't indulged her FBI-level inquisitions for details as of yet.

"No dirty details for you, but he asked me to go skiing in Colorado with them the week after Christmas. I know we've never been apart that long but—"

"Maybe...you should go."

If she grew a third eye right now, I think I'd be less shocked than I am at that response.

"What? Really? I thought you were going to throw a fit."

"It sounds like fun." She twists her mouth nervously. "And... umm...Cheetah asked me to go home with him for Christmas. I was planning to talk to you about it."

I think my jaw must drop to the floor. "Seriously? Are you together?" I know she occasionally has sex with him, but I haven't known her to do anything more than sleep with someone in over a decade.

She shakes her head. "No, no. Nothing like that. Don't give me that damn hopeful look. He has, like, a hundred siblings who are all married with kids. His mother constantly pesters him about getting married. Apparently, she's even got the woman picked out. Cheetah asked me to come home with him to pretend to be his girlfriend for the week. I told him I'd let him know. I can't imagine spending Christmas without you, and the prospect of flying without you is making me sick to my stomach, but he promised me an all-expenses paid trip to Jamaica afterward if I go with him."

"Wow. His family lives in Texas, right?"

"Yes. I think near Galveston." She nervously runs her hands through her hair. "I don't know if I can do it. Fly without you. Be without you for that long. I haven't slept since he asked me."

"You haven't slept in twenty years."

She smiles. "True."

I rub her back. "You should definitely go, and so should I. This could be good for us, Kam. We're too old to have never spent time apart. We're eventually going to have to learn how to do that."

Tears sting her eyes. "You're my soulmate, Bails. You jump, I jump." She tugs at her collar. "I'm sweating just thinking about it."

I hug her. "I know. You're my soulmate too, and I'm equally nervous, but we need this. We both know it's time. It's probably way past time."

We both have tears streaming down our cheeks when my FaceTime rings. I pull away and look at my phone to see that it's our father. It's odd that he's calling us considering we spoke with him yesterday.

"It's Daddy."

She smirks. "Which daddy?"

I roll my eyes and answer. "Hey, Daddy. Is everything okay?"

TANNER

I'm getting things ready for poker night when the doorbell rings. I wonder who's here early. *Very* early. It's unlike any of them.

I open the door to Bailey in tears. My face falls. "What's wrong?"

She looks behind me and around the house. I shake my head. "No one is here. We're alone."

She throws herself into my arms and starts sobbing. I hold her tight and caress her back. "What's the matter, sweet girl?"

"It's my mom. She's sick. Our father just called and said

that she has some sort of liver disease caused by all the years of drinking. They gave her a year to live."

I pull her tighter into my arms. "I'm so sorry." I know they're not close, but I imagine it still hurts. "Do you need to fly down there?"

She shakes her head in my arms. "No. She doesn't want to see us. She said we didn't care about her in life, and she doesn't want us to come now that she's dying. Dad said to give her a few weeks to absorb everything and then we'll revisit. Kam doesn't want to go, but I do. I just...I can't leave things unsettled like this."

I pull her inside and close the door, still holding her in my arms. I don't think she needs me to say anything. She just needs me to be here for her, though I wonder where Kam is. I'd think Bailey would want her at this time.

After she finally calms down, she breathes, "I'm sorry I bothered you. Kam was just acting so cold about our mother dying. She wouldn't talk about it. Then she took off saying she had plans. I needed a little comfort. I know you have poker night. I should head out. Maybe it's finally hit her, and she needs me."

I squeeze her hard, not letting her go. "You're never a bother. I'm glad you came to me. You bottle things up, always needing to be the brave one. It's okay to be vulnerable. It's okay to be the one needing to be taken care of."

Her face is buried in my neck as she nods her head and mumbles, "Thank you."

Her hands are fisted in my shirt. I simply hold her close as the remaining tremors of sobs begin to dissipate.

When I'm confident she's completely calmed down, I hold her cheeks and lift her face so that our eyes meet. "Are you okay?"

She whispers, "I think so."

"Let me cancel tonight."

She shakes her head. "No, I'm sure they're on their way. You need this time with your friends. I should probably go find Kam anyway, though I doubt I'll have any luck. When she wants to disappear, she fully disappears."

She looks up at me with an expression that threatens to break me. "Just a few more minutes of you. It helps."

I hold her in my arms, trying to give her whatever it is she needs, secretly loving that it's my arms providing her comfort.

She begins kissing my chest, eventually trailing those kisses up to my neck. Her fingers run through my beard. She loves doing that.

Before I know what's happening, she's standing on her tippytoes with her lips brushing over mine. "I need you. We can be quick. Don't hold back. Make me forget, even if just for a few minutes."

In an instant, my mouth is on hers. I feel the warmth of her body relaxing into mine as her arms circle my neck. My hands move around the back of her thighs. I lift her and she wraps her long legs around me.

She breathes, "Tie me up. Do whatever you want to me. Just make me feel good. Please."

I do the only thing I can do right now. I nod and begin kissing her again.

In a frenzied state, she unbuttons my shirt and opens it. Without breaking the kiss, I move us upstairs to my bedroom, and we fall onto my bed. I grind my covered cock through her center. She moves her hands all over my back. All over my body. I've never felt her more needy than she is right now.

Why do I like her dependence on me? I've never liked that in women, but with Bailey, it's only serving to make me want her all the more. But I hate the notion of giving it to her hard and fast and then sending her on her way. There's something so wrong about that.

An idea occurs to me. I reluctantly pull away, loving that she audibly whimpers at the loss.

I command, "Get your ass naked."

The corners of her mouth raise and her eyes flash with mischief. "And if I don't?"

"I'll take that ass in my hand and make it red."

She runs her lower lips through her teeth. "What if I want that, Daddy?"

My fucking cock threatens to poke through my pants at her word choice. This woman will be the death of me.

I calmly respond, "You think you know how to push my buttons, don't you, sweet girl?"

"I know I do." She happily removes her top and then her bra. I watch each of her tits fall heavily with a slight bounce as they're freed from their confines. So full. So perfect. So mouthwatering.

She then lifts her hips enough to remove her leggings and panties in one movement before turning over onto all fours and wiggling her ass. "Give it to me."

I place my palm over her ass. She lets out a moan in anticipation. But I don't spank her. I lean over and whisper in her ear, "Do you want to be punished?"

She pants, "Yes. Please."

"Get on your back and spread your arms and legs."

She hesitates for a moment, likely in surprise, before obliging me. I unlock the chest and remove the fluffiest ties I own.

After securing her arms and ankles—tightly—I pick up my shirt from the floor and begin to rebutton it. Her eyes widen. "What are you doing?"

"I have guests about to arrive."

She pulls on her cuffs and adorably harumphs in frustration. With a lot of edge to her tone, she spits out, "Fine, I'll leave. Untie me."

"No, I want you here all night. You'll wait here for

me. I'm feeling generous though. I'll turn on the television." I lean over her and very slowly run my tongue through her pussy, only grazing her clit. I rub my beard through her a bit too. "I'll keep your taste on me for the evening, reminding me what's up here waiting for me."

She unsuccessfully pulls on her restraints. "Tanner, let me go. I'm not waiting here all night, naked and shackled, while you circle jerk with the boys."

I smile. "That's a lot of sass. I have a special punishment in mind for sassy girls. One I'm more than sure you'll enjoy, but if you don't want to stay, all you have to do is say *payoff pitch* and this can end."

Her lips twitch. I see it on the tip of her tongue, but she won't give in. Leaning over her, I whisper into her ear, "I'll make it worth your while. I promise."

Her nipples immediately harden, and she exhales a long breath in frustration but doesn't use her safe word. I've got her right where I want her. She wants to forget her sorrows? I'll make that happen for her.

I run my thumb over her lower lip. "I want you frothing at the mouth when I return."

She sucks my thumb into her mouth and playfully bites it.

"Ooh, that will cost you, Ms. Hart."

She thrusts her hips up to attempt to rub herself against me, but I pull away and nonchalantly use the remote control to turn on the television. "What does it for you, Ms. Hart? Do you prefer *Fifty Shades* or *9 ½ Weeks*?"

She scoffs. "Is that question for real? One hundred percent *9 ½ Weeks*. It's not even close."

I chuckle as I turn on the movie for her, close my bedroom door, and head downstairs just in time for the doorbell to ring.

I open it to see Layton, Cheetah, Trey, Vance, and

Daylen. With a frown, Trey mumbles, "Gemma made me come. I'm only staying for a few hands."

I look at Layton, leaning on his crutches, and roll my eyes at how Trey is about Gemma. He shrugs his shoulders. "Sorry, man, if my girl was in town, I'd want to get home to her too."

I shake my head. "You're all pussy-whipped." Then I think of the delicious pussy I have waiting for me upstairs and have a drop more compassion for them.

As we're walking down to my mancave, Layton nods at Cheetah. "You were the last one in the front door. We need a fun fact from you."

Cheetah smiles. "I've got a good one. McCaffrey will love it."

Vance practically growls, and Cheetah smirks as he says, "The state of Montana has three times as many cows as it does people." Vance is originally from Montana.

Daylen chuckles. "That explains McCaffrey's prom date. The photographer had to tell her to moooove to the left. Mooooove to the right."

The guys all laugh except Vance. He gives Daylen the finger and mumbles, "Assholes. Why do I come to these nights?"

Everyone pours drinks and makes plates of food. I hear Cheetah mention Ezra's name. I know he has a thing for Bailey and calmly ask, "How's he doing these days?"

Cheetah shrugs. "You know Ezra. Slightly socially awkward. He's the kind of guy who, when he goes to the gas station, if the card reader says *see cashier*, he gets in his car and leaves."

I chuckle. "That's funny."

He nods. "Yet true. His childhood friend, a cool chick, was here a few weeks ago. They were touchy-feely, but he said that's just how they are. She apparently has a boyfriend. Anyway, he went home for a few weeks. He'll be back in the new year as our off-season workouts ramp up a bit."

I can't say I'm sad to see Ezra out of town and out of sight for Bailey.

We begin playing cards, and I enjoy the usual banter, though my mind is on the naked woman waiting in my bedroom. I decide it's time to check on her. Standing, I hold up my phone and say, "Play a round without me. I need to check on Harper. She's at a friend's house."

I quickly make my way upstairs and open the bedroom door to a relieved Bailey. "Oh thank god. Untie me."

I shake my head. "Nope. We haven't had our fun yet."

I rub my pointer finger over her lips before sliding it into her mouth and commanding, "Suck."

She briefly hesitates before she does as I instructed.

"Good girl. Next time I come up here, this will be my cock."

Her eyes widen. "Next tim—"

"Shh."

I pull the finger out and slowly drag it down her body. Down her neck, through her tits, over her now trembling belly, and then through her pussy. "You're wet, sweet girl."

She breathes, "More."

I slide the finger deep into her tightness, and she cries out, "Yes."

Still with my finger pumping in and out of her, I bend and flick my tongue over her tiny bundle. Her hips buck, though I never break stride.

It takes only a minute or two before her legs begin to shake and I know she's almost there. I then pull away.

She yells, "No. Please. I'll do anything."

She's trying desperately to rub her legs together but can't with how I have her restrained.

I give her a hard, open-mouth kiss before standing

again. "You're so beautiful when you're at my mercy." I wink. "Back to my game."

"Please, Tanner. Stay. Make me come. Just once, and then you can go back."

I blow her a kiss before sucking on the finger that was inside her. "See you in a bit."

I close the door and head back downstairs, smiling the whole way.

Forty-five minutes later I return and she's in tears. "What's wrong?"

She turns her head to me. "I forgot how sad the ending of this movie is."

I can't help but let out a laugh. "Only you, Bailey Hart, would cry during *9 ½ Weeks*."

"If it helps, I'm also unimaginably turned on by it. Is your game over?"

"Nope. I'm just here for a little fun before I head back."

Her face falls. "I can't do this anymore."

"All you have to do is say the words and I'll let you out."

Her lips start to form a P, but the words never spill from her mouth. She briefly closes her eyes. "This better be the best orgasm of my life."

"It will be. For now, I'll take one because sitting down there with my friends, knowing you're in my house naked, tasting you on my lips and fingers, has my cock on overdrive." I start unzipping my pants. "Open your mouth, sweet girl."

Her lips curl in amusement. "Yes, Daddy."

I have to squeeze my newly freed cock to tame the throb. What is wrong with me that her words affect me so much?

I climb onto the bed and begin tracing my tip around her wet lips. She flicks her tongue over it. "Hmm, you taste good, Mr. Montgomery."

"You're going to swallow me down like a good girl, aren't you?"

She looks up at me with those innocent big eyes of hers and nods.

"Open wide."

She does, and I slide my cock all the way in until it reaches the back of her throat.

"Wrap those beautiful lips around me."

Again, she does as she's told as I begin my thrusts in and out of her mouth until I come down her throat.

"You're being very compliant."

"Reward me."

I smile as I remove the nipple clamps from the chest at the end of my bed. Her eyes widen. "What the hell are those?"

"Only pleasure, Bailey. We can stop this anytime."

I spend a few minutes teasing and sucking on her nipples, preparing them for what's coming next.

Pinching her nipples with my fingers, I ask, "Does that feel good?"

She moans, "Yes. I want you. Make me come."

I shake my head. "So impatient. Not yet." Warming each clamp with my hands for a brief moment, I then attach them to her nipples.

Her eyes practically roll to the back of her head as her back arches and she yells out, "Oh my god."

"Shh. We don't want my guests to know you're here. Let me go wrap things up downstairs, and then I'll give you what you crave."

"No. Don't go. Stay."

I fiddle with the remote control again and put on *Outlander* for her. I remember Fallon's obsession with that show when we were married.

I'm again downstairs. I'm not wrapping things up quite yet. I want to allow the clamps to get her teetering on the edge to the point where detonation is the only option for her.

Trey is gone, so it's just the five of us. I look at Layton. "How are you managing?"

"Day by day. The fucking cast sucks, my girl isn't here, Quincy disappeared, and my career is over, but I'm sick of my pity party. I've got some things in the works that I'm looking forward to."

"What do you mean Quincy disappeared? Weren't you at his house last night?"

He nods. "Yep. But he texted us this morning that he was heading out of town and he wouldn't be reachable for the foreseeable future. Dinner was awkward as fuck last night. He doesn't get along with his parents. Ripley, Kam, and Bailey were all pissed at him for some unknown reason. Arizona doesn't know he took off yet. She's going to be worried. I hope he comes back before she returns home in a few weeks."

Cheetah nods in agreement. "It was definitely awkward."

We spend a little time chatting about the Christmas holiday. Vance and Daylen are in season, so they'll be in town. Cheetah mentions that he invited Kam to come home with him, but she hasn't given him an answer yet. I hope that means Bailey is free to spend that time with me in Colorado.

The boys all eventually head out, and I make my way up to my bedroom. When I open the door, she's breathing loudly. She whimpers, "I swear to god, if you brush by my clit, I'll come. I'll do anything. Don't leave again. I'll suck your dick every day for a year if you make me come right now."

I smile as I begin unbuttoning my shirt. "I'm not going anywhere until you have the greatest orgasm of your life. I promise."

She lets out a breath in relief. "Thank duck."

I inwardly laugh. Even in this moment, she won't curse. So dedicated. So disciplined.

The more clothes I remove, the more her breathing increases and she pulls on the cuffs. She's not kidding about being on the cusp. I need to play this carefully. I want this to be the best orgasm of her life.

I undress painfully slow for her. I know that drives her nuts. She's always frantic with need. Making her wait is half the fun. Well, less than half, but it's still fun.

Finally down to my boxer briefs, my cock strains against its confines. It's been hard to keep him under control all night knowing who was waiting for me and her current state of being tied naked to my bed.

Running my fingers around her reddened nipples, I ask, "How do the clamps feel?"

"I don't know if they were sent from heaven or hell. I'll let you know in a few minutes."

I smile as I lean over and taste her smart mouth. She loves kissing, and I love the effect my kisses have on her.

My tongue slowly explores her mouth while hers rapidly ravages mine. She sinks her teeth into my lower lip and bites down, mumbling, "I'm not letting you go until you make me come."

I reach for one of her breasts and squeeze the clamp. She lets out a scream, releasing my lip.

"You're a bad girl." I slap her pussy, and she bucks her hips and yells out.

My lips meet the scorching skin of her cleavage as I slowly drag them down her body. I can't help but inhale her. I love her scent. I love the way she feels. I love everything about her.

She begins to visibly tremble with anticipation. She's so on edge.

Eventually I get down to her center, gently kissing it

before lightly running my tongue through her. I whisper, "Is this where you need me, sweet girl?"

Tears leak from the corners of her eyes as she squeezes them shut and nods.

Another soft, slow lick through her, and her back arches off the bed. "That's it, sweetness. Daddy is going to make you feel good. Relief is coming. This pussy is going to sing for me tonight."

My tongue meets her center again and I can tell she's about to come, so I pull away.

She writhes under me and screams, "No!"

I run my lips back up her body, to her favorite spot on her neck. She again bucks her hips, desperately seeking any type of friction. It won't take much to bring her over the cliff into the sea of ecstasy.

With my lips still pressed to her neck, my fingers make a winding, long trail down her body until I reach her opening. Slipping two fingers through and then into her, I push deep until I reach the spot I've come to learn drives her wild.

Her body begins to squeeze around my fingers, and I again pull out. More tears leak out of her eyes. *She sucks in a short breath.* "Please." *Short breath.* "I'll do." *Short breath.* "Anything." *Short breath.*

I reach over and sheath myself in a condom. This orgasm is going to be explosive. I want to feel it on my cock, not my tongue or fingers.

Her eyes are shut. She's in a different world right now, having no clue what I'm going to do to her next. I get off on the control I have over her body.

We've experimented with some of the toys and edging over the past few weeks, but this is the furthest I've taken things with her.

I know the end will be worth the long journey. Giving her new experiences and pleasure is so hot. I love opening her eyes to a new world, one she seems to be enjoying.

I hover over her on my hands so as not to disturb the clamps. I know they only add to her enjoyment.

Bringing my tip to her entrance, I tease it for only a few seconds before thrusting all the way in. She yells out, "Ah, Tanner!" I can feel her begin to convulse around me.

One, two, three deep, hard thrusts, and her pussy squeezes me so damn tight. It's a miracle I don't come. She screams at the top of her lungs as fluids gush from her body in a way I haven't seen from her before.

I continue my strokes. Her orgasm hasn't ended yet. She's completely out of control. I think if she weren't tied down, she'd either be hovering above the bed or have fallen to the floor. I'm not sure she's fully conscious.

She's writhing and jerking as much as she can within her confines. The orgasm rolls on and on. It's not until I feel the tremors begin to subside that I push in deep and give in to my own release.

We're both sweaty and breathless. I'm not sure she knows what planet she's on. I want to collapse, but I need to carefully remove the nipple clamps first.

I gently remove them, sucking on each nipple as I do so to soothe them. Aftershocks work through her body each time my tongue barely grazes her nipples.

Her eyes are still shut as I untie her. She wraps herself around me like a koala bear and begins to weep.

I hold her and rub her hair. "Shh. It's over. I'm here. I'll take care of you, sweet girl."

She sobs into my chest, her body clinging to mine for dear life.

"Are you hurt?"

She shakes through her continued tears. "It was incredible. I don't know why I'm crying."

"It's emotional. That's okay. Did it feel good for you?"

"It was perfection."

"Are you hungry?"

"Famished. I feel like that orgasm took everything out of me."

"Let me feed you."

I try to stand, but she doesn't let go, so I stand with her wrapped around me and walk downstairs to the kitchen.

I gently place her ass on the kitchen counter, and she screeches. "Ah, cold."

"Sorry. Stay put. Let me grab you something."

She peels herself off me and leans back on her hands, completely exhausted and completely exposed to me.

After quickly removing and disposing of the condom, I open the refrigerator and pull out a bowl of sliced pineapples. We've been keeping a steady supply on hand since Bailey started working here. She eats them all the time, and now Harper and I do too.

I stand between her legs, but as soon as I offer her one, she giggles.

"What's so funny?"

"Do you know why I eat pineapples?"

"Because you like them?"

She smiles. "Because Kam told us it makes your..." she points between her legs, "taste better."

My face falls. "Are you serious? My whole family is now pineapple addicts because of Kamryn's crazy?"

She lets out a laugh. "Yep."

I rub a slice over her lips. "Perhaps I should punish you for that too."

She licks the juices from her lips before taking a bite. "I might be up for that."

I rub it over her lips again, but this time I lick it off. "Hmm. I must say, you do taste very sweet. Maybe she's onto something."

"Maybe." She lets out a moan. "That was the most drawn-out orgasm of my life. It lasted forever."

"Worth it in the end?"

Her lips curl up. "Also the *best* orgasm of my life."

I can't help but smile in satisfaction.

She looks up at me. "Were you always like this with women? What got you into this type of sex?"

I raise an eyebrow. "Do you really want me to talk about other women with you?"

She nods. "Yes. I'm curious."

I rub her thighs because I can't seem to keep my hands off her. Contemplating her question for a moment, I eventually answer, "Something happened in high school that took an emotional toll on me. I felt like I lost a bit of control in my life. The only good news for me at the time was that I still had the interest of girls."

She smiles. "I bet you did."

I raise an eyebrow.

"You're gorgeous and so damn sexy. I have no doubt women did and do throw themselves at you."

I roll my eyes at the compliment. "Anyway...that's when I began experimenting. I liked the control it afforded me."

"What happened where you lost control?"

"Nothing I want to talk about."

"Was Fallon into it? The way you are in bed?"

"I'm not discussing my sex life with Fallon with you."

She feeds me a pineapple slice. "I'll take that as a yes."

After I finish chewing and swallowing, I admit, "Let's just say that our physical relationship fizzled along with the marriage."

She shrugs. "Her loss is my gain. You're undoubtedly a tough act to follow. That's probably why she doesn't date."

"She doesn't date?" That's news to me. I assumed someone like Fallon has an unlimited supply of men pursuing her. "How do you know that?"

"She told me once when we were having dinner. You weren't home yet. She said between her job, her parents, and Harper, she doesn't have time."

My face falls. "I'm sorry to hear that. That's not what I want for her. She has a lot to offer."

"She's a beautiful woman who's warm and smart. I'm sure it's only a matter of time."

I cup her cheek. "Speaking of warm, smart, beautiful women, is this one ready for another round?" I thrust my growing cock against her center.

"You've got a lot of energy, Mr. Montgomery."

"You're irresistible, Ms. Hart." I lean in for a kiss.

She smiles into my mouth. "One more slice, and then I'll be ready."

As I feed it to her, I say, "Cheetah mentioned taking your sister home for Christmas. Does that mean we're on for Vail?"

She nods as she swallows. "Yep. Kam and I talked about it. She's leaving before Christmas though. My friends are all gone. I need to figure out what I'm doing, but I'm definitely free the next week."

Without thinking, I offer, "Spend it with us."

She pinches her eyebrows together. "How would that work with Fallon?"

"The truth. You don't have your family or friends around. If she knew, she'd insist on you spending it with us anyway."

"What do you guys do?"

"This year we're doing Christmas Eve at Fallon's with her parents. We alternate years. Harper will sleep there this year. They'll do Christmas morning at her house first and then she'll bring Harper here for another Christmas morning. Then we leave for Vail later that day."

She smiles. "So I can stay with you on Christmas Eve? Or will your father be here?"

I roll my eyes. "He won't come the years we do Christmas Eve at Fallon's. He's stubborn, blaming her for the divorce. He's planning to visit after New Year's for Harper's birthday."

She smiles. "I can't wait for her party. I told her I'd make the cake. She wants something *softballish* but said to otherwise surprise her."

I lift her up and she giggles. "Enough talking. Time for *my* favorite cake."

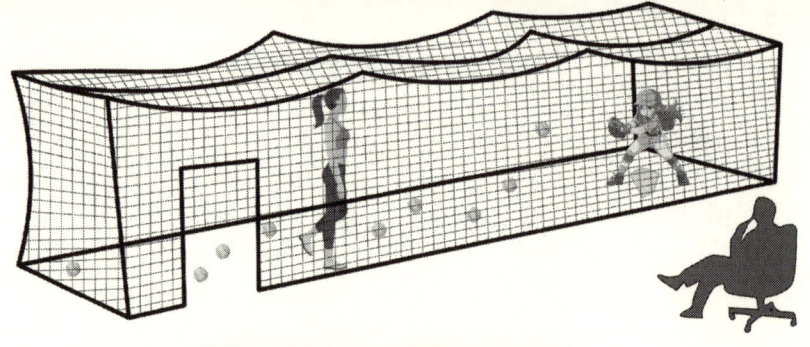

CHAPTER SIXTEEN

BAILEY

Poor Cheetah. Kam was such a mess when I sent her off this morning. I gave him a rundown of how to handle her on the plane but I'm sure nothing prepared him for how crazy she gets when flying. But she officially took her first flight without me. She texted that they landed safely. I've got my first flight without her tomorrow.

It's Christmas Eve, and we're on our way to Fallon's house. I've been there a handful of times over the past few months, but I haven't met her parents. Her father had some complications with his broken ankle and was bedridden longer than expected. Apparently he's fine now.

Tanner turns to me. "I have a nanny-appropriate gift to give you tonight. It's from both Fallon and me. She called me with the idea, and of course I said yes. I have a gift from me that I'll give to you in private."

"A dirty gift?"

He chuckles. "Your mind is in the gutter."

"I have a dirty old man doing unspeakable things to my body all the time. You've turned my mind as gutter-like as Kam's."

He raises an eyebrow. "Old man."

I smile at him as I gently scrape my fingernails across the gray in his beard. The sexy as hell gray in his beard. "I've never been with a man with gray hair until you."

"Are you looking for a spanking later?"

I bite my lip. I will never understand why that turns me on so much, but it does. I better change the topic before we end up on the side of the road having sex. "You didn't have to get me a gift. This trip is more than a gift. I'm excited to try skiing. I never even saw snow until we moved to Chicago."

"You're still young, and you're a world-class athlete. You'll pick it up quickly. I have no doubt."

"Is Harper a good skier?"

He smiles. "When they're young they have no fear. It's the best time to teach them. She's great. Dylan has been skiing since she could walk, so she's good too. I arranged for the two of them to go to ski school in the mornings. You and I can take our time in the mornings. I figured I'd teach you how to ski. Then we'll ski with them in the afternoons. There are tons of good restaurants around. It's a beautiful town. The cabin I rented has four bedrooms. I'll leave the master for Fallon. This way you and I will have an adjoining bathroom to come and go as we please."

"Are you going to sneak into my room at night, Mr. Montgomery?"

He briefly closes his eyes as he squirms in his seat. "You know it makes me hard when you call me that."

"It makes you hard when I call you Daddy."

He leans his head back on the headrest and groans. "Fuuuck. It makes my cock leak when you call me Daddy. Hard when you call me Mr. Montgomery. *Both* names get me riled up. Don't do that to me before we head into my ex-wife's house."

I can't help but smile. "Me too."

He grabs my hand and kisses it. "Who am I kidding? Everything you do gets me riled up. This desperate need to be close to you at all times isn't waning. It's only growing."

I don't know how to respond to that. I feel the exact same way, but he's always been clear about what we are. Is he changing his mind?

Before I can overanalyze his words, we arrive at Fallon's beautifully decorated home. I haven't seen it with Christmas lights. It's stunning.

Tanner knocks on the front door. I'm surprised he doesn't just walk in like she does at his house.

"Don't you have a key? I even have a key to this house."

He scrunches his face. "I don't like to just walk in. It feels invasive even though I'm happy Fallon does it at my house... except when I'm in bed with you."

I smile just as the front door opens. Harper runs out and jumps into my arms. "Bailey's here!"

I squeeze her tight. "Merry Christmas, angel."

Tanner grumbles, "What about me?"

I joke, "Merry Christmas to you too, Mr. Montgomery."

He narrows his eyes at me. Harper and I both giggle, and she wiggles her way down from my arms and into his. "Merry Christmas, Daddy."

"You too. Are you all packed for our trip?"

She nods enthusiastically. "Yes. Mommy said the cabin you rented has an outdoor hot tub. Is that true?"

"It sure is. It's cold out, so you have to run really fast to get in and out of it. Can you do that?"

"Yes! I'm superfast."

He nods. "I agree. The hot tub overlooks the Rocky Mountains. It will be beautiful." He winks at me. "Think of all the fun we can have in that hot tub."

My heart starts beating faster. This man.

I notice the candy necklace around Harper's neck. "Ohh, is this fancy jewelry new?"

She smiles. "Yes. My grandparents got it for me."

"I love it. They know you well."

The door widens and Fallon's beautiful, grinning face

appears. "Merry Christmas. Come inside." She shivers. "It's freezing cold out here."

I walk in and hug her. "Wow. You look gorgeous." I've never seen Fallon in anything but scrubs and leggings. She's in flattering jeans, a tight sweater, and boots, with her hair blown out and makeup on tonight. She's an undeniably stunning woman.

She rubs my arm. "You're beautiful, as always."

I hand her two bottles of wine. "Thank you for having me."

She takes them. "We're thrilled to have you. Harper is excited to introduce you to her grandparents. And I'll open the wine for you and me."

Harper grabs my hand. "Come on, Bails. They're dying to meet you."

I let her drag me through the house into the living room. There's so much Christmas cheer in this house. It's such a contrast to what I grew up with. My father did his best, but he was basically on an island doing everything with limited resources. Fallon's tree is enormous and looks like it was professionally decorated. In fact, all of her holiday decorations look like a professional did it.

I squeeze Harper's hand. "Wow. This is beautiful. You're a lucky little lady that your mommy did all this for you."

An older woman, likely in her sixties, very much resembling Fallon, waves her hand dismissively. "Nonsense. Joel and I did it all for her." She holds out her hand. "I'm Doris. This is my husband, Joel. Harper never stops talking about you. It's a pleasure to finally meet you. I'm sorry it's taken so long. We've had a bit of a rough fall season."

I take her hand. "I'm glad he's healed. It's so nice to finally meet you."

She holds my arms and looks my body up and down. "Aren't you a pretty thing? You must have a line of suitors out the door."

I let out a laugh. "Something like that, though I think the same can be said about your daughter."

Doris raises an eyebrow at Fallon. "I couldn't possibly agree more. If only she'd open that door and let them in."

Fallon blows out a breath and jokingly grits out, "Bailey, you're supposed to be on my side. Girl code."

We all smile as Tanner walks into the room and kisses Doris's cheek. "You look well, Doris. You never seem to age."

She rubs the gray in his beard. "I wish I could say the same for you, Tanner."

Fallon shakes her head. "Be nice, Mother."

Doris bats her eyelashes. "I'm always nice."

I meet her father too, who still seems a little squeamish on his feet. I hear a bit about everything he's been through the past few months from infections to casts that were too tight. It doesn't sound fun.

Harper insists on exchanging gifts. I gift her the bat from the game-winning hit in the league championship game, signed by the entire team. Harper starts crying from excitement, calling it her most prized possession.

Fallon hands me an envelope. "This is from the three of us." She seems so excited to give it to me.

I open it and my eyes nearly bug out of my head. It's front-row seats to Coldplay when they're in town this spring. It includes backstage passes.

"Oh my god. I can't believe you guys did this."

Tanner shrugs. "Fallon insisted that they're your favorite band. I hope she was right."

She remembered. "They are. This is honestly one of the most thoughtful gifts anyone has ever given me. Thank you, Fallon."

She hugs me and whispers into my ear, "Thank you for all you do for Harper. For loving her the way you do."

Tanner grumbles, "They're from me too."

I smile and move to hug him in gratitude. I need to keep it appropriate. "Thank you, Mr. Montgomery."

I gently hug him but can feel and hear him turn his nose into my neck to inhale me. I doubt he meant to do it, but it happened.

PAYOFF PITCH

Quickly pulling away, I look around. Fallon didn't notice, but her mom definitely did.

A FEW HOURS LATER, Tanner and I are in bed enjoying our after-sex glow. He reaches over and hands me another envelope.

"What's this?"

"Your real gift."

"Coldplay was more than real. With the way you were talking in the car, I thought it was going to be a sweater, not backstage passes to see my favorite band. It was over the top."

He shrugs. "This gift is for both of us."

I twist my lips. Admittedly, I'm excited to see what he came up with. "Fine." I excitedly open it and see that it's a skydiving session for two. I shake my head. "There's no way—"

He interrupts, "You said that Kam is the wild one and you've always had to be the sensible, motherly one. It's time for Bailey Hart to have a little fun of her own. I've gone several times. It's one of my favorite things to do, besides you."

"You skydive? Mr. Business Suit and Tie. Mr. High-end Whiskey On the Rocks. Mr. I've Never Seen Your Clothes Wrinkled."

He chuckles as he nods. "Yes. Do you have any idea how incredible it is to let go and freefall from thousands of feet in the air? It's a rush like no other. One of the only irresponsible things I still indulge in. I want you to experience it."

I take a few breaths. "Wow. I don't know what to say."

"I'm certified. You'll be attached to me while I control the parachute." He smirks. "Your life will be in my hands. It's the ultimate act of submission for you."

"Did you just make skydiving sexual?"

He wiggles his thick eyebrows. "Oh, sweet girl, you have no idea."

Tanner

We've had an amazing week in Vail. Not surprising at all, Bailey picked up skiing very quickly. She's such a naturally gifted athlete.

We've settled into a routine. Harper and Dylan go to ski school in the mornings, leaving Bailey and me to have coffee and then ski on our own.

We have lunch with the girls and then ski all together during the afternoons. We go out for dinner every night. If there's time afterward, we play board or card games, and when the girls go to bed, Bailey and I sit in the hot tub and talk. We then go at it for hours and fall asleep together. She wakes at some point during the night and sneaks back into her room. Just to be safe.

It's been heavenly, and I don't want it to end but it is. Fallon arrives tomorrow, so this is my last night with Bailey. We can't risk any sneaking around tomorrow night.

We're in the hot tub with drinks, and she smiles. "This was one of the most relaxing weeks of my life. Thank you for bringing me."

I chuckle. "A vacation with two kids was relaxing?"

"It was. They were great. They're so fun. And obviously getting this uninterrupted time with you has been perfect." She lets out a laugh. "Do you realize that this is the longest Kam and I have ever been apart?"

I shake my head. "That's incredible. Hard to believe."

"It is. I love my sister. Not having her around feels like a limb is missing, but there's also a little bit of peace I don't always get to enjoy with her being...her."

"She's a character, for sure. Have you spoken with her?"

"Of course. She and Cheetah are up to all kinds of shenanigans."

"No doubt about that. Do you think there's something genuine between them?"

She shrugs. "Who knows? If there was ever anyone perfect for my sister, it's him. I'm not sure she's the settle-down type though."

I blow out a breath. "I'm not sure he is either."

She bites her lip. I know she wants to ask me the same question, but I don't want to talk about this right now. She won't like the answer.

I continue, "I think this is a healthy break for you and her. The codependency is a lot. You're getting too old for that. You've lived your life for her. It's time you live it for you."

Her face falls. "I live it for me."

"Is that so? Why aren't you teaching? Oh, because of Kamryn. She needs you to play softball with her. At twenty-eight. Why do you live in Philly? Because of Kamryn. What about your books? You've mentioned two drafts sitting on your computer. You have time to work on them. Why haven't you? Let me guess. Kamryn."

Her stare hardens. "You have a lot of opinions for a man who keeps everyone in his life at arm's length."

"No, I don't."

"You do. Besides your monthly poker game with clients, you don't really socialize at all. And you're only forty-three. Why won't you consider getting married again and having more children?"

I start to speak but she holds up her hands. "I'm not talking about doing it with me. I mean in general. There's no reason for you to close that door and seal it shut the way you have."

"I'm not interested in talking about this."

"Right. Because anytime things get too emotionally intimate, you turn away. You deflect. I've watched you do it for as long as I've known you. You'll talk about me, judge me, but not you. I don't really know that much about you. We've been doing this," she points her finger back and forth between us, "for months. I've been in your house three or four days a week for nearly six months. I know about your marriage ending, but nothing substantive beyond that."

She looks like she wants to say even more but then thinks better of it and stops herself.

My jaw stiffens. How dare she. "I don't owe you my deepest, darkest secrets, Bailey. We're fuck buddies. I've been clear about that from day one."

Tears rise in her eyes at my cold words. Ones that pain me to say but I know she needs to hear.

She steels herself. "I know we have no future. You've made that *crystal* clear. You've asked me to open up, and then you opine on my life. I'm only asking for the same in return."

I exhale a long breath, feeling like the dick I know I am. "I'm sorry. I honestly feel like I've opened up to you more than most. I'm not ready to give more."

"Then my personal life is off limits too, including your thoughts on my loving relationship with my sister. I'm sorry you can't relate to a strong sibling bond, but I won't apologize for having one with my sister."

I nod. "Fair enough."

She tilts her head to the side. "Do you know what it's like to have someone in your life who you trust one hundred percent? Someone who will have your back no matter what? Who loves you so unconditionally? Who would undoubtedly take a bullet for you?"

I answer the truth. "No. I don't have that. My brother is a piece of shit. My wife cheated on me. My best—" I stop myself, unwilling to talk about this with her. It's too much. "No, I've learned the hard way that I can only truly rely on myself."

She shakes her head. "That's sad, Tanner. I know my

sister is a lot to take, but she's that for me and it's everything." She stands. "I think maybe I should go to bed. I don't want to say anything else I might regret."

My shoulders fall. "It's our last night. It's been a great week. I don't want it to end like this. Don't go to bed angry." I pull her to straddle my lap, pinning her to me when she fights it. "It's been nice having this time with you. Away from Philly. Away from work. Away from real life. I want to enjoy every second of you that I can get."

I bend and kiss the spot on her neck that she loves. I whisper, "Don't pull away. You can hate me tomorrow. Not tonight. I don't want a wonderful week to end this way."

She relaxes her body and tentatively wraps her arms around my neck. She's still mad at me but nods in agreement. "I know. I feel the same. I don't want to fight with you."

"I don't want to fight with you either." I softly kiss her lips, and then we hear a noise. We both snap our heads toward the open sliding glass door but don't see anything.

She attempts to pull away, but I hold her tight. "Please stay with me."

"The girls could come out."

I wiggle my eyebrows. "They can't see what's going on underwater."

She sighs. "I'm not up for this tonight. I'm sorry."

"Are you mad at me?"

"Maybe a little. Let me sleep on it." She pulls away and stands. "I need to call my sister and check in on her. You know, the whole codependency thing. I'll see you in the morning."

As she towels off, I grab the glass of whiskey sitting next to me and down it in one go. She stares at me for a second and then looks at the bottle of whiskey sitting on the ledge of the tub. The one that's nearly empty. "Typical. Go drown your sorrows at the bottom of that."

"What the hell is that supposed to mean?" I challenge.

"You know exactly what it means. When was the last night you didn't drink?"

I can feel my whole body tense in an instant. "Don't project your mother's shit onto me. I'm not an alcoholic. I'll have a glass or two, not a bottle or two."

"Do you think she started by drinking two bottles a day? No. It started when she couldn't get through a single day without a drink, Tanner. Sound familiar?"

I turn around, throw the glass out into the snowy abyss, and then shout, "There. Happy?"

"Good night, Tanner. Maybe you'll grow up a little by the morning."

Once I'm alone, I take a deep breath and run my fingers through my hair in frustration. How dare she insinuate that. I'm a fucking grown man. I can have a glass of whiskey in the evenings.

Without even thinking, I grab the bottle and take a long gulp. As I pull it away from my lips, it hits me what I just did. Fuck.

The fact is that Bailey sees right through me in a way no one ever has. She challenges me in a way no one ever has.

I don't want to lose her. I need to make this right.

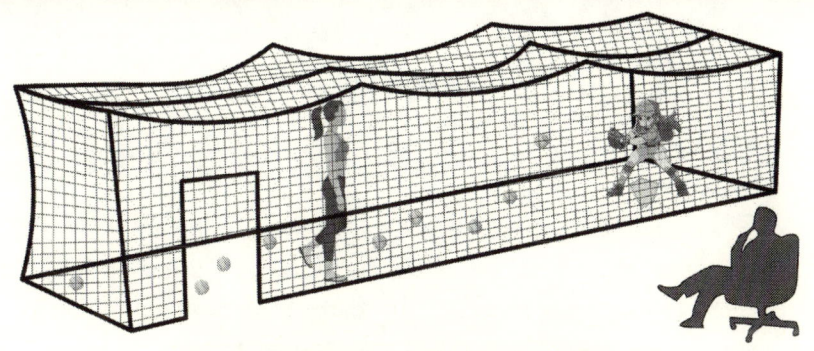

CHAPTER SEVENTEEN

TANNER

Fallon arrived this afternoon following a morning filled with the cold-shoulder treatment from Bailey. I tried to apologize multiple times, but she found a way to ensure she was never alone with me. Now that Fallon is here, I won't get Bailey to myself until tomorrow when we leave.

She and I are supposed to fly home tomorrow morning. She offered to stay longer to help Fallon, and probably to avoid me, but Fallon insisted that Bailey go home and enjoy her New Year's Eve with her friends.

I'm taking them all to dinner at a restaurant where you pick your own steaks and then you get to cook them yourself on the lava rock grills. We come here every year. It's Harper's favorite restaurant out here and she wanted to wait for Fallon to come so we could all enjoy it together.

As we grill our steaks, Fallon asks Bailey, "Any big New Year's Eve plans?"

She shrugs. "I'm not sure. I've never spent one without my sister before. Some girls on the team mentioned clubbing. It's not really my scene, but maybe I'll make an exception."

I had asked her to spend it with me. This is her way of telling me she's not. I wish it didn't hurt as much as it does.

Fallon appears surprised by the fact that Bailey doesn't enjoy clubbing. "I would think you guys would be out drinking and dancing all the time. How do you meet men?"

I can't help but flinch at the question. Fallon immediately notices. For someone who prides himself on being a good poker player, my real-life poker face needs a lot of work.

Fallon closely watches me while Bailey answers, "Here and there."

About twenty minutes later, we're at the table enjoying the fruits of our labor. Fallon is staring daggers at me when Bailey's phone rings. She rejects the call without looking to see who it's from and gives us a sheepish smile. "Sorry. I didn't realize the ringer was on."

Just then, it starts ringing again. I nod toward it. "Someone needs to get in touch with you. Answer it."

She looks down and her eyebrows pinch together. "It's my dad. That's strange. He knows I'm here with you guys. It must be important." She stands. "I'll be right back." She walks out the front door of the restaurant.

Fallon asks Harper, "Did you and Dylan use the outdoor hot tub? I can't wait for that. I love watching the snow fall from the confines of a warm tub. I bet it's beautiful."

Harper nods. "Yes, we went in every day when we got back from skiing. Daddy and Bailey used it every night after we went to bed."

I do my best not to choke on my food. I didn't realize she knew that. "Umm...yep. My old bones needed it after a day on the slopes."

Fallon gives me a forced smile, "I'll bet your bone needed it."

She glares at me. I know a big talk is in my future, and I have no idea what I'm going to say.

I'm fumbling for the right words when Bailey returns with tears streaming down her cheeks. I immediately stand. "What's wrong?"

She visibly swallows and fairly calmly says, "My mother passed today."

Uncaring where we are or who we're with, I wrap her in my arms as she begins silently sobbing into my chest.

Fallon looks at me. "Get the car and bring her back to the cabin to pack. Take care of whatever logistics she needs. I'll finish up here and we'll Uber back."

"Are you sure?"

She nods. "Of course. Bailey, I'm so sorry for your loss."

Bailey nods and croaks out, "Thank you."

I help her out the door with my arm around her. I don't care if Fallon has a problem with it. Bailey needs comfort right now.

The drive back to the cabin is done in silence. I hold her hand while she stoically stares out the window.

Eventually breaking the silence, she admits, "He said a year. I thought I had more time. I never gave up hope that we'd all make amends. I wanted it, but Kam *needed* it. I'm worried for my sister."

I pull her hand to my lips and kiss it. "I'm sorry, baby. I know it's hard, and I know you worry about her, but right now, it's okay to think about yourself and your feelings on this."

She looks at me. "I don't know how I feel. I'm sad, but she hasn't been a real mother to us in such a long time. My father has done all the parenting for as long as I can remember."

"How is he?"

"Kind of emotionless. I think he was in shock. I told him I'd call Kam. She's not going to have a normal response, and I don't want him to have to deal with her. I honestly don't know if she'll come to the funeral."

"I'm sure she will. For your sake." I don't know if that's true, but Bailey needs to hear it right now. "What can I do to help?"

She stoically responds, "I need to call her and pack. Would you mind changing my flight tomorrow morning to Florida instead of Philly? I also need to figure out my clothing situation. I only have winter clothes with me and nothing for the funeral. I guess I can buy something there."

"I'll take care of clothing for you, and I'll change our flights. Don't worry about a thing."

"*Our* flights?"

I turn to her. "Yes. I'm coming with you."

"I don't think that's a g—"

"I'm coming. Who knows what Kamryn will do? Even if she's there, she'll be a handful, and you'll spend all your time taking care of her and your father. Who will take care of you? I want to be there for you. Harper is gone all week with Fallon. No argument. I'm coming with you."

She nods as we pull into the driveway of the cabin. I quickly exit the car and walk around to help her out.

Once her feet are on the ground, she looks up at me. "I know we're not really together, but I want you to know how much I appreciate this. It means a lot to me."

I wipe her tear-covered cheeks with my thumbs. "No matter what we are and aren't, I care about you." *More than I should.*

I take her hand. "Let's get inside and get everything sorted."

We walk in and she holds up her phone. "I'm calling Kam. Wish me luck."

"She'll come. I know she'll do the right thing." She better.

Bailey nods as she disappears into her bedroom.

PAYOFF PITCH

I first call Shannon and instruct her to take care of everything, including flights, hotel, car rental, and an assortment of clothing for Bailey.

I then text Cheetah.

> Me: No matter what you have to do, get her to that funeral.

> Cruz: She's not emoting over this. It's weird. I'll try.

> Me: I told Shannon to book us two suites at a nearby hotel. One will be in your name. If you need her to take care of anything else, just text her.

> Cruz: Thanks, man. How's Bailey?

> Me: Worried about Kamryn.

> Cruz: Sounds about right.

> Me: Our flight arrives in the late afternoon. Get. Kamryn. There.

> Cruz: I'll do my best. Let me run. They're getting off the phone. I'll keep you updated.

Bailey's still in her room when Fallon returns with the girls. She says to Harper, "It's late. Why don't you two get into your pajamas and brush your teeth? I'll come read you stories in a few minutes."

Harper's little brow furrows. "But I want to make sure Bailey is okay."

I reply, "She's sad, honey. Why don't we give her a little space tonight? You'll see her in the morning before she goes. I'm sure she could use a big hug from you."

"Okay, Daddy."

She and Dylan head to their room. Fallon looks at me. "How's Bailey?"

"Upset. She had a strained relationship with her mother. I think not getting closure will sting for a bit. It's worse for Kamryn. She had a lot more animosity toward their mother than Bailey did. Of course, Bailey is more concerned about her sister than herself."

"I'm sorry for what she's going through. It can't be easy."

"It's not."

She blows out a breath. "Not to sound insensitive, my heart genuinely breaks for her, but maybe you should stick around an extra day or two so we can chat about the fact that you're fucking our daughter's nanny." She shakes her head. "My mother was right. I told her she was mistaken, that neither you nor Bailey would be so selfish, but she saw it. I was ignorant, but she knew right away."

I pour myself a drink and take a long gulp. Shit. I wasn't going to drink tonight. Fuck that. The situation warrants it. "We didn't plan this, Fallon. It just happened."

Her lips tighten into a thin line. "When you hire a woman who looks like a swimsuit model as a nanny, and you look like...you, this kind of shit is inevitable. I explicitly expressed these concerns to you before you hired her, and you assured me it wouldn't be a problem. I don't care who you fuck, Tanner, but I care if it could hurt Harper. When you dump the poor kid in a few weeks, where does that leave Harper? You know she loves Bailey. She'll be devastated when Bailey leaves her. Heartbroken."

I take another sip, letting it smooth out the edges. "What do you want me to say? We've agreed to be casual. To not let it impact Harper."

She rolls her eyes. "Oh please. Don't play ignorant. I see the way she looks at you. I assumed it was unrequited puppy love. I didn't know you were so weak. This isn't casual for her. I barely know Bailey, but I know enough to realize that a girl like her probably doesn't do casual. Maybe when she gets back from Florida, the three of us should sit down and figure out what's best for Harper."

"I'm...I'm going to Florida with her."

She freezes and simply stares at me for a few moments. Her hand moves over her mouth. "You have feelings for her." She whispers to herself, "Holy shit. I'm such an idiot. How could I be so blind?"

I'm getting angry but doing my best not to raise my voice to her. I calmly yet clearly state, "You know what, Fallon, my love life is none of your concern."

"I don't disagree, but when it impacts Harper, it is. How could you be so careless about who you sleep with?"

I scoff. "Isn't that the pot calling the kettle black? At least I didn't—"

I stop myself from finishing that sentence when I see the tears streaming from her eyes at the uncharacteristic shot fired. I've never once thrown her affair in her face. I pride myself on that fact.

I hold up my hand. "I'm sorry. That was uncalled for."

Her lips tremble as she shakes her head. "No, you're right. I'm the dirty whore of the two of us, not you."

"You're not a dirty whore, Fallon."

Tears continue to fall from her eyes. "I broke up our marriage. I lost the only man I've ever loved because of a foolish decision. One that I replay over and over every single night of my life, wondering if I made a different choice, what our lives would look like. Would we have gotten past the distance and found our way to happiness again? Would Harper have married parents? I suppose we'll never know, and I'll be left..." She doesn't finish her thought.

"Be left how?"

She shakes her head. "It doesn't matter." She takes a

deep breath, gathering herself. "I'm going to read to the girls. Go help Bailey with whatever she needs. We'll talk more when you get back from Florida."

IT'S EARLY MORNING, and we're about to leave for the airport. Harper is clinging to Bailey for dear life.

Fallon looks at me with worry written all over her face. I know she's concerned about Harper's attachment to Bailey. She's not wrong.

Harper whimpers, "I'm sorry you're sad, Bailey."

She kisses Harper's head. "I'll be okay. Don't worry about me. You know what would make me feel better?"

Harper looks hopeful. "What?"

"If you promise to have the best week with your mommy." Tears fill her eyes. "You're very lucky to have such a good mommy."

Fallon wraps her arms around Harper from behind. "We promise, right, baby?"

Harper nods. "Y...yes."

Fallon reaches for Bailey and hugs her. She whispers something in her ear, but I can't make out what it is.

Bailey simply nods when they break apart.

Later that afternoon, we land in Florida. Bailey sighs. "I didn't think about a car, a hotel for you, or anything. I'm sorry. My brain has been in a fog since last night."

"Don't worry. I took care of everything. I wasn't sure of the situation at your parents' house. I booked big suites for both us and for Cheetah and Kamryn. I gave Cheetah all the info."

"Oh. It's probably best that we stay in a hotel. I guess I assumed Kam and I would stay with my dad, but she probably won't want to sleep in that house.

She swore she never would again. Thanks for doing that."

"Of course. Why don't we head to the hotel first? There should be clothes waiting for us. It's a little hot down here for sweaters and jeans."

As we're driving to the hotel, I ask, "What did Fallon whisper to you before we left?"

She smiles. "How many hours have you been dying to ask me that?"

I chuckle. "Every minute since it happened. She was...a little worked up about us last night."

"Yep. I realized she figured it out. I'm sorry."

"Don't worry about it. I'll handle her."

"I get her concerns. She whispered that she's thankful to me for loving Harper the way I do and she hopes no matter what happens with us, I'll put Harper first."

"I have no doubt that you will."

"Always."

We arrive at the hotel and change clothes. She suggests that she go to see her father alone. She takes the rental car keys and heads to his house.

A few hours later, well into the evening, she's still gone and I'm busy working at my laptop when there's a knock at the door. I open it to see Kamryn and Cheetah. Kamryn pushes her way in. "Where's my sister?"

"Hello to you too, Kamryn. Nice to see you. I'm sorry for your loss."

"I'm just glad the suffering is over."

"Oh. Was she in pain? I didn't realize that."

Kamryn deadpans, "No. Not her suffering. Ours." She scoffs. "It's no loss. The world is a better place without that lowlife. Where's my sister? She's the only reason Cheetah talked me into coming to this charade. Our appearance will probably double the number of people who attend her funeral." She narrows her eyes at me. "Why are *you* here?"

"Because she wasn't sure you'd come, and I didn't want her to have to do this alone."

"Hmm. Do you care about all of your employees this much? If Shannon's mother passed, would you accompany her to the funeral too? It's quite an employee perk program you're running."

"If Shannon's sister was crazy, yes I would go."

Cheetah barks out a laugh. "He's got you there."

Bailey suddenly appears in the doorway. She wraps her arms around Kamryn from behind and sinks her nose into her back. "Thanks for coming."

Kamryn turns around and hugs her back. "I'm here for you and Daddy, not her."

Bailey nods. "I know. I'm still happy you're here. I missed you."

"I missed you too." Kamryn pulls back. "How's Daddy?"

Bailey twists her lips. "He's surprisingly calm. He's all business about it. It's weird."

Kamryn nods. "He's probably relieved to be rid of the witch."

"The house is different. It's like he was already packed up and ready to sell it. I don't think they were sleeping in the same room. All his stuff was in our old room."

"Who would fuck her? I hope he had a side piece he was bringing into our room at night. He deserves it."

Cheetah chuckles. "Kam bam, you're the only person on the planet praying for her father to get side action."

She smiles. "I am. And I plan to put the *fun* in this funeral. It's more of a...celebration. Daddy is free at last. It's a holiday miracle."

Bailey sighs. "Behave for two days. For him. He said he knows you won't stick around for long. He wants to come up for a visit next month to talk to us about some things."

"Good. I want to get the fuck out of this shitty town as soon as I can. We're leaving tomorrow."

"Fine. I didn't tell any of our friends. It's the holidays, and I don't want anyone to feel obligated to fly down here. I assume you're good with that?"

Kamryn nods. "For sure. Don't make anyone come in for this shitshow. They're busy with their own crap." She looks around. "I see you have a two-bedroom suite as well. Interesting."

Bailey rolls her eyes. "Don't start. Not today. How were your trips to Texas and Jamaica?"

Kamryn smiles. "Texas was great. Cheetah's family is awesome. There are a million of them, and almost all are fun like him. He's the only one with blue eyes though." She winks at Cheetah. "Right?"

He shakes his head in exasperation. "It's been family fodder for years and Kam bam joined right in on it."

Bailey smiles. "I have no doubt."

She continues. "We weren't in Jamaica for long, but it was the most beautiful place I've ever been."

Bailey nods. "Sorry your vacation got cut short." She yawns and stretches her arms. "I'm beat. I'm headed to bed."

"What? It's New Year's Eve. Let's go party. We can celebrate the new year and the end of an error."

"An era?"

"An error. Beverly Hart's existence was an error of grand proportions."

Bailey shakes her head. "I'm not up for going out. Our mother's funeral is tomorrow. Do you have anything to wear?"

Kamryn smiles and nods. "I've got the perfect dress for the occasion, sis. Don't worry."

Bailey sighs. "Oh Christ. Remember, we're here for him. It's about him."

"Sure thing. So, Bails, which room are you sleeping in tonight?"

Bailey pushes her and Cheetah out the door. "Good

night. Have a good time tonight. Don't get too blitzed. See you in the morning. Be ready to leave by nine."

Kam laughs as they leave. "Oh, we'll have fun."

Once they're gone, I pull Bailey into my arms. "How was he?"

She relaxes into me. "Oddly at ease. I hate to admit it, but Kam might be right. I think he's relieved. He was sad—they have a long history together—but he seemed at peace. Maybe he can move on and live a fuller life."

"How about you? How are you feeling?"

"She was a terrible person, but she was still my mother and she's gone. In some ways, we lost her to the bottle nearly twenty years ago. And I hadn't seen her in a very long time."

"When was the last time?"

"Our high school graduation. She showed up trashed and belligerent. It was really embarrassing. Kam made our father promise not to bring her to our college graduation."

"How are you so maternal and perfect coming from that situation?"

She lets out a laugh. "I'm far from perfect. Like I said to you before, sometimes you have to see what you don't want to know what you do."

I tuck her hair behind her ear. "Why don't I draw you a bath? Have you seen the tub? It's enormous."

She rests her head on my chest. "Hmm. That sounds good. Will you join me?"

"I thought you might want some time alone…away from me."

"I know we're sort of in a weird place, but you're here and I'd rather be with you. I know things might change when we get home. I just want to enjoy it while it lasts."

I grab her face. "We will continue to spend time together as long as we both want to do so. Fallon has no say in that."

"She has a say in who spends time with Harper though."

"She knows there is no one better to be Harper's nanny than you. She'll put Harper's needs first. She always has."

Fifteen minutes later we're sitting in the tub with her leaning back into my chest. I'm rubbing her shoulders, and she sighs. "I'm in heaven. I've never been taken care of like this in my life."

"That's a shame. You deserve it."

"Is it wrong that I'm here to bury my mother and yet I've never felt more relaxed?"

"Not at all. I'm happy that I'm here with you."

She turns her head and kisses my jaw. "Me too. Tell me something about you. It doesn't have to be deep. Maybe tell me what you were like in high school. I bet you were so handsome."

"*Were* handsome, as in past tense?"

She giggles. "You know what I mean."

"I suppose I did alright with the ladies. I was focused on baseball. Being a professional player meant everything to me. A lot of people, my father included, thought it would happen. I was initially a pitcher being recruited to several top college programs."

I get a wave of emotion. There's a reason I never talk about this with anyone.

"And something bad happened?"

"Yes."

"Was this the incident you mentioned to me a little while ago? The one where you felt you lost control?"

I nod. "It was. My shitty coaches overused me, and I threw my arm out when I was sixteen. My elbow was a mess. I needed surgery. I was out for a year."

"Oh, Tanner, I'm so sorry."

She turns around in the tub and straddles me, taking me into her comforting arms.

"I lost my division-one-level throwing speed after that

and was never able to get it back. That's how I became a shortstop. The division-one offers went away. I decided to play division three with thoughts of working my way up. I was a great defensive player, but my hitting wasn't there. When you're a pitcher, you spend time on that, not hitting, so I never developed that properly."

"Yep. I've never even seen Ripley pick up a bat. All she does is pitch."

I pinch my lips together. The pain feels as fresh as it did back then. "By the end of my sophomore season in college, I knew the realities of my situation. I was never going to be a major league baseball player. I didn't want to give up on having baseball in my life though. I loved it so much. I still do. My father is the one who suggested becoming a sports agent. It's easier to break into the field if you're both a former athlete and an attorney, so that's how I ended up in law school. I live vicariously through my clients. Layton was among the first I signed. That's why his career means a lot to me. *Meant* a lot to me. I suppose it's over now."

She grabs my face and gives my lips a soft kiss. "Thanks for sharing all that with me. I know it's not easy for you."

She kisses me again. I know she intends for it to be innocent and comforting, but I deepen it. I think we need each other right now, but I don't want to push her if she's not up for it. We've had a rough few days.

She doesn't pull away though. She kisses me back every bit as much as I kiss her.

I run my hands down her body to the spot between her legs. "I can help you relax even more if you'd like."

She smiles into my mouth and spreads her legs as wide as they can go in the tub. "Do your worst, Mr. Montgomery."

At that, I slip two fingers into her. Her eyes flutter. "Oh god. That feels nice."

"Nice? I'm not aiming for nice."

She smiles playfully. "Your fingers are nice. Your dino-dick is a whole other story."

I chuckle. "Dino-dick?"

"You're so big, like a dinosaur. Were you always big?"

"Hmm. I've never thought about it."

She gives me an incredulous look. "You have the biggest dick I've ever seen, by far. You must know how unusually... gifted you are."

I can't help but smirk. "I suppose I am fairly...gifted. It's been many years since I've been in a locker room comparing johnsons."

"Let me promise you, you're at the head of the class. When does that happen for a guy? Is it like feet? They grow first and then the body grows into them. Did you have this giant dick and small body causing you to topple over all the time?"

I let out a laugh. "I love your pillow talk."

She smiles as she plays with the back of my hair. "Tell me. I want to know."

I squeeze her breast. "You're pretty top-heavy. How did it work for you?" I joke. "Did they grow first, causing you to *topple over*?"

She giggles. "Point taken."

I grab her hand and wrap it around my now-hardened cock. "He's fully grown with you sitting on my lap. He's looking for somewhere wet and warm. Can you help him out?"

She runs her lower lip through her teeth. "I can but I don't have a condom in here, do you?"

I shake my head. "No. I know you have the IUD. I assume there's no one else?"

She rolls her eyes. "You know there's not."

I squeeze her ass hard. "I should spank you for rolling your eyes at me."

She lifts one eyebrow. "I might be up for that."

I stroke my cock a few times and run the tip through her slippery flesh until it rests at her opening. I push in just an inch or two.

She closes her eyes. "Hmm. That feels good. I've never had anyone bare inside me before. When was the last ti—"

"Not since Fallon."

"And you're not—"

I echo my words from the first night we were together. "Sweet girl, there's no one else. You're all I see."

Seemingly satisfied with my response, she wiggles her hips, slides all the way down on me, and breathes, "Tanner," before her lips meet mine.

My cock is fully seated but completely still inside her as I sweep my tongue through her mouth. She scrapes her fingernails across my scalp before beginning to swivel her hips over me.

This feels intimate. Too intimate for what we're supposed to be. I shouldn't have done this, gone bare with her, but there's no stopping us now.

She tilts her head back and closes her eyes as she begins to ride me harder. "Oh yes, Daddy, I like that."

Fucking hell. Why does it drive me nuts when she calls me that? I thrust my hips up, desperate to get as deep inside her as possible.

It's been many years since I've gone bareback with a woman. I nearly forgot how incredible it feels.

I reach back out of the tub toward the ice cubes sitting in the bucket with an unused bottle of wine. I sat it there for her in case she wanted a drink, but I'm committed to not drinking on this trip.

Grabbing a cube, I rub it around her nipples. She gasps before looking down at what I'm doing. Her peaks pebble into hard balls before I drop the cube into the warm water and take her nipples one at a time into my warm mouth.

PAYOFF PITCH

She looks down at me with so much damn heat and passion that it threatens to break me.

We make very slow, passionate love in that tub, and I feel like the entire earth shifts when I come inside her. There's something happening inside me, but I have no words to describe what the hell it is.

One particular word drifts unbidden through my mind, but I ignore it because that will never happen. I won't let it.

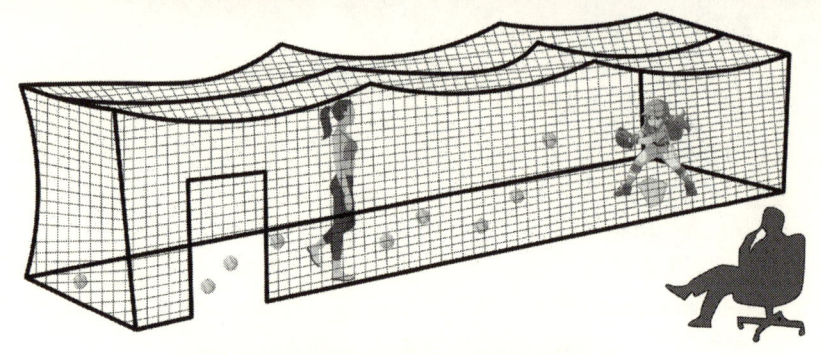

CHAPTER EIGHTEEN

TANNER

"And then Kam showed up to her own mother's funeral in a hot-pink dress with hot-pink stiletto heels?" Layton asks.

Cheetah and I both nod, and all the guys start laughing hysterically. Vance shakes his head. "Damn, Cheetah, she's fucking nuts. She must be a real wildcat in the sack."

We're sitting around my poker table with our cards in hand. Cheetah remains tight-lipped, something I've never before seen from him.

Vance's mouth widens. "No jokes, Cheetah? Wow, you must have it bad for this chick."

Cheetah twists his lips. "You want a joke? I've got one for you. How do you know a car mechanic has a girlfriend?"

Vance asks, "How?"

He holds up his hand. "Two clean fingers."

We all burst out laughing. I know that was his way of deflecting the interrogation about Kamryn, but it was still funny as hell.

We've been playing for a few hours. These guys always bring a smile to my face.

Daylen pushes all his chips into the pot. "I'm all in. You motherfuckers are going down like my prom date. This is *my* night to win."

Layton whistles. "Damn, Daylen. Did you just come into a lot of money or something?"

I recently negotiated a substantial new contract with a huge signing bonus for him. Everyone knows that he just came into millions of dollars, making him among the highest paid tight ends in professional football.

Daylen smiles innocently. "I did, in fact, recently come into a lot of money. It's so odd because I usually do it into a sock."

We all start laughing again. This is just what I needed the night before Fallon and Harper get home from Colorado.

As I'm cleaning up a little while later, Layton wobbles over to me on his crutches and knocks on his cast. "I get this off tomorrow."

"Your *wife* must be excited."

He smiles. "She is. We're flying out to LA for her appearance."

"Oh right. Good luck with that." I shake my head. "I can't believe you two pulled off getting married on the sly. But I've never seen you happier, and I'm happy for you." I'm one of the only people who knows about it. They're waiting to reveal it publicly.

"Thanks, buddy. We're going to have a big reception to celebrate with everyone. Quincy is still MIA, or we'd have it before the season. If he doesn't get back soon, we'll push it until after the Cougars and Anacondas' seasons are over."

"No matter when it is, I'll be there with bells on."

"Will you be there with Bails on?"

I'm quiet.

"Ooh. Do tell. How are things on that front?"

I consider my words for a brief moment. "I have feelings for her, but I know I'm not the long-term guy for her. We're having fun while it lasts."

I hate the pain in my gut at saying those words out loud. I don't want her with anyone else, but it's inevitable. I can't give her what she needs.

He winks. "We'll see."

"We might have issues sooner rather than later. Fallon found out about us and blew a gasket."

His eyes widen. "Oh shit. What happened?"

"It was out in Colorado when everything went down with Bailey's mom. We didn't really get a chance to talk about it. Fallon and Harper get back tomorrow. I'm in for it. Wish me luck."

He pats my back. "Good luck, buddy. You're gonna need it."

I'm at the airport baggage area waiting for Fallon, Harper, and Dylan. As soon as Harper sees me, she takes off in a dead sprint and leaps into my waiting arms.

I squeeze her tight and pepper kisses all over her face. "I missed you, bug."

She giggles. "I missed you too, Daddy." She wipes her face. "Stop kissing me."

"Never. Did you have fun?"

She nods. "Yes. Mommy took us back to make our own steaks four times." She holds up four fingers.

"Four times? I hope you ate some veggies with all those steaks."

"I did. Bailey says veggies are important for athletes, and I'm an athlete."

I look up at Fallon at the mention of Bailey's name, but she remains fairly stoic. I can't get a read on her mood. She's a foot shorter than me and weighs half of what I weigh yet I'm terrified of her.

Trevor walks into the baggage claim area, and Dylan runs into his waiting arms. "Daddy!"

He smiles as he hugs her. "We missed you, firecracker. Life is bo-ring without the famous Dylan Knight to add some color."

She nods and dances in his arms as she sings, "'Cause the party don't start 'til I walk in."

He winks at her before he holds out his hand for me. "Thanks to you both for having her. I hope she wasn't as much trouble as her mother is."

The girls giggle, and I smile. "No trouble at all. She's a great skier."

He nods. "With my father originally being from Colorado, skiing has always been a part of our lives, though Cassandra prefers the hot tub to the slopes."

Dylan smiles. "The hot tub is awesome."

Fallon gives a big, fake smile. "I know Tanner loves it."

Yep, I knew that was coming.

An hour later, I'm pulling into Fallon's house. Harper is coming home with me, but we're dropping Fallon at home first.

She turns back to Harper. "Daddy is going to help me bring in my suitcase and we have to talk about your party this weekend. He'll be out in a few minutes."

Harper doesn't even look up from her book as she wordlessly nods and throws a few Skittles into her mouth.

I carry Fallon's bags inside and run them up to her bedroom. As I walk back down, I cover my balls with my hand, bracing for impact. "Give it to me. I'm ready to be kicked."

She lets out a laugh. "I'm not going to kick you in the balls. I'm not the bad guy here, Tan."

"I know you're not."

"Bailey called me after you guys got home."

"She did?"

"Yes. We had a long talk. She assured me of her commitment to Harper no matter where things head between you guys. She said she knows you two are short term, but that won't impact anything with Harper. She loves Harper and wants to stay on as long as we'll have her." She takes a breath. "I know she believes her words, but I equally know how hard it is to lose you. I suppose we'll see how things go. All I ask is that when things go south, please keep Harper in mind when you decide how to conduct yourself."

I pinch my eyebrows together. "That's it? I've developed a twitch all week for that? I thought you were going to key my car or slash my tires."

"I'm *not* the crazy jealous ex-wife in this scenario. I'm trying to be reasonable. *All* I care about is Harper and what's best for her. It's such a catch-22. You want your daughter's nanny to love and protect her like she's her own, but then you equally fear too much attachment and eventual heartbreak. I gave it a lot of thought this week. At the end of the day, I couldn't possibly ask for a more perfect person to have around our child. Do I wish she was the ugly duckling? You bet I do. But she's not. She's a stunning, talented, wonderful young woman." She smiles playfully. "Honestly, Tan, she's too good for you."

I chuckle. "I'm aware."

"Does she know you're done having kids? She's the kind of woman who probably wants ten."

"I told her from day one that I have no intentions of

ever getting married again or having more children. I told you; she knows what we are. I'm not misleading her."

She studies me carefully. "If you say so. Have fun with Harper. I'll see you at her party. I look forward to our parents' annual trading of the barbs."

I smile. It's true. My father doesn't get along with her parents at all.

"Bailey is bringing Kamryn and Arizona to surprise Harper."

She responds, "That's nice of them. She'll be over the moon."

DAD ARRIVED THIS MORNING, just in time for Harper's laser tag party. The three of us drive to the venue and arrive at the same time as Fallon and her parents. I look back at my father. "Play nice in the sandbox."

Harper innocently answers, "I always play nice, Daddy."

"I wasn't talking to you. You're a good girl. I was talking to Grandpa. He's a bad boy."

Harper giggles and pats his head. "Be a good boy and I'll let you have some of my cake."

Dad rolls his eyes. "I'm always a good boy. It's your Nanny and Poppy—"

"Dad," I warn.

He straightens his shoulders. "I'm very much looking forward to seeing Nanny and Poppy. They're...lovely. And I'm most excited to meet this Bailey woman you've been talking about nonstop, Harper. She must be very special."

She sure is.

Harper nods. "She's transcendent."

Dad smiles at her use of the word. "I look forward to meeting this transcendent nanny of yours."

Harper whispers, "She's also my best friend in the world."

I clutch my chest. My heart.

We step out of the car, and Fallon's parents immediately gush over Harper. They give my father and me significantly less warm welcomes. I see Fallon give them a look of warning similar to the one I gave my father. This is going to be an interesting day.

The party is just underway when Bailey walks in with Kamryn and Arizona. She's holding a cake and smiling at me.

My father coughs. "What the hell is happening? Do models frequent the laser tag facilities? I need to find one in Florida."

My lips curl in amusement. "That's Bailey, her twin sister, and their friend. They're all professional softball players."

He mumbles, "No wonder Philly has become a softball town. Holy shit."

I mumble back, "Behave yourself, old man."

Bailey places the cake on a nearby table, approaches me, and smiles. "Hi, Mr. Montgomery."

Dad stands in front of me and holds out his hand. "I'm the original Mr. Montgomery, but you can call me Stan, or anything you want, just call me."

She lets out a laugh. "Stan works just fine. I see where your son got his charm from."

Dad shakes his head. "Tanner charming? No, no, no." He takes her hand and kisses it. "Allow me to open your eyes to a true Montgomery Casanova."

Kamryn flashes her mischievous grin and throws her arm around my father. "And I'm the charming Hart. My name is Kamryn. You and I should hang out, Daddy Stanley."

Bailey narrows her eyes at Kamryn. "What did we talk about in the car, Kam?"

"That I have to be a good girl." She turns to Dad and bats her eyelashes. "You think I'm a good girl, right, Daddy Stanley?"

He links his arm through hers. "I most certainly do. Allow me to get you a drink and tell you about my manscaping."

Kamryn lets out a laugh. "I love a man who isn't afraid to talk about his manscaping."

They walk away toward the sodas, and I shake my head. "Sorry about that. He's kind of a dirty old man."

She giggles. "She's kind of a dirty young woman. They're a perfect match."

"They sure are. Show me the cake I've been hearing about."

We walk toward the table where she left it, and I look at it. It's a professional-looking cake of a softball field and players with *Happy 8th Birthday Harper* written in the outfield. The shortstop even has Harper's number and hair color. No detail is missing.

"Wow. Incredible."

Fallon walks over and shakes her head. "Holy shit, Bailey. I knew it would be nice but not like this. It's amazing. I'm afraid to cut into it. This must have taken forever. Thank you."

Bailey looks both relieved and happy. It's the first time she and Fallon have seen each other since Colorado. "It was my pleasure. I hope Harper likes it."

Fallon's parents walk over. Doris nods toward Dad fawning all over Kamryn and mumbles, "Like father, like son."

Fallon briefly closes her eyes. "Mother, go make yourself useful and take pictures of Harper and her friends."

They leave, and she sighs. "Sorry, Bailey. The cake is amazing. Harper is going to flip. Having you and your friends here alone is enough to make her day." She turns to me as she digs through her purse. "I forgot to tell you." She finds a business card and hands it to me. "A man approached us on the airplane. He's from a talent agency and said he thought Harper and Dylan were stunning and asked us to call him if they want representation. I looked him up. He's legit, but—"

Bailey shakes her head emphatically. "No. No way. I don't want Harper involved in any of that."

Fallon's smile fades as she turns to Bailey. "No offense, but sleeping with Tanner doesn't give you a say in what Harper does and doesn't do. You're not her mother."

I grit my teeth. "Fallon. Watch yourself."

Bailey slowly nods. "I'm sorry. You're right. Just take it from someone who did that kind of stuff at her age, it's not as glamorous as it seems. I care about Harper, and I don't want her to experience anything I experienced. It's long days being manipulated by dozens of adults. She'll have to miss things like softball games, school, and sleepovers. It robs you of your childhood."

Fallon considers her words. "Thank you for your input. If you had let me finish, I would have told you that Harper said she wasn't interested, but Dylan was. Before I flip the card to them, I was going to ask Tanner to check out the company."

I take it from her. "I'll look into them and call the Knights."

The three of us stand there in silence. That got awkward fast. Fortunately, Harper and her teammates run over and gush all over Bailey, Arizona, and the cake.

I see my father and Fallon's parents in a heated discussion. Somehow Kamryn is also involved. I can only pinch the bridge of my nose. This day is a disaster.

PAYOFF PITCH

LATER THAT NIGHT, my father and I are alone at my house sipping whiskey when he smiles. "I can't believe you're diddling the babysitter."

I sigh. "Don't cheapen her like that. It's not tawdry."

He chuckles. "I got an earful from Doris about it. Even no-personality Joel chimed in."

"It's really no one's business, with the possible exception of Fallon, and only because of its impact on our daughter. Honestly, Fallon has been pretty cool about it. She likes Bailey."

"As do you, son." He wiggles his eyebrows. "A little too much."

"Cut it out. We're simply having fun together. It's casual."

He holds up his hands in surrender. "No judgment from me. I'm happy for you. Her sister is a pistol."

"She's nuts. They're complete opposites."

"Speaking of opposites, your brother called me this week."

I roll my eyes. "Did he want money or money?"

"Both. A lot of it. Said he's in *dire need*."

I roll my eyes at Lincoln's dramatics. "You didn't give it to him, did you?"

"Hell no. I told him if he held a respectable job for a year, I'd match the salary. He wouldn't even consider it. Can you imagine that?"

"It's a generous offer."

"I only did so to make a point. I knew he'd never do it. He's never held a job for more than a few months. It's amazing how different my two sons turned out. He's such a disappointment on every level."

I slowly nod. "Are you disappointed that I never made it

to the big leagues? You were so happy when I was in my pitching glory. I feel like I let you down."

He jerks his head in surprise. "Where did that come from after all these years?"

"Bailey thinks I bottle things up inside and avoid deeper conversations with people. She got me to open up about that time in my life and how it shaped me. It's had me thinking about it."

"Opening up to your *casual* paramour, are you?"

He gives me a playful look, and I roll my eyes.

He continues, "It's good to talk about things that weigh on you. To be clear, I was never disappointed *in* you; I was disappointed *for* you. It was your dream, not mine. Nothing is more fulfilling as a parent than seeing your child achieve their dreams. Nothing is as horrible as seeing that dream slip away. But dreams change. Do you know how many little boys dream of being professional baseball players? A lot more than achieve it. You've succeeded where most don't."

"But I didn't succeed."

"The hell you didn't. You're forty-three, almost forty-four. If you had played, your career would be long over. You love baseball and sports in general. You get to advocate for the best athletes in the world every single day. You run a business that's afforded you a beautiful home, good food on your table, and your daughter will never want for anything a day in her life. Speaking of your daughter, she's smart, stunning, kind, and so damn special. It all sounds like success to me. Disappointed in you? Not for one single minute of your life. You're my pride and joy. The best thing I've ever done. The only thing left for me to wish for you is happiness."

"You don't think I'm happy?"

"I think you're unfulfilled in certain parts of life."

I'm about to ask what he means by that, but I'm pretty sure I know the answer. I stand and stretch. With a bit of a

PAYOFF PITCH

yawn I say, "I'm getting tired. I think I'm going to head up to bed."

He chuckles. "I guess that Bailey is pretty smart."

I pinch my eyes together in confusion.

"About avoiding deeper conversations."

I twist my lips and mumble, "Baby steps."

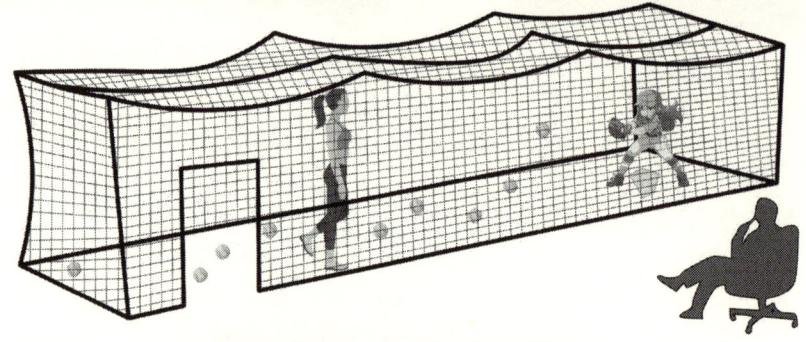

CHAPTER NINETEEN

BAILEY

I'm in my car, well, Tanner's car, but it's sort of become mine, waiting for Dad at the airport. I see him walk out, and I wave to get his attention.

He smiles as he sees me. It's been a few weeks since the funeral. He looks well, not like a man who has been home crying his eyes out. I'm relieved to see him this way. I wasn't sure what to expect.

After placing several large bags in the trunk, he gets into the car and leans over to hug me. "Hi, love. Wow, this is a nice ride."

I place the car into gear and head out of the airport. "It belongs to the Montgomerys. I drive Harper a lot, so they prefer her to be driven in this. And I need transportation to and from his house."

"*His* house?"

I nod. "Yes, they're divorced. He's a single father, though sometimes I help out the mom too if she's stuck at work."

"I see. And he flew to Mommy's funeral with you. That's... interesting. I didn't get to chat with him at all. You guys left so quickly after the funeral."

"I was helping him with Harper and her friend out in Colorado when you called about Mom. I told you I was going there. His ex-wife had just arrived for her week out there with Harper. We were supposed to fly home to Philly, and he moved our flights. He was concerned Kam wouldn't come. He was offering a shoulder to cry on. We're friends."

"Hmm. And your sister was with...a boyfriend? I only met him briefly."

"I'm not sure what they are, but he's kind of perfect for her. He matches her crazy."

"Was it Cruz Gonzales, the baseball player? She introduced him as kitten."

I let out a laugh. "Yes, it was Cruz Gonzales. His nickname is Cheetah so she calls him kitten to mess with him."

"Well, that sounds like your sister. Are you seeing anyone?"

I hate lying to him, so I keep it vague. "Now and then. Nothing serious."

I nod my head toward the trunk. "Not that I don't welcome a long stay, but you said it was going to be two nights. That you couldn't get any more time off work. Why all the luggage?"

"I brought some of Mommy's things and other household items that I thought you and Kamryn might want. If you don't, we can donate them."

"It looked like you were emptying the house when I was there, and now all this stuff. Are you moving?"

"Let's talk about that when we're with your sister."

"Okay. I made up my room for you. I'll sleep with Kam in her room. I assume you have no interest in her waterbed."

He lets out a laugh. "I can't believe she finally has one. She asked for that every single year for her birthday. That and a puppy."

"I wouldn't bring up the puppy." We had one for a few weeks until my mother's antics were the end of that. Kam is still salty about it twenty years later. "It's her second waterbed since we've been here." I hold up my hand and smile. "You don't want to know what happened to the first."

He chuckles. "Your sister. Out of control since day one." He pats my hand. "It's a good thing you're always so sensible. She's lucky to have you looking out for her. She'd probably be in jail if not for you."

Truer words have never been spoken.

We park and head up to our apartment. Kam is waiting with takeout Chinese food boxes spread all over the kitchen table. She pulls Dad into a big hug, but I place my hands on my hips. "I thought you said you were cooking tonight since I'm cooking at the Montgomerys' house for everyone tomorrow night."

Tanner invited us over with Dad.

She shrugs. "When have you ever seen me cook a meal in our entire lives? Cooking is a man's job. It's pronounced coo*KING*, not coo*QUEEN*."

"You're absurd."

"We're not ten. You don't need to kiss his ass. You're fine with Chinese food, right, Daddy?"

Dad smirks. "I've missed the two of you and your bickering. You used to go at it constantly. And it feels like years since we've sat down to a meal. I don't care what it is. I'm just happy we're together."

Kam crosses her arms in satisfaction. "Told ya so. And, Daddy, we haven't eaten together in years because you always carried around that baggage called Beverly. Now that the witch is burning in the pits of hell, we can be a normal family who eats meals and spends holidays together."

He blows out a breath. "Let's move past the Mommy-bashing. You two hadn't seen her in ten years."

Kam waves her hand. "It's fine. She and I had a little graveside chat. I said everything I needed to say to her. First time she listened to me her whole life."

Kam stayed behind at the grave. I could see her yelling and

screaming at our freshly buried mother. It was hard to watch. Tanner pulled me away, and Cheetah dealt with Kam that day.

We sit and begin eating before Dad clears his throat. "Listen, girls, I want to talk to you about something. I've wanted to talk to you about it for a long time. There were a few things about your mother you never knew. Before you jump down my throat, I am *not* condoning her behavior. She was a shitty mother, plain and simple."

Kam and I look at each other. He's never admitted that to us.

He continues. "She was sick. She suffered from mental illness, depression, abuse of pain meds, and alcoholism. The booze only made her depression worse. It was a vicious cycle with no end. She wasn't the woman I knew when we were kids. The one I fell for. Her diseases and demons overtook her until she was unrecognizable, even to me."

Kam grabs his hand. "Why didn't you leave her, Daddy? You could have found someone else. You could have had more kids."

He briefly closes his eyes. When he reopens them, I see they're filled with tears. "I did find someone else. After you girls left for college, I started seeing someone. Your mother knew about this person. I stayed with your mom as a caretaker, not a husband. I've been with a wonderful companion for about ten years now." He swallows. "I hope you don't think less of me."

Tears spill down my cheeks as Kam and I silently communicate. I know she's thinking the same thing I am. "We would never think less of you. Honestly, we're relieved. We want you to be happy. You deserve a woman who can give you that."

"That's the thing. It's not a...woman."

Kam's face lights up. "You're into men?"

He nods.

"I'm a chip off the old block. Best day ever. Let your freak flag fly, Daddy. I'm with you."

He shakes his head at her and then looks at me for a response. I admit, "It actually makes a lot of sense. If you found someone who you love and you're happy, I personally don't care if it's a man, woman, or anything else. But, Daddy, why after all this time? How long have you known?"

My heart breaks for him that he's been in the closet all these years.

"I grew up in a different era. I think I always knew but didn't always accept it. Your mother was beautiful back in the day. You girls look so much like her."

Kam scrunches her face. "Ugh. She looked like a saddlebag with eyes."

"The years of alcohol abuse took their toll on her. You know full well that when she was younger, she was stunning like you two."

Kam rolls her eyes. She knows he's right.

"We were high school sweethearts. She followed me to college. I experimented a bit while there but always maintained a relationship with her. When she fell pregnant with you two, I did the right thing. I married her. I don't regret any of it because it gave me the two most precious gems in the world, but when you two left for college, I decided that I would no longer hide myself. That's when I met Ray. I spend most of my free time with him, but I couldn't leave your mother to fend for herself. She had no other family, and I couldn't afford a hospital. I took care of her and spent time with Ray. He's been understanding, but now I'm going to officially move in with him. I'm selling the house. The bags I brought are a lot of our belongings and some of your awards and trophies from over the years. Take what you want and do as you please with the rest. Ray's house is beautiful. I don't need to bring anything but my clothes."

Kam wiggles her eyebrows. "Is he hot? Can we see pictures? When can we meet him? I need to meet the man who makes my father happy. Maybe a little interrogation too. I need to make sure his intentions are honorable."

Dad sighs. "Perhaps I'll bring him with me on my next visit, or perhaps you two will actually come home now that...things are different."

PAYOFF PITCH

I stand and wrap my arms around him. "I'm so happy for you. I love you."

"I love you too."

Kam hugs him too and loudly whispers in his ear, "Want to get matching rainbow flag tattoos?"

Dad simply shakes his head at her like he did a million times when we were growing up.

TANNER

Bailey's father is in town and, without thinking it through, I invited her to bring him over for dinner. She loves to cook in my gourmet kitchen and was excited to do so for him. She was equally excited to introduce him to Harper.

I suppose I knew he had her when he was young, but I didn't think about it until I met him. Chris Hart is only a few years older than me. Bailey and Kamryn look like him, with dark brown hair and big brown eyes, though Bailey has mentioned resembling their mother when she was much younger. His hair is graying similarly to mine. He's a good-looking guy with an athletic build like the girls, though I think living a tougher life has worn on him a bit more than usual.

After seeing her childhood home and from some things Bailey has said in the past, I know they grew up with more limited means. I wanted to provide them with a great meal but didn't want to insult him by paying for dinner at a fancy restaurant. I went all out in my grocery shopping though, hoping that was more palatable. And Bailey loves to cook here.

Bailey mentioned to me once that she and her father are

the ones who made dinner for her family since her mother was never sober enough to do so.

Kamryn and Harper are playing cards at the kitchen table while Bailey and her father work together to make the meal. They move around each other as though they've done it a thousand times before. It's endearing. The mutual affection they share is clear.

I'm trying to be helpful, but I'm in the way more than I'm not. I decide it best to simply stand back and observe.

I catch Kamryn talking about a full house. I snap my head toward them. "Are you teaching her poker? I thought you were playing Go Fish."

Kamryn rolls her eyes. "Go Fish is for babies and it's mindless. Any idiot can play. Right, Harper?"

Harper nods. "Yeah. Any idiot can play Go Fish. Kam says that poker is a thinking person's game and I'm too smart to play kid's games."

I see their father smile at the interaction. "I taught the girls how to play poker when they were around Harper's age. Maybe even a little younger. Their minds were always way more mature than their years. They took to it quickly." He chuckles. "They've hustled quite a few decent players out of cash over the years."

I smile as I look at Bailey. "I didn't know you played."

She raises an eyebrow. "You never asked."

I mouth, "Brat," to her and she winks.

I admit, "I suppose I didn't. We'll have to play sometime."

I catch her smirk while looking down. "You don't stand a chance, Mr. Montgomery."

Chris nods. "I'm telling you, Tanner, the girls are very good. Better than I am at this point. And Kam can count cards. I always swore I'd take her to Vegas one day."

Kamryn yells out from the table, "We should all play

PAYOFF PITCH

after dinner. It will be better for Harper to learn in a big group."

I nod. "Game on. I play with a group of clients every few weeks."

Kamryn scoffs. "Clients as in Layton, Cheetah, Vance, and Daylen? Those morons wouldn't know a good hand if it smacked them in their faces. Dad played a weekly game when we were really little. Then he started bringing us, and we'd wipe those nimrods clean. They never knew what was coming. Suckers. They stopped inviting him after a while."

Chris smiles as he shakes his head. "They stopped inviting me because you two hustled them out of their paychecks. And you were nine. They saw two young girls and assumed they knew nothing. The girls would tank the first few games and lose a few dollars. Then they'd insist on upping the ante with their modeling money and take those guys for hundreds of dollars." He chuckles as he says it with a huge dose of pride. I don't blame him. I'd feel the same if it were Harper.

Kamryn and Bailey share bemused looks. Kamryn says, "We did it in college too. All the time. That's how we made beer money. It was like taking candy from a baby. Men are idiots. Always underestimating the Hart girls."

My lips twist. "Hmm. Perhaps we should play with candy instead of cash tonight."

Bailey giggles. "Are you scared of little ol' us, Mr. Montgomery?"

I admit, "A little."

Bailey looks around like she's searching for something and then innocently says, "Can you grab me the big spatula, Daddy?"

Without thinking, I answer, "Sure," at the exact same time their father answers, "No problem."

Bailey's eyes immediately widen. Kamryn spits out in laughter and mutters, "Holy shit."

Harper gasps, fortunately blissfully unaware of what just happened. "That's ten dollars in the swear jar, Kam."

Kamryn grins widely as she pulls a ten-dollar bill out of her pocket and hands it to Harper. Staring straight at me, and with a wide grin, she announces, "Totally worth it. Best ten dollars I ever spent. We used to have one of those swear jars growing up. Right, *Daddy*? To be clear, I meant Chris Hart, not you, *Mr. Montgomery*."

I mumble something about being used to Harper calling me Daddy. I can't look Chris in the eyes right now. I feel like he'll see right through me and know all the dirty things I'm doing to his daughter.

AFTER A SLIGHTLY AWKWARD dinner where I could practically see Chris's eye twitching, we're playing poker now. Bailey told him she'd drive and that he should enjoy some of my good whiskey and cigars. It seems to have relaxed him. That, or he's doing a better job masking his warranted contempt for me.

He looks around my man cave. "This is a great setup, Tanner."

"Thank you. It's my sanctuary. I'm a bit of a workaholic and—"

Bailey interrupts, "Only when you don't have Harper. Otherwise, you're an attentive father, just like ours was. Trust me, it matters."

Kamryn asks, "Is your ex-wife a deadbeat mother like Beverly was?"

Chris gives her a disapproving look. "Cut it out, Kamryn."

Bailey motions toward Harper indicating that Kamryn needs to zip her lips, and then says, "Fallon is a wonderful mother. She misses nothing. She works like a dog when Mr. Montgomery has Harper so she's completely available to Harper when she has her. And regardless of where Harper is staying, Fallon comes to every game and recital." She smiles at Harper. "I hope to be as good of a mom one day as your mom."

I squeeze her leg under the table in appreciation. And then her words sink in. Bailey wants to be a mother one day. What the hell am I doing with her? I'm done having kids. Maybe it's time to end this for Bailey's sake. She won't see anyone else while she's with me. How will she find the right man if she spends all her free time with me? I know I'm being selfish, but I'm just not ready to let her go yet.

BAILEY

I throw my would-be winning hand on the table face down as I fold. Shaking my head, I say, "Darn. You win again, Harper. Are you sure you haven't played before?"

Harper has a huge smile on her adorable little face as she proudly displays her two pairs. "Read 'em and weep, suckers." Something she learned from my sister tonight.

Kam is about to interrupt with a better hand when I grab her arm and grit out, "You should fold too, sis."

She narrows her eyes at me. She hates losing, especially fake losing, but eventually relents and throws her cards down. "Fine. Last time I *lose* though."

I smile innocently. "No problem. It's past Harper's bedtime, and we should get going. I'm sure Mr. Montgomery has work to do."

Dad stands and holds out his hand to Tanner. "Thank you for having us. This was quite a treat."

Porterhouse steaks were definitely not a regular dinner in our house growing up. Tanner went overboard on the food tonight.

Tanner smiles and shakes his hand in return. "My pleasure." He places his hand on Harper's shoulder. "We consider ourselves lucky to have Bailey. She's remarkable. I see the apple didn't fall far from the tree."

Harper walks over and hugs my waist before pouting. "I go to Mommy's tomorrow, so I won't see you for three days. I'll miss you."

I bend down and hug her back. "I'll miss you too, baby girl. Remember, you can FaceTime me from Mommy's phone whenever you want. I'm only a call away."

She nods. After we say our goodbyes, we head out to the car. Kam offers, "Daddy, why don't you sit up front? I'm sure you have *lots* to talk to Bails about."

I narrow my eyes at her, but she simply smiles.

We get settled in, and I pull the car out of the driveway.

He blows out a breath. "Bailey, you've always been so level-headed. Do you think spending time with a much older man is a good idea? One who you work for."

Kam makes a sound of disgust. "Ugh, that's it? I waited all night for this conversation and the best you can do is," in a deep voice she repeats, "'do you think spending time with a much older man is a good idea?'"

Dad rarely gets angry, but he turns back to Kam. "Butt out and mind your own damn business, Kamryn. I expect this shit from you but not from her."

Kam sucks in a breath. I can count on one hand how many times in our lives my father has spoken to either of us this way. She leans back and remains quiet. Both are waiting for me to respond.

Tears fill my eyes at the thought of disappointing him. "I'm sorry you feel that way. You, more than anyone, know that you can't help who you love."

Kam spits out, "Love? Are you fucking nuts? Bang him and

get it out of your system. You don't fall in love with a guy like Tanner Montgomery."

I briefly turn back and glare at her. "A responsible, kind, smart, handsome, sweet man?" I sarcastically add, "I must truly be crazy to fall for a man like that. Maybe it's not headed anywhere, but there are real feelings involved. Is it better to hop around from meaningless encounter to meaningless encounter like you?"

Kam counters, "You don't know shit about me."

Our father rubs his forehead. "Girls, don't fight." His face softens as he looks at me. "I'm worried about you, sweetheart. You're from separate worlds and at different points in your life. He's so much older than you. You're still a kid."

I squeeze the steering wheel in frustration. "I'm not a kid. I'm a twenty-eight-year-old grown woman. I can more than handle myself. Right now, he makes me happy. I make him happy too. As long as we're both happy, there's no reason to change things."

Kam shoots back, "Then why keep it a secret? Why are you ashamed?"

"I'm not ashamed, but there's Harper to consider. She's attached to me. I would never jeopardize her well-being. There's no reason for her to know anything right now. It's still newish and our future is uncertain."

Not completely the truth, but I'm not getting into a deeper discussion with them about this when I'm not exactly sure what we are myself.

The problem is that she's not wrong. It's getting harder and harder to hide. I know he's said he doesn't want anything real, but like it or not, we're real. He must feel it too. Maybe it's time to talk to Tanner about telling Harper and the world that we're together.

Dad asks, "And you don't feel pressured because it's your job, right? You feel safe?"

I roll my eyes. "Of course, Dad. I made the first move, not him."

He scrunches his nose in disgust. "I didn't need to hear that."

Later that night, Kam and I are in bed together, staring at the ceiling, when she takes my hand in hers. "Are you sure you know what you're doing? I thought you were just fucking around. I should have known you'd catch real feelings. I don't want you to get hurt."

I squeeze her hand in return. "I'll be okay. Thanks. I'm happier than I've ever been with a man in my entire life. There's something special about the way we click."

"And the sex?"

I turn toward her and can't help the smile that creeps onto my lips. "The best of my life. By a mile. He's kind of a freak in bed. Like BDSM shit, Kam. Can you believe I'm into that?"

"Umm, no, I can't. Thank fuck you're finally telling me. I didn't know what to make of your secrecy." She turns and smiles at me. "Dad's going to sit home every night tossing and turning over your safety, meanwhile you'll be tied up in Tanner's bed begging him to spank and choke you."

I burst into laughter. "It's funny 'cause it's true."

Her face turns a bit more serious. "It's not your orgasms I'm worried about. It's your heart. You have the biggest heart of anyone I know. You still believe in fairy tales and happily ever afters. I don't want you to become jaded like me. Hardened. Love is pain. Look at Ripley. She's a mess."

"But look at Arizona. She's living proof that fairy tales happen. That happily ever afters exist."

"I don't know any fairy tales that begin with, *so...I started banging the father of the kid I babysit.*"

"I'm not saying this is my happily ever after, Kam." Though I'm hopeful. "He's my happy for now. We'll see what happens."

"Okay. I'm here for you. Whatever you need, whenever you need it. You jump, I jump."

"I know."

It's quiet for a moment before she asks, "Do you really call him Daddy?"

I can't help the smile that finds my lips.

PAYOFF PITCH

She fans her face. "Fuck, that's so hot."

I bite my lip. "You have no idea. He's so domineering. He knows how to make me see stars."

She blows out a breath. "I just want to make sure you're okay and that we're not headed toward a disaster. I feel like this might be as dumb as Ben and J Lo not having a prenup."

I smile at her attempt to lighten the conversation. "No matter what happens with Tanner and me, *nothing* can ever possibly be as dumb as Ben and J Lo not having a prenup."

We giggle as she talks me into giving her a few more details about our sex life.

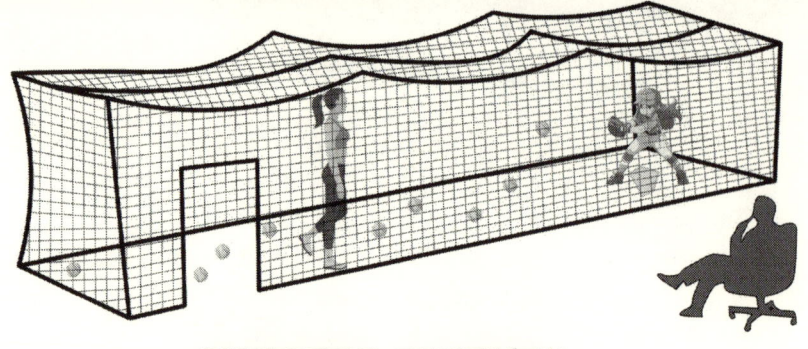

CHAPTER TWENTY

BAILEY

It's been a crazy few weeks. Ripley went into premature labor in California. Arizona, Layton, and Quincy have all moved out there for the time being to help her and the baby, who's currently in the NICU but seems to be headed in the right direction.

Kam and I offered to fly out, but Arizona said they're only letting family members see the baby and that Ripley will need help once the baby comes home, so we should wait. It could be months before that happens.

The Cougars are down in Florida for their spring training, so those guys haven't been around. We do hang out with some of the local football players sometimes, but most of my free nights are spent with Tanner. I've fallen for him and even though he hasn't expressed it, I think he's fallen for me too.

Things between us have taken on a new level of intensity since we returned from Colorado and Florida. I know we're so much more than originally intended. I've chickened out on having a serious conversation more times than I can count, but I'm hoping that it happens soon. I'm just waiting for the right moment. At least, that's what I'm telling myself.

I'm with Tanner tonight ahead of our skydiving adventure tomorrow. He asked me to play poker which has morphed into strip poker. While he has a drink sitting there, I notice that he's barely touched it. He's definitely making more of an effort since I mentioned it to him in Colorado. Before then, I was never with him at night when he didn't have at least two or three glasses. Since then, it's maybe half the time and never in excess. I'm happy he's changing his ways.

We're both sitting across from each other at his card table with cigars in our mouths. I've never had one before, but the taste makes me think of Tanner and I'm loving it.

I'm holding what I know will be another winning hand when I ask, "Do you keep in contact with any college friends? I never hear you mention them or any friends who aren't clients."

His face looks pained. I've struck a nerve.

"I used to have a close friend. He moved to New York too. We were close but have...drifted in the past few years."

I ask, "Did something happen?"

He tosses his cards on the table with disgust, meaning he's folding. He knows I have a winning hand. "Yes, you won another hand, and I'm losing another article of clothing."

We've been playing for all of forty-five minutes and he's nearly naked. Kam and I have truly spent a lifetime being underestimated by men at the poker table. I think Tanner thought he'd have me naked and at his mercy in no time. It's just the opposite.

He makes a show of pulling his socks off, leaving him in only his boxer briefs and his tie. I'm fully clothed. He playfully lifts an eyebrow. "I can't believe you've won every single hand. I'm questioning my manhood."

I lean my body forward so I can peek over at the bulge in his boxers, and say, "You should *never* question that manhood," as I lay my winning hand on the table with a small smile of satisfaction. "Flush. All hearts for Bailey Hart." I blow a plume of smoke into the air in victory.

He smirks as he licks his big lips. "As the...*owner* of this casino, it's come to my attention that there might be some cheating going on."

I lean back in my chair and let out a laugh. "Is that the only way a woman can win? Cheating?"

"I need to frisk you for cameras and other contraband. Standard operating procedure. If you're innocent, it shouldn't be a problem."

I place my cigar in the ashtray and raise my arms in the air. "Frisk away, Mr. Montgomery."

He stands and walks around the table toward me. I notice his bulge is becoming more pronounced with each step as his boxer briefs begin to ride up his thick, muscular thighs. He may actually be the sexiest man in existence.

He makes his way to me until he's standing behind my chair. "Stand, Ms. Hart." I do. "Place your hands on the table where I can see them."

I make a bit of a show of spreading my legs and bending over before placing my hands on the table. I'm wearing spandex shorts and a cropped T-shirt, so plenty is exposed to him when I do so.

He achingly slowly pats down my entire bottom half, leaving no inch untouched. He pays particular attention to the inferno between my legs. All I really want is for him to tear my clothes off and fuck me on this table, but rushing into things isn't his M.O. He prefers the slow seduction, and I'm a more than willing victim.

His fingers trickle up the bare skin on the sides of my waist and stomach until they cup my breasts. "What cheating device could possibly be in there, Mr. Montgomery?"

Spank.

I let out a moan. God, I love when he spanks me.

"Watch your mouth, Ms. Hart. We don't like brats at the Montgomery Casino. They're dealt with sternly."

I reach between my legs and grab for his bulge, which is currently poking me in the ass. Squeezing his now fully hardened cock, I say, "You seem to like it a lot."

Spank.

My eyes roll back in my head. A gush of wetness shoots from my core. My panties are immediately soaked.

"That will earn you a *full-body* examination."

Yes please.

He slides my shorts and panties down and off my legs. I can't see him, but I hear him inhale deeply. "These panties tell me that something naughty is going on down there."

It certainly is.

He reaches around my body and shoves my wet panties into my mouth. I've never done that before. I can both taste and smell my arousal. So hot.

I feel him drop to his knees. He spreads apart my ass cheeks and licks through me. I gasp at the unexpected and never-before-experienced move.

His thumb then teases my back entrance. "Has anyone been here before?"

The truth is no. I lied to Kam about it a while ago. She was all over me about how great anal sex is, so one day I told her what she wanted to hear. I felt bad lying, but she was relentless, and I couldn't take it anymore.

I won't lie to him though. "No, Daddy. I've saved it for you like a good girl."

He lets out a loud grumble from deep in his chest. I guess he liked that.

He applies open-mouth kisses to both my ass cheeks a few times before his tongue again finds my back entrance. I can feel a mixture of his saliva and my juices dripping down my inner thighs.

Suddenly I feel his finger prodding my back entrance before he slips it in an inch or two. I suck in a breath at the new and unexpectedly pleasurable sensation.

"What do we have in here, Ms. Hart?"

He pushes further, and the backs of my legs start to tingle. I collapse my front onto the table causing the piles of poker chips to fall and scatter. Holy heck, this is good.

I let out a loud moan. I don't recognize my own voice when I rasp out, "Deeper."

He sinks in to the knuckle. I can feel my clit throbbing from it. Pulsing. If he touches it—

Before I can finish the thought, the fingers of his other hand begin rubbing my clit as his finger in my back entrance begins thrusting in and out of me. The dual sensation is blowing my mind. Damn, I hate when Kam is right.

I'm gripping the far side of the card table as he expertly works me over. My vision begins to darken, illuminated only by the starry lights beginning to take form. I yell out so freaking loud into my orgasm that I start to feel light-headed like I might pass out. And then darkness overtakes me.

"Bailey! Sweetheart. Are you okay?"

I blink my eyes open and find him sitting in a chair with me cradled in his lap. I whisper, "What happened?"

He smiles. "You blacked out from your orgasm."

My mouth forms an O. "I didn't know that was a real thing. It felt so ducking good I couldn't see straight. I lost consciousness. Holy shitake."

He chuckles. "Best day of my life. I've never made a woman black out before. I want to do a happy dance right now, but my cock is about to explode from how fucking hot that was." He gives me a huge smile. "I'll forever replay that when I'm sitting here with my friends at this poker table, with them blissfully unaware, bragging to me how good they are in bed."

I wiggle my ass over his cock and he lets out a groan. I can't help but run my fingers through his sexy beard. "How about I take care of Daddy?"

His face twitches, as does his cock.

I slip down to my knees between his legs and do just that.

REAGAN DAULTON SUMMONED me to her office. I told her I have plans this afternoon, but I could come by in the morning. I didn't bother to tell her that my plans include jumping out of an airplane strapped to Tanner's chest with my life in his hands.

I head downtown to Daulton Holdings. Even though she has offices in both the Anacondas and Cougars' stadiums, this is her main office. It's in an enormous skyscraper. Her company occupies every single floor. I know she's the CEO of one of the biggest companies in the world, but I don't think I appreciated just how big it was until I walked into the building and saw how many people work for her. It must be in the thousands.

The security man at the front desk tells me which floor to go to and that I should ask for Sheila, Reagan's assistant. I ride the elevator and eventually find my way to an adorable middle-aged woman in trendy eyeglasses. She smiles at me. "You must be

Bailey. She said for you to go in when you arrived. She's in a meeting but is fine with you interrupting."

I knock on the door and walk into what must be the biggest, nicest, executive office in creation. It's got a huge marble desk, a full bar, an area that looks like it's for a toddler, and a full living room complete with sofas, chairs, and a television. She's seated there with two attractive blonde women with a bunch of files spread on the coffee table. All three are in very fashionable business suits. I suddenly feel underdressed in jeans and a sweater.

She smiles when she notices me. "Bailey. Thanks for coming." She points to the blonde with green eyes and says, "This is my sister, Skylar."

Oh, I see the resemblance.

Skylar holds out her hand. "Nice to meet you, Bailey. Congratulations on all your success this past season. I'm hoping to bring my kids out to more games this year."

I smile in return. "Thank you. It's nice to meet you too."

Reagan then turns to the other woman. She's unusually tall, but otherwise very much resembles Reagan. "This is our cousin, Jade."

Jade is holding a can of something. It looks like it has the word *pussy* on it, but I must be mistaken.

Jade smiles in a mischievous manner that reminds me of Kam. "Nice to meet you, Bailey Hart. I met your teammate Ripley last year. I heard she gave birth prematurely. I hope she's doing well."

I nod. "Thank you. She and the baby seem to be headed in the right direction."

She notices my line of sight and smirks. "Yes, it's Pussy Juice. It's a natural energy drink." She winks, "I don't prefer the bitter taste of coffee in the mornings, I like the sweetness of a good Pussy Juice."

Reagan rolls her eyes. "She drinks it just to get a rise out of people. Ignore her. It tastes like shit." She shoos the back of her hand at Jade. "Get your Pussy Juice out of my office. I'll talk to you two later."

The three of them giggle as Skylar and Jade walk out.

Reagan shakes her head. "Honestly, I think she does it to make all the men in this office uncomfortable. She's a bit of a button-pusher. She totally gets off on ruffling feathers."

"She'd probably get along with my sister."

"Ha. No doubt." She motions toward one of the sofas. "Please sit." I do. "Can I have Sheila get you something? Food, drink? Anything but Pussy Juice."

I smile nervously. "No, I'm good."

I think she notices my nerves. "Don't worry, Bailey, this meeting has absolutely nothing to do with your contract with the Anacondas. It's a side project, and I think you're the right person for the job."

I breathe an audible sigh of relief. "Phew. I've been on edge since you asked to see me."

She scrunches her face. "Sorry. I should have said something. Sometimes I forget that people are scared of me."

"I'm not scared of you, per se, more the power you wield."

The corners of her mouth raise in amusement. "Touché. Point taken. Anyway, I don't want to waste your time. Let's get right to it. Have you been watching college basketball this season? I know you were a great player at one point. I think you even have a few state records in Florida."

I nod. "I've absolutely been watching. What's happening with women's basketball right now is very exciting."

It's getting more attention than it ever has in the past. There's a specific player, Sulley O'Shea, who is breaking records and garnering attention never seen before in the sport. Attendance and viewership have been way up over years past. Her jersey is a best seller.

She nods. "I agree. What I'm about to tell you is confidential for the time being. Can I trust that it will stay between the two of us?"

"Of course."

"The Anacondas have honestly exceeded my expectations. I

had a few tricks up my sleeve to get things kickstarted, but you ladies won over this town with your grit, great play, and heart. I can't tell you how rewarding it is for me to be a part of shining a light on women's sports. Giving you all the opportunity to play professionally for a living is worth every bit of time I have to spend on this." She smiles. "I'm just lucky that I work with my husband and my son goes to daycare in the building or I'd never see them."

I shake my head in disbelief. "Honestly, I don't know how you do it all."

She deadpans, "I don't get much sleep."

I let out a laugh. "I bet."

"I don't want to stop at softball. I want to bring women's professional basketball to Philly. I think the timing is ripe. If we move things along quickly and become an expansion team this year, guess who has the first pick in the draft?"

I nod my head up and down in realization. "You'd get Sulley O'Shea."

She wiggles her eyebrows up and down. "Bingo. The draft is coming up. I'm willing to push this new team along a year earlier than I had planned just to get her. The problem is that Sulley comes from a small town. If we weren't involved, the first pick was going to a much smaller town than Philly. I'm worried about her willingness to come to a bigger city. I see you as the heart and soul of the Anacondas. You're probably my favorite player to watch. You're unassuming. You're not flashy. You put your head down and give every ounce of yourself to your team. You don't do it for the glory. I can't even get you to consider endorsement deals. You've got a...small-town heart. From my research into Sulley's background, it seems like you two are a lot alike. I think you'd be a great liaison for Sulley, both as an Anaconda and a former basketball player. You have common ground. I'm willing to pay you for your time. We can call you a consultant."

It's not lost on me that Tanner said something similar to me about being the heart and soul of the team months ago. It's a really nice feather in my cap.

I take a moment to consider her words and her request. "Wow. I'm flattered by the compliment, but I don't think I'd feel comfortable taking money for that. What if Sulley found out I was being paid to spend time with her? I'd feel terrible. Why don't you just tell me when she's in town, and I'll reach out to her? It's more organic that way. I can introduce her to a ton of people and help her feel at home. I don't need to be paid to do it. It's the right thing to do."

She stands and holds out her hand for me to shake, which I do. "You're a good cat, Bailey Hart. I won't soon forget this."

"It's honestly my pleasure. You've already done so much for all of us."

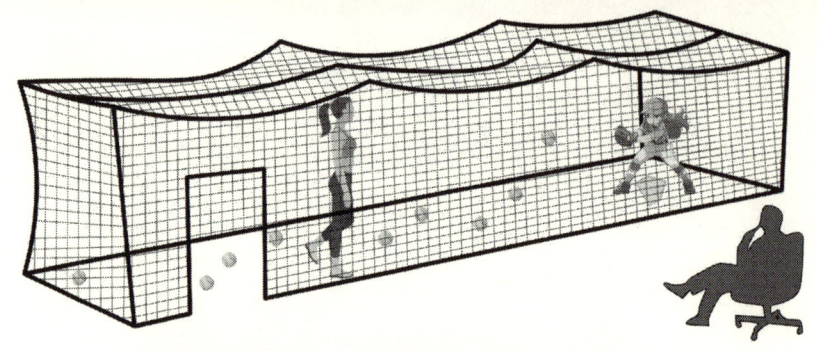

CHAPTER TWENTY-ONE

BAILEY

"Holy. Ducking. Shitake," I yell.

I can't believe I'm about to jump out of an airplane.

The door of the plane is open, and we look out at the open space of western Pennsylvania from ten thousand feet in the air.

We drove a little over two hours west after my meeting this morning. I feel like we're in the middle of nowhere, though I suppose you need open fields to land.

I had to take a safety course where they taught me a bunch of things that are currently jumbled in my mind because it's hard to think of anything while you're this high up, the door is open, and you're expected to jump in a few minutes.

Tanner chuckles. "It's such a high, isn't it?"

We're in blue jumpsuits. I'm practically glued to his arm, afraid of falling, even though we're tethered to the interior of the plane.

He grabs my face. "We're going to get you attached to me now. You've got this." His golden eyes bore into mine. "Thank you for trusting me. You have no idea what it does to me."

PAYOFF PITCH

I look down at his cock clearly stirring in his jumpsuit. "I think I have a pretty good idea what it does to you."

His lips smash into mine as he pulls me into his arms. I whimper into his mouth as our tongues meet. He's so hot.

A throat clearing breaks us apart. The man from the skydiving company gives us an awkward smile. "Sorry. It's time."

Tanner nods and they spend a few minutes tethering my back to Tanner's front. Tanner has them check the safety of every connection at least ten times. I can tell the guy is getting annoyed with it.

We've got our helmets and goggles on. They take a few pictures. I didn't tell Kam I was doing this. She would have recited some random statistical facts to me about how likely I am to die. I didn't need that negativity going into this. I trust Tanner. He wouldn't do this with me unless he was sure it was safe.

I want to just randomly text her a picture of me in the sky to see her reaction. Given her fear of flying, she's going to flip her shit.

We're standing at the door of the plane now. Tanner whispers in my ear, "You jump, I jump."

I gasp at his word choice. I can't believe he just said that to me. It's my thing with Kam. This is my sign that it's time to talk about our future. That's if I have one after jumping out of the plane.

He shouts, "One, two, three!"

We both fall forward as we were taught in the class. My heart must be beating two hundred times per minute.

The cold wind immediately assaults my face and my stomach drops. I'm screaming at the top of my lungs as Tanner manages to maneuver both of our bodies how he wants them.

I look around and absorb all that's happening around me. I can't believe I'm doing this. It's the biggest high I've ever experienced. And I do trust him completely. I know he'll take care of us and pull the cord. In Tanner's arms. That's where I belong. That's where I feel safe and at home. I want this.

As the ground draws closer, he shouts, "I'm going to pull the cord. You'll feel a sharp pull."

I nod. "I'm ready."

"Don't close your eyes. You'll miss too much."

He's said that to me multiple times today.

He motions to the other man who jumped with a camera and has been snapping pictures of us, and yells out, "It's go-time."

The man nods and holds up three fingers, counting down to one. As soon as his fingers all close, I see him pull a cord, and then I experience a sudden jerking sensation.

I can't help but briefly close my eyes. A failed parachute is the fear in this moment. I ask, "Did it work?"

He lets out a small laugh. "It did. Take it all in. Enjoy every moment."

I open my eyes and look around, realizing we're now floating in the sky. It truly is an unimaginable feeling of bliss, freedom, and a few nerves, though they're better now that the parachute has been successfully deployed.

We sail through the beautiful sky until a huge target begins to come into view. The landing field.

Oh god. The ground is getting closer and closer.

Tanner shouts, "When I say now, do what they said to do with your legs."

I nervously respond, "Okay."

I'm definitely closing my eyes for this part. I'm terrified.

Tanner manages to position us so that we're about to land precisely on the big, painted target area. I have no idea how he did that.

The ground isn't far now. Oh my god. He yells, "Now."

I hold my legs up and squeeze my eyes shut until I feel him running on the ground, eventually coming to a complete stop.

Peeling my eyes open, I see the ground is here. We made it. We're alive. I think.

His arms immediately surround me. "Are you okay?"

I breathe, "Wow. Can we do it again?"

He laughs. "Not today, but another time for sure."

He works to unhook me and as soon as he does, my adrenaline practically bursts. I turn around and tackle him to the ground, smashing my lips to his.

I'm straddling him while we kiss. I'm on such a high. I want him. Badly.

A throat clearing again breaks us apart. Why won't this guy go away?

I mumble, "Cockblocker," into Tanner's lips, and feel him smile into me.

We sit up, and the man takes a few more photos of us while we wait for the skydiving company to pick us up by van.

An hour later, we're armed with photos and in Tanner's car on the way home. It's a two-lane highway through the seemingly secluded cornfields of western Pennsylvania. My adrenaline is still pumping through me.

"Tanner, pull over."

"Why? What's wrong?"

"Do it."

He does, worry written all over his face. "Are you okay?"

I start unbuttoning my jeans.

"Umm, what are you doing?"

"I need you. Right now."

"Here? We're in bumblefuck. Anyone could drive by and see us."

"Don't care."

I pull down my jeans and panties and then practically leap into his lap. I kiss him as my hands work his belt and jeans down enough to free his cock.

He slides his fingers between my legs. "Let me get you ready."

I slap it away. "Trust me, I'm ready."

Frantically, I grab his dick, lift my body, bring him to my entrance, and sink down onto him. We both let out moans as I do so.

I have to take a few long breaths as I get used to his size and the euphoric feeling of having him inside me coupled with the rush of what we just did.

He rubs his hands over my body and runs his nose along my cheek. "Nothing feels better than being inside you, sweet girl. I never want this feeling to go away."

If I didn't know it before, I know now. He loves me like I love him. This has turned into something very real. It's my sign to finally talk to him about it.

I begin my up-and-down movements on him. He's almost always the one in control of the sex we have, but he's letting me have the reins right now as I take what I need from his body.

I'm so desperate for him. Our eyes meet as I move my body over his. Despite the frantic way this started, we're making love now. The intensity of our connection is special. I know he must feel it too.

I'm completely in love with him and I'm confident he feels the same. That thought alone causes my body to ripple around his as I find my release, followed shortly thereafter by his.

Two hours later, we're pulling into his driveway. Once we're in the garage, he cuts the engine. Before he can get out of the car, I stop him. "Can we talk for a minute?"

His jaw tics just a drop. "Of course."

I swallow as I try to form the words I need to say. "Tanner, I know what we were supposed to be, but, honestly, I've completely fallen for you. Everything you say and do makes me think you're feeling the same. I'm not looking to get married tomorrow, but can we have a talk where we actually consider having a real future together? I can't imagine mine without you and Harper anymore."

His face falls as he takes my hand in his. "Bailey, I won't lie and tell you that my feelings for you aren't strong, stronger than I ever imagined they could be, but—"

"But what?"

"But there is no future for you and me. I've always been clear on this."

"Yes, you said that, but you've said and done a lot of things contrary to that."

"Because you're so damn perfect and so damn hard not to fall for."

"So you *have* fallen for me?"

"It's complicated."

"It's not."

He runs his fingers through his hair. "I...I can't give you what you want."

"All I want is you."

"That's not true. You want a big family, and I could never take that away from you. A woman like you should have a dozen kids."

"We can have kids one day. You and me."

His mouth opens and closes a few times. He attempts to steel himself, but I know better. With pain written all over his face, he says, "As I've said before in very clear terms, we have no future. I will never get married again. I will never have any more kids."

"I don't understand. You're an amazing father. You have so much to offer. Why wouldn't you want more—"

"I had a vasectomy."

The air is sucked out of my lungs. My head starts spinning. "What!? You had a vasectomy?"

He nods. "Yes."

"When?"

"Years ago. Just after Fallon and I separated."

My whole body starts trembling. Tears immediately freefall from my eyes. This feels like such a betrayal.

"W...why didn't you tell me?"

"Why would I? I told you we had no future, that I wasn't getting married, and that I was never having more kids."

My heart feels like it's breaking into a million pieces. I have physical pain shooting across my chest.

He tries to take my hand, but I pull it away. For months I've been thinking he was falling for me like I was falling for him. That he wanted a future with me, despite the words he had said about us not having one. I thought his heart would overrule them. I was so wrong.

"A lie by omission is still a lie. You're not naïve. You know I've been falling for you, and you said nothing. You let me believe this was real."

"It *is* real."

"Bullshit! That's right, I cursed."

"Bailey, can't we just stay—"

I shake my head as everything around me is blurred by the excessive tears in my eyes. "I've had you on this pedestal the whole time, but at the end of the day, you're nothing but a coward. I can't believe you withheld this from me."

Suddenly, this car feels suffocating. I need to get out. I need my sister.

I open the door and practically fall out of it, not having full use of my limbs. My whole body is shaking.

He immediately exits the car and runs around to me. I'm having trouble walking. The ground feels wavy. I don't think I've ever felt so betrayed or heartbroken in my life.

He again tries to touch me, but I pull away. "Don't touch me. Don't ever touch me again. You're a liar and a fraud. You can't tell me things like, *I never want this feeling to go away.* You can't tell me that I'm all you see. You can't spend months making love to me with nothing between us. Coming inside me. Claiming me." I point at him. "I know you told me that we would never be more, but everything else you've said and done suggests otherwise and you fucking know it."

He does nothing but hang his head. He knows I'm right.

I wipe my eyes and try to channel the inner strength of my sister. Holding my head up, I say, "Goodbye, Mr. Montgomery."

Tears fill his eyes. "Baby, don't leave like this."

I shoot him an icy glare. "Don't call me baby or sweet girl or anything that makes me think you give a shit about me. I know you don't."

"That's not—"

"What were you going to say? *That's not true*? What do you know about truth? You don't care about me. You made a twenty-eight-year-old woman fall in love with you when there was never any remote hope for the future. This wasn't a one-night stand or a casual hookup and you know it. It's been six months. Six fucking months of me falling in love with you. You sat back and said nothing as I fell a little harder each and every day." I poke him in the chest. "You knew. Don't pretend you didn't."

He closes his eyes. He knows I'm right. He knows what he did.

"Tell Harper that I'll pick her up from school on Monday for softball practice. You can contact me as it pertains to Harper, but otherwise don't call, don't text, don't even talk to me."

I turn and walk toward my car. *My* car. That's not even really mine. I need to buy one of my own. I don't want anything from him.

THIRTY MINUTES LATER, I walk into our apartment. Kam's face is buried in her computer, but she says, "Are you fucking kidding me sending me those photos and then going radio silent? Did you jump out of a fucking airplane? Are you insane?"

She lifts her head. Her smile immediately fades when she sees my tear-stained face. She jumps up and runs to me. "What's wrong? Are you hurt?"

I fall into her arms. "He had a vasectomy. He strung me along, making me feel hopeful about a future when there is none."

She squeezes me tight into her comforting arms. "Oh, Bails. I'm so fucking sorry."

"I...I thought he loved me too." I weep into her chest. She has to hold me upright or I'll collapse to the ground.

She rubs my hair. "I know you're hurting, but didn't he tell you from the beginning that you guys weren't long term? That he didn't want marriage and more kids?"

I nod into her chest. "Yes, but the way he acts with me didn't match those words. Other things he's said to me don't line up with that. No man has ever treated me with more love, compassion, and tenderness. Everything he did told me he was falling the same way I was."

"You're right. Want me to burn down his house? I'll do it and not think twice about it."

I let out a laugh through my tears. "No, but thanks for offering."

"I'd do anything for you. *Anything*."

TANNER

It takes me all of fifteen minutes to decide that I need to go see her. I can't let things end like this. I need to tell her that she's right. I fell for her too. I'm a coward. I knew what was happening between us, and I let it go on. I knew that me telling her about the vasectomy would be the end of things, and I withheld it from her.

I arrive at her apartment and pound on the door. Kamryn opens it, and her eyes just about pop out of her head when she sees me.

She shoves me into the hallway and quickly closes their door behind her. She then takes me by surprise by punching me so damn hard in the stomach that it knocks me to my knees.

She grits out, "How fucking dare you come here!"

I hold my hand up in surrender, breathlessly pleading, "Please, just let me talk to her. Let me make things right."

"The time for that has passed…by about six months. She is literally everything that is right in this world. She's a fucking ray of sunshine in a shitty, fucked up world. She doesn't have a bad or deceitful bone in her body. You're a fucking jerkoff who never has and never will deserve her. Don't ever fucking step foot in this building again. I swear to god, I'll call the police. I mean it. Leave her alone."

She turns, opens their door, walks back into their apartment, and slams the door shut. It feels like she slammed it directly on my heart.

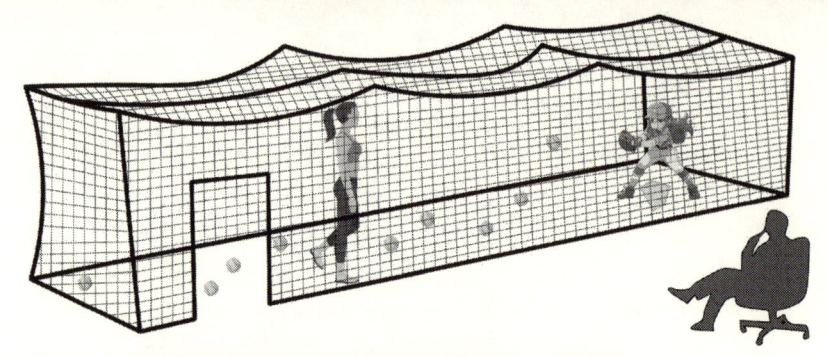

CHAPTER TWENTY-TWO

BAILEY

After a long weekend of crying, Monday afternoon rolls around. I finally emerge from the safe confines of my bedroom and head into the kitchen. Kam is sitting at her laptop. She's barely left my side for a single second. She's truly the only person in the world I can rely on.

That's not totally true, I have good friends, but they're on the other side of the country right now. My sister is here and taking care of me. She even attempted to cook my favorite meal last night. It was an epic failure, and the fire alarm went off, but she tried, and that's what matters most.

She looks up at me from her computer and examines me in my sweatshirt, leggings, and sneakers. "Where do you think you're going?"

"I need to pick up Harper from school, and then we have softball practice. You know I'm coaching her team this spring."

Her chin drops. "Are you fucking kidding me? You need to quit your job."

I shake my head. "No. I'm not doing that to Harper. She's innocent."

"So are you."

"I gave my word that if things went south with Tanner, I wouldn't abandon Harper. I intend to live up to that. She's my happy place right now. Honestly, I think I need her. And I committed to the team. Their season has only just begun. I won't jump ship on them. It's not right."

She closes her laptop and stands. "Fine. I'm coming with you. I'll be your assistant coach."

I eye her skeptically. "You can't curse in front of the girls."

"I'll fucking try. By the way, cursing is a sign of intelligence."

"That's the dumbest thing I've ever heard."

"It's a sign of social intelligence, knowing when and where to use it."

"Well, then be socially smart enough to realize that a softball practice with twelve eight-year-old girls isn't the time and place. I mean it. And remember they're little kids. Keep things fun and age appropriate. They're not training for the Olympics."

She narrows her eyes at me. "The last game I attended, I watched little innocent Harper Montgomery charge a ball and throw from the slot with perfect precision and technique. Most college players can't do that. Was that age appropriate?"

I twist my lips. "Hmm. Valid point." I cross my arms. "Seriously, you can't treat them like adults. They're kids."

She sighs. "I always preferred to be treated like an adult. Remember that dumb fuck on the cereal commercial we did once who tried to give us a lesson on how to hold a spoon like we were two, not ten?"

"I remember you taking said spoon and flicking the cereal all over his face and then saying something along the lines of, *is that how I'm supposed to hold it?*"

She lets out a laugh. "I've always been so iconic, even back then."

I can't help but smile. "You're something, that's for sure."

Her face lights up. "Ooh, your first smile in three days. Progress."

"I suppose. I'm fresh out of tears. It's time to put one foot in front of the other."

"I'm glad you feel that way because I made plans for us tomorrow night."

"I have Harper tomorrow night."

"You have Harper until seven. You're coming. Don't think about fighting me on this. We're going out with Vance and crew. There's a new Camel, and they want to introduce him to people and show him a good time."

I sigh. "Fine. Put on a bra and let's go. I don't want to be late."

"Why do I need a bra?"

I point to her bedroom. "Bra. Now."

***

"Sapphire, get your ass down. Bend those knees."

I snap my head toward Kam. "Mouth."

She throws her hands up. "Ass isn't a bad word. It's a part of the body."

"It is a bad word, and you can't tell a little kid to get her ass down. Her parents will throw a fit."

"Her parents gave her a stripper name. They must expect things like this."

Fuck's sake. Why did I bring her? Admittedly, the girls on the team were beyond excited to learn that she's the new assistant coach but keeping her in check will be a full-time job for me.

Kam shouts, "Alright, let's work on turning two."

"Kamryn! They're eight. There's no chance that they'll ever turn a double play in a game. We need to work on fundamentals."

She shakes her head. "We've been doing that the whole time. Since Harper moved to second base, I think there's a chance. She has a really good arm."

Harper has decided that she wants to be like me and play second base. I almost burst into tears when she told me.

"Fine. We can end practice with that as a fun activity." I turn to Harper. "It's different than when you play shortstop. At short, you swipe the bag with your right foot. At second, you tap it with your left before planting and throwing."

She enthusiastically nods her head. "Got it, Coach Bails. Easy peasy lemon squeezy."

I go on to show her how to do it before giving her the opportunity to do so. Kam shows Sapphire the proper way to toss the ball to Harper from shortstop.

After only a few attempts, they actually do a good job. It would take a perfect throw from Sapphire at short and a super slow batter for them to get it in a game, but it's not out of the realm of reason.

I call them all into an end-of-practice huddle. "Great practice girls. We've got a big game this weekend. What's the best way to prepare?"

Andie raises her hand, and I point to her. She happily answers, "Get lots of sleep and eat healthy."

I nod. "Excellent. Throw your hands in the middle." They do. "Snakelets on three. One, two, three," and they all shout, "Snakelets!"

Kam mumbles to me, "Snakelets is a shitty name. Who wants a small snake?"

"It's a baby snake, and they did that because of the Anacondas."

"Still sucks. It would be better if there was a cool name for baby snakes. Like cygnets are baby swans. Cygnets is a badass name."

"Perhaps you can make one up? You love making up words."

"Perhaps I will."

The girls are returning the equipment to the shed for storage when I see Fallon waiting on the sidelines. I approach her. "I didn't realize you were coming. I thought I was driving her to Tanner's?"

She shuffles nervously on her feet. "Umm...Tanner mentioned that you two are...no longer an item. I thought it might be easier for you if I picked her up tonight and drove her there. So you don't have to see him."

"I appreciate it, but I'll be there tomorrow night. I'll see him when he gets home, and I'm going to have to see him in the future."

"Do you need me to come by tomorrow? Maybe for a few weeks until emotions simmer down?"

I shake my head. "No. I promised you that I would be devoted to Harper no matter what, and I am."

She nods. "I appreciate it. If you have any issues, we can try to figure something else out. We don't want to lose you, Bailey."

"You won't. I'm committed. I promise. I can manage my emotions."

She bites her lip. "I told him a hundred times to tell you about the vasectomy. To give you all the information before you got in too deep."

"Yeah, well, he didn't listen to you. I certainly wish he did. I don't know if it would have changed anything, but him keeping it from me feels very calculated."

"You're completely right." Her face is full of nothing but compassion. "I don't know that it will make you feel better, but he's hurting too. Despite his behavior, he does care for you."

"Thanks, Fallon. Can we just keep things about Harper moving forward? The wounds are a little fresh for me to be having this conversation with you right now."

Her face falls. "I'm sorry. Of course. If you have any issues or need a little time away, just reach out."

I give her a small smile. "I will. Thank you."

"I'm here, so I'll take her tonight. And you're sure you're good for tomorrow night?"

"I'm fine. I promise."

PAYOFF PITCH

It's just before seven, and I instruct Harper, "Only set two places at the table."

"I thought Daddy was coming home for dinner."

"He is. I'm leaving."

Her face falls. "Why? You always stay for dinner."

"I'm sorry, sweetie, I have plans tonight. I need to leave as soon as Daddy gets home." *Like two seconds after he gets home.*

She looks so sad. "Okay. Will you stay tomorrow night?" she asks hopefully.

"I'm sorry, I have plans tomorrow too." I don't, but my days of dinners here are over. It will take a little time, but she'll get used to our new normal.

I see the headlights of his car beaming through the front windows. I quickly place the food on the table and gather my jacket and purse.

Giving Harper a hug, I tell her that I left Skittles for her inside the drawer in her night table. I knew she'd be a little upset at me leaving, so I left them as a happy surprise for her.

When he walks in through the garage door, the pain feels as fresh as if it just happened. Shit. I thought I was making progress. My heart physically hurts at the sight of him.

Harper runs to hug his leg. He hugs her back but maintains eye contact with me.

I force out a small smile and beg the tears to stay away. "Dinner is on the table. I'll see you tomorrow."

His face looks pained. "You're not staying for dinner?"

Harper shakes her head. "She has plans tonight." She loudly whispers, "I think she has a date."

Tanner's jaw tightens. I have no idea where Harper got that from.

"I'm just going out with some friends, sweetie. Have a good night."

I practically sprint out the front door. It takes all of two seconds for him to follow me out, closing the front door behind him. "Can we talk without Mike Tyson around?"

I stop and turn around to face him. "Mike Tyson?"

"Your sister beat the shit out of me when I tried to come see you."

I didn't know that, but I can't say that I'm disappointed to hear it. "Good for her. I have nothing to say to you." I turn toward the car but stop again and turn toward him. "I'm going to buy a car this week. I don't feel comfortable using yours anymore. It doesn't feel right. I'll make sure to get something safe for Harper."

"That's ridiculous. I don't ever use this car. Keep it."

"No." He approaches me, but I hold up my hands. "Don't. Just leave me alone."

He tries to grab my arm, but I pull away and rush to get into the car, quickly closing the door. He speaks through the window. "You're going to have to talk to me at some point."

Maybe, but today is not that day.

WE'RE OUT WITH VANCE, Daylen, a teammate named Beau, and the new guy on their team, Champ Williamson. He's a star running back and was just traded here from the Fort Worth Wranglers down in Texas. He's attractive, with mocha-colored skin and huge brown eyes with exceedingly long lashes. His curly hair is longer on top and is bleached.

Beau has practically been forcing Champ on me all night. While I'm not ready for anything along those lines, I'm hitting it off with Champ. He's so sweet and funny. Hopefully, we can be friends.

Girls have been hitting on him all night, but he acts

completely disinterested. The girls in this club are so obvious and forward. I can't ever imagine acting that way. One woman came up to our booth and introduced herself as Lana. She then said, "It's easy to remember my name if you spell it in reverse," before winking at the boys.

Kam "accidentally" spilled a drink on Lana, and she left in a huff. The guys were all hysterically laughing about the whole scene.

Kam was in my ear on the way here that the best way to get over someone is to get under someone else. Fortunately, she hasn't been pushy since we arrived. She knows it's just not my style to jump into bed with someone else to nurse a broken heart.

Their teammate, Presley, walks in. I'm surprised to see him. His wife just had their first baby. I've only met him once before.

Vance lifts an eyebrow. "Elvis?" Their nickname for him. "What are you doing here? I thought you'd be knee-deep in diapers and shit."

Presley runs his fingers through his blond, messy hair. "Layla kicked me out."

Daylen chuckles. "What did you do?"

He scrunches his face. "She doesn't care for my sense of humor. She had her four-week checkup with her OB today. When she came home, she said he told her we still can't have sex for another two weeks. I asked her what the proctologist said."

We all burst out in laughter though I feel my face flushing, knowing what Tanner did to me last week.

He nods. "It's funny, right? It was a joke. But she got mad and told me to leave for a few hours." He sits down and rests his head on the table. "All I really want to do is sleep. Fatherhood is exhausting. The baby cries and shits all the time."

Champ leans over and whispers in my ear, "Let's get away from Debbie Downer. Want to dance, sexy?"

"Sure. Why not?"

He grabs my hand, and we walk out of the booth toward the

dance floor. Every female eye moves to Champ as he glides to the dance floor. He's a physical specimen, that's for sure. I think I'm the envy of every woman here.

Champ twirls me around for a few songs. We're both laughing and having a great time. He's easy to be with. I'm glad Kam made me come. I needed a fun night like this.

As a slow song begins, he pulls me into his giant arms but not too close. He's being respectful, and I appreciate that.

He looks down at me. "I'm glad we met, Bailey. You'll officially be my first friend in Philly."

I smile. "I'm glad we met too."

He blows out a breath. "Since we're besties now, can I tell you something?"

I giggle. "Of course, *bestie*."

"I'm...umm...I'm not into women *that* way. The guys, particularly Beau, have been very obvious in trying to play matchmaker tonight. I don't want you to expect anything from me along those lines. I really like you and don't want to give any mixed signals."

"Oh. Why don't you just tell them? You're not out?"

"Honestly, I don't feel like I should have to announce it to people. Did you come out as heterosexual?"

"Hmm. Valid point. I never thought of it that way. You can tell Vance and Daylen. They're great guys. I'm sure the others are too, but I don't know them well."

"You're probably right, but I'm not sure everyone in the league will feel the same. I'm not looking to be the poster child for gay men in professional sports. My private life should remain just that. Private."

I zip my lips. "Your secret is safe with me. Are there any men here tonight who interest you?"

He scrunches his face. "I left someone behind in Texas. I'm nursing a broken heart right now. I'm not ready for that yet."

I nod. "So am I. Maybe we can just be there for each other, so everyone leaves us alone."

He gives me a million-dollar smile and then kisses my cheek. "I like that idea, bestie. Maybe we can go out for dinner in the next few weeks and get to know each other better. Just the two of us."

I can't help but smile. "I'd like that."

He kisses my cheek again. He's very kissy. "Great. I need to scout the local steakhouses to find my favorite. We'll hit one of them."

"Perfect. I love a good piece of steak."

We make our way back to the booth. I expect Kam to crack jokes about me dancing with Champ, but she doesn't. It's kind of odd. I wonder if she sensed his sexuality. She's got much better radar for that than I do.

She slides out of the booth. "The waitress is taking forever. I'm going up to the bar to get another round for everyone."

She returns a few moments later and places a huge tray on the table. Suddenly I see Cheetah appear, but he brings his finger to his lips indicating that I should keep quiet about his arrival.

I subtly nod that I will.

He walks up behind Kam, cages her in with his arms, and speaks into her ear, "Want to play Titanic?"

Her lips curl in amusement before she answers, "Fine, but I'm going be the iceberg this time, and you're going to be the ship that goes down."

They both smile as she turns around in his arms. His hands move down to her ass, pulling her close to him. They're practically nose to nose.

She places her hands on his shoulders. "You're back early, kitten."

He wiggles his eyebrows. "I am. Our final game in Florida scheduled for tomorrow was canceled with the forecast of rain, so a few of us flew back tonight. Trey practically sprinted to the airport as soon as he found out, but I wasn't far behind. I missed you, Kam bam."

"How did you know where I was?"

"Find My iPhone."

"Stalker."

He nods. "Don't lie to yourself. You get off on me stalking you. Happy to see me?"

"Hmm."

"Use your words, Kamryn."

"Parts of my body are extremely happy, including my lips."

"I like your lips."

"There are twenty-five billion lips on this planet. Are my four your favorites?"

He chuckles. "I think so, but it's been a few weeks. I'll need a refresher to make sure."

"That can be arranged. Which two do you want first?"

He smiles as his mouth meets hers. It starts off innocent enough, but in true Kam and Cheetah fashion, it doesn't stay that way for long.

Kam said they're "casually fucking" but she didn't "casually fuck" anyone else the entire month he's been gone. That must be a record for her. I wonder if they're more than she's letting on.

The over-the-top kiss eventually ends after everyone in the booth catcalls and whistles.

She pulls away, though their faces and bodies remain close together. "I think you were the last to arrive tonight, kitten. You know what that means."

He grins widely. "I've got a good one for you. The clitoris is made up of the same tissue as a penis. It expands and engorges when aroused, so technically women get erections too."

"That makes sense for what I'm feeling right now."

He rubs his nose along her cheek. "Let's get out of here, Kam bam."

She turns her head to me. "We're going to take off. Are you okay to get home?"

I nod. "I'll be fine. Have fun."

Champ wraps his arm around me. "I'll get her home. Don't worry."

PAYOFF PITCH

Kam gives him a skeptical look before turning back to me. "Are you good with that?"

"Yep."

"Okay. I'll see you tomorrow."

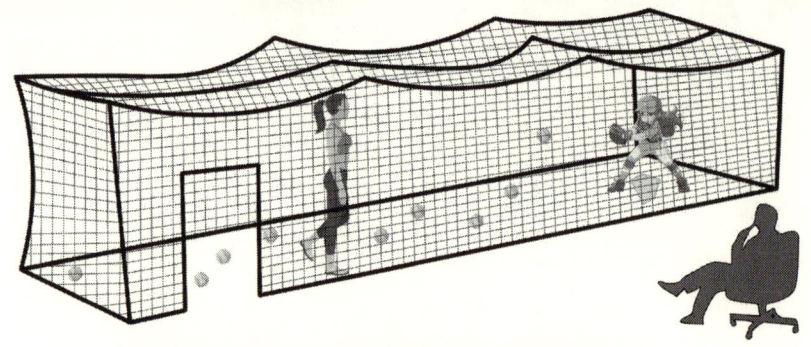

CHAPTER TWENTY-THREE

TANNER

The past few weeks have been difficult. It's so hard to see Bailey and have her be cold and distant. She leaves the second I get home. One foot is practically out the door when I step in.

I miss her. It's got me questioning everything I thought I wanted.

On a happy note, she's done a great job with the Snakelets. The girls have all improved so much. They're dominating the league. Surprisingly, Kamryn is a decent coach. She treats the girls like peers, and they seem to enjoy that.

The best part of the games is that they give me the ability to sit and watch Bailey. If not for that, I'd only see her as a blur when she rushes out the door at night.

My heart is aching for her. I miss touching her. I miss talking to her. It was more than physical, and I knew it. I'm such an idiot. I hate myself for hurting her.

Fallon has tried to talk to me a few times about it, but I shut her down. I want to wallow alone in my misery.

My daydreaming is broken up by Layton walking into my office. He and Arizona recently returned from California. Ripley and Quincy had a baby. I didn't even know they were together. In fact, I'm not sure they are together, but she's living with him in Philly now as they care for their daughter.

I force a smile. "Hey, bud. I don't think we have an appointment. Is everything okay?"

He nods. "Yes. I sent over a few swimsuit company contracts for you to review for my wife and me. The offers are pouring in. I don't know why."

"You two are the proud owners of the best-selling *Sports Illustrated* cover of all time. You're an exceedingly attractive couple, outwardly in love. You're both looked up to as superstars in your respective sports. And your bodies are flawless. I'm not a genius, but I'm guessing those are the contributing factors."

He lets out a laugh. "Yep, my wife is a hottie."

"You really like using the words *my wife,* don't you?"

He smiles dreamily. "I do."

Layton was one of the biggest playboys on the planet, and now he's the most whipped man I've ever met. I never thought I'd see the day, and it happened so fast after he met her. It makes me wonder about people growing and changing.

"What can I do for you?"

"I just wanted to check on you. Arizona told me that you and Bailey are no longer sneaky links."

"What the hell is a sneaky link?"

He twists his lips. "I guess it's secret sex partners."

I grimace. "You make it sound so cheap."

"Were you ever forthcoming about your relationship?"

"No."

"Were you having sex?"

I exhale a breath in resignation. "I guess we were sneaky links."

"Yep. Are you okay?"

"Not really. I hate that I hurt her, but I suppose it's for the best. Maybe she'll find the right person." I have to choke out that last sentence.

"Why can't that be you?"

I hold up my hands. "Enough, Dr. Layton. I need to get going."

He simply shakes his head.

"What?"

He pinches his lips together as if choosing his words carefully. "You always do this."

"Do what?"

"When conversations get a little deep for you, you deflect. It's probably a skill you acquired in law school. It's okay to be vulnerable sometimes. It doesn't make you less of a man. It makes you more of one. Look at what I've been through. I wouldn't be okay right now if not for the help of Arizona and my friends. You can trust me with your feelings. I'm your friend, Tanner. I promise."

I'm silent.

"You obviously care about her more than you let on. Probably more than you expected to."

Every instinct I have is to run away from this conversation. Bailey was right about me. Layton is right too.

I look at my watch. "I really do have to get going. Yes, my feelings for her run deeper than I had anticipated. Yes, I'm having a hard time letting go." I stand. "Thanks for checking in. I'll be fine. I really do have a dinner interview. I need to get across town."

"Interview for what?"

"I want to bring in a female agent to run my new

women's sports division. I want to get these girls better contracts. The kind they deserve."

"Oh, cool. You'll be the Billie Jean King of the twenty-first century."

I let out a laugh. "There are certainly worse things I could be."

He smiles. "I guess the Beavers coming to town will be good for business."

The owners of the Cougars and Anacondas just announced that they're bringing an expansion women's professional basketball team to the area. The Philadelphia Beavers. They have the first pick in the upcoming draft and will undoubtedly pick Sulley O'Shea. She's the biggest star in the sport right now.

I nod. "Yes, I have calls in to a few of their prospective players."

He smirks. "Sulley O'Shea."

"That's an obvious one."

"Arizona mentioned that she's coming to see Philly next week, and Reagan asked Bailey to show her around."

"Really?"

He nods. "Yep. The girls are all planning to take her out and about, but Reagan wants Bailey to be the main point of contact."

"I suppose that's smart. Thanks for the intel."

"Sure thing. Also, my wife and I set a date for the reception this fall. Will you be one of my groomsmen?"

I smile. "I'd be honored."

Two hours later, I'm sitting at a fancy steakhouse with a woman I know isn't right for the position, but I can't be rude and leave. We have to at least finish dinner.

She's an attorney who said she was an athlete, but it's clear she wasn't. At least not at a high level. I need someone who can speak the language of these female athletes. A no-nonsense, strong woman who doesn't take shit from anyone. Someone I can train to effectively advocate for these women.

She's droning on and on about irrelevant topics. I'm simply sipping my whiskey when a body I know as well as my own walks through the door. She's in a black dress, with her hair down and makeup on her gorgeous face. I've rarely seen her dressed up like this.

Because you're an asshole who never took her out.

I see the hostess talking to her and then pointing toward a specific table. My eyes toggle to it. Sitting there waiting is Champ Williamson in a jacket and tie. He's a star running back. The Philly Camels just traded with the Wranglers to bring him here.

He stands when she approaches, smiles widely, pulls her into his arms in a familiar way, and kisses her cheek.

She smiles and hugs him back. What the fuck? Are they on a date? Is she already dating? What happened to being in love with me? Why does my tie suddenly feel so damn tight?

"...is single?"

I turn to the woman I'm sitting with. "I'm sorry. What did you say?"

"I asked if Vance McCaffrey is single."

Is she fucking kidding me? "I'm not sure that's my business, and I *know* it's not yours. I also know that it's not an appropriate question to ask at a job interview."

Her face falls in horror. "Sorry, just trying to make conversation." She mumbles, "This is awkward."

I sip my whiskey again as I turn my attention back to Bailey and Champ. He's holding her hand across the table, and she's laughing at whatever he just said.

Why is he touching her? I should be the one touching her from across the table at a fancy restaurant. Anger brews from deep within and sweat starts forming on my brow. I suddenly feel like I can't breathe. I think I'm having a panic attack. I need air.

I scooch my chair back a little too hard and it falls over backward. Fortunately, I don't.

Bailey turns her head at the loud interruption, and our eyes meet. She then looks at the woman with me and tears fill her eyes.

She stands, says something to Champ, and then walks quickly toward the bathroom area with her head down.

I toss my napkin on the table. "Excuse me for a moment." I grab a handful of hundreds and slap them on the table. "In fact, you can head out. I'll be in touch." Or not.

I rush toward the bathroom area and straight into the women's room without giving a shit. I immediately lock the door behind me. She's leaning her hands on the elegant marble vanity. Her head turns to me, and I see tears spilling out of her eyes. She looks so sad.

I walk toward her and blurt out, "It's not a date. It's just a job interview."

She shakes her head. "It's not my business anymore. I suppose it never was."

My fingers twitch. Every instinct of mine tells me to touch her. To comfort her. To be close to her.

I approach her and wrap my arms around her from behind. Our eyes meet in the mirror. "I miss you."

She shakes her head. "Don't."

I inhale deeply, needing her scent to survive.

She's not relaxing into me like she normally does. Why not?

"Are you dating Champ Williamson?"

She pinches her eyebrows together before she straightens her shoulders and steels her face. "That's none of your business."

Pushing her hair to the side, I kiss the spot on her neck that I know drives her wild. "Does he know how much you like to be kissed here?" I kiss and then lick the spot again.

Her eyelids flutter.

I run my hands up her bare legs until they're under her dress. Her whole body shivers. I can see her nipples harden through the flimsy material of her dress.

"Does he give you goosebumps from a simple touch?"

Her breathing intensifies.

I run my fingers across her panty-covered pussy and apply a little pressure. "Does he know how much you like my beard right here? Rubbing against you. Pleasuring you."

She whimpers.

I slip her panties to the side and run my fingers through her wetness while simultaneously grabbing her hair with my other hand and pulling it hard. "Does he make you as wet as I do? Does he know you like to be dominated in bed? Does he know that you like to give up control?"

Our eyes are like laser beams to one another in the mirror. She breathes, "Tanner."

"I prefer it when you call me Daddy."

Her whole body shakes. Her juices drip down on my fingers. I need to be inside her.

Removing my hands, I quickly unfasten my belt and pants, pulling out my cock. I run my tip through her wetness a few times. After grabbing her chin hard, I bark out "If you don't want this, use your safe words."

She briefly closes her eyes. When she reopens them, there's a pained look in her eyes as she breathes out, "I want it."

That's all the invitation I need. I slam into her.

She lets out a scream that morphs into a moan. She tilts her ass toward me, and I immediately begin my deep, hard thrusts inside her body. It feels so right to be back inside her.

Our eyes remain connected like they usually are when we have sex. It's one of my favorite things about her. The fact that it's through a mirror doesn't lessen the intensity.

My pounding into her body quickly turns animalistic. I've never been so rabid for a woman in my life. I've never felt so out of control with need.

I can feel her walls constricting around me in sync with her moans of ecstasy. I growl, "No one will ever fuck you like I do.

"Oh god."

"Come for me, sweet girl. Come hard and long. Make that pussy sing for Daddy."

Her eyes roll back in her head, and she does just as I instructed, coming long and hard. As soon as she's finished, I give her five more long, hard pumps and groan into my own release, filling her with my semen.

As I gradually still inside her, the only sounds in the bathroom are our ragged breaths. There's so much to say to her, yet I'm at a complete loss for words.

I look down and see a drop of my come drip down her leg. There's something primal about it. She's marked as mine. When did I turn into a fucking caveman?

Someone knocks on the door. "Anyone in there? You're taking forever. Are you okay?"

Bailey shouts, "One more minute."

I pull out and tuck myself back in with a huge smile on my face. She narrows her eyes at me. "Why are you smiling?"

I lick my lips before admitting, "I'm going to enjoy watching you on your date knowing you're full of my come."

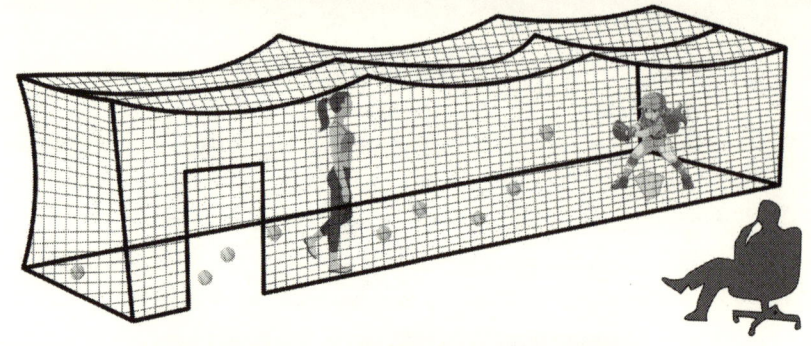

CHAPTER TWENTY-FOUR

BAILEY

"Wow, this is such a beautiful city," Sulley O'Shea expresses with a genuine smile on her pretty face. Sulley has jet-black hair and light blue eyes. She's tall, probably as tall as Ripley, who stands at six feet. With her paler skin and a smattering of freckles, I'm guessing she's of Irish descent.

I let out a laugh. "You seem shocked."

She nods as she takes another bite of her cheesesteak. Taking someone to one of the famous cheesesteak restaurants is the first thing you have to do when they visit Philly. With a mouthful, she says, "I am. I was expecting dirty mayhem, but it's not like that at all. It's kind of peaceful, not overrun with people."

"It's a city and certain sections are better than others, but in general, no, it's not overpopulated. I genuinely like it here. Are you sure you're okay heading out to my friend's house? We can do something else. Something more touristy, if you want."

Even though we've already done a small handful of touristy things, I think it best to make sure she enjoys some interpersonal connections as well. I know that will help her become more comfortable here than seeing a few more landmarks. There's time for that if and when she moves here.

It's a warm spring day which only adds to the beauty of the city. Ripley invited us over to Quincy's house to sit by the pool. The Cougars are away on a road trip.

Her eyes brighten. "Meeting Arizona Abbott, Ripley St. James, and your sister? Count me in. You guys are my inspiration. I was glued to the television last year during your playoffs. Do you think you guys can win it again?"

"I hope so. Practices start back up this week. Ripley having her baby early means we might get her back this season when we assumed we wouldn't, at least not to start the season. I know she's working her ass off to get back into pitching shape."

Her mother moved out here with her to help her with baby Kaya and to help her get back into pitching shape. Her mother was an Olympic pitcher and coached both Ripley and Arizona throughout high school.

"Awesome. I packed a bathing suit like you said. Ready when you are."

We climb into my new car and drive twenty-five minutes into the suburbs to Quincy's palace. That's exactly what it is. A palace.

Sulley's eyes practically bug out of her head when we pull in through the front gate. "Holy shmagegies, this place is huge."

"Quincy had it custom built. It's got everything you can possibly imagine." I mean *everything*. It's what's considered a smart house. You can yell any instruction, and the house does it for you.

I let us in and notice that the back glass panels to the pool area are wide open. We walk out and see Arizona, Kam, and June, Ripley's mother, lying out in bikinis. Ripley is in a T-shirt and shorts holding baby Kaya on a chair in the shade. I immediately grab for Kaya. "Gimme, gimme, gimme."

Ripley laughs as I take Kaya into my arms and smell her baby scent. I love it so much. Kaya is the spitting image of Ripley, with red curly hair and blue eyes. She's so adorable. I want to eat her up.

I introduce Sulley to everyone. Kam looks her up and down. "You look like a taller Eve Hewson." She's an up-and-coming actress in a handful of movies and television shows.

Sulley answers, "I get that all the time. Thank you. It's a nice compliment."

Kam asks, "Did you know that she's Bono's daughter?"

Sulley pinches her eyebrows together. "Bono from U2?"

Kam nods. "Yep. His real name is Paul David Hewson."

"I didn't. That's cool."

Arizona asks Sulley, "I know where you went to college, you can't turn on a television these days without seeing your awesome plays, but where are you originally from?"

"A small town in Montana. The same one as Vance McCaffrey."

Kam wiggles her eyebrows. "He's so hot, in a broody, mysterious kind of way. Did you bang him in high school?"

Sulley scrunches her face. "He's eight years older than me."

Kam shrugs. "So?"

"So, when he was a senior in high school, I was ten."

Kam scrunches her face in disgust. "Oh. Right. Whoops."

Sulley offers, "He was friendly with my older brother though."

Her face falls as she says that. Kam must catch it too because she turns her attention to me. "Speaking of banging older men, what's your current status?"

My steakhouse romp with Tanner weeks ago somehow managed to thaw the iciness between us. We've gotten back to semi-friendly terms. It's easier for Harper this way and holding onto anger isn't really my style. I still don't stay for dinner, it's too personal, but we're able to engage in polite conversation before I go.

June has her eyes closed on the chaise lounge chair but says, "Nothing wrong with banging older men. I preferred them at your age. They know what they're doing in bed. I've seen that fine man. I'm sure Bailey was getting it pretty good."

Sulley's eyes widen, but the rest of us are used to the way June St. James talks.

I sarcastically respond, "Thanks for the support, June."

"Anytime, sweetie."

Looking at Kam, I answer "We're friends. It's gotten back to a cordial place. I'm fine with it as is."

"Friends with benefits? It's weird that you went from love to hate to friendship. It sounds like you banged it out to me."

"Can we please keep things PG in front of Sulley? We just met her."

Sulley giggles. "I think you guys are a riot. I come from such a conservative town. No one outwardly talks about this stuff. It's nice that you all are so open."

Arizona snort-laughs. "If you want open, you're in the right place, Sulley. I'm married to my brother's best friend. Ripley had a baby with my brother. Kam bangs everything in sight, both men and women, and then tells us about it in graphic detail. And June is, well, June. In high school, I'd bump into her naked body in their kitchen in the middle of the night letting out her latest bedfellow. She'd simply offer me a high five as she went about her business."

June giggles as she fixes her red hair into a messy bun. "There's nothing wrong with a healthy sexual appetite. I've always had one."

Ripley rolls her eyes, but Kam nods in agreement. "Preach, Mama June."

I cover Kaya's ears. "You guys aren't going to be able to talk like this in front of her for long. Poor baby will be scarred for life. You should see how Kam talks to the girls we coach. I can't believe I don't have more parent complaints."

Kam scoffs. "They don't complain because we're undefeated. We're running a well-oiled machine. I'd take this team on the road to local high schools, and we'd probably kick their asses."

I turn to Sulley. "Kam and I coach a softball team for eight-year-olds. One of the players is the little girl I nanny for. Our championship game is tonight. Arizona said you can hang with her during the game and then we can all meet up later."

Sulley smiles. "Can I come to the game? I want to watch them play. It sounds cute."

Kam raises her eyebrow. "We're not cute. We're a killing machine taking no prisoners on the way to winning the championship and collecting our trophies tonight."

I remind her, "We get trophies, win or lose."

Kam's jaw drops. "Are you kidding me? Second place gets trophies too? What a joke. How will they learn to be competitors in this participation-trophy society?"

I smile at Sulley. "Kam used to toss all second-place trophies."

Kam shouts. "It's not like there were a lot of them. I'm a champion. First place or bust. You don't want these kids living in their parents' basements at thirty years old, clinging to ninth-place shit-brown ribbons, do you?"

Sulley giggles. "Now I really need to see this team in action."

Arizona nods. "Cool. I wanted to go anyway. We'll sit together."

Actually, Arizona and Sulley being there could be good for the team. I look at the two of them. "Why don't you two give the pre-game speech? The girls will flip for both of you."

They both happily agree.

"LISTEN, bitches, it's your time to shine. This is war, but we're not taking any prisoners. It's kill or be killed in the dog-eat-dog world of Little League softball. Make those fuckers bleed."

The kids all giggle at Kam. Annoyingly, they freakin' love how she talks to them in a straightforward manner.

I smile at the absurdity. "Most importantly, have fun."

Kam scoffs. "Fun? They can have fun at the afterparty, not during the game."

I sigh. "Anyway, we brought in two special guests to talk to you tonight." I motion toward Arizona and Sulley, who have been hiding behind a tree so we could give them their grand entrance. "I give you Arizona Abbott and Sulley O'Shea."

The girls all scream like they're rock stars as they approach our huddle. Four of the girls are so starstruck that they start crying.

Arizona smiles. "I've seen a few of your games this season. You guys are even better than mine and Ripley's team when we were your age." The girls all gasp. "Ripley has been my teammate since we were five. Kam and Bailey since we were eighteen. Trusting your teammates is very important. Make sure you all love and support each other no matter what. Mistakes are part of the game at every level. It's how a team supports one another, and moves on, that separates the good and the great teams."

Sulley nods in agreement. "Arizona is right. Being a good teammate is important. Loving what you do is important too. Make sure you have fun out there."

Kam tries to interrupt, but I cover her mouth. The girls all giggle.

I place my hand in the middle, and the team follows suit. "Hiss on three. One, two, three," They all collectively hiss. Hissing was my compromise with Kam because she can't stand the name snakelets and the only substitutions she could come up with were perverted and completely inappropriate for this group.

We're in the last inning. This is the tightest game of the season. We're only up by one run. The other team brought a few new players tonight. I can't know for sure, but I think some of them are a few years older than they're supposed to be in this league. I've been hearing our parents chirping about it in the stands all night. I had to go over at some point and tell them to simmer down since the girls were feeding off that negative energy.

Our pitcher has thrown a good game, but she's getting tired. The bases are loaded and there's only one out. I call a timeout and walk toward the mound as I motion for the entire infield to join us. I look at our pitcher. "You're looking a little tired, Stacey. You've pitched a great game. Maybe it's time for me to bring in someone else."

She takes a breath and then shakes her head. "I want to finish, Coach Bails. I can do it."

I nod. "Alright. This batter is their best one. She's been hitting line drives all night. Can you keep the ball low in the zone? We want to induce a ground ball. You don't have to try to strike her out. Trust your team behind you."

She nods. "I'll try."

I look at Andie, who we moved over to shortstop when Sapphire was struggling earlier this season. "You and Harper pinch the middle. Let's see if we can't induce a double play."

They look at each other with uncertainty. We haven't turned one the entire season. They've tried three times, but the runner at first base always beat it out.

"This batter isn't fast. I think this is our best chance to win the game. Stacey is gassed. We don't want them to score a run and have to go to extra innings. We need this. I believe in you both."

They pound their gloves and nod. Harper says, "We'll do it."

I walk back to the dugout. Kam looks at me. "Why aren't we playing shallow? The play is at home."

I shake my head. "Stacey only has enough left for one batter. This girl hits too hard. It will get through if we play up. I'm having Andie and Harper pinch the middle. I told Stacey to throw low. I'm going for broke on your double play."

She twists her lips. "It's risky."

"It's our best shot."

One of the parents sitting in the stands yells, "You guys need to come in. The play is at home."

Kam narrows her eyes at him and shouts back, "Shut up, Norman. You're not the coach. Spare all of us and put on some deodorant for once."

PAYOFF PITCH

The parents all chuckle. He's definitely the overly sweaty, smelly dad.

Five pitches later, there are two strikes and three balls on the batter. A full count. That makes this next pitch the payoff pitch. One of the fathers on the other team even yells about it. I turn and look at Tanner after the man shouts it. His eyes meet mine, and he gives me a small smirk in acknowledgment of the term. God, I miss him. I miss his kisses. I miss the way his body feels on mine. I miss being in his arms. His scent. All of him. I can see in his face that he's feeling the same. In fact, I see it every time I'm with him. He doesn't bother to hide it.

Kam mumbles, "Stop ogling Tanner and focus."

I snap my head back to the game. "Sorry." I shout, "Come on, Stacey, you've got this. No free rides." Walking this girl would tie the game and put the winning run at third.

She nods as she steps onto the pitching rubber. She winds up and throws the pitch. It's coming in low. The batter swings and hits a hard ground ball. It's heading toward the left side of second base. I don't think Andie can get there, but she proves me wrong. She lays out for the ball, and it skips right into her glove. From the ground, she tosses it up to Harper at second base who secures the first out, plants her left foot, and then throws as hard as her little body is capable of toward first base. So hard that she falls to the ground afterward.

It's a bang-bang play at first. All eyes move to the umpire who signals the final out. Kam gasps. "Holy shit, it worked. Fucking A, they did it."

Kam and I are hugging, screaming, and jumping up and down in excitement. The girls all start running over to Harper. The parents are all yelling in both shock and happiness.

Kam and I run out to the girls. Harper leaps into my arms and hugs me. "This is the best day of my life, Bails. Thank you. I love you."

I start crying as I hug her back. "I love you too. I'm so proud of you. All your hard work has paid off."

Kam rubs her head. "Harper, you're a stud."

She then hugs Andie. "That play was next level, kiddo. I don't know if I could have made it. Way to get it done."

Andie has a huge grin on her face as she's lifted onto Kam's shoulders. I'm proud of Kam for how far she's come with these kids this season. It doesn't come naturally to her, but she found a way to connect with them, albeit unconventional, and it worked.

We briefly join the team pizza party. All the parents express their extreme gratitude for all our time this season. We then head home to get dressed for our night out.

Sulley is dressed and waiting in our living room. I'm looking in my mirror applying my makeup when Kam walks in and asks, "Can we talk?"

I nod. "Of course."

She plops down on my bed. "I see the way you're always looking at Tanner and the way he looks at you."

Tears threaten my eyes. "I know. I'm trying not to, but I can't help it. It's hard to explain. I miss the closeness to him. I feel so empty without him."

She blows out a breath. "I'm not stupid. I know you're eventually going to end up back in his bed. It's only a matter of time."

I'm silent. I'm not sure she's wrong.

She nods once. "At least you're not in denial or lying to me. Thank you for that." She leans back on her hands. "Can I give you a few rules of casual sex that I think would be best for you? I'm not sure you're capable of it, but if you're going to do this, I need to at least do everything I can to safeguard your heart from being broken again."

"Okay. Tell me."

TANNER

It's one in the morning and I'm too wired to sleep. I'm still not over what I watched tonight. Harper blows my mind. She's got more work ethic at eight than most adults ever have. Proud isn't a big enough word for what I'm feeling for my special little girl.

We all celebrated at a local pizza parlor after the game. Harper then went to Fallon's. The Windsors are hosting a huge team party at their house next week.

Kam and Bailey only stayed at the celebration for a short time. They said they had plans. It means she'll be out and about with a line of men wanting to get into her pants.

I hate that the season is over. I won't get to see Bailey as much. With her own season starting back up again soon, she won't be able to coach the Snakelets in their summer league, and she won't be at the house as much. I feel...empty without her.

She's such a bright, shining light. There's a dimness and an ache in my chest when she isn't around. It's confusing for me. I've never been emotionally reliant on anyone, not even Fallon.

I consider going downstairs to pour myself a glass of whiskey, thinking that maybe it will settle me down enough to fall asleep, but then I remember Bailey's words to me. I don't want to turn into a man who's reliant on booze. I've cut back a ton since that conversation, trying to only be a social drinker, not a solo drinker.

I can't get our night in the restaurant bathroom out of my mind. It was so hot. That might have been the hottest sex of my life. I'm not addicted to alcohol. I'm addicted to Bailey Hart.

I'm happily running through each detail of that night when I hear my front door open and then close. What the hell?

In only my boxer briefs, I get out of bed and quietly tiptoe toward the staircase. As I approach the top of the stairs, I see Bailey at the bottom of them pacing. She doesn't see me at first. She's mumbling to herself about whether or not she should come upstairs.

I can't help but smile. She's so adorable.

"Hey, stranger."

Her head snaps toward me. "Hi. Sorry. Did I wake you?"

I shake my head. "I was up. What are you doing here?"

She nervously chews at her lower lip. "Honestly? I'm not sure." Her fingers fidget with the bottom of her skirt. "I just miss you."

"I miss you too." I motion for her to come upstairs. "Come here. Let me hold you."

She hesitates briefly before eventually walking up the stairs. She's in a short skirt with a very small, revealing tube top. She looks like sex on a stick.

I pull her into my arms, and she immediately relaxes into me. "I don't know what to do, Tanner. I can't shake you. There's this ache in my body without you."

"I know. I feel the same." I tilt her chin up so we're looking at each other. "For now, can I kiss you? I miss your lips and your taste so fucking much."

She nods, and my lips immediately find hers. As soon as my tongue touches hers, she mumbles into my mouth, "I don't want to want you, but I do. I need you."

I lift her legs to wrap them around me and then push her against the wall. Her skirt is naturally lifted so that my cock can press against her pussy with only the thin threads of our underwear between us. She's so warm. I'm realizing how cold I've been without her. Like a chill I can't shake.

Our kiss turns frantic as we practically swallow each other whole. It's been so long since I've kissed these beautiful lips.

I lower my boxers enough to free my cock, desperate to

be inside her. When I push her panties to the side, she grabs my wrist and breaks the kiss. "Condom. I can't do it bare with you anymore. It's too intense."

My jaw tightens. Does this mean she's been with others? I don't like that at all, but I won't argue with her right now. We both need this. I wordlessly move us toward my bedroom.

Rummaging around my drawer until I find a condom, I take one out and start to place her on the bed so I can sheath myself.

Her arms squeeze tightly around my neck. "No, not on the bed. The wall is fine."

"Why are you cheapening this?"

"Just fuck me, Tanner." Her big brown eyes meet mine with so much need written all over them. "Fuck away the pain that's been here since we broke up."

Because I can't deny her and I want her beyond measure, I sheath myself and then fuck her hard against the wall until she comes.

Once I do the same, I gently place her feet on the ground but keep my body pressed to hers. I don't want the contact to end, but she gently pushes me away, immediately fixes her panties, and then pulls down her skirt. "I'm going to head out."

"What? No. Stay with me. In my arms."

She shakes her head. "No. I can't."

"It's the middle of the night. Just stay. Please."

She shakes her head. "No, Tanner. I want to be with you...physically. For now. I can't do anything else and risk my heart breaking all over again. If you find someone else, this ends. If I find someone else, it ends. It's physical. That's it. It's in no way, shape, or form any other kind of relationship. No movies, no dinners, no in-depth conversations, and definitely no sleepovers."

"Is this about Champ?"

She rolls her eyes. "Champ is just a good friend. Do you honestly think I'd be here right now if he and I were more? Would I have let you fuck me in that bathroom if he and I were together?"

I shake my head. I know she wouldn't.

I run my fingers through my hair, pulling at the ends. "So you just want to be...fuck buddies?"

She winces. "I'm not a huge fan of that term, but yes. We can never be more than that, so it's a purely physical relationship or none at all. The boundary needs to be crystal clear this time. It's up to you. I've told you what I want."

This is so unlike her. "Are you sure this is really what you want?"

She swallows. "In an ideal world, no. In the world we live in, yes. It's all I can handle. I have to protect myself as best I can. And this is what you said you wanted, right? So it shouldn't matter to you."

I'm silent, feeling so conflicted about it. Of course I want her, but like this? Then I think about what I've put her through. How could I possibly ask her for more?

I whisper, "Okay."

She nods and pats my chest. "Great. I'll be in touch. Thanks for tonight. It's just what I needed. I'll see you when I'm back on duty with Harper."

What. The. Hell. Just. Happened?

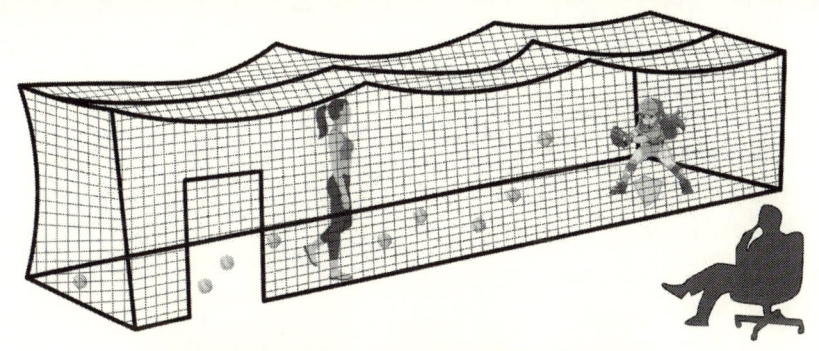

CHAPTER TWENTY-FIVE

FOUR MONTHS LATER

BAILEY

I walk out of my room in the morning to Kam sitting in the same spot on the couch where I left her last night, still with her head buried in her laptop.

"Did you sleep?"

"Meh. I wasn't tired. I'll catch a few hours tonight."

I shake my head. "I don't know how you function. What are you always doing on your laptop?"

She shuts it. "Nothing. However, I did learn that female snakes have a clitoris. Isn't that shocking?"

"I can't say I've ever put any thought into that topic."

She smiles as she nods. "I have and they do. Now you know."

"I'm sure it will come in super handy should the need ever arise for me to help a snake get off."

She laughs, realizing the absurdity of it.

"You should save that for one of Quincy's random facts. I promise you no one else thought to research that topic."

She shrugs. "I'm a wealth of useless knowledge. You know that. I always come up with something interesting when I'm the last to arrive."

"I know you do. The depths of your brain will be studied in a scientific lab one day."

"Probably."

I point to her bedroom. "Go get dressed. Let's grab a quick breakfast at the diner before practice. I'm jonesing for their blueberry pancakes."

Her face lights up. "With a side of pineapples?" I nod. "Sounds like a plan. Give me five."

I'm waiting for her when my text tone pings. I look down at my phone and smile.

> Tanner: Fuck buddy isn't feeling very fucked lately.

For the past few months, Tanner and I have managed the whole fuck buddy thing. I've channeled my inner Kamryn and am happily in a purely sexual relationship.

We meet at his office, our cars, kitchen tables, bathrooms, stairwells, and we even once did it in his garage when he got his new sports car because it's the hottest car ever and I couldn't wait another second for him to be inside me.

> Me: Been busy. I'll stop by Daddy's office after practice.

> Tanner: Such a good girl. I'll be waiting.

Kam walks back out. "What are you smiling at?"

"I might stop at Tanner's office after practice. Have someone give you a ride home."

She rolls her eyes. "This isn't you. I never should have given you the rules. You're going to get hurt again."

I place my hands on my hips. "Admit it's lasted longer than

you thought. You didn't think I could be in a purely sexual relationship, and I have been."

"I *absolutely* didn't think you'd go through with it. What if he told you tomorrow that he met someone?"

"I'd be fine."

"Bull-fucking-shit. You'd be heartbroken all over again. And you won't even look at another man. You're basically in a relationship. Just because you don't call it one doesn't mean it isn't."

"If I'm interested in someone, I promise I'll go on a date. It's going well with Tanner though. I'm happy, and I've managed to adhere to all your rules."

Kam gave me a list of casual sex rules she thought I needed to abide by in order to keep this casual. Never in a bed, never unprotected, never more than once a week, keep it on my terms, don't be too available, keep the post-sex talking to a minimum, and never actually fall asleep together. I always leave as soon as it's over. I think that last part upsets Tanner more than anything, but it's too intimate. I can't stay.

Kam told me that it's all about control. I told her he likes to be in control, but she said it's not about what goes on in the bedroom. It's about what goes on out of the bedroom. I definitely control everything except the actual sex. I'm not sure if she's a genius or completely diabolical, but Tanner is always begging for it by the time I agree to meet with him.

She rolls her eyes. "Whatever. Let's just go. I can't have this conversation for the thousandth time."

"No one will sit on these snakes, right ladies?"

We're in the huddle with Coach Billie giving us her daily dose of inadvertently sexual snake comments.

We all start giggling as practice comes to an end and we do our final cheer. The Anacondas' season can best be described as dominating. Ripley came back with a vengeance. She's happy and it shows in her pitching. Her mother is now our team pitching coach. She's fantastic and has Ripley throwing the best she ever has in her life.

The Olympic committee has been to several of our games. It's still three years out, but they're starting to put thought into who they want on the team.

They've interviewed Arizona, Ripley, Kam, and me. The three of them were bouncing off the walls with excitement. I'm still a little indifferent about it. Maybe I just don't want to get my hopes up only to be heartbroken if I'm not selected. I'm probably the last of the four of us who they'll consider, and taking four players from the same team seems unlikely to me.

Arizona pulls us aside after practice. "Sorry for the late notice. Are you guys free this afternoon for a bridesmaid dress fitting? The woman just called and said there was an issue. She needs to see everyone to make sure the right sizes arrive in time for the wedding. Gemma said she'll meet us there."

Even though they're already married, Arizona and Layton are throwing a ceremony and wedding reception right after our season ends in a few weeks.

Ripley and Kam both answer that they can come.

I check on the time. "I need to make a quick stop. I'll meet you guys there."

Kam gives me a look of warning, but I don't care. I'm going to see Tanner.

FORTY-FIVE MINUTES LATER, I walk out of the elevator toward Tanner's office. His assistant, Shannon, smiles as I approach. She knows why I'm here. I was embarrassed the first few times, but I simply don't care anymore. I'm a grown woman taking what I want from a sexy man. I won't apologize or feel bad about it. Not when it feels so damn good.

I innocently return her smile, as if she doesn't know I'm about to get defiled in the office right behind her desk, and cheerily say, "Good afternoon, Shannon."

"Good afternoon, Bailey. He's expecting you. He said for you to come right in when you arrive."

I respond, "Great. Thank you."

As soon as I walk through the door, it closes. He pins me against it with his big body. His delicious scent immediately invades my nostrils, setting my body on fire. I swear, his smell is my orgasm trigger.

He grabs my wrists and quickly wraps a telephone charging cord around them before holding them above my head with one of his hands.

He barks out, "Leave them here. Don't move them."

I innocently bat my eyelashes. "Yes, Daddy."

He growls and then falls to his knees and roughly pulls my leggings down and off before sinking his face straight into my pussy.

I smile. "Hungry, Mr. Montgomery?"

He mumbles, "Famished."

He lifts one of my legs over his shoulder while his tongue plunders in and out of me like he can't get deep enough. He's always excited for our rendezvous, but he's on a different level right now. I've left him hanging for longer than usual. I think it might have been worth it to get this ravenous reaction from him.

Without thinking, I lower my arms and grab onto his hair. He immediately pulls his face away, appearing angry.

"What did I tell you?"

I breathe, "Sorry," before my lips curl up in amusement at what I know is about to come.

He stands and straightens his tie before making a bit of a show of licking around his lips and beard. Fuck, he's hot.

With a giant tent in his pants, he calmly walks over to his desk and sits in his big, leather executive chair looking every bit as demanding and in charge as he likes to think he is. Without any words, he simply spreads his legs and pats his lap knowing full well that I'll obey his every command.

I feign indignance and hide my excitement as I make my way over to him. I can't help but inwardly laugh at my appearance right now, all of two minutes since I walked in the door. I have nothing on from the waist down. I'm wearing a hoodie. And my wrists are bound by his iPhone charging cord. It's kind of ridiculous, yet I'm beyond turned on by it all.

When I approach, he runs his hands under my hoodie and then closes his eyes. "No bra?"

I shrug. "I thought it would be faster."

"Very smart. Now take your punishment like a good girl."

"Yes, Daddy."

He grabs his dick and squeezes it before gritting out, "Do it. Now."

I lay on my stomach across his lap and stick my ass right in the air. Before I know it, his hand is striking my fleshy backside, and I almost come on the spot.

He does it three more times, and I'm dripping like a leaky faucet. My clit is engorged and throbbing. The sounds reverberate throughout the room. What must poor Shannon be thinking right now?

Picking me up, he places me on his desk. "Lie back, keep those hands above your head, and spread that pretty pussy all over my papers. I want to smell you on them later."

As if I have a choice, I happily obey. He moves his chair forward and wraps his arms around my thighs. He briefly pushes his tongue back into me before eventually latching onto my clit and bringing me to orgasm in no time at all. He knows my body so well and always gives me exactly what I need.

I'm still in the blurry clouds of my post-orgasm bliss when I feel him slam his sheathed cock into me. Again, bringing me to orgasm in no time. Again, acting like he's a man possessed.

When we're done, I slip back into my panties and leggings and shake my head. "What got into you today?"

He looks angry. His jaw looks like he might grind his teeth off. "Nothing. It's just been a while."

"It's been less than two weeks. You know I had a long road trip, and I've been...busy." I do my best to act unaffected.

His jaw releases a drop and he gives me a hopeful look. "It's fine. Do you want to stay for lunch?"

I shake my head. "No, I don't. In fact, I have lunch plans with Champ. I should go." Obviously I don't, but I know it pisses him off.

"I thought—"

"I told you, he's my friend." I wiggle my fingers at him. "Bye, fuck buddy."

His mouth opens and closes a few times like he wants to say something else but decides against it.

I inwardly giggle as I walk out the door. This is fun.

TANNER

"Tan? What are you doing here?"

I'm about to step off the elevator at the hospital only to see Fallon about to get on.

"I was coming down to see if you have time for a cup of coffee."

Surprise is written all over her face. I've never done this before. "Oh...umm...I was just about to go upstairs for my late afternoon sugar fix. I have about thirty minutes before my next patient. Is everything okay with Harper?"

"Yes. Fine. I had an appointment upstairs and just came down to chat with you about something."

Her face falls. "Are you okay? Is something wrong?"

"I'm fine. Let's go find a quiet corner in the cafeteria so we can talk in private."

After we make our way up there and I buy her a few snacks and myself a coffee, we're sitting at a table away from any prying ears.

She bites into a huge candy bar. "So? What's up?"

I scrunch my face. "How do you keep your figure eating that shit every afternoon?"

She's always had a sweet tooth, and she seriously has a flawless figure. I've never once seen her go to a gym. We both know where Harper's sweet tooth comes from.

She shrugs and, with a mouthful, answers, "Good genes, I guess. Look at my mother."

Doris has a very good figure too.

I pat my stomach. "I hope Harper gets your genes, not mine."

She raises an eyebrow. "Yep, you look exactly like Norman. Smell like him too."

I let out a laugh at her referring to one of the fathers on Harper's team. "He really does have a strong body odor, doesn't he? What grown man doesn't use deodorant? Who does he think he is, Matthew McConaughey?"

She giggles as she takes another bite of her Snickers bar and nods her head. "He sure does. He's probably the most *unfuckable* human being I've ever met."

"I can't say I've ever thought of him that way."

She leans back in her chair and nods her head again. "When you have sex as infrequently as I do, you rate every man you come across. He ranks at the absolute bottom next to your brother, but Linc's low ranking is for personality, not grotesque looks and smell."

I ignore the warranted dig at my brother, instead focusing on her love life. "You're still not dating?" I hate to hear that.

"Dating and sex aren't one and the same but don't

worry, I've gone on a few dates. You know who just asked me out?"

"Who? I'll hire a private investigator to check him out."

She lets out a laugh. "Not needed. You know him. Jett Jeffries."

"As in the coach of the Camels?"

She nods. "Yep."

"I didn't realize they got divorced."

"A year or two ago."

"He's a decent guy. Women on social media certainly like him." He garners a lot of attention for his good looks.

She sighs. "He's attractive. I told him I'd let him know. I feel like it's a little...close to home. You have a lot of clients on that team. It's weird."

"I see your point. It doesn't matter from my perspective, if that's what you're worried about. Whatever makes you happy."

She finishes the rest of her candy bar and tosses the wrapper. "I'm not really asking your permission, being that you banged the nanny and all, but it's good to know you approve."

I smile. "You're a certified ballbuster, Fallon. Speaking of my balls, my appointment today was with Dr. Berkley."

"The urologist?"

I nod.

"Is something wro—" And then it hits her. "You're finding out if you can have your vasectomy reversed, aren't you?"

I blow out a long breath. "I am."

"Assuming this is for Bailey?"

"It is."

"I thought maybe you two started back up again but wasn't sure."

I shake my head. "We're not together. It's...physical."

"That's what you said last time."

"Trust me, it's purely physical this time. She won't allow anything beyond that."

"Allow?"

"Without going into much detail, let's just say she doesn't…stick around afterward."

Fallon smiles. Widely.

"What are you smiling at? I thought you'd be pissed."

"It's your life, Tanner. I just think it's funny that sweet, innocent Bailey Hart has you so fucking wrapped around her little finger that you're considering this. She's got you panting like a dog. Fuck, I respect her for it."

My mouth opens in shock. "This conversation isn't going how I thought."

She shrugs with a bit of indifference. "What do you want me to do? Carry on like a crazy ex-wife trying to hold on? Divorce sucks. I don't have the mental energy for ours to be anything less than the amicable way it's always been. It's not like I spent my life imagining myself as a middle-aged lonely divorcée, but here I am, living and breathing it every day."

"You're not middle-aged. I'm fucking middle-aged. That's why I didn't want any more kids."

"I call bullshit. You got that vasectomy in your thirties, about five seconds after we split. It was an emotional, knee-jerk reaction to the way our marriage ended and what I did to you. You decided to never let a woman in again and that was your way of ensuring it wouldn't happen. In comes Bailey Hart, slowly cracking the hard shell you built around that heart of yours. You fell for each other, but you always had your foot out the door. You were so wrong not to tell her from the beginning. It took a year, but you're finally realizing that you might just want more than a life sitting home alone with your precious bottle of whiskey."

I'm silent as I consider her words.

"Why are you even telling me this? It's not my business anymore."

"Because you're Harper's mother. It impacts her, so it impacts you. And, I don't know, it just seems like the right thing to do. Your opinion matters to me."

"Well, if I'm being honest, my preference would have been for us to stay together as a family. I didn't cheat on you because I fell out of love with you. I cheated because I was lonely in our marriage and had a terrible moment of weakness. You've changed since then. Your priorities have changed. I'm happy you're growing as a person. I wish it happened about six years ago, but it didn't. That being said, if I had to pick a stepmother for our daughter, it's not like anyone better exists."

"Hmm."

She twists her mouth. "Obviously, if you go public, people will have opinions. You're kind of a cliché for banging the much younger nanny, but that's your bed to sleep in, not mine."

I can't help but let out a laugh. This isn't the reaction I expected at all.

"What does Bailey think about all this?" she asks.

"I haven't discussed it with her. I don't want to do so until I get my results. If it can't be reversed, I won't put her through the heartbreak. And...she's changed. She's colder toward me. I'm not even sure she wants us anymore, but I'm not having that conversation until I find out if I can give her what she needs. I can only hope she still wants me."

Fallon rolls her eyes. "Just when I thought I couldn't respect her anymore, she's got you feeling like an insecure schoolgirl. I think I'm in love with her too."

I chuckle. "I think we have the weirdest divorce ever."

She smiles. "We just might."

"As long as our little girl is a happy one."

She nods. "She most definitely is. She's perfect. I love everything about the young lady she's becoming."

"I mostly agree with that statement, but is she calling you *Mom* instead of *Mommy* all of a sudden? She started calling me *Dad* and it's driving me nuts."

She giggles. "Yes, I hate it too. At least it's not *bruh*. Cassandra said that Dylan has started calling her *bruh*."

I chuckle. "Yep. That's worse."

Fallon sighs. "She's growing up too fast. She'll be off to college in the blink of an eye."

I suck in a breath. "Bite your tongue. I hate that thought. What about you? Do you want more kids?"

She shrugs. "In an ideal world, yes. I'm getting dangerously close to it being too late. It's not like I have any prospective fathers."

"You're a catch, Fallon. You need to get out there."

"I'm at a weird age in the dating world. It's the age where you can either date a guy or his father and both are socially acceptable."

I let out a laugh.

She smirks. "No judgment from you."

I hold up my hands in surrender. "No judgment at all."

"Though I was thinking about Jett after he reached out. I can't believe I'm at an age where the coach is more appealing to me than the players."

I wiggle my eyebrows. "Somehow, I'm back to the players. I'm not sure how that happened. It was never my plan. I know you're not asking for my permission or my opinion, but I think you should give things a chance with Jett. At least I know he's a good guy who will treat you right."

She's silent for a moment before she takes my hand. "I know we've never truly discussed it, and I know you prefer it that way, but I'm genuinely sorry for how things ended. I sometimes feel like part of the reason I rarely date is to punish myself for what I did." Tears fill her eyes. "I'm honestly happy that you're considering something real with Bailey. I've always felt like it was my fault that you closed yourself off. That I damaged you beyond repair. Hearing that you're opening your heart again is...is...liberating for me."

I squeeze her hand in return. "I didn't know you felt that way. Fallon, I'm just as much, if not more, to blame for what happened to us. Your infidelity was a result of my actions. My neglect. I was a bad husband to you. If I end up doing this again, I know I need to be better."

"But—"

"But nothing. When I say that what happened is water under the bridge, I mean it. I'm sorry if I've held you back. You're a wonderful woman with so much to give. You deserve happiness. While the type of love I have for you has changed over the years, I will always love and care about you. Hear me. Nothing would make me happier than to see you happy. I want you to find someone who thinks the world revolves around you. Even after everything we've been through, that's what I think you deserve. I know you want more kids. I want that for you too. Hear me, Fallon. You deserve that. Stop punishing yourself."

Tears stream down her cheeks as she wordlessly nods. I had no idea how much she needed to hear this. I had no idea how much I needed to have this conversation with her for both me and her.

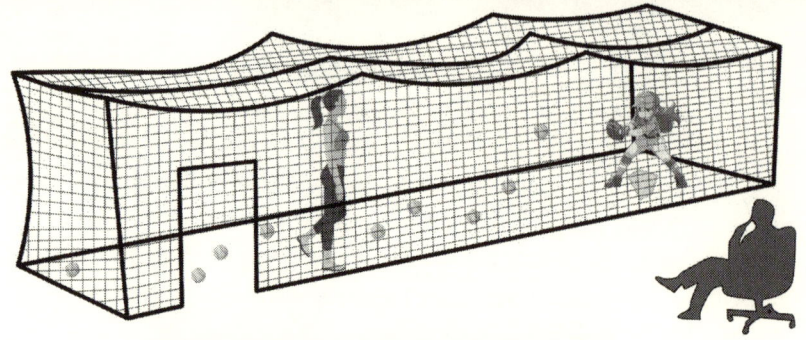

CHAPTER TWENTY-SIX

BAILEY

We're awakened in the morning to Arizona running into our room shouting, "It's my wedding day!"

Kam mumbles, "Oh Christ. Don't be one of those brides."

I kick her under the covers before smiling at Arizona. "We're so excited. Are you nervous?"

She shrugs. "I mean, we're already legally married and I've already got a bun in the oven. This is just the icing on the cake."

Arizona became pregnant right at the beginning of the season. She's only a few months along and is barely showing. If you didn't know, you wouldn't know.

She insisted on playing the whole season. We all held our breath anytime she was in a physical play at home plate, but the pregnancy is healthy, and she's feeling great. She's finding out the sex in a few weeks.

We won another league championship last week, and now it's finally her wedding day. Her second wedding day.

Ripley walks into our bedroom in the two-bedroom suite Arizona rented for us and lovingly wraps her arms around Arizona. "I'm so happy for you. To think you spent our teen years staring at posters of Layton on your ceiling, and here we are all these years later with him being your forever."

Arizona gives us one of her larger-than-life smiles. "I know. I'm so lucky. I feel like I live in a fantasy world sometimes."

Ripley's eyebrow raises. "He's the lucky one, though neither of you are lucky when it comes to weather. I can't believe how cold it's gotten." It's been unseasonably cold this week. I've even had to battle a few icy roads.

Ripley walks over to the window and opens the curtains. "I hope the snow holds off. That would suck if people can't get here."

Arizona nods. "I don't want snow at my wedding but wouldn't mind nine inches on my honeymoon."

We all laugh as we hear the front door of our suite open and close. A few seconds later, Gemma appears in the doorway looking like she just walked off a photoshoot. She shimmies for us. "You four ready to get your glam on?"

Kam narrows her eyes at Gemma. "Why do you look like you already got your glam on? The four of us are battling eye boogers, knotted hair, and morning breath while you're ready to walk the runway."

Gemma giggles. "I have a horndog husband who woke me early with a morning delight." She winks. "My favorite way to start the day."

Arizona smiles dreamily. "I hope after five years of marriage we're just like you and Trey."

Doesn't everyone want a marriage like Gemma and Trey's? I'm hit with a pang of sadness. I'll never have that with Tanner. Maybe Kam is right and it's time for me to accept it and completely move on from him. The truth is, I don't look at other men. I don't accept dates from other men. I know I'm only hurting myself, but the thought of not having Tanner in my life hurts more. I'm so torn.

I feel my sister grab my hand under the blanket. She always

knows what I'm thinking. I look over at her and she nods. "It's time to let go."

I nod in agreement. Maybe it is.

WE'RE GETTING our hair and makeup done when Ripley asks Gemma, "How did you and Trey meet? I've never heard the story. He played for New York then, right?"

My sister gives a knowing smile like she's heard this story before. Weird.

Gemma nods. "It's a crazy, long story. Almost unbelievable. I might write a book about it one day. The severely shortened version is that he saw me in a drunken social media video and swears he contracted an incurable case of love at first sight. He basically stalked me and weaseled his way into my life and then eventually into my heart. Before him, I spent a lot of lonely nights at home writing about the kind of men we all want, never truly believing men like that could be real. Let me tell you something. The swoony, sexy, romantic fictitious men have absolutely nothing on Trey DePaul. He's every fantasy you can imagine come to life. There is nothing, I mean nothing, that man wouldn't do for me. And they're not just words. He shows it in his actions too. He fulfills every need of mine and then some. I'm so thankful for him and the life we have together."

I clutch my heart. "That might be the most romantic thing I've ever heard in my life."

She gets a little emotional as she nods her head. "Every bit of it is true."

Is it wrong that I want that too? I'm definitely barking up the wrong tree with Tanner. I'll never find Mr. Right if I continue to spend time with Mr. Wrong.

After a day of glam that took an interesting turn into Gemma talking about a scene in her upcoming book with a car blow job that she said is one of the hottest she's ever written, the ceremony is finally beginning.

The music starts playing and we're getting paired off with our groomsmen counterparts. I don't see him yet, but I can feel Tanner's eyes on me. They light up my body in a way I can't imagine anyone else ever doing for me. But maybe that's because I'm not bothering to give anyone else a chance.

Kam takes Cheetah's arm, and then I see *him*. If Tanner Montgomery in his daily suits is sexy, Tanner Montgomery in a tuxedo is orgasmic. He's truly the sexiest man I've ever seen in my life. I struggle to imagine ever being attracted to anyone the way I am to him. My body is drawn to his like a magnet.

He holds his big arm out for me. I take it as I'm hit with a waft of his aftershave. It immediately makes my nipples tighten.

His warm, whiskey-scented breath hits me as he leans over and whispers, "You're beautiful."

I smile as I look up into his eyes, which are burning in a way I'm not sure I've ever seen. "You're not so bad yourself."

His eyes move up and down my body, even as we take our first steps down the aisle. "You're coming home with me tonight so I can tear that dress off you."

I thought he had Harper tonight. Fallon is out of town. I'm pretty sure her plane will arrive very late tonight, not in time to see Harper. "What about—"

"She's sleeping out."

I take a deep breath. One last night with this man. One last night to enjoy the passion and pleasure we share together. I'll be thirty next year. I can't continue to spend my time on a man with who I have no future. But I'm giving myself tonight. The big goodbye. The grand finale.

We take our places next to Layton and Arizona, and the ceremony begins. They wrote their own vows. Layton talks about how he felt the first time he laid eyes on Arizona. I remember that night. She outwardly showed zero interest, though we all knew it wasn't true. She was afraid.

Is that all this is? Am I afraid?

I know the answer is no. It's not fear. It's common sense, the fact that we want two different lives. I'm not willing to compromise being married and having a big family. I don't know that I could ever truly be happy without that.

Layton continues, "All these guys used to say I'd never get married because I love myself more than anyone else." Everyone laughs. "Well, a wise man once told me that you can tell how much you love yourself by the partner you choose." He takes a deep breath. "I guess I'm the bomb. I must love myself *a lot* 'cause my wife is the best there is."

There's a huge mix of laughter and *awws*. Arizona smiles giddily with tears in her eyes and pure happiness on her face.

Tears spill out of my eyes, not only for the joy of the love I'm witnessing but for the loss I'm about to sustain. What about Harper? I can't let her go. I love her like she's mine even though she never will be.

I try to blink away the tears. I need to set aside my own shit so that I can properly celebrate one of my best friends and her new husband.

Shortly after the ceremony, Layton and Arizona share their first dance to the first song they ever danced to, "Until I Found You." The way they stare at each other is like a dream.

My tears start back up again. They're such a magical couple.

As always, Tanner is keeping a distance from me in public. For some reason, it's bothering me more tonight than it usually does.

My friends and I dance the night away, having a blast, until a slow song begins. This is when all the couples pair off and I'm left alone.

My eyes catch Ezra's. Why can't I feel for him half of what I feel for Tanner? My life would be so much easier.

He takes two steps in my direction. Even though he has someone now, he's still putting my needs first. My heart warms for the kind of man he is.

Suddenly his movements stop, and his eyes glance behind me.

Before I can turn, I feel a warm hand on my arm. It gives me shivers. I'd know that touch anywhere. Tanner.

With our bodies close, I turn and look up at him. "People will talk."

He runs his fingertips up and down my arm and breathes, "What people? No one else is here."

I'm processing what he's saying when he jerks my body tight to his. I nearly gasp at the surprise move before giving in by leaning into him and moving my hands to the nape of his neck.

With his big hands on my waist, his lips move to my neck, peppering it with kisses.

I'm dumbfounded. "What's gotten into you tonight?"

He audibly inhales me. "It's me who will be getting into you. In fact, let's get out of here and start that process now. I'm feeling particularly insatiable."

I let out a laugh. "I'm not leaving. It's too early. She's one of my best friends."

He lifts his head and furrows his brow. "And what am I?"

Without any hesitation, I answer, "My fuck buddy. You're supposed to be my *secret* fuck buddy, but you're not doing a good job of hiding it tonight."

He shrugs. "Half the people here know anyway."

"And the other half?"

"I don't care."

What is happening? I pull his head away from my neck until our eyes meet. I'm so confused.

Before we can continue the conversation, the song ends and Kam pulls my arm, likely realizing I need a rescue. "We're doing shots." She narrows her eyes at Tanner. "Get lost. Act like she doesn't exist, per normal." She hasn't remotely thawed to him in the past few months.

We make our way toward the bar. She grits out, "You need to end things with him. You're in too deep."

I nod. "I know. You're right."

She stops short. "Excuse me? Say that into my good ear."

"You're right. It's time. We have different plans for our futures, and I can't find what I need while I'm still doing what I'm doing with him. I want one more night with him. We've spent a year together. I need tonight. I'm going to break things off tomorrow."

"I think you should quit your job with him. You can still be in Harper's life. Maybe even coach her team, but being in his house a few days a week isn't best for you."

"We'll discuss it. Perhaps we can keep things professional."

"No, you can't. I know you adore her, but you can't be in his house and see him, expecting to keep things platonic. You're in way too deep for that."

"We'll see." I grab her arm. "Come on. Everyone is waiting."

We get to the bar area where our team stands with a line of blow job shots ready for us. One of our teammates giggles. "This isn't even my first BJ of the evening. I gave one to Greg on the way here."

Kam smiles. "Nothing beats a good old-fashioned car BJ. It's like a contest to see if you can make him lose control."

Hmm. That's not the first time car blow jobs have been mentioned today. I've never given one in a car while it's moving.

I END up having the best night. We drink and dance all night celebrating Layton and Arizona.

The second they wave goodbye to all of us, Tanner grabs me. "Let's get out of here."

I step back. "Seriously, what's gotten into you tonight?" He must be horny, drunk, or both. "You're acting weird. Have you been drinking?"

He assures me that he hasn't and is just missing me.

Missing me? "It's been four days." We had sex earlier this week before the wedding festivities began.

PAYOFF PITCH

He exhales a long breath and looks around as if in contemplation before grabbing my face and kissing me. Hard. He's never once kissed me in public and here we are doing it in the lobby of one of the fanciest hotels in Philadelphia.

And it's no sweet, ordinary kiss. His demanding tongue forces its way into my mouth. Because I can't help myself, I pull him close and kiss him right back. I'm going to miss this. Him. I want to savor every last moment.

He eventually pulls away, leaving me breathless. I'm so powerless against him when he's all domineering. I nod my head. "Okay, let's go. Now."

I lick his delicious taste off my lips. His eyes follow my tongue and his already hard dick visibly twitches in his pants. I can only shake my head. "You're thinking about me sucking your duck, aren't you?"

He gives me a sexy smile. "Why do you know that?"

"Because you're a filthy man, *Mr. Montgomery.*"

The bulge in his pants further intensifies. It drives him wild when I call him that. If I called him Daddy right now, I think he'd pull me into a closet and fuck me senseless.

He removes his jacket and places it in front of his pants, hiding his massive erection. I'm aching for that erection to be inside me. To fill me one more time.

I'm contemplating calling him Daddy when the valet pulls up in Tanner's new car.

The valet fawns all over it as he hands Tanner the keys. But then the man practically eye-fucks me.

Tanner isn't happy about it and lets him know, growling at him like a caveman pissing around his territory. I've never seen this territorial side of him. Yes, he's jealous of my friendship with Champ, but he's never done anything to Champ to let on. Not like what I'm seeing right now.

The valet apologizes and scurries off. Tanner opens the car door for me while I place my hands on my hips. "Was that necessary?"

He scowls. "Yes, it was. I didn't like the way he was looking at you."

"And how was that?"

"Like he wants to fuck you."

I can't help but give a big, exaggerated smile. "You look at me like that all the time," though usually only in private.

He confidentially nods. "And I want to fuck you all the time."

I let out a laugh as we both get into the car.

We joke around for a few minutes, and I poke him about his age. He shakes his head. "You're not being very nice to me, sweet girl."

I look over at the gorgeous man driving an expensive sports car. The whole scene is hot, and I'm feeling inspired by my earlier conversations with my friends.

I bite my lip. "Maybe I don't feel like being so sweet tonight."

I move my hand to his lap and feel the thick muscles of his thigh. There's nothing I love more than the sight of him naked with me tied up as he uses those thick thighs to drive himself in and out of me.

I'm so wet right now. I'm aching for him.

I move my hand up to his dick. It's still hard. I can practically feel it between my legs.

Feeling inspired and wanting this last night to be everything, I unbuckle my seatbelt and lower my head to his lap, kissing his dick through his pants before unzipping him and pulling out his length.

He stutters, "W...what are you doing?"

I stroke him while licking his tip. "I'm here to service you, Mr. Montgomery."

I take my sweet time to give him the best blow job of his life. He's always the one in control in the theoretical bedroom, but tonight he's bordering on losing control. It feels good to make him come undone this way.

It's always been him fucking my mouth, but right now it's me sucking in his cock until it hits the back of my throat. I can't help but moan at the satisfaction I'm feeling. If he slid his hand up my dress right now, he'd easily discover just how turned on I am.

In what may be the record for how quickly he's come, it takes only a few minutes before his warm seed fills my mouth and I swallow it all down.

I think I need to touch myself before we get to his house. I'm so on edge.

Given how low his car is, I don't want anyone to see him when I pull away. I quickly tuck him back into his pants before lifting my head. His eyes are glazed over as he stares at my swollen lips.

As soon as my head is up, I see that we're about to slam into the car in front of us. I scream, "Watch out!" before the world goes dark.

DARKNESS. I can't see anything. I can't feel anything. But I hear Tanner's voice telling me to wake up.

Despite the pounding in my head, I manage to blink my eyes a few times. Realizing I'm snuggled into Tanner's lap, I croak out, "What happened?"

He frantically moves his hands all over my body like he's checking it for damage. Worry is written all over his face. "We crashed. Are you okay?"

Pound. Pound. Pound. I must have hit my head. It feels like a heavy metal band is playing the drums in there.

"My head hurts, but I think I'm okay." I gingerly look around and see what's become of Tanner's new car. It's wrecked, and I start to get hysterical. "I'm so sorry, Tanner. This is my fault."

He squeezes me and rubs my hair. "No, it's not."

He keeps asking if I'm okay. I feel like I'm going in and out of consciousness, but I'm trying to be present.

Suddenly there's a loud bang at the window. It makes my head hurt all the more. Stop the banging. Please.

I think it's a police officer. He's asking Tanner a bunch of questions. I don't hear much with the ringing in my ears, but I do hear him ask, "How did this happen?"

Tanner can't bite back his smile as he whispers to me, "Do you want to show him?"

If I wasn't feeling like death, I'd laugh. Or maybe slap him.

He goes on to tell the officer about swerving to miss a car, after which the officer asks him to reach behind me and turn off the ignition.

Tanner attempts to do so, but because of the damage to the car and me on his lap, he can't reach it and asks me to do so.

That's when I realize just how bad this is. My top half is wracked with pain, but my bottom half feels nothing. Absolutely nothing.

"Tanner, I…I can't feel my legs."

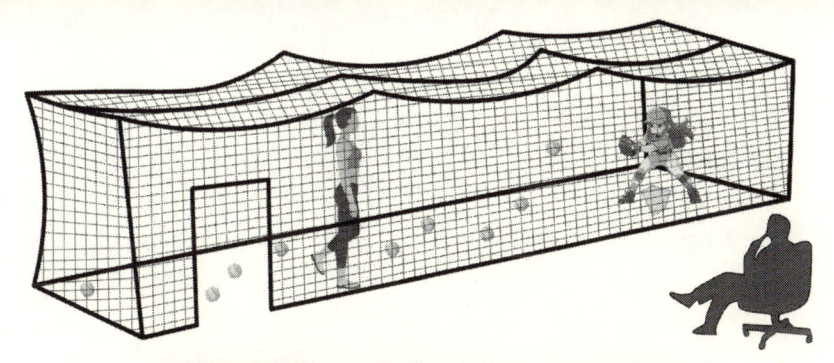

CHAPTER TWENTY-SEVEN

TANNER

The next ten minutes are probably the worst of my life as a fear I've never before known sets in. The policeman first instructs me to keep her immobilized until the medics can arrive and properly move her.

Tears leak from her eyes, and she's shaking, but she otherwise says nothing. I think she's in shock. I do my best to reassure her when I'm anything but confident right now.

I whisper reassurances in her ear, reassurances that I don't know to be true but know she needs to hear.

The ambulance finally arrives. They immediately immobilize her neck with a brace. It takes a little time, but they eventually carefully transfer her from the car onto a boarded stretcher.

At this point, I have blood dripping from my head, but that's the least of my concerns. They want to put me on a stretcher too, but I refuse. They want to put me in my own ambulance. Again, I refuse.

"Sir, we need to check you out."

"I'll be in the ambulance with Bailey. You can check me

in there if you must, but that woman is going nowhere without me."

I grab her purse from the car before finally exiting the vehicle. My legs are wobbly, but I do my best to muscle through.

Shit, I might be concussed, but I don't want to let on. I don't want her to be alone.

I step onto the ambulance and end up sitting above her head so they can do whatever they need to do for her. They won't let me take her hand. I gently rub her hair and face as space permits, praying to god that she's okay.

She eventually whimpers, "Call Kam. I need her. Tell her not to tell Arizona. I don't want to ruin her honeymoon."

The cell phone in her bag starts ringing, and I pull it out. It's Kamryn, so I answer. "Hello, Kamryn."

"Something happened to my sister. I can feel it. Is she with you?"

"Yes. We've been in a car accident. She's conscious but hurt. She...she can't feel her legs. We're in the ambulance. Meet us at Philly Hospital. She doesn't want you to tell Arizona."

"I swear to god, Montgomery, if this is as bad as it sounds, I will kill you with my bare hands."

There are mumbled sounds of Kam and Cheetah arguing before I hear Cheetah's voice on the phone. "Sorry man. She's hysterical. Just worried about her sister. We're on our way. Text me a room number when you get one."

"I will."

As soon as we arrive at the hospital, there must be thirty staff members waiting for us. What the hell?

They carefully remove her from the ambulance and set her on a gurney, wheeling her inside. I'm trying to keep up, but my vision is getting a little blurred. My legs are having trouble walking a straight line.

A tall blond man about my age approaches me. "Tanner Montgomery?"

"Yes."

"My name is Brody Cooper. I'm the chief of the neurosurgery department, specializing in spinal injuries. Reagan Daulton is my sister-in-law. She seemed to know you were coming in and called ahead demanding we do everything we can for Bailey."

I'm starting to see spots, and he grabs my arm. He instructs, "Linda, grab a wheelchair. Tanner, did you hit your head?"

"I...I don't know. Maybe."

He carefully helps me sit in the wheelchair before applying a soft item to the throbbing section of my head. He then flashes something in my eyes.

"Tanner, your head is bleeding and your pupils are blown. We need to get you a head CT to make sure there's no internal bleeding."

I slur, "No. I'm staying with Bailey."

"She needs to get her imaging too. You're not allowed in there with her. I'll tell you what. You get the CT, and then I'll have the nurse drop you in Bailey's room. Technically you're not allowed in because you're not family, but if you cooperate, I'll get you in."

I feel like I'm falling asleep, desperate to keep my eyes open but losing the battle. I simply nod, unable to do anything else before everything goes dark.

I'M AWAKENED to the beeping sounds of a hospital. I look around and see that I'm in a hospital bed with machines hooked up to my body. The room is dark, only slightly illuminated by the lights of the hallway.

My head is throbbing, and it takes a bit for my eyes to gain focus.

As soon as they do, I see Fallon sitting at my bedside with red-rimmed eyes. I croak out, "Where's Bailey?"

Her eyes meet mine. "You're awake. Let me call the nurse."

She presses a button over my head.

Again, I ask, "Where's Bailey?"

I hear a different voice. "She's in surgery, you motherfucker." I gingerly turn my head and see Kamryn. She's hugging her knees in an empty bed next to mine, looking like she's been crying for hours. Cheetah, Ripley, and Quincy are sitting in chairs by that bed. "How did you crash your car? Why wasn't she wearing a seatbelt? She *never* goes without wearing a seatbelt. She fucking yells at me about it all the time." She begins rocking back and forth and getting more hysterical. "How did you let this happen to her? It should be you in there, not her."

Fallon bites out, "Enough, Kamryn. It was an accident. He's injured too. Give him a minute. Why are you so fucking accusatory? Do you honestly think he did this on purpose?"

"But he—"

"I've sat here for two hours listening to you bash him. E-fucking-nough. Just shut your mouth. I can't listen to you bitch and whine anymore. It doesn't help anyone, especially Bailey."

I catch Ripley, Quincy, and Cheetah all trying to hide their smiles. They all stand. Ripley grabs Kamryn's hand. "She won't be out for a little while. Let's grab a snack. We'll give Fallon a chance to catch Tanner up on everything." She then looks at Fallon. "Do you want anything?"

Fallon shakes her head, no, but I mumble, "Get her a Snickers bar."

They all walk out, leaving me alone with Fallon. She

looks at me. "I need you to tell me the truth right now. Were you drinking? Don't lie. They took your blood. The truth will come out regardless, and if it's worst-case scenario, we need to call a lawyer and get ahead of it."

I try to swallow away the dryness in my throat before gently shaking my head. "I had two drinks hours ago, before the ceremony. There is zero chance I was above the legal limit. I swear to you. I've cut back on my drinking significantly this year."

She nods, looking relieved. "Thank god for small miracles." She takes my hand in hers. "You have a bad concussion. You need to rest, but you'll be okay. There's no brain bleed or anything along those lines. You're lucky because you apparently hit your head pretty hard. Hard-headed bastard."

"And Bailey?"

She blows out a breath. "The doctor will explain it better, but if she had to fracture anything in her spine, it's the best-case scenario."

My heart sinks. "Oh god. Her back is broken?"

"Yes, but it's not as bad as you're thinking. In layman's terms, it's the spot on the highest part of her lower back." She shows me on her body exactly where it is. "It will be a long process, but she'll recover enough to live a normal life. I'm not sure about playing ball though. There's a big difference between being a functional person and being a professional athlete. Her surgery is tomorrow. Well, today, but you know what I mean."

"I thought she's in surgery now?"

She pinches her lips together. "She also had some internal bleeding, and they discovered something else. She'll...umm...she'll probably lose an ovary."

Tears fill my eyes, and I cover my mouth.

"Kam gave them permission to salvage as many eggs as they can from the ovary being removed. She's not infertile.

Don't freak out. Plenty of women have children with one working ovary."

Before she can continue, a nurse walks in. "I see you're awake, Mr. Montgomery."

I can only whisper, "I am." I almost wish I wasn't.

"I don't want to shine light in your eyes, but can you look at me?"

I do. She's in my face, manipulating it for a few seconds before she smiles. "Your pupils look much better. Stay off your phone. No televisions, computer screens, or any other bright lights for the time being. Bright light will bother you for a few days. The doctor will come by in the morning with your discharge information and explicit instructions about how to manage your concussion."

I nod. "Thank you."

She walks out, and I turn back to Fallon. "What will Bailey's recovery look like?"

"Put simply, she's going to have back surgery. She'll need a few screws. It will take a little time, but she should make a full recovery. Spinal injuries aren't black and white, and you never know what they'll find when they're in there, but her prognosis is a good one. Probably as good as it could have been given that she broke her back and lost feeling in her legs. We could very easily be having a different conversation right now. She'll need to stay here for about two weeks but will start physical therapy and occupational therapy right away. Within a day or two of the surgery. She's going to need a lot of PT and probably a good amount of OT for a long time. There are rehab facilities equipped for all that. I can get you some names. She'll need to stay at one for at least three months and, if things are going well, then she'll be able to do outpatient therapy."

"No, I'm not dropping her at some random hospital. I want you to help her."

"We don't have all the equipment needed in this hospital. That's not exactly what we do here."

"You have my credit card. Use it."

"We're talking about hundreds of thousands of dollars in equipment. Maybe more."

"Do I look like I care about the costs? Buy her whatever she needs to get better."

"She can't stay here, and she shouldn't be transported back and forth. That could be dangerous for her. These facilities are all in-patient. That's what she needs."

"Renovate my home gym with every piece of equipment she needs. You'll both move in."

She sighs. "I'm not moving in with you. If you insist on doing this at home, I can find you someone to help her."

"No. You're the only person I trust with her."

"I have a job."

"I'll double your salary."

"Tan—"

"Please. I'm begging you. You. I only want you to help her."

Her eyes fill with tears, and she kisses my hand. "Give me a minute. It's been a long night. When I got the call, I thought I lost you." She begins sobbing. "From the airport until I arrived, I didn't know anything other than you wrapped your car around a pole."

I squeeze her hand. "I'm fine. I had my seatbelt on."

"Thank god for that. Why didn't she?"

I look away. "You don't want to know the answer to that."

"Oh cheez. Kamryn might cut off your manhood when she finds out. That kid is a fucking handful. She and Bailey are night and day."

"That's the understatement of the year."

"I texted Cassandra and Trevor. Your accident is all over the news and social media. I asked them to keep things away from Harper. I'll pick her up in the morning and explain everything. She's obviously going to be distraught."

"I'm glad you thought to text them. Bring her here so she can see that I'm okay. I have no idea what Bailey will and won't be up for." I look around. "What time is it?"

"It's four in the morning. Reagan Daulton called every member of the hospital board. There are probably fifty doctors treating Bailey right now. I'm not sure I've ever seen anything like it. She was here earlier but had to get home to her son. She knew Bailey wouldn't be out for hours. She said she'll be back in the morning."

"She'll offer her resources to help get whatever equipment we need as quickly as possible."

"What makes you say that?"

"That's just the way she is. And she happens to adore Bailey, though I think she'd do it for anyone who plays for her. Please do whatever is needed and coordinate with Reagan. Shannon can help, but you know better than anyone. The home gym is big. Do you think we can fit everything she needs?"

"This is crazy. We don't need to decide anything right this minute. No matter where she ends up, she'll start her therapy here."

"I'm not kidding, Fallon. The nurse said no phone. I need you. Get things rolling on the equipment. Pay whatever is needed to get it as quickly as possible. Tell Shannon to call my housekeepers and have them make up three guestrooms."

"Three?"

"Do you think there's a chance in hell that Kamryn isn't moving in too? I don't have it in me to fight her. Bailey will need her anyway."

"To be clear, you're asking me to move in with you, my ex-husband, so I can help our daughter's nanny, who's your lover, and I need to take a leave of absence from a job that I love? Add in the fact that your lover's batshit crazy sister will also be there. Oh, and I have to handle all the logistics because you're not allowed on the phone or a computer right now?"

I can't help but smile at the complete and total absurdity of it all. "Correct."

She smiles in return. "Like I've said before. Weirdest. Divorce. Ever."

BAILEY

I awaken in a hospital bed. There are wires and tubes coming out of my entire body. Every inch of me aches. My mouth feels like I swallowed a bag of cotton. A bag of cotton that a skunk slept on.

I see Kam asleep on Cheetah's shoulder. I can only manage a whisper. "Kam."

Her eyes pop open, and she sits up straight, immediately taking my hand in hers. In a soft voice, she asks, "Hey. How are you feeling?"

"Like the morning after you made me take twenty-one shots on our twenty-first birthday."

She smiles. "That was a fun night."

"But a terrible morning after."

"Hmm. Possibly." She reaches up and presses a button above my head. "They said to ring when you're awake. By the way, your surgeon was so hot. Like he belongs on *Grey's Anatomy* hot. McSteamy-level."

I sigh. "How thrilling." I smack my lips together. "I think something died in my mouth."

She leans forward and takes a few sniffs before scrunching her face. "Ooh. I'm not sure whether to get you a mint or toilet paper for that situation."

Cheetah lets out a laugh. I roll my eyes. "Water. I need water."

She fills a cup for me and helps me drink water through a straw. Several cups. I think I down about two gallons.

I move my tongue around, desperately trying to get some saliva in there.

After finally feeling a bit more hydrated, my memories start to come back. Memories of being unable to feel my legs. "Am I going to walk again?"

Her face falls. "You don't remember talking to the doctor last night?"

"No. I know they said something about two surgeries. I was in and out. I don't remember much else."

The door opens. Tanner walks in with the man I'm assuming is the doctor since he is, in fact, extremely attractive. As if it matters. He's also in a white coat. Tanner has a bandage around his head and is wearing sunglasses.

The doctor smiles. "Hello, Bailey. How are you feeling?"

"Like I was in a car accident."

He nods. "I have no doubt."

Tanner walks over. He takes my other hand and kisses it. "I'm going to take care of you. I promise. Everything is going to be okay."

Kam scoffs. "You already failed at taking care of her. I still want to know why she wasn't wearing a seatbelt."

The doctor interrupts, "Bailey, I'm Dr. Cooper. As your friends and family know, Reagan Daulton is my sister-in-law."

"Oh. I met your wife. She works with Reagan."

"That's their other sister, Skylar. My wife works at this hospital."

Kam's phone pings. She looks down. "Shit. It's Arizona. They just landed and saw the news. They want to fly home."

I attempt to shake my head but can't seem to move very well. "No. They're on the other side of the world. Tell her they're not allowing visitors or something along those lines. They need to go enjoy their honeymoon. There's nothing they can do for me right now."

Cheetah stands. "I'll call them. Ripley and Quincy were here all night. They needed to get home to Kaya but asked that I call when you're awake. I'm gonna step out. I'm happy to see you awake, Bails."

He looks exhausted, but I know my sister probably needed him. I can only imagine how she was behaving. "Thanks for being here."

He nods, knowing exactly what I mean by that.

I look back at the doctor. "Tell me everything."

"You sustained an abdominal injury. That was your first surgery. It was determined that your right ovary was beyond repair, and it had to be removed."

Tears immediately fill my eyes. Kam squeezes my hand. "They think you'll still be able to have kids. As a precaution, I had them harvest every available egg in the ovary before they removed it. Don't stress. I'll have the fucking kid for you if you have any problems. I promise you'll be a mother one day."

I nod, unable to form words. I notice tears streaming down from underneath Tanner's sunglasses.

Dr. Cooper nods his head. "She's right. Many women still get pregnant with one ovary. Though that's not my specialty. I can have someone come talk to you more about that. As for your spine, you suffered a thoracolumbar junction L1 unstable burst fracture. It's in your mid-back just below your ribs. You've got a drain in there now that we'll remove in a few days. You had what we call a spinal decompression laminectomy with stabilization using pedicle screws at T11 and L3. In layman's terms, we fixed what was broken. From my perspective, the surgery was a success. I'm going to check a few things. Don't freak out if you still don't have feeling in your lower body. The anesthesia hasn't completely worn off yet, and some residual swelling could still be pressing on your nerves."

He lifts my blankets and runs a device over my feet and legs.

Fortunately, I'm able to feel all of it. I can't move my legs much, but I feel everything he's doing, and Dr. Cooper seems thrilled with that.

He smiles. "That's great, Bailey. Already ahead of the class. Either later today or tomorrow morning we'll get you going on PT and OT. You're going to stay with us for a bit. About two weeks. And then we'll find you an appropriate in-patient rehab facility where I'm guessing you'll spend three or four months before you'll be able to switch to outpatient."

Tanner interrupts. "I've made other arrangements for her."

I turn to him in question. He nods. "We'll talk about it in a minute."

Dr. Cooper continues, "Spinal injuries aren't full of certainties. I can't make you promises, but I have no reason to think you won't make a full recovery. The harder you work, the quicker your recovery will be. I wholeheartedly believe that you'll be able to live a normal life doing normal things."

"And softball?"

His face falls just a drop. "With these injuries, there's always the risk of something being a little off. A finger that doesn't work properly. A toe. Or worse. Being a professional athlete is so much more than being able to function in daily activities. If you work hard, I think it's possible." He briefly pauses. "What I should say is that it's not impossible."

Kam scoffs. "You don't know my sister. She's the strongest person I know. She'll be wearing a gold medal around her neck in three years. I can promise you that."

He nods and gives a small smile. "I look forward to watching it happen. I need to go make my rounds. I'll check on you a little later."

"Thanks, Dr. Cooper."

"You're very welcome. You have an amazing support system. There are a lot of people who care about you. Don't be afraid to lean on them. You're going to need them for the next few months."

"I understand. Thank you."

As soon as he leaves, the tears break free. Kam grabs my face so we're eye to eye. "Don't cry. I meant every word. You're the strongest person I know. We'll get through this. I'll be with you every second of every day."

I let out a laugh through my tears. "I'll physically recover and then be institutionalized from spending too much time with you."

She smiles through her own tears. "Every damn day until you're back to your perfect self. You jump, I jump."

I attempt to nod but have never felt more terrified in my life.

Kam notices and takes my hand. "It could be worse."

"Does it really get worse than this?"

She gives me her special smile. "You could have dementia and diarrhea. Imagine starting to run to the bathroom and then forgetting where you're going."

How could I possibly not laugh at that? I lost an ovary, I don't know if I can have kids, I broke my back, I don't know if I'll ever walk properly again, but my sister just managed to make me laugh. I love her so much.

She kisses my cheek and whispers, "Unbreakable Harts. We've got this, big sis."

I nod before I turn to Tanner. "You mentioned arrangements. Did you find a hospital that allows crazy sisters to stay too?"

He kisses my hand again. The same hand he hasn't let go of since he walked in. "I'm having all the necessary equipment delivered to my house as we speak. Reagan Daulton called in some favors, and everything is being expedited. You'll stay with me. Fallon is going to move in and give you everything you need."

I pinch my eyebrows. "You bought all the equipment?"

He nods.

"And Fallon agreed to this?"

He nods again.

"What about her job? Her life?"

He squeezes my hand. "We're all here for you, baby. We're

going to get you through this together. You'll be stronger than ever."

Kam clears her throat, and he lifts his head to her. "I've already had a room made up for you too."

I shake my head. "This is too much, Tanner. I can't ask this of you."

"You didn't ask. And it's already done."

Kam wiggles her eyebrows. "Looks like we're having a slumber party at Daddy Tanner's house."

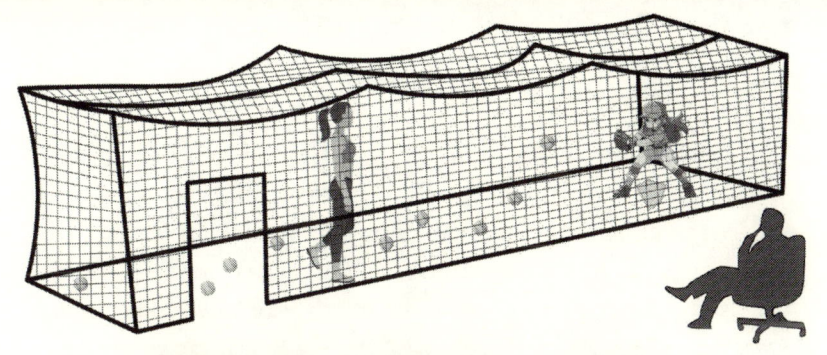

CHAPTER TWENTY-EIGHT

BAILEY

The past few weeks have been difficult. I'm frustrated with my progress, even though Fallon and the doctors tell me I'm doing remarkably well and ahead of where they expected me to be at this point.

Kam and Tanner are at each other's throats. It's like a pissing contest between them as to who can do more for me. They're both driving me nuts even more than they're driving each other nuts.

I'm trying my best to shelve my emotions over the lost ovary and the fear of what it could mean for my future. They had a specialist come in and explain everything to me. She said as long as my other ovary is healthy, they have no reason to think I'll have any problems becoming pregnant when the time comes. They did an ultrasound to confirm the health of my remaining ovary, and the doctor was optimistic. Kam has repeated a thousand times her willingness to carry for me if needed, but I know she doesn't want that. She's always been adamant that she doesn't want to ever be pregnant or have kids. I don't know that I could ever ask that of her.

My future fertility is the least of my concerns right now. Walking and functioning independently is my sole focus. Needing help from others for every little thing is so damn frustrating.

Arizona and Layton canceled their honeymoon and came right home. I cried my eyes out when they walked in. I hate that it was ruined for them, but she said there was no way they would have been able to enjoy themselves knowing what I was dealing with. They promised to take a real honeymoon when I'm able to walk them to their gate at the airport.

Kam, Arizona, and Ripley spent all day, every day with me at the hospital. I feel both loved and like a burden. The hospital suggested I talk to someone given how this type of injury can take its toll on your mental health. I've been talking to a psychologist almost every day. It helps.

Even with a full-time job and a little one at home, Gemma stopped by the hospital every few days. Since I already read all her books, she brought me signed copies of books from her author besties, Libby Cox, Bella Valentino, and J. Estes. They all even made me several hysterically funny get-well videos.

My happiest moments at the hospital each day were when Harper came to visit after school. She stayed through dinner. I loved having dinner with her every night. She's what I needed to push through during my darkest moments full of self-loathing and fear.

Fallon has been nothing short of a godsend. She's pushing me on the physical front, she plays referee between Tanner and Kam, and she seems to have the best understanding of what I'm going through. It makes sense considering what she does for a living.

The Camels are in season, but Champ comes to as many of my physical therapy sessions as he can. He and Ezra are the positive cheerleaders that I need. Tanner gets crazy jealous when they're with me. His over-the-top reaction is honestly the humor I need at times.

My father and Ray visited for a bit. Dad offered to move here to help out, but I know he can't really afford to be away from work that long, so I told him I'm fine and already have more help than I can handle. He calls every single day to check in on me.

We're finally out of the hospital and back at Tanner's house. It feels like a million people are living here. There are two guest rooms on the first floor. That's where Kam and I sleep.

Fallon is in the upstairs guest room next to Harper's room. Tanner's home gym is completely unrecognizable from before the accident. It must rival the nicest therapy facilities in the world. I can't imagine what it cost him, and he won't talk about it. He simply says that he and Reagan together made sure I'd be given every opportunity to succeed as soon as possible.

The news outlets have all speculated as to what Tanner and I were doing in the same car, but Reagan issued a statement that he was giving me a ride home after I had too much to drink. Fortunately for Tanner, his blood alcohol level was below the legal limit, so there are no issues there. He and I both know the real reason we got into an accident. Kam went ballistic when she found out, and somehow Fallon knows, but that's it. No one else. It was below freezing temperatures that night and people assume we slipped on ice.

I've been feeling crowded, so I begged Tanner to go to his office in the mornings. That's when I do most of my physical therapy. I don't need him then. Fallon is obviously with me, Kam doesn't leave my side, Arizona and Ripley are usually here, Champ comes when he can, and Cheetah, Layton, Quincy, and Ezra always manage to pop in and out. I need at least one person out of the house, so Tanner isn't here for my PT anymore. And being around him is hard. I was a minute away from ending things, and now all of a sudden, I'm living in his house being catered to every single minute. I need breathing room.

"That's it, Bailey. Five more steps and then we're done," Fallon encourages.

Most of my weight is on the bars next to me, but each day I'm able to put a little more on my legs.

I'm exhausted. Who would have ever thought that walking would be so damn tiring?

For some reason, I don't feel much progress today. I'm frustrated and it's showing. My cheerleading squad is yelling for me, trying to encourage me, but it's a struggle. I want to tell them all to shut up, but I won't. I know they're doing this because they care.

With sweat covering my face and body, I make it the last five steps, and they all jump up and down like we just won the championship game. I equal parts appreciate it and find it condescending. I feel like a toddler taking his first steps with his mom and dad standing there cheering.

Kam takes me to shower while everyone else prepares lunch for us. Yes, my sister has to help me shower. Actually, it's one of the things she and Tanner fight most about. I've threatened to have Champ or Ezra shower me if he doesn't chill out with Kam. That usually gets him to back off.

I have a shower chair that is the bane of my existence. It symbolizes my need for help to do something as simple as cleaning myself. I will cheer the day I can throw that piece of shit out the window. I swear my body has a visceral reaction every time I see it taunting me. I think I'll have nightmares about it for the rest of my life.

We're all having lunch together. They're yapping, and I'm quiet. I feel like today is the first day that I didn't experience any real progress, and I'm frustrated.

Kam notices. She grabs my hand. "Are you okay?"

I shrug. "It was a tough day. I have nothing to show for it."

She nods in understanding. "Tomorrow is a new one. Tomorrow will be better."

I shake my head as tears fill my eyes. "I'm already sick of this shit. I want to run away, but I can't run. I want to throw everything against the wall, but I can't even throw properly. I need a fucking straw in my cup because I can't hold a damn glass of water."

Her face tightens. "Being negative isn't the Bailey Hart I know. Don't be a Karen. Don't be the person who complains when you order a Diet Coke and the restaurant only carries Diet Pepsi. I hate those people. It fucking tastes the same."

I start laughing. Hysterically laughing. My sister can make anyone smile. It's her gift in life.

She leans back in her chair in satisfaction knowing she made me smile. "Bails, you know what attracted me to the sport of softball?"

I shrug. "Because you look cute in the tight pants?"

She lets out a laugh. "Ha. It's true. My ass looks amazing in those pants. I don't know why you played basketball. Is there anything more unflattering for a woman than a basketball uniform? Baggy long shorts and an oversized tank top? Whoever designed that combo is a moron. At least tennis, field hockey, and lacrosse have cute skirts. Equestrians all look super-hot in those tight pants. But basketball, ugh."

Arizona shakes her head in disgust. "I think you just set feminism back fifty years."

"Maybe, but I'm not wrong." She turns back to me. "I'm being serious. Why do you think I chose softball?"

I shrug. "I don't know."

"Because it's the best sport on the planet."

I roll my eyes.

"No, it is. In no other sport can you fail more than you succeed and still be considered successful. It's a sport of failure. It's how you respond to that failure that makes you great. What do you call a professional baseball player who only gets hits three out of every ten times he steps up to the plate?"

"What?"

"A fucking Hall of Famer."

I think about that for a moment. A .300 batting average is considered elite in professional baseball. She's right.

She nods her head. "Yep. He failed seven of ten times, and he's still one of the greatest and sits in the damn Hall of Fame. One of the best to ever play the game. It's been about twenty days since you started PT and you've been hitting it out of the park. You just had your first strikeout. Bails, you're batting, like, .950 right now. So you had an off day. So what? Failure is part of this. Tomorrow you'll succeed. I have no doubt about it."

Fallon smiles. "That's a really healthy way to look at it, Kamryn." Turning to me, she says, "Your sister is right." She winks. "Don't tell Tanner I said that. You've been moving at a statistically unheard of pace. There will always be plateau days. You've had a crazy run being this far in and it being your first hiccup. There will be more. Stay mentally tough. Tomorrow is a new day."

I nod. "You guys are both right. Thank you. I appreciate all your support. You all don't need to be here every day."

Ripley shakes her head. "There's nowhere else we'd rather be, Bails. If this happened to any of us, you'd be by our side every step of the way. We won't stop until you're Olympics ready. I don't play on teams that don't have Bailey Hart on them."

I blow out a breath. "I just want to walk again. I don't know if I'll ever play again, and I certainly don't know that I'll play at that level."

Arizona reaches over and takes my hand. "It's all four of us or none of us. So unless you want the three of us to sit out the Olympics, you better get your ass in gear, Hart."

I look at Ripley and Kam. They both nod in agreement.

I'm not sure whether I feel so entirely loved or feel like the pressure of the world is on my shoulders, but I do know that I don't want to let them down.

Everyone except Fallon and Kamryn eventually heads out for the day. I love having them here, but a little peace and quiet is welcome. I usually lay down in the afternoons given how hard I work in the mornings. Sometimes, I Zoom with the psychologist, but not today. She's out of the office.

I'm helped into my room. As it does every day, the desk and laptop area Tanner set up for me stare me right in the face. He suggested working on my books during my downtime. When I reminded him that I'm unable to type, he bought me some audio program that allows me to dictate. The words I speak supposedly then appear on the screen.

I can't bring myself to try it though. I'm not in the right headspace.

Fallon and Kam lay me down in the middle of the bed, and then they both plop down next to me. Kam and Fallon have gotten along extremely well, which is fortunate because both rarely leave my side. Fallon laughs at everything Kam says, and I think Kam is crushing on Fallon.

Fallon lays back with her hands behind her head, closes her eyes, and lets out a little moan. "Hmm. I can't tell you the last time I laid in bed during an afternoon. It's kind of nice."

Kam looks her up and down. "You're a full-fledged hottie. I'm into blonde women if you're ever looking to bat for the other team. Or, ya know, test the waters of the kitty pool. I'm an excellent guide."

Fallon opens her eyes and pinches her eyebrows together. "I thought you were with Cheetah."

"I'm an equal opportunity pleaser."

I turn my head to Fallon. "She's bi."

She asks me, "Are you bi too?"

Kam scoffs. "Nope. She's not into cranberry farming. She's only been having her oil checked by your ex-husband for the past year."

Fallon deadpans, "I'm aware. Thanks for the reminder, Kamryn."

"Why do you call me Kamryn? Everyone else calls me Kam."

"Tanner calls you Kamryn."

"That's because he hates me. It's how he depersonalizes me."

I roll my eyes. "Thanks, Dr. Phil. He doesn't hate you. He tolerates you. Kind of like I do."

She reaches over, about to tickle me, but stops herself. Fallon nods. "Careful. She's still healing. No twisting or sudden movements."

Kam sighs. "Then who's Tanner gonna have sex with? Bails is out of commission, and he doesn't like me. That just leaves you, Fallon."

Fallon lets out a laugh and shakes her head at Kam's antics. "You're a troublemaker, *Kam*. Tanner and I haven't had sex in about six years. I promise it's not happening now."

I scrunch my nose. "He must be a hard act to follow."

She blows out a long breath. "You have no idea."

Kam shakes her head. "You two have a fucking weird relationship."

Fallon and I both giggle.

Kam happily announces, "Well, Bailey will find out soon enough, right, Bails?"

I shake my head. "Don't start. Not now."

Fallon pinches her eyebrows together. "What does that mean?"

My shoulders fall. I don't know why Kam had to bring this up right now. "It's not like anything has or will ever change for Tanner and me. I want to get married and have kids one day, assuming I still can. He's been very clear that he doesn't want any of that. At some point, we'll have to part. I had been thinking about it a lot before the accident. As long as I'm spending time with him, my life is at a standstill. At some point, I need to put on my big girl pants and try to move on from him."

Fallon twists her lips. "You should have an honest conversation with him. Maybe everything isn't as set in stone as you think."

"What does that mean?"

"Talk to him. Do you love him?"

My eyes fill with tears. Kam answers. "Yes, she does."

Fallon bites her lips and nods. "When you're ready, talk to him."

I sigh. "I can't even have a normal conversation with him right now. He's treating me with kid gloves. It's driving me nuts. I know he'd say whatever he thinks I need to hear in the moment. I don't want his pity."

She shrugs. "Maybe sometime in the future then, but talk to him. Trust me, communication is key." She sits up and pats my leg. "You did a lot today. Probably more than you should have. You need to take a nap. *Kam* and I will leave you alone."

I whine, "Ugh. I feel like I'm eighty. I need a nap from trying to walk. Can we watch a movie? I promise to rest my body. I don't want to sleep all day though. It keeps me up at night, and then I can't shut off my mind from the negativity."

Fallon grabs the remote. "Sure. As long as you relax. What do you guys want to watch?"

At the same time, we both answer, "*Titanic*," and then giggle.

Fallon turns on the movie. She pulls me over her body a little. "I'll rub your shoulders. Your muscles are tight. They're being overworked."

I lay back on her and she begins rubbing them. "Hmm. This is nice."

Kam wiggles her eyebrows. "Can I get a turn too, Fallon?"

TANNER

Cheetah stands in the doorway of Bailey's room with his mouth wide open. "I'm going to jerk off to this image every day for the rest of my life. You're the luckiest man I've ever met."

Kam, Bailey, and Fallon are all asleep in Bailey's bed. The back of Bailey's head is on Fallon's chest with Fallon's arm wrapped protectively around her, and Kam is curled up with her head on Bailey's leg.

He elbows me. "At least you've slept with two of them.

I'm only at one. Do you think I've got a shot with Fallon? I might like to try an older woman."

I narrow my eyes at him, and he silently laughs, loving to bust my chops.

I see Kam stirring before her head lifts and she notices us. She sleepily stretches before quietly walking out of Bailey's room and closing the door behind her. "It's totally normal that your ex-wife and your girlfriend are cuddled together in bed."

Cheetah asks, "Should I go replace you in that cuddle sesh?"

Kam smiles. "You'll probably jerk off to the image of the three of us lying together."

Cheetah winks at me. Kam knows him well.

I ask, "How was today?"

She scrunches her face. "Probably her worst one yet. She was upset about it. We gave her a pep talk. I think she felt better afterward, but this isn't easy."

I exhale heavily, sad that she's going through this. "I wish she'd let me help more. She's shutting me out. I know we're in a weird place, but I want to be there for her."

"You two have been in a weird place for months."

"She's changed, and I don't mean since the accident. She was so sweet and loving our first time around. She became so much colder the second time."

Kam looks at me with pure venom. "At first, a woman treats you how she wants to be treated. After a certain amount of time, when she reaches her breaking point, she treats you how you treat her."

"I've always treated her well."

"Is that so? You lied to her for months and made her fall in love with you even though there was zero chance of a future."

"I told her from the very beginning what we were."

She rolls her eyes. "Don't bullshit a bullshitter. You

know what, Tanner? I've got a new word of the day for you. It's called acuntability. Taking accountability for being a cunt." She holds up her hand before I can respond. "I'm done with this conversation. You got something to say to my sister, say it to her. Don't treat her with kid gloves right now though. That's not what she wants or needs."

"I'm trying to help her."

"Then treat her like a normal person. That's what she needs. She hates all the pussyfooting around her."

I nod. Maybe she's right. I need to normalize things for her.

Cheetah looks her up and down. "You need to get out of this house for a few hours. Want to go out for dinner?"

She turns to me in question, and I nod. "You should go. I've got her. Fallon's here too."

She sighs. "Okay. I guess I could use a night out. Where do you want to go?"

He fiddles on his phone. "I just googled the best place to eat out and look what came up."

He holds up his phone to a picture of Kamryn.

She giggles. "Good one, kitten."

He twists his lips. "Hmm. Since it's your first night out in a while, I'll take you for fondue, the worst food on the planet."

"Bite your tongue. Fondue is the best food in the world." She quickly pecks his lips. "Thank you. We can even get the dessert to go. I'll let you eat the chocolate off me."

"Deal."

"I need to shower. I won't take too long."

Cheetah offers, "I need to shower too. We should save water and shower together. You can do my back, and I'll do your front."

She gives him her mischievous smile. "I like it in the front and back. Can you accommodate that request?"

"I believe I can."

She grabs his hand, and they head toward her bathroom. They have a bizarre relationship.

I make my way to the kitchen. Fallon appears a few minutes later, sleepily rubbing her eyes. I nod at her. "Hey. Kamryn said Bailey had a rough day."

She plops down in the chair by the kitchen island and yawns. "She did. Physical and emotional ups and downs are normal. Unfortunately, she had a down day on both fronts. As crazy as she can be, Kamryn is very good with her. She makes her laugh and keeps things in perspective. She doesn't let Bailey get away with a pity party. I know you two butt heads, but she's been there for Bailey every single second and always knows what she needs."

As I scoop ice cream into a bowl, I say, "She's...well-intended. She's just a lot to take. And why the fuck doesn't she sleep? She sits in here all night on her laptop."

I place the bowl of rum raisin ice cream in front of Fallon with a spoon, knowing she needs her afternoon sweet fix.

She smiles. "Thank you."

I nod.

She places a big spoonful of the ice cream into her mouth and mumbles, "I didn't realize that Kam is up all night. I'm usually zonked out after Harper goes to bed. What about you? Are you sleeping?"

"Not really. I've tried to get some alone time with Bailey, but she's been shutting me out. I don't want to push her right now."

"You need to tell her about the fact that you're willing to give her what she needs. I think she's emotionally distancing herself from you because she assumes you have no future."

"Until I know for sure, I won't say anything."

Harper walks in the front door, ending this conversation. Since the accident, the Windsors or Knights drive her home every day so we have one less thing to worry about. "Is Bails in her room?"

I open my arms in invitation. She rolls her eyes, gives me a short hug, and robotically says, "Hello, Dad."

I raise an eyebrow at Fallon, and she smiles before standing and pulling Harper into a hug. "Did you have a good day, sweetie?"

"Not really." Her shoulders fall. "I got into trouble. I wasn't allowed to go out to recess today."

Fallon and I exchange glances. Harper has never gotten into trouble before. I ask, "What happened?"

"I called Mrs. White an ignoramus."

Fallon and I do everything we can to bite back our smiles.

I gather myself first and ask, "Why did you call her that?"

She purses her little cherry-red lips. "Our music teacher was playing a song on the piano. Mrs. White was sitting in the circle with us. As the music began to fade away, the teacher asked if anyone knew what it was called when the music gets softer and softer. I raised my hand right away." I know exactly where this is going. "I said a smorzando." Yep, that was one of her toilet paper words of the day last week. "Mrs. White told me I was making up a word. I told her I wasn't. She immediately looked it up. She was embarrassed that I was right and told me to apologize for being disruptive to the class. I told her she should apologize for being an ignoramus." A word of the day a few months ago.

Fallon and I look at each other and burst into laughter. Harper scrunches her face. "It's not funny. I missed the kickball game. I've been practicing for that all month."

Fallon wraps her arm around Harper. "But you won the battle of wits with a sixty-year-old woman."

I raise an eyebrow, and Fallon corrects herself. "Harper, there will be times in life when you're significantly smarter than people in positions of authority. You have to respect them no matter what."

She crosses her little arms. "Kam says respect is earned and that most people are fuckwits who never earn it."

Fallon covers her smile with her hand. I pinch the bridge of my nose. I need to get Kamryn out of this house and away from my kid.

I take a deep breath. "Bailey is probably awake now. Why don't you grab the Monopoly set and see if she wants to play?"

Harper's frown quickly turns into a smile, and she runs to gather the Monopoly set before leaving to go to Bailey's room. I know spending time with Harper makes Bailey happy, so I try not to interrupt. Every day they end up playing games or cards until dinnertime when I help Bailey into the kitchen.

When dinner's over, Bailey always asks to go back to her room. She hangs with Kamryn and her friends until bedtime. I feel so helpless.

When Harper disappears, Fallon looks up at me with a spoonful of ice cream in her mouth. Her lips curl up as she admits, "Kam isn't wrong."

AFTER A FEW WEEKS of the same mundane routine, I decide that Bailey needs a fun night. We can't go out with all the press attention on her, and I don't know that she'd want to be seen in her wheelchair, so I invite everyone over for a big poker game full of good food, good drink, and hopefully a few laughs for her.

Just before everyone is set to arrive, Fallon stands there with her mouth widened. "You're letting girls play in your precious *boys-only* poker game? I never thought I'd see the day."

Kamryn smiles. "It's only because Bailey and I are the best poker players around. These dipshits don't stand a chance against us."

Fallon nods toward Bailey's room. "I don't know if she'll be able to hold the cards properly. Why don't she and I play as a team? I'll tell her that I want to learn how to play."

My face falls. "I never thought of that. Shit. I was trying to create a fun night for her."

Kamryn nods. "It's a good idea. She needs a normal, chill night with friends and laughs. I'll bring my A game, don't worry."

"Oh Christ. God help us all."

An hour later, my poker table is fuller than it's ever been. Everyone showed up tonight even with it being last minute. I'm so grateful to all of them.

I brought down a big chair for two for Fallon and Bailey to share. Cheetah motions toward the two of them with their heads huddled together and winks. He's deranged.

Harper played a few hands with Kamryn and then went to bed. She's actually getting quite good at it. As much of a pain in the ass as Kamryn is, she's highly intelligent and has taught Harper nearly every advanced card game.

We're all into a groove now, with Kamryn or Bailey winning every hand.

Kamryn asks, "Anyone watch that Menendez brothers miniseries?"

They're two privileged men who famously killed their parents more than thirty years ago. There have been several movies about them, but a new series has them back in the media spotlight.

Vance nods. "I watched it. They definitely did it."

Kam nods. "Without a doubt, but that's not what stands out to me. Did you know that both brothers have gotten married since they've been in jail? One of them even got divorced and remarried."

Daylen chuckles. "Seriously? Maybe it's for the conjugals."

Kamryn shakes her head. "They're not allowed conjugal visits. These are women who started letter-writing relationships with these murderers and then married them. I think one has been married for twenty-five years. I want a miniseries about these crazy bitches. That's more interesting than the actual case."

Daylen nods. "That's a valid point. I had an ex-girlfriend once who used to write guys in prison. I think it's a fetish."

Kamryn lifts an eyebrow. "She admitted that to you?"

Daylen shakes his head. "Nah, I read about it in her diary. Incidentally, she broke up with me because she said I didn't respect her privacy. Isn't that crazy?" He wiggles his eyebrows up and down with a small smirk.

Bailey starts giggling. It's music to my ears. I desperately want her to forget about her sorrows for a few hours.

Kamryn lays down cards on the table. It's a royal flush, the best hand in poker. She grabs the pile of chips in the middle with a big smile. "This is like taking candy from a baby. I can't believe you guys claim to be good poker players."

I honestly don't know how she does it. Every. Single. Time.

All the guys moan in malcontent. Trey mumbles, "I used to think I was smart."

Kamryn shakes her head. "Men are only smart during sex."

Cheetah nods in agreement. "Because our little heads are smarter than our big heads?"

"No, because it's the only time you're plugged into a genius."

Everyone laughs while Fallon looks at Kamryn. "Do you have a list of jokes on hand at all moments?"

Bailey nods. "Her mind is a wealth of useless information."

Daylen throws his arm around Kamryn. "Don't listen to them. In my heritage, it's considered a sign of greatness to make people laugh."

Heritage? He's from Maryland.

Kamryn turns to him. "What's your heritage?"

"My father is Welsh, and my mother is Hungarian. It makes me...well hung."

Kamryn bursts out laughing. "Oh shit, that's a good one."

Gemma starts typing on her phone. "I agree. I need to use that in a book."

Bailey smiles all night, and my heart warms. I look around the table and realize how many good friends I've accumulated throughout the past few years. I'm feeling very fortunate.

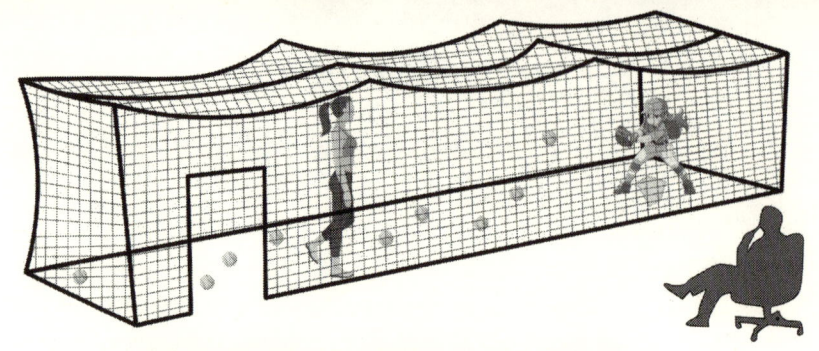

CHAPTER TWENTY-NINE

ONE MONTH LATER

TANNER

Bailey is doing much better. She can walk short distances without a cane but still needs one for longer distances. Fallon said she's worked harder than any patient she's ever seen. It doesn't surprise me at all.

While she's advancing quickly from a medical perspective, it's not fast enough for her. She overworks herself and still has moments of extreme frustration. She fell on her way back to her bedroom tonight but fortunately wasn't injured. She was upset about it, but Kamryn calmed her down.

As much as I want to strangle Kamryn at times, she truly is an amazing sister. She's completely devoted to Bailey's recovery, never missing a single moment. She cheers when Bailey needs cheering and pushes when Bailey needs pushing. She offers both soft and hard love, always seeming to know which is best in that given moment. There's a bond between the two of them that's hard to understand unless you see them in action.

It's made me think a bit about my own brother and how different our relationship is. I've never been able to truly connect with him. I always assumed it was due to our age difference of thirteen years, but seeing Kamryn and Bailey has made me realize it's more than that. Lincoln would never be here for me the way Kamryn has been here for Bailey. He's inherently selfish. He always has been. He's only met Harper twice, and that last time was years ago. I can't imagine a scenario where Kamryn wouldn't be a huge presence in the life of Bailey's children.

Bailey's children. Another thing I've been thinking about. I want so badly to give her that so we can be together, but first I need to break free from this coexisting zone we've settled into. I can't ever get her alone. I'm keeping my distance because it seems to be what she wants, but it's hard. What I want most right now is for her to recover, and if keeping me at arm's length for now helps, then so be it.

It's the middle of the night, and I can't sleep. I'm often awake at night contemplating my future with Bailey.

I tiptoe downstairs in a pair of athletic shorts and a T-shirt. I don't see Kamryn in the kitchen. Maybe the insomniac is finally sleeping. I've never met a person who sleeps so little.

I pour myself a whiskey but simply stare at the amber fluid. It's been a while. I've barely touched it since the accident. Only on the occasional night when everyone else is imbibing too.

I'm trying not to depend on it to get me to sleep like I used to. Bailey opened my eyes to the dangerous road I was headed down, but tonight I feel like I deserve one.

I continue to stare at it but can't seem to take the sip I'm craving, hearing Bailey's voice in my head. I've committed to only being a social drinker. *Alone in the middle of the night certainly doesn't qualify, Montgomery.* I squeeze my eyes shut and eventually pour the contents down the drain.

I'm considering braving the cold out back to have a cigar. I should be safe from the water gun brigade during the middle of the night. I need to run upstairs to get warmer clothes. I'm contemplating doing just that when I hear a cry coming from Bailey's room. I run down the hallway, rush into her room, and find her sweating and shaking. Her clothes are soaked.

"What's wrong?"

She breathlessly rubs her eyes. "I had a nightmare. And then I woke up and realized that reality is worse than the nightmare."

Her fists curl before she punches the bed and begins sobbing. My heart breaks for her.

I'm not sure if she wants my help, but I can't not go to her. I sit down on the bed and pull her up and into my arms. She lets me hold her as she cries into my chest. I'm realizing this is the first time I've truly held her since before the accident. It feels so nice. I desperately want to be the one to comfort her.

She mumbles into me, "Can...can you get Kam?"

I swallow down the lump in my throat. "Let me be here for you. I'll hold you until you fall back asleep."

She shakes her head. "I'm covered in sweat. I want to take a shower. Please get her. I'm sure she's walking around somewhere."

"I didn't see her. I think she's finally sleeping. She must need it. I'll help you."

She hesitates briefly before nodding.

I carry her into the bathroom, and together we remove her clothes. It's been so long since I've seen her body. I can't help but run my eyes up and down her perfect form. She's so beautiful.

PAYOFF PITCH

After doing my best to get her hair into a bun, I start to position her shower chair when she stops me. "I'm so fudging sick of showering in that damn chair. Can you...can you come in with me? Hold me so I don't have to sit in it? Make sure I don't fall again."

It feels like Christmas morning. "Of course I can. Whatever you need." I'm so freakin' happy she asked, I can barely contain myself.

I quickly strip, set out the towels, and we step into the shower together. Holding her naked body close to mine feels so fucking good I want to weep.

Her arms are wrapped around my waist and mine around her whole body. I can feel her relax into me with her head buried in my chest. We simply stand there and silently let the water beat down on us. It's our most intimate moment in nearly a year. We might have had plenty of sex in that timeframe, but nothing that felt this intimate. I want this with her. I need it. It feels like she needs it too.

Without moving her, I manage to squeeze a little of her body wash onto my hands and rub it over her back, shoulders, and anywhere I can reach without releasing my hold on her. The scent is strong and familiar. It's uniquely hers.

I hold her with one arm and, with the other, I rub it over her front. She doesn't flinch when my hands run over her breasts and through her legs.

She eventually lifts her head and looks me in the eyes. Even though her long lashes are covered in water, I can see tears in her eyes. She croaks out, "I miss you. I wish I didn't. I've been trying so hard to be strong. I want to let go of you, but I can't."

I brush back a few strands of hair that have fallen to her face and look her in the eyes. "What if I don't want you to let me go?"

Tears stream down her face. She looks so pained.

I want to kiss her but equally don't want to do anything to cause her to pull away.

After a brief stare down, she reaches back and turns off the water. "Take me to bed."

My shoulders fall. "If that's what you want." Reaching for the towels, I dry both of us before lifting her like a bride and carrying her to her bed, carefully lying her down.

I'm about to gather my clothes from the bathroom when she grabs my arm. "When I said *take me to bed*, I meant for you to stay."

I want to jump up and down in glee. I don't think I've ever been this happy in my life. I don't have any idea exactly what she wants, but anything that involves me being in the same bed as her works for me.

With a towel wrapped around my waist, I climb in next to her in bed. She reaches for the top of her towel and removes it. She then rolls toward me and opens my towel too.

I've been hard since the second she took off her clothes in the bathroom. It's not like she doesn't know, it's obvious, but now it's this big thing physically hanging between us.

She tentatively climbs up on top of me, straddling my lap. "I'm so sick of all the sadness. Of all the pain. Of all the emotions. I need you to make me feel something. Something happy. Something good."

"Whatever you need, sweet girl."

"What I need is to feel you inside me again. I've never been happier than when you and I were together like that... the first time around. That's my happy place. Take me there again. Even if it's just for one night."

I nod. "I promise to make you feel good. Do you need me to take over?"

She shakes her head. "I want to be in control. I need to take back some control in my life. It probably won't be very good for you. I need to go slow, and I'm not very mobile, but I want to be on top."

I can't help but smile. "I promise it will feel good for me. Anything where your body is on mine feels good. But I don't have a condom with me."

Her face is close to mine as she breathes, "I don't want one. You have no idea how much I need to feel you moving inside me. All of you."

I nod. "Do you need me to get you ready?"

She shakes her head. "Being this close to you again has me more than ready."

With a little assistance from me, she lifts her body, places my tip at her entrance, and slowly sinks down onto me.

Oh fuuuck. It's been so long since we've been together and a lot longer since I've been bare inside her. It's so damn perfect. This is where I belong.

She's seated to the hilt, not moving at all, while tears leak from the corners of her eyes. She breathes a sigh of relief. "This still feels good."

I can't help but smile. "Were you afraid it wouldn't?"

She nods. She's so adorable.

I can't help myself. I lift the top half of my body so I can kiss her. Chest to chest, with my arms wrapped around my girl, and without our bodies otherwise moving, we gently kiss for minutes on end, both savoring every second of it. Neither of us is in a rush to move this along as we finally reconnect.

"Bails, have you seen my—"

We break our kiss and turn our heads toward the opening door. Who else? Kamryn.

She looks at us and smiles. "Ooh, plot twist. I suppose she needs this. Though I sort of imagined you'd be tying her up. Anyway, have you seen my AirPods?"

Bailey sighs. "I'm a little busy here, Kam. Can you come back later?"

Kamryn waves her hand dismissively. "Nah, I'll find them. Just give me a second."

The lunatic starts opening drawers and crawling on the floor looking under the bed. She even fucking flips through the blankets right next to us on the bed, searching. As if my dick isn't very clearly inside her sister.

My patience is officially gone. "Kamryn, get the fuck out of this room right now! You want to see someone tied up, you crazy fucking bitch? I'm going to handcuff you to your bed at night if you don't get out of here. This. Second."

Her lips curl up in amusement as she winks at me. "Save that fire for my sister. Fine, I'll go. Let me know when you're done. I need them as soon as possible...but not too quickly."

She begins to walk toward the door but then turns her head back at us. "You have a good body, Tanner. Maybe I should develop a Daddy fetish like my sister."

I point to the door. "Out!"

She giggles as she mercifully exits the room and closes the door behind her. My eyes meet Bailey's again. I think we both have a brief moment of shock before we simply start laughing. It doesn't get more absurd than Kamryn Hart.

"Your sister is certifiable."

She smiles as she nods. "I know. But I love her more than anything."

I place her hand over my heart. She can undoubtedly feel it beating hard and fast. Looking her in the eyes, I admit, "I know the feeling of loving someone so completely and fully that there's literally nothing in the world you wouldn't do for them. So much that you would gladly switch places with her to take away her pain. Willing to do anything just to put a smile on her face."

Her brow furrows in question. "Are you talking about me?"

I can't help but smile at her naivety. "I am. It's impossible not to love you. Trust me, I tried." I squeeze her hand on my chest. "This is where you reside. You always will. I think I've known all along, but I was afraid." I run my thumb along her lower lip. "I'm not afraid anymore. I want you. I want us."

She moves her hands up my body until she's rubbing her fingers through my beard. It's something she always used to do, something I've missed. I can smell her sweet breath mingling with mine. I could stare into her face all day long.

Her hair is up but messy. Her eyes burn with both love and desire. Her cheeks are flushed. She's my everything. I have zero doubts about that.

Our lips finally meet again. Our kiss before Kam-interruptus was slow and sweet. This one is immediately full of passion, need, and longing. Warmth floods my entire body as her tongue caresses mine and our chests rub against each other.

My hands explore every inch of her back. Her skin is soft and smooth. She briefly flinches when they move over the scar from her surgery, but I set her at ease right away. "Shh. It's nothing but a reminder of your strength and resilience."

She nods as she finally begins her movements on me, slow at first, but once she gains a little confidence, it turns into something much closer to a full-blown bounce than I would have expected. Every instinct in my body wants to flip her over and fuck her senseless, but I know she wants to be in control, and I want to give her the temporary reprieve she desperately craves.

Before her lips meet mine again, she breathes, "You don't have to be gentle."

I immediately dig my fingers into her hips and thrust

up. She sinks her teeth into my lower lip and mumbles, "Yes, like that."

We eventually find a groove with us both giving and taking. Our bodies work together like a perfectly choreographed dance. They always have.

The sounds in the room are a beautiful symphony of her wetness, our bodies slapping together, and our mutual moans of pleasure. It's music to my ears.

I feel the telltale signs of her impending orgasm as her pussy flutters around me. "Oh god, Tanner, so good."

"Let go, sweet girl. Come all over Daddy."

Her head tilts back, and she lets out a loud moan as she digs her nails into my shoulders. As soon as I bend my head and suck her nipple into my mouth, her pussy grips my cock and she comes. I immediately let go and gush into her with a low growl.

I breathlessly fall back with her on top of me and dot kisses all over her face. "I've missed this. I've missed *you*."

She lets out a simple yet satisfying, "Hmm."

Her body is like Jell-O right now. It's been a long time since she didn't pull away from me right after sex. I'm holding her for as long as she'll let me.

She happily sighs before starting to pull away. I squeeze her. "Don't go. Let me hold you." I don't want this closeness to end.

"I need to get cleaned up."

"Stay here. I'll clean you."

She nods, and I gently place her back on the bed before going to her bathroom and grabbing a wet, warm washcloth. She allows me the autonomy to do what's needed. I love the intimacy of it.

Afterward, I crawl back into bed, and she lets me hold her all night. Sans one more interruption from her crazy sister needing the damn AirPods, we sleep blissfully wrapped in each other. I've never been happier.

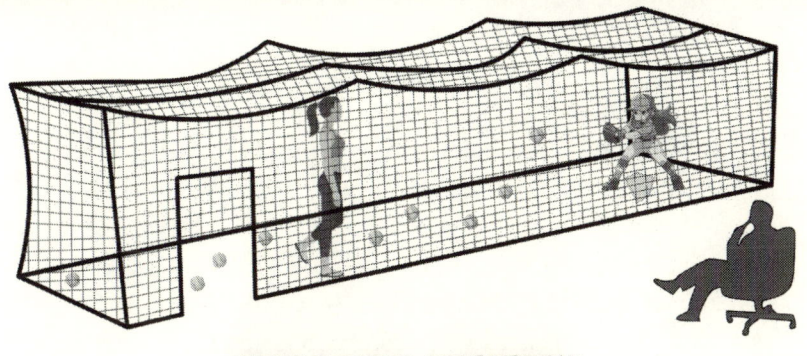

CHAPTER THIRTY

BAILEY

It's been over a month since I let Tanner back into my bed. I'm not sure I realized just how much I needed him until I had him again. He's with me every single night, loving me, giving me anything and everything I need. It's been breathing life back into me, making me feel whole in a way I haven't in nearly a year.

The intimacy between us grows every single day. Even Kam hasn't been on my case about it. She sees how much I need him and how much my closeness to him has helped me.

On the recovery front, I feel like I'm getting stronger every day. I'm finally able to be more independent. We had a bonfire to burn that damn shower chair. I never want to see one of those again.

My friends have all been amazing. I think they must have some sort of schedule because the house is always full of people and laughter.

Even though my workouts are getting more strenuous and lasting longer, I don't get as tired as I used to. My fingers are working, enabling me to get back into writing. I initially resented Tanner for pushing me on that front, but writing in the afternoons has become therapeutic for me. One book is just about done, and I've come up with a new concept for my second. Tanner said he knows a few publishers and will happily contact them on my behalf.

Kam mentioned us moving back into our apartment. I know we need to have this conversation with Tanner. He'll be more than happy to get rid of Kamryn, but I don't think he'll warm to the idea of me leaving. The truth is, I don't want to leave this house. My mind has been swirling with thoughts of my future maybe not looking exactly like I always thought it would. Do I need marriage? Do I need children of my own when Harper fills me with so much joy?

With my physical strength and abilities gradually coming back to me, I'm able to do some of the smaller things that bring me happiness, like getting up early and making breakfast for Harper every morning. I can't believe how much I missed cooking for her. I've also been making dinner for everyone at night. It's equally as therapeutic for me as anything else I do. I love our big group meals so much. I feel like we're back to a general place of happiness as opposed to feelings of sadness over the accident.

It's a Saturday morning. I'm at the stove in Tanner's huge T-shirt and my shorts, making a big batch of pancakes for our full house. Tanner is behind me in only flannel pajama pants, unable to keep his hands off me. That's something that he's become more liberal with as the weeks have gone on. Except in front of Harper, he's always touching me and no longer cares who's around. I can only hope no one realized what he was doing to me under the blanket while we all watched a movie the other night. I drew blood on the inside of my cheek as I bit it, trying to keep quiet through my orgasm. The crazy man then sat there subtly sucking on his fingers. All it served to do was turn me on again. I can't seem to get enough of him. I don't think I'll ever have my fill.

I slap his hand as it slips up my shirt to grab my braless boob. "Stop distracting me. Don't you want breakfast?"

In his sexy, gravelly morning voice, he responds, "I already had breakfast. It was delicious."

I smile. "Not *that*, you sex maniac." I reach back and make a small grab for his very hard cock. "You better take care of this before anyone else wakes up."

He thrusts it onto my ass, kisses my neck, and mumbles into it, "Why don't *you* take care of it?"

I giggle. "I already did."

Suddenly I see Fallon's legs appear, walking down the stairs. I try to push him away, but he doesn't budge. Maybe he hasn't seen her yet.

Nope, it's obvious. He just doesn't care.

She arrives at the bottom of the steps and stops short when she sees us. "Umm, sorry." She fidgets a bit. "Ooh, this is awkward, but it's a good opening for me to tell you that I'm moving back to my house tomorrow."

Tanner doesn't make any attempt to remove his body, currently glued to mine, but looks up. "Do you think it's time?"

She nods. "Bailey is more than ready for outpatient treatment. She's doing great. I'm not going back to work for another two weeks. I'll come by in the mornings for physical therapy until then."

I wish he wasn't groping me in front of her. It feels disrespectful. I elbow him away a little to create some space.

He softly whispers, "I like when you're rough with me."

I try to ignore the sex machine attached to me and look at Fallon. "I'll never be able to repay you for everything you've done. You gave up your life for me over the past three months. I'm so appreciative of you and know I wouldn't have come as far as I have if it wasn't for you."

She smiles. "Tanner didn't really give me a choice in the matter, but it was honestly my pleasure. You're a medical marvel at how quickly you've recovered. I've never had a patient work this hard. It's not surprising that you're an accomplished professional athlete."

"I feel like a normal person now, but I still have a long way to go to get back into game shape. I can't grip the bat quite right." I make a show of my reduced grip strength. The doctors had mentioned to me that minor things might take longer or might never return. My ability to grip smaller items tightly seems to be one of those things.

I've been in that batting cage every afternoon trying to get my swing back. It's not even close yet. The bat keeps flying out of my hands.

"Give it time. You're still healing. Your body is working on reconnecting everything. Playing any sport will be tough for a little while longer, but if you keep up with your therapy, I truly believe you can get there. Your being in such fantastic shape beforehand was certainly a contributing factor to your accelerated recovery time."

"Speaking of playing sports, guess who's coming over today for a little one-on-one rehab on the basketball court?"

Fallon's face lights up. "Sulley?"

Sulley moved back to her hometown during the off-season but did visit once shortly after my accident. She checks in with me all the time though. She's very sweet.

Fallon fangirls over my friendship with Sulley and is dying to get on the basketball court with her.

I nod. "Yep, I told her she was going to have some major competition in Fallon Montgomery."

"Eek. I'm so excited." She jokingly narrows her eyes at me. "I'm still going to work you hard this morning. You're not getting out of that."

I smile. "I wouldn't want it any other way."

We hear the familiar footsteps of Harper running down the stairs. She's surprisingly loud for a little kid. Tanner backs away from me just before she comes into sight.

Her eyes light up. "Pancakes?"

I nod. "Yep."

"Pineapples in mine, please."

PAYOFF PITCH

"As you wish. You're going to turn into a pineapple."

"I want to be like you and Kam. You two always eat pineapples."

Tanner smirks. "Yep, Bailey sure does eat a lot of pineapples."

I ignore the innuendo and ask Harper, "Did you go to the bathroom?"

"Yes. Dad definitely won't know the word today."

Tanner grumbles, "It's Daddy, not Dad, and you haven't stumped me yet, bug."

Harper rubs her hands together and raises an eyebrow. "Taradiddle."

Fallon, Harper, and I all turn to Tanner. His face falls. Oh my god. He doesn't know.

Fallon and I look at each other wide-eyed. Holy. Shit.

Realization hits, and Harper's face breaks out into the biggest grin I've ever seen.

Kam walks in and winks at Harper. I think she may have had something to do with this word.

She pops a pineapple slice into her mouth. "Looks like you stumped him, Harper. Tell your ignoramus father what it means. Better yet, use it in a sentence."

Harper crosses her arms. "When someone says Daddy knows *every* word in the dictionary, that's a bit of a taradiddle."

Kam nods emphatically. "Truth."

TWO HOURS LATER, we're in the gym where Fallon has been kicking my ass. Kam had plans this morning. It's rare she misses a session. It actually makes me feel good, like she thinks I'm progressing and don't need constant support from her anymore.

I'm doing a few free weight drills when I look at Fallon. "I'm really sorry about Tanner being so handsy with me in front of you. I've told him to stop, but he doesn't listen."

She shrugs. "You two should act how you want in your house. I'm the outsider now."

"It's not my house, and you're never an outsider here. You belong here more than I do."

She exhales heavily. "He's different with you than he was with me. He's a...better partner."

"Does it bother you?"

Her lips twist a bit. "I'm not going to lie and tell you that I don't have moments of hurt, because I do, but it's not because I still want him or anything along those lines. I'm under no illusion whatsoever that I'll be getting back together with Tanner, whether you're in the picture or not. I irrevocably broke our marriage. It's on me. Frankly, I'm happy to see him this way. I was afraid that I broke him in my shame spiral."

"He doesn't blame you for anything."

She tilts her head to the side. "What has he shared with you about the end of our marriage?"

"He told me that you were unfaithful one night, but that he was an absentee husband and father leading up to it. He feels he's equally, if not more, to blame for the destruction of your marriage."

Tears fill her eyes. "He's always been so classy about it." She shakes her head. "I don't deserve it."

I start to defend her, but she holds up her hands.

"He's spent the past six years against marriage and more kids because of my actions. That's very clear to me. It's a burden I've carried for what feels like forever."

"Fallon, you had a moment of weakness with a stranger. Stop beating yourself up about it."

She takes a few calming breaths. "Have you heard the name David Schumaker?"

I shake my head. I haven't.

"He was Tanner's best friend. They were close since their freshman year of college, and they originally moved to New York together. He was the best man at our wedding. He always had a bit of a thing for me, but I laughed it off as harmless flirting. Tanner wasn't the jealous type over me, and he, too, thought it was innocent." She pinches her lips together, overcome with emotion before continuing. "I can't begin to express my feelings of loneliness at the time. I lived in a city with no family and very few friends of my own. After grad school, all my friends moved away from New York. My husband was never around. One night, Tanner and I were supposed to go out to dinner. I was so excited. I planned a whole fun evening and even bought a new dress. I had a babysitter and was standing by the door ready for him to come home and pick me up. He texted that he was caught up and needed to cancel. That was it. A text. At the time we were supposed to be leaving. I was so embarrassed in front of the babysitter that I pretended like he was downstairs waiting, and I left. I took a cab to a place we had been to a million times. Here I was, out at a bar, drowning my sorrows over the state of my marriage, and in walked David. He sat with me and let me cry as he fed me drink after drink. He kept saying things along the lines of *he's never realized what he has. I would never treat a woman like you that way. You're one in a million, Fallon.* Before I knew it, we were in an alley around the corner where I let him fuck me against a brick wall." Her eyes drift away as tears leak from them. She whispers, "I cried the whole time."

I pull her into my arms. "Oh, Fallon. It sounds like you were forced into it."

She shakes her head on my shoulder. "No, I knew what I was doing. Was I trashed? Yes, but part of me wanted to hurt Tanner as much as he hurt me. I don't blame David. Is he a piece of shit for doing that to his best friend? Absolutely. Am I equally a piece of shit for doing that to my husband? One hundred percent."

She pulls away and wipes her eyes. "I came home, and he was reading some contracts in bed. He didn't ask me where I was. He didn't apologize for missing dinner. He didn't even look at me. Here I was, doing something terrible to our marriage and my husband didn't care enough to stop reading his damn contracts. It made me snap. I've never felt more unseen. I first got into the shower and physically scrubbed my body clean until it was red and raw. Then I walked out and scrubbed my conscience clean. I told him what had happened. I think I wanted him to yell and scream at me, to show that he cared, but he didn't. He calmly got up, got dressed, and went to David's to beat the shit out of him." She lets out a laugh. "I think he was more impacted by the end of his friendship than he was by the end of our marriage."

"I'm so sorry, Fallon. You didn't deserve any of that."

She gives me an incredulous look. "Me? You feel sorry for *me*? *I* was in the wrong. *He* was the victim."

I shake my head. "I think you were both in the wrong, and you were both victims. Neither of you are bad people. It was an unfortunate situation. Maybe the marriage didn't work out, but you got Harper out of it. Something wonderful came from it. You shouldn't regret anything."

She wipes her eyes. "Christ, you're like a damn ray of sunshine. Is there any situation where you can't find the positive?"

I giggle. "I haven't been feeling very sunshiny and positive the past few months."

"You've handled it with grace. We're all entitled to our moments."

"Back at you, Fallon."

She nods in understanding.

Suddenly realization smacks headfirst into me. "I suppose I now better understand Tanner and why he keeps people at arm's length."

"He does. You've made a lot of progress with him on that front. Don't give up on him. Honestly, Bailey, when I see him happy with you, it helps my own recovery. For over half a decade, I've carried around this guilt that I ruined his chance at happiness, but he's happy with you. I want that for him."

Our conversation leaves me wondering if we can't one day be more than what we've been.

PAYOFF PITCH

TANNER

I'm standing at the window watching Sulley, Bailey, Fallon, and Harper all happily play basketball on the outdoor court. It's a little cold out, but it doesn't seem to bother them at all.

Bailey looks so happy, even though I can see that some movements are still a little off for her. It's clear she takes joy in playing. She has a great shot. I know she was an all-state basketball player growing up.

Kamryn walks into the kitchen. I turn to her. "You don't want to play with them?"

She scrunches her face. "Nah. I suck at basketball. That was her thing."

"Why didn't she play in college?"

"Because we wanted to play together." She toggles her head from side to side. "Well, I possibly wanted her to play softball more than she actually wanted to play softball. The prospect of going to separate colleges wasn't palatable for me. I had to do something about it. She'd be good at any sport. She's the better athlete of the two of us."

"As much as it pains me to compliment you, you're an elite athlete, Kamryn. I'm sure you know that."

"I have my days, but it's true that she switched to softball because I begged her to."

"I'd make a comment about her always doing everything for you, but there's no denying you've been here for her the past three months."

"I'd do anything for her."

"I realize that." I smile. "It's why I tolerate you."

"You tolerate me because you're in love with her."

"Hmm. I suppose that's true."

"Listen, I want to tell you how much I appreciate what you've done for my sister. This environment was so much better for her than a rehab hospital would have been. I know that's why she's doing so well."

"I'd do anything for her too."

"I'm glad you feel that way because I think it's time for her and me to move back to our apartment."

My face falls, and she notices.

"I assumed you'd be happy to get rid of me."

"You? Yes. Her? No."

She blows out a breath. "Again, I'm appreciative of what you've done for her. Don't take what I'm about to say as any lack of gratitude for everything. The rekindling of your relationship has been good for her mental health during this difficult time, but it's not good for her long-term mental health. I'm asking you as someone who just said he'd do anything for her to please let her go. It's time."

My jaw tightens. "I can't do that." I nervously scratch through my beard. "I was planning to call your father soon, but I bought a ring. In fact, I bought it before the accident. I want to marry her."

Her eyebrows pinch together. "What happened to you never getting married again?"

"Bailey happened."

"What about kids? She loves Harper like her own, but she's meant to mother a gaggle of kids, not just one."

"Can I ask you to keep something between us for one more week?"

"I can try. I'm not very good at secrets."

"Fair enough. Also, before the accident, I had my vasectomy reversed."

She's got a look of pure shock on her face. "What?"

"When you guys were in the playoffs, a few weeks before the night of the accident, I had a procedure done to reconnect things in hopes that I could give her the children she should have."

"Why doesn't she know this?"

"I was supposed to go back a month after the surgery for them to test me to see if...the pipes are reconnected properly. At first, I didn't go because of everything going on with her. Then I just wimped out. If the answer isn't what I want, I know I need to let her go. But the appointment is set for next week. I'm going to find out one way or the other. If it's what I hope for, I'm going to ask her to marry me."

She sits down. I think she's in shock. "Wow. I didn't see this coming."

"I love her, Kamryn. I want to be with her. Whatever it takes."

She's quiet for a few long beats before she stands, seemingly eager to get away from me. "I...umm...have a few errands to run. Tell her I'll be home for dinner."

She walks out the front door, but the doorbell rings less than five minutes later. Maybe she forgot her key.

I open it and nearly fall over in shock. "Linc?"

He smiles and opens his arms. "No hug for your baby brother?"

BAILEY

I've had the best afternoon shooting hoops. I can't do everything I once could, but my shot isn't bad. For some reason, it makes me happy to know that I haven't completely lost it.

It was Sulley and Harper against me and Fallon. Fallon is great, and Harper isn't bad. She's such a natural athlete. I smile at her as we walk back toward the house. "You got your mom's basketball skills. You should play on a team."

She shakes her head emphatically. "I love softball. I'm a softball player."

"You're young. You can play both. In fact, at your age, you *should* play both."

She turns to Fallon. "Do you think I'm dexterous, Mommy?"

"Yes, baby, and I agree with Bailey. You should play lots of sports."

Sulley blinks a few times. "What word did she just use?"

Fallon and I giggle. I answer, "Harper learns a new word every day. She amazingly remembers them and uses them appropriately in conversation."

"What does that word mean?"

Harper answers, "Having skill at something with your hands or limbs. Like ambidextrous is having skills with both hands."

Sulley twists her lips. "Hmm. I think I need to study more if I'm going to hang out with you, Harper."

We're all laughing as we walk back toward the house. I invite Sulley to stay for dinner, but she says she has plans. Before leaving, she turns to Fallon. "Have you ever considered working with athletes?"

Fallon nods. "I work with them all the time."

Sulley responds, "I mean on a permanent basis. I know the Beavers are in the market for a full-time dedicated physical therapist. We told management we want it to be a woman. A woman like you with a basketball background would be perfect. And look at what you did for Bailey. Obviously it's more intense during the season, and you need to travel with the team, but you'll be able to set your own hours in the off-season. Something to consider. We'd love to have you."

Harper's face lights up. "Does it mean courtside seats for her daughter?"

Sulley laughs. "I don't see why not."

Harper jumps up and down. "Yes, Mommy. You should do it."

Fallon smiles. "I'll think about it. Thanks for asking, Sulley."

Sulley nods and says her goodbyes as she makes her way toward her car.

When the three of us walk back inside, I notice a familiar-looking man sitting with Tanner.

Fallon stops short and her face falls. "Linc? What in the hell are you doing here?"

Harper gasps. "Mommy. Language. That's ten dollars."

Linc. Linc. It takes me a second, and then I remember that it's the name of Tanner's younger brother. The one he rarely sees. The one he doesn't think highly of. I don't remember seeing a photo of him beyond the age of eight, but I feel like I've seen him before. Maybe it's because he resembles Tanner, though he's not nearly as attractive.

Linc rolls his eyes. "Warm as ever, Fallon. I didn't think I'd see *you* here," he wiggles his eyebrows, "but I certainly don't mind the view."

He then oddly stares at me. It's kind of making me uncomfortable, but perhaps I'm reading too much into it. I hold out my hand. "Hi, I'm Bailey. It's nice to meet you."

He tentatively shakes it. "You too...Bailey? Did you say your name is Bailey?"

"Yes."

Tanner stands behind Harper. "Bug, you probably don't remember him, you haven't seen him since you were really little, but this is your Uncle Lincoln."

Harper shakes her little head. "I don't remember."

He smiles at her. "Maybe we can do something to get to know each other. Do you have dolls? We can play with them. Or maybe a make-believe kitchen? We can have a tea party."

Harper scowls at him. Fallon and I smile at one another. Harper doesn't have a single doll or engage in tea parties. She's a tomboy through and through.

Tanner bites back his own smile. "Linc, she's not four, and she happens to be into sports. Mostly softball. She probably throws harder than you ever did."

"Oh, I didn't know. Aren't sports for boys? You should play princess dress-up, polish your nails, or other things like that."

I mouth to Fallon, "He's a douche."

She nods and mouths back, "Yep."

Fallon grabs Harper's arm and grits out, "Why don't we go get cleaned up for dinner? Perhaps we can find some noise-canceling headphones for you." She gives Lincoln a death stare.

I point toward my room. "I think I'll go get cleaned up too. Nice to meet you."

His eyes move up and down my body. It's creepy as hell. Tanner definitely notices. I can see him getting uptight.

After I shower, I'm sitting on my bed in my towel when there's a knock at the door. Assuming it's Harper, I say, "Come in."

Linc walks in. I immediately tighten my towel around my body, feeling very exposed and uncomfortable. "Oh, I thought you were Harper. Can you please wait outside? I need to get dressed."

He gives me a smug smile as he disregards my request and steps further into my room. "Nothing I haven't seen before, sweetheart. Tanner tells me you're a bit of an item. Are you going to tell him we've had sex, or am I?"

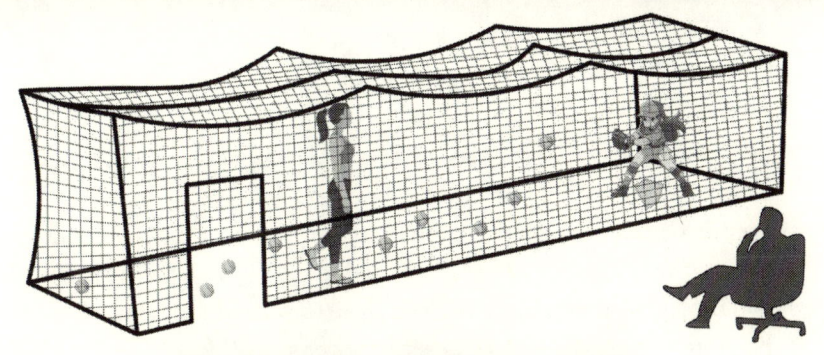

CHAPTER THIRTY-ONE

BAILEY

I'm speechless. I have no words for this. I think I'm in shock.

"Excuse me?" I hear Tanner's deep voice bellowing in the hallway. "What did you just say to her?"

Tanner walks into my room and takes in my state of undress. His eyes practically bug out of his head.

Linc shrugs. "Sorry, man. I know you're into her, but we slept together a decade ago. You went to UCLA, right?"

I can only nod.

He winks at me. "Best lay I ever had. I never forgot it. And she gives great head."

I'm not sure what Tanner is going to do right now, if his anger will be at me or his brother, but he grabs Linc by the shirt and shoves him against the door. "Watch your fucking mouth. Don't disrespect her. Ever."

I cry, "Tanner. I've never touched him. I swear. I have no idea what he's talking about."

He nods. "I know. You'd never stoop so low as to let a guy like him near you." He then turns his attention back to Linc. "Why are you here? What do you want?"

405

"I wanted to reconnect. To spend time getting to know Hailey."

"It's Harper, you fuckwit, and you've had nine years to connect with her. Stay away from my kid. Is it money you want?"

Linc smiles awkwardly. "I'm a little low. If you're offering, I'd be up for that. Dad has become a scrooge in his old age."

I hear the front door open and close. Kam stops at my doorway to see the commotion, easily assessing that it's a contentious situation. She looks Linc up and down. "You look familiar."

Linc's head toggles between me and Kam as things start to make sense to both Tanner and me.

Kam slowly nods. "Oh, right, I remember you. Rocco's Tavern in LA. Worst lay I ever had. You never forget your worst. Why are you here?"

I answer, "He's Tanner's brother."

She lets out a laugh. "Holy shit. That's crazy. I guess Tanner got the sexual prowess genes in the family." She looks down at Linc's crotch area. "And the girth. And the length. This fucker was blowing up my phone for months. Remember when I had to block a guy who I was afraid was going to boil a bunny in our kitchen? This was him. He wouldn't take no for an answer. What a loser."

I remember that. She was actually a little freaked out. She showed me a picture of him so I knew to steer clear. That's why he looked familiar when I saw him.

Tanner tightens his jaw. "I think this little visit is over, Linc. I don't want you in my house ever again. And stay away from my daughter, Bailey, Kamryn, and Fallon. This is your one and only warning."

He pulls him away from my doorway toward the front door. Kam walks into my room and shuts the door.

"That guy is an asshole."

I nod. "Yep."

"I'm guessing he and Tanner aren't close?"

"No, not at all. He was a dick to Harper earlier. It's certainly clear Fallon doesn't like him. Poor Tanner."

"Poor Tanner? What about me? I had sex with the shithead."

"You've had sex with a lot of shitheads. That's nothing new."

She lets out a laugh. "True. Good ones are hard to find, both men and women. I swear there are more crazy people than normal ones out there."

"And which category do you think you fall into?"

She smiles. "You're feeling salty today. I like it."

I sigh. "I'm just realizing why Tanner is the way he is. I may have been too hard on him."

"Maybe I have too."

My jaw drops. "What?"

She rolls her eyes. "Look at all he's done for you. I know we clash at times, but he's obviously gone above and beyond for you, Bails."

"I know he has." I motion toward her shopping bags. She's got three big ones. "I see you were shopping. What did you get?"

"I needed a few things." She reaches into one, pulls out a box of condoms, and throws it on my bed. "I got you some more condoms. You two have been having so much sex, you must be running low, right?"

She stares at me oddly, waiting for a response. This feels like a test. One I'm about to fail.

I scrunch my face. "I know it's against your rules, but we haven't been using condoms."

She pinches the bridge of her nose. "Bails, didn't the doctor tell you they had to remove your IUD when they removed your ovary?"

I shrug. "Yes, but Tanner is shooting blanks. It doesn't matter. He hasn't been with anyone else since me. I needed to feel all of him. I needed things to be like they were the first time around." Holding up my hands before she argues with me, I say, "I know you think I'm in over my head, but I truly needed him the past month. He's my happy place. You know it's helped me."

She takes a few deep breaths and rubs the spot on her forehead like she does when she's stressed. I'm not sure why it's a big deal.

"Kam, I need to talk to you about something and you're not going to be happy."

She visibly swallows but simply nods her head. I think on some level she knows what's coming.

"I know you mentioned us moving back home."

"And?"

"Kam, I love him. I'm in love with him. I know I'll never love a man more than I love this one. If the ups and downs of the past year have taught me anything, it's that. And I know he loves me right back. You can't possibly argue with that."

"What are you saying?"

"I'm saying that maybe I can be flexible. Maybe I don't need marriage and kids of my own if I have him and Harper. Sometimes life doesn't go exactly how you plan. You've got to go with it. Look at what happened to me. It's given me some perspective." I run my fingers through my hair. "I just...I need him. My heart belongs to him. I can't be without him anymore."

She has an unreadable look on her face. I thought she'd yell and scream about me giving up on what I've always wanted for a man. It's basically against everything she stands for.

In the wake of her deafening yet odd silence, I continue, "I think you should move back to the apartment. I'm going to talk to Tanner about telling Harper about us and giving this a go. My heart is telling me that this is where I belong. He's my home."

She remains silent. Kamryn Hart has never been silent about anything in her entire life.

"Say something. You not screaming at me is unsettling."

She lets out a nervous laugh before pinching her lips together. "I think I need to sit on it for a minute. Let me know when dinner is ready. I...umm...need to do some research on my computer."

What?

"Oookay. If that's what you want. I'm happy to talk about it whenever you're ready. I need you to be okay with it before I move forward. I need your support. I can't have the two people I love the most playing tug-of-war over me. I want us all on the same page."

She nods. "Just give me time to process. I want to react... appropriately."

She's legitimately the knee-jerk-reaction queen of the world, but if this is the first time in her life she wants to take a step back and process, I'll certainly let her do so.

She starts to leave, but I stop her. "Hey, Kam?"

She turns her head back and answers, "Yeah?"

"Thanks for being here with me the past few months. I couldn't have gotten through it without you."

Tears fill her eyes, and she walks over and hugs me. "It's been an honor. You've taken care of me for thirty years. It was about time I returned the favor. I love you, Bailey, more than anything in the world. I truly want you to be happy. You deserve it."

"I love you too. And I want you to be happy too. That's why I want you to go home and get back to your real life. You probably miss sex."

She scoffs. "I've been having sex. I might be a good *sister*, but I'm not a nun."

I giggle. "That was a good one."

She squeezes my arm. "Don't make any rash decisions about your life until we've talked, okay?"

I feel like she's speaking in code. "Umm, okay."

She leaves, and, as I'm getting dressed, Tanner walks back in with pain written all over his face. "I'm sorry about that. He's... umm...not a good guy. Never has been."

I shake my head. "I don't care from my perspective; I just didn't like the way he talked to Harper."

He sighs. "Neither did I. It doesn't make the way he talked to you remotely acceptable. I'm truly sorry you had to endure that."

He sits on my bed looking a little distraught.

I'm seated next to him, rubbing his back. "Are you okay?"

He shakes his head. "Even though I want to wring her neck at times, you're lucky to have Kamryn. I've grown to envy your relationship with her. So much so that I was planning to reach out to Linc to see if we could rebuild our relationship. When he showed up at the door, I allowed myself a moment of hope that we could turn things around, but I see now that it will never happen. He's not a good guy and no amount of optimism will ever change that."

I lean my head on his shoulder. "I'm so sorry. It can't be easy."

"It's not. You're so fortunate to have someone you inherently trust. Someone you know will *always* be there for you."

I want to reassure him that I can be that for him forever if he wants, but I want to wait to talk to Kam more about it. She asked me to wait, and I want to give her that. I need her support. I hate seeing him like this though. It makes me sick to my stomach. In fact, I'm actually getting sick to my stomach.

I sprint toward the bathroom, fall on my knees in front of the toilet, and puke up everything I've eaten today. Where did that come from? I hope I'm not coming down with something.

Tanner is suddenly there holding my hair, rubbing my back. "Are you okay?"

I nod. "Sorry. That came out of nowhere."

"Why don't you get into bed? You may have overdone it today. I'll order dinner."

He's right. I'm exhausted. I did a lot today. Getting into bed suddenly sounds like the best plan ever.

TANNER

I order Chinese food and extra soup for Bailey. When I call everyone to dinner, Kamryn asks where Bailey is.

PAYOFF PITCH

I answer, "She wasn't feeling great. I think she did too much today. She's in bed."

"She seemed fine an hour ago when I was in there."

"Right after you left, she puked. That's why I ordered dinner. I didn't want her to have to cook. And I stocked up on plenty of soup for her."

Kamryn chokes on her water. "She puked?"

"Yes."

Harper asks, "Can I bring Bails her soup? She's probably hungry."

I nod. "Sure, bug. I'm sure she'd love it even more coming from you. Grab some crackers."

Kamryn mutters, "Bring the whole box of saltines. She's gonna need it."

Harper leaves with a tray of soup. Kamryn appears nervous and on edge. I've never seen her this way.

I stare at her. "What's wrong with you? Are you sick too? We don't need a sick house."

She wordlessly shakes her head.

I ask, "Is this about our conversation from earlier today?"

She widens her eyes and motions toward Fallon.

I shake my head. "Fallon knows. You can speak freely."

"She knows you had a vasectomy reversal?"

Fallon pinches her eyebrows together. "You already had it? You told me you were thinking about having one. I didn't know it was done."

I nod. "I thought I told you I had the procedure. I guess not. I had it months ago, shortly after we originally spoke about it."

"Oh. Did it take?"

"I find out next week. I'm waiting to tell Bailey, hoping it's good news."

Fallon's head jerks before her eyes rapidly move from

Kamryn to Bailey's room and back to Kamryn again. Her mouth widens. "Didn't Bailey have her—"

Kamryn blurts out, "Yes, she did."

I shake my head in confusion. I feel they're speaking a different language. "What the hell are you two talking about?"

Kamryn stands and grabs Fallon's hand. "We need to talk. We'll be right back."

They run out of the kitchen toward Kamryn's room, slamming the door behind them.

Has everyone lost their minds?

Harper reemerges. She and I end up having dinner alone. I have no idea what Kamryn and Fallon are doing. I know they've gotten close, but I'm clearly missing what's going on under my sorority house roof.

Suddenly, the doorbell rings. I open it and find Arizona and Ripley. Arizona is holding her belly, heavily pregnant now with her and Layton's daughter.

Ripley looks nervous. "Umm, Kam called us." She points toward her room. "We need to go see her."

I open the door wider. "Please, join the Montgomery looney bin. Everyone is off their rockers tonight. Must be a full moon."

They run toward Kamryn's room, open her door, and then quickly close it behind them. I look back toward Harper, and she shrugs. "They're all maniacal, Dad."

I nod. "I can't argue with that. I think I have too many women in my life."

She giggles. "Girls are the best."

I smile. "You're right, they are, but I don't think I ever imagined this many living in my house."

Harper and I have just cleaned up dinner when the psycho sorority sisters all reappear, dragging an unwilling Bailey with them.

Kamryn nervously chews her lip as she moves her

pointer finger between Bailey and me. "Umm, we need to talk to you two." She nods toward Harper. "Almost all of us. Rip, can you take Harper upstairs?"

Ripley shakes her head with a huge grin on her face. "No way I'm missing this."

Kamryn sighs. "Arizona, can you?"

"Heck no. I'm staying right here."

Fallon rubs Harper's arm. "Sweetie, I'm sorry, but we have a few adult things to discuss. Can you go take your shower now? You can stay up past your bedtime tonight if you do."

"Can we watch a movie?"

Fallon smiles. "Anything you want."

Harper agrees and happily runs upstairs. When we hear her bathroom door close, Fallon points toward the living room and cryptically says, "I think we should all sit for this."

As we're walking, Bailey glances at me, and I shrug. She's clearly in the dark like me.

I pull her to sit next to me. I've given up pretending we're anything less than what we are. I love her, and I don't care anymore who knows. It's not like everyone sitting here doesn't know anyway.

I stare at the firing squad. "Can someone clue us in on what's happening?"

Everyone turns to Kamryn. She laces her fingers together and places them in her lap. "I think there's been a little...miscommunication, but I'm pretty sure the result is a good one, even if unexpected."

Bailey pinches her eyebrows together. "What in the world are you talking about? You're acting so ducking weird tonight."

Kamryn looks at me. "Tanner, I'm going to go ahead and assume that you did not know that Bailey's IUD came out with her ovary." She raises her eyebrows like something should be clicking for me.

"No, I didn't know tha—" And then it hits me. I whisper, "Holy shit."

Kam nods. "Yep." She pops the P.

My mind starts spinning. No IUD, a vasectomy reversal, no condoms, a lot of sex, and she just threw up with no real reason. She's pregnant. Bailey Hart is pregnant with my baby.

A huge smile finds my face. I honestly wasn't sure how I'd feel about it if the moment ever came, but now that it's here, I couldn't be happier. Ecstatic. Thrilled. Elated.

I turn to Bailey, the only one still in the dark, and hold up a finger. "Give me one minute. I need to go get something."

I run to my office and open my safe, grabbing the box that's been sitting there for many months before practically sprinting back to the living room.

I stand in front of Bailey and grab both her hands. "Sweet girl, I love you so fucking much."

Her eyebrows pinch together in confusion. "Umm, okay. I love you too, but I feel like Kam was just about to tell us something. Can we discuss this later?"

Without another word, I drop down to one knee.

Her jaw drops with it. She swivels her head and looks at everyone else with their giant grins before turning back to me. "W...what are you doing?"

"I know we took the road less traveled, but I love you and want to spend my life with you."

"I...I thought you didn't want to get married again?"

"You've brought color to the parts of my life I thought would forever remain gray. I'm a changed man from living under the light of your love. I want to spend every single day of my life loving you back. Marry me."

I think she's toggling between emotional and confused.

"Why right this second? What am I missing? I love you, and I want to be with you, but I feel like everyone is in on a big secret but me."

"Do you want to spend your life with me? As husband and wife?"

Tears begin streaming down her cheeks. "I do. And I know what I'm giving up, but I'm willing to give that up to be with you. And I'm not really giving it up. I gain Harper and I love that little girl as much as I would if she were mine."

"I know you do. It's one of the million reasons I love you."

"Tanner, we don't have to get married. I'm okay to just be with you."

I grin. "I want to marry you. More than anything."

She turns her head to Fallon. "Are you okay with this?"

Fallon has tears in her eyes. "I love you for thinking of me during your special moment, but I'm more than okay. Another person loving and protecting Harper sounds good to me." She smiles. "To be clear, I'm not going to be one of those ex-wives whose entire TikTok personality is videos of her and her baby daddy's new wife getting along." She exhales a breath. "Fine, one TikTok a month together. But that's it."

Bailey and all the girls laugh. I don't know what any of that means, but I think it was nice.

She looks back at me with all the love in the world and nods her head emphatically. "Yes, I'll marry you."

I kiss her hard and place the ring on her finger. Rubbing her face with my thumbs, I look into her big brown eyes and shock her to her core. "One more thing. Sweetheart, you're pregnant."

BAILEY

Tanner looks at me with all the love in the world. "Sweetheart, you're pregnant."

I'm frozen in place. I can't move a single inch. He said pregnant, right?

I hear Kam's voice. "Don't piss yourself." She mumbles, "She pissed her bed until she was eight."

I blink a few times, turn to her, and deadpan, "Perfect time to bring that up. Thank you."

She smiles and winks at me.

I look back at Tanner, who has an enormous grin on his handsome face, and say, "I'm pregnant?"

He nods. "Yes."

"How?"

Again, Kam's intruding voice says, "It happens when a penis goes into the vagina and—"

"Kam! Not now!" I snap.

The four of them giggle.

Tanner squeezes my hands. "I didn't know about your IUD being removed. And you didn't know that I had a vasectomy reversal."

"A what? When?"

"A vasectomy reversal. A few weeks before your accident."

"Why didn't you tell me?"

"I was going to wait for them to run tests to make sure it worked before I told you. I didn't want to get your hopes up only for you to be heartbroken."

"You haven't had the tests yet?"

He shakes his head. "No."

"Then I might not be pregnant."

Kam interrupts, again, "I did research on it. Reversing it isn't that big of a deal. The success rate is high. That, along with your lack of birth control, the number of times I heard you orgasm through the thin walls the last several weeks, and the vomiting all tell me you're pregnant. I'm also your twin. I can sense it." She grabs her boobs. "I think my tits have sympathy tenderness."

I'm still processing. "I think we should go buy a test."

Kam nods. "That's where I was earlier. I bought, like, a dozen pregnancy tests for you."

"Okay. I'll take one in a minute." I look at Tanner. "Is that why you proposed? Because you think I'm pregnant?"

He raises one of his thick eyebrows. "And I just so happened to have had a ring for you? No. I bought this ring before your accident, at the same time I decided to get the procedure. I was waiting to propose until I found out if I could give you babies. I won't take that from you."

I take his handsome face in my hands. "Whether I'm pregnant or not today or ever, I still want to be with you. I love you. I will always love you, no matter what."

He places his hands over mine and looks at me with all the sincerity in the world. "Maybe the pregnancy changed my timeline, but I want to marry you. I have for a long time." He smirks. "I promise it's not a taradiddle."

I can't help but smile.

He stands and pulls me to him. "Let's go find out. Whether you are or aren't, I want to marry you and will do my best to give you everything you want and deserve. I can think of nothing better than filling this house with you by my side."

My heart feels like it might burst. I love him so much. I can't help but bring my lips to his.

Ten minutes later, six pregnancy tests are sitting face down on the bathroom countertop, because it's totally normal for each person to want to read their own. It's a good thing I had a huge bowl of soup and therefore plenty of pee inside me.

Kam giggles. "This is like our senior year in college when all four of us were late and took pregnancy tests."

Fallon asks, "All four of you? That's odd."

She nods. "Turns out we're all dumbasses and took our birth control pills a week earlier than we were supposed to."

Arizona shakes her head. "I still don't know how we managed that. We took our pills together at breakfast each day and not one of us noticed that we started a new pack a week early. Idiots."

Ripley smiles. "We were planning a *Golden-Girls*-like baby commune. All living together with our babies."

Fallon's eyebrows raise. "Ooh, that sounds like fun."

Kam nods. "It would have been. We had this whole *Golden-Girls* theme planned, but it was going to be Olympic gold, not old-age gold."

Tanner shakes his head in disbelief. "Can we focus on the task at hand?" He glances at his watch. "It's time."

My mouth is dry. My heart is beating fast. Everyone takes a test and holds it face down in their palm. Tanner flips his over first. A big smile finds his handsome face. "Pregnant."

I look at mine, and a moment of absolute bliss takes over. Warmth floods my body. I whisper, "Pregnant."

Everyone else flips theirs over.

"Pregnant."

"Pregnant."

"Pregnant."

"Pregnant by Daddy Tanner's new and improved swimmers."

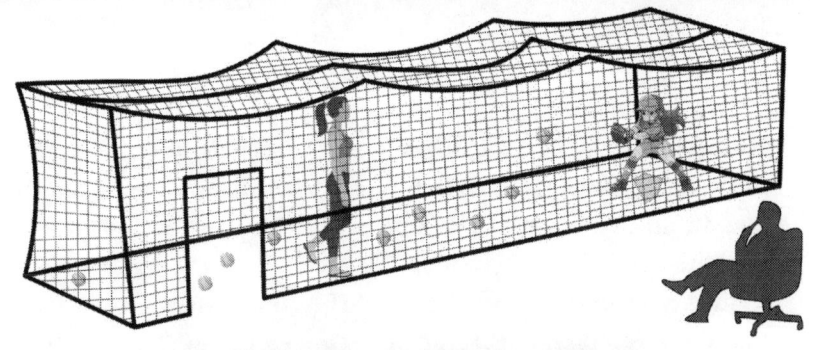

CHAPTER THIRTY-TWO

FOUR MONTHS LATER

TANNER

We're walking into my wife's twenty-week ultrasound. And by we, I mean Bailey, me, Harper, Kamryn, Arizona, Ripley, and Fallon. It's a damn army of women. It always is.

Despite my initial hesitation, Bailey insisted that Fallon be here. Aside from the fact that the two of them are extremely close, she said our babies are Harper's siblings and Fallon should be with us. Yes, babies. We found out at nine weeks that it's twins.

The evening we discovered that Bailey was pregnant, Bailey, Fallon, and I sat down with Harper and told her that Bailey and I were together and getting married. We decided not to also throw the pregnancy at her that night.

Harper was understandably a little confused at first. Fallon giving her full support helped put Harper at ease. And then she became exceedingly happy at the prospect of

Bailey being in her life forever as her *bonus mom*. That's the term Fallon used. Bailey burst into tears when Fallon said it, and the two of them cried and hugged for minutes on end.

We got married quickly. Within two weeks of that night. Bailey didn't care at all about a big wedding. She wanted something intimate at the house. It was family and close friends. She let Harper and Kamryn plan most of it, which made parts of it...interesting, but Bailey was happy, and therefore, I was too.

No bride has ever looked more beautiful and happy than Bailey that day. She wore a simplistic silk white gown with spaghetti straps. It almost looked like a nightgown as it hugged her curves perfectly. The emotions I felt as she walked down the aisle were like nothing I've ever experienced.

I spent a lot of time considering my vows, remembering how impactful Layton's were. As he stood beside me as my best man, I got to recite my own vows to my bride.

Bailey, as you know, I wasn't searching high and low for someone to share my life with. I spent years closing myself off to that possibility. I never let people in. I never opened my heart.

As it turns out, I was waiting for you, sweet girl.

In you walked that first day, a ray of sunshine. Beautiful, perfect sunshine. That's what you are. You light up the lives of everyone around you. You're mature beyond your years. You're kind, selfless, loving, compassionate, and so stunningly beautiful that here we are more than a year and a half later, and I still can't take my eyes off you. I love everything that you are.

You seem to know what I need exactly when I need it. You challenge me. You make me a better man. I've always prided myself on being the boss. Being in charge. Being in control.

Yes, she both smiled and blushed at the control comment.

But with you, I don't have to be all those things all the time. You're my true partner. My equal. My everything.

I know I'm supposed to make you feel secure and cherished, but it's you, sweet girl, who makes me feel those things. I will strive every single day to be worthy of your love and return it back to you a million times over.

It's my absolute privilege to build a family with you, go through life with you, and to grow old with you, though I'll be doing that well ahead of you.

That line earned me a lot of laughs.

I love you today. I'll love you tomorrow. I'll love you forever.

When we returned from our honeymoon, we told Harper about the baby. She was so happy that she burst into tears. I don't think I ever realized how much she ached for a sibling. The next day, we found out it was *siblings*.

Bailey will be taking this season off from softball. It's easy to say that it's because she'll be heavily pregnant during the season, but the reality is that she's not fully recovered from the accident and we don't know if she ever will be. There's still something slightly off with her fingers. Her doctors have said to give it more time and hard work, but that it's more likely than not that her playing days are behind her. She can lead a completely normal life, just not one as a professional athlete or as an Olympian. She was calm as they told her the prognosis. Oddly enough, I think it made her more determined than ever to get back into playing shape and to make that Olympic team. She has time to decide whether or not she'll make that push. I'll support her efforts in any way I can.

Here we are at the ultrasound. Kamryn is pacing, doing her daily dose of driving me nuts. The technician is moving the wand all over Bailey's stomach until our two little babies come into view. The sounds in the room are music to my ears. Their heartbeats are strong.

Harper gasps. "Wow. That's prodigious."

The technician stops what she's doing and stares at Harper. The rest of us smirk at yet another person in awe of Harper's vocabulary.

Kam asks, "Well?"

The technician gives a fake smile. "I take the videos and photos. The doctor will be in to discuss the results."

"Just fucking tell—"

"Kamryn!" I bark out. "Let her do her job. I swear to god, I will kick you out. Nothing would make me happier."

She bats her eyelashes at me. "Yes, Daddy Tanner."

I pinch the bridge of my nose. "I can't believe I'm stuck with you for the rest of my life."

"Pft. Just be glad I'm not living with you...for now."

I mouth, "Never again," to her, and she smiles.

Arizona can't contain her excitement. "I hope it's girls. They can be teammates with Ryan."

Arizona and Layton had a baby girl named Ryan. She's got the blondest hair, bluest eyes, and is beautiful, just like her mom.

Bailey squeezes her hand as she takes a deep breath. "All I care about is health. Healthy babies."

We're now waiting for the doctor, and all the girls are fussing over Bailey. I wish this was just the two of us. It's our moment, and I'm standing behind five other people. I can't even touch my wife from here.

The doctor walks in and her eyes widen. "Wow, we've got a big crew today."

I mumble, "Too big."

Bailey reaches her hand for mine. "Tanner."

I happily part the sea of women and make my way to my wife to grab her hand. She's got her other arm around

Harper's waist as Harper bounces up and down with excitement.

The doctor smiles. "I reviewed all the scans, and everything looks perfect. The babies are healthy and growing as they should."

Bailey exhales a breath of relief. "Thank god. Thank you so much."

Her eyes toggle between me and Bailey. "Do we want to know the sex?"

I nod. "That's why we've got an army of women here."

She smiles. "Brace yourself, Dad, because you're about to add two more women to the crew."

Bailey has tears of joy dripping down her face. I can't help the big grin on mine. "I'm more than happy to spend my life surrounded by spectacular women."

Kam throws her arm around me. "Just think, at least one of them could be like me."

Dear god...

LATER THAT NIGHT, I'm in bed in boxer briefs reading through a few contracts while Bailey is in the bathroom. When she emerges in nothing but her short, light-pink silk robe, I nearly lose my breath. She looks like an angel.

I immediately toss my paperwork and reading glasses aside as I watch her roll her shoulders and wince. "Are you in pain?"

She stretches her arms across her body. "My shoulders are tight. Physical therapy while pregnant is kicking my butt."

I crook my index finger. "Come here, beautiful. Let me rub them for you."

Her face lights up. "Ooh. That sounds nice."

I spread my legs and pat the space between them. "Let Dr. Montgomery take care of his favorite patient."

She gives me a sexy smile before sliding onto the bed and leaning back into my waiting arms. After slipping her robe down a bit, I begin rubbing the soft, smooth skin of her shoulders. I bury my nose in her hair, taking in her intoxicating scent. Every little whimper and moan she makes causes my dick to stir.

My hands begin to take on a life of their own, and she slaps one. "My nipples are well beyond my shoulders. You're a little out of your jurisdiction, counselor."

I chuckle at her use of legal lingo. "Whoops. My hand must have slipped." I begin to kiss her neck. "You might enjoy it though."

She shakes her head in exasperation and then leans back into me. I love the feeling of her soft, bare back on my hard chest.

She tilts her head up and kisses my jaw. "Keep rubbing my shoulders. It feels so good."

"I know something that might feel even better."

She giggles. "A little longer, hornball. I want to talk to you about something, and I know once we start things, there will be no talk. At least not by me."

"True." I go back to massaging her shoulders.

"I know I can't fully commit until after my pregnancy, but, if I'm still up for it after the girls come, are you really on board for me to give my career another go? It's going to be hard on all of us." She sighs. "But I think I'll always wonder if I don't at least try."

I pepper kisses over her neck. "I'm a thousand percent on board if you choose to pursue it. I think it's amazing that you're even considering it. You know I'm putting infrastructure in at the office so that I can take a step back if needed. I want this for you if you decide you want it.

What could be better than our daughters seeing their mommy working her ass off to achieve her goals?"

She whispers, "What if I fail?"

"I don't think you will. I know my wife."

"The doctors don't think it can be done. What if they're right?"

"They don't know the heart in Bailey Hart Montgomery. And if the committee doesn't select you, we'll simply go cheer on your sister and your friends. I'll be proud of you for leaving nothing on the table. You don't have anything to prove to anyone. You were an all-American athlete with national championships and world championships. A gold medal would be nice, but it doesn't define you or your career."

She nods while opening and closing her fist. "I just wish my grip would come back. It's driving me nuts."

I take her hand and place it on my cock, now standing at full attention above the band of my boxer briefs. "Your grip feels good to me. I'm always happy to provide a little after-hours physical therapy for you."

She giggles. "You're a pervert."

"My wife is sexy as hell. I can't help myself."

"You used to make fun of Layton all the time for referring to Arizona as *my wife*, and now you do it all the time too."

Hmm. She's right. "I never thought about it. I think I'm just so happy that you are, in fact, my wife. I know how lucky I am, and I'll never take it for granted. I've learned from past mistakes in my life. I'm laser focused on us, our family, and our happiness. That's all that matters to me. Or at least it matters the most."

She reaches up and runs her fingers through my beard. "Are you happy? Was today okay for you? Are you disappointed to not have a son?"

I run my hands down and over her belly several times.

"Not even a little bit. In fact, this is what I wanted. Two more Harpers? Sign me up."

She smiles. "It could be two more Kams."

I suck in a breath. "Bite your tongue."

She lets out a laugh. "Even I couldn't handle that."

I can't stop rubbing her belly, loving that she's growing our girls inside her. "How about two Baileys? Then I'll want a hundred more."

She looks up at me. "You'd consider more after these two?"

I think about it for a moment as I continue running my hands all over her body. "Unbelievably, yes. I can't imagine anything better than watching you be a mother or seeing more products of our love. We'll have to stop at some point though. I don't want to be eighty when they're in kindergarten."

She reaches her hand back again and gives my cock a squeeze. "You feel young and healthy to me."

I nibble on her ear. "How about you sit on him and find out just how healthy he is?"

She nods. "In a minute. I enjoy this intimacy with you. Laying in your arms with your hands all over me. I love you, Tanner. So much."

"I love you too, my sweet, sweet girl. My life had a lot going on before you came into it. The count was full and it could have gone in a lot of different directions."

She let out a laugh. "Are you telling me I was the payoff pitch?"

I smile into her hair. "Yes you were, and I hit a grand slam."

EPILOGUE

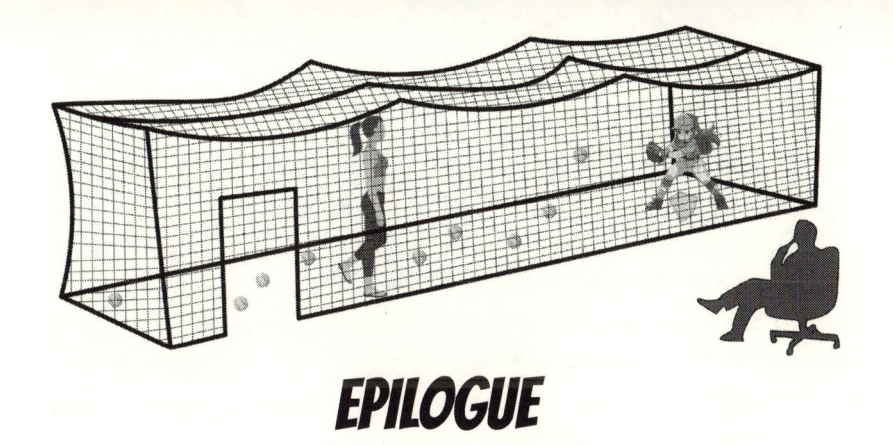

TWO YEARS LATER

BAILEY

I'm huddled up with Kam, Ripley, and Arizona. Our arms are lovingly wrapped around each other as we absorb everything and try not to let the emotions overcome us. We're about to take the field for the gold-medal game of the Olympics. Win or lose, this is the last career game for me, Ripley, and Arizona. Kam is on the fence, but I think she'll retire too. She has so many good things going on in her life right now, but that's a story for another day.

We all have tears in our eyes. This is truly the end of an era. I love these three women so much. Kam might be my only blood sibling, but I consider all three of them my sisters.

I take a few calming breaths so I can try to form the words needed. "It's truly been an honor and a privilege to play with you three. We all know that I wouldn't be here without you. Thank you for everything you've done to support me."

When it came time to choose the Olympic team, the

committee was on the fence with me because of my injury. I sat out a season, technically because of my pregnancy, but we all know my recovery wasn't far enough along at the time that I would have been able to play even without the pregnancy.

Sitting out a year ended up being the absolute best thing for me. It reignited my passion for the game. Suddenly, getting back into playing shape and making this Olympic team became extremely important to me. I think I needed to prove to myself that I could do it, and I also wanted to show my three girls, especially Harper, all about hard work, dedication, and perseverance.

It wasn't easy, and it didn't happen overnight, but I eventually got myself there. Last year, my first season back, certainly wasn't my best. It's hard to be out of the sport for so long. But this past season, I think I was pretty close to how I was before the accident.

The Olympic committee was choosing between me and another infielder. A much younger, accident-free, kid-free infielder. Without an ounce of hesitation, Kam, Ripley, and Arizona let them know that their acceptance of this team was dependent on the committee making *the right decision*. They went into a whole thing about team chemistry and the like. I wasn't sure how I felt about it at the time, but I was selected for the Olympic team, and I've worked my ass off every day since to make sure they don't regret it.

I eventually earned the starting job at second base and haven't sat a single inning in the Olympics yet, happily contributing to our path to the gold-medal game.

After a tear-filled final pregame huddle, I do a quick scan of the crowd searching for my family. I spot them waving at me, all in my jersey. Tanner is talking to someone, but his eyes are on me. He blows me a kiss when our eyes meet. He still gives me butterflies in my stomach.

I then find our three girls right next to him. Lorelei is on Harper's lap and Aurora is bouncing between Fallon's lap and my father's.

Fallon and I get so many eyebrows raised at our close friendship. We're more like sisters now. Tanner jokes that he's usually the odd man out of the three of us. But the fact is, we share a daughter. We're family. What's the alternative? For us to have animosity between us? That only hurts Harper, something neither of us are willing to do. And, if I'm being honest, I genuinely like Fallon. I always have. She's not just Harper's mom or Tanner's ex-wife. She's my good friend.

Fallon has been my biggest cheerleader after my husband and my sister. She's been a constant presence in my physical therapy and has been a huge help with all three girls when I needed to train. The twins call her Aunt Fallon, and she showers them with love and affection. Like Fallon said the night Tanner and I got engaged, the more people who love your children, the better.

Not all families look the same. It doesn't make one better than the other. This is ours, and, while maybe it isn't what I imagined when I was younger, I wouldn't want it any other way.

We've got about five minutes until the game officially begins. I sneak off in their direction. We had to stay with the team this week, so I've barely seen them.

I walk straight over to Tanner. He leans over the stands, grabs my face, and says, "I've missed you, sweet girl," before he softly kisses my lips.

I run my fingers through his beard, which is a little grayer now, but I refuse to allow him to shave it off even though he's mentioned it a few times. It's too damn sexy to disappear. I mumble into his lips, "Me too. I hope we can find some alone time tonight."

He smiles into my mouth. "Fallon said she'd take the girls."

"Best. Sister. Wife. Ever."

He chuckles. "I suppose."

I hear Harper's voice. "Ugh. Will you two stop the PDAs? It's repugnant."

Harper might have a few years until she's officially a teenager, but sometimes it feels like those years are already upon us. She does, however, still hold onto her word of the day toilet paper. She won't let go of that part of her childhood. I don't know what she's saying half the time. I keep a pocket dictionary on hand. Her little sisters can't wait to potty train so they, too, can have "Harper toilet paper."

I hug all three girls and then Fallon. I whisper in her ear, "How do you feel?"

She whispers back, "Like if the wind changes and I catch a single whiff of the hot dog over there, I'll lose my breakfast all over Rory's head." Rory is what we call Aurora.

I giggle. "Me too."

We're both newly pregnant. She's the only person besides Tanner and Kamryn who knows about my pregnancy, and I think Kam and I are the only ones who know about hers. It's very early on for both of us, but I'm excited that we get to do this together and that our kids will grow up together.

The game finally gets underway. I do my best to take in the moment. How many people get to play in a gold-medal game in the Olympics? Knowing the journey I took to get here, and that it's my last game ever, makes it all the more special. I'm walking away from the game on my terms, no one else's. Whether the medal around my neck is gold or silver, just being here makes me a winner.

IT'S BEEN a defensive battle of a game. Kam and I turned a huge double play last inning during a big moment. We smiled at each other as we ran off the field together. We've turned thousands of them over the years, but we both realize that it was likely the last one.

We're down one run going into the bottom of the sixth inning. Ripley has pitched an amazing game, but the other team got lucky and scored one run at the beginning of the inning. We've only got six outs left to make this happen.

Arizona leads off the inning, gets on base, steals second, and then Kam bunts her over to third base. I'm kind of surprised our coach didn't have Kam swing away, she's one of the best hitters in the world, but I guess she wanted Arizona at third base.

This is the first runner we've had at third all day. We can't strand her there. Unfortunately, the next batter strikes out. Shit. We needed her to put the ball in play for Arizona to score, but it didn't happen.

There are two outs as I step up to the plate for what will likely be the last at-bat of my life. It's simple. I need a hit to tie the game. Making solid contact. That's all I'm focused on.

I drown out the noises of the capacity crowd, doing my best to avoid the weight of the moment. It's just me and the pitcher in a theoretical game of chess.

The first pitch comes in a little low and I don't swing, but it's called a strike. Deep breaths, Bailey, deep breaths. It's only a gold medal on the line.

The second pitch comes in; I'm set to swing but pull back at the last second when I see it's coming in high. The ump calls it a ball. Phew.

I'm dripping sweat. I can feel it covering me like a blanket. Everyone is depending on me. Score Arizona. Score Arizona. Tie the game up.

I swipe my cleats through the dirt and get myself set in the box. I lift my bat just above my shoulders. You've done this thousands upon thousands of times, Bailey. Just watch the ball hit the bat.

The pitcher winds up. I peek down and see the catcher set up inside, meaning the ball was likely called to be an inside pitch. I need to turn on it. I track the ball as the pitcher releases it, get my bat out in front, and *crack*.

The sound is almost deafening. I know the second I make

contact that it's gone. Time momentarily freezes as I stand there in awe watching the ball easily sail over the left field wall. A home run. I just hit a home run to give our team the lead. In the Olympics.

My jaw drops and my hands find my head as I stand in disbelief. Arizona, approaching home plate, laughs and yells out, "You might want to take your trot around the bases, girlfriend. Smile pretty for the cameras."

Oh shit. I need to move. I take off in a dead sprint, even though I don't have to. I think I might even twirl once or twice. The crowd is going berserk. As I'm rounding second, I find my family, who are going absolutely insane. Harper looks like she's going to jump out of the stands. Tanner has tears streaming down his cheeks with the biggest smile I've ever seen. The twins don't truly know what's going on, but they're feeding off the excitement around them and jumping with Harper. How special is it that all three girls got to be here to witness this moment?

As I round third, I see my entire team waiting at home plate for me. They're screaming in excitement, encouraging me to come to them. I charge at home plate with my fist held up proudly in the air.

As soon as I slam my foot down on it, it feels like a hundred hands are slapping my helmet, arms, and back. Kam lifts me up and twirls me around, screaming out, "My sister, the hero. The unbreakable Bailey Hart Montgomery." She then pulls me close and whispers, "I'm so fucking proud of you."

So am I.

She places me on the ground and tearfully hugs me. "You're the eighth wonder of the world, Bails."

I hug her back. "I love you."

With two outs in the seventh inning, Kam makes a defensive play to end the game that she's probably the only shortstop in the world capable of making.

And then absolute mayhem ensues. There are screams of joy, a dogpile, and lots of tears. We did it. It's almost hard to believe. Our group has been talking about this day for fourteen years.

Since our first day of college. Here we are, all these years later, and it's come to fruition. All four of us had huge hands in the victory. We couldn't have scripted it any better.

As we break apart, I'm pulled into what feels like a thousand media interviews with just as many cameras on me. Kam is standing behind them with a huge grin on her face.

Unable to wait any longer, I motion for my family to join me. Harper sprints onto the field and into my waiting arms. She's getting too big for this, but I certainly won't deny her this moment.

The twins aren't quite as fast as they waddle out and both latch onto my legs. Tanner smiles as he approaches. New tears find his eyes as he leans down for a short, hard kiss. Damn, his kisses still make me weak in the knees.

He stares at me, looking sexy as sin in his aviator sunglasses, USA hat, my jersey, and jeans. "My wife, the hero. I never had a doubt."

I can't help but stare back. He's just so—

The reporter I'm currently being interviewed by interrupts my thoughts and says, "Tanner Montgomery, we'd love to chat with you about your thriving women's division. You've been instrumental in getting female athletes better pay."

He lifts his head and curls his lips in amusement. "Today I'm merely a husband proud of his wife. She just had one of the biggest clutch moments in Olympic history. Let's focus on that right now. She's living proof of someone overcoming obstacles. Defying the odds. Hard work. Sacrifice. She's a role model for millions of young girls, our three included, both on and off the field. Keep your eye on the ball, Karen." Her name isn't Karen. "Celebrate my wife. She deserves it."

The reporter doesn't know what to say, so the next one takes her turn. She asks what my plans are for the future. I've been super clear that I'm retiring after this game. I have nothing left to prove. All I want is to be with my family.

I smile at Harper. "I plan on doing a lot of coaching. I've

coached this little prodigy during the off-season for years, but now I want to coach her in the summers too. Next year she'll be eligible for the Little League World Series, and you can bet on us making it there."

The reporter looks surprised. "Oh, she must be very good to play at that level."

Kam interrupts by throwing her arm around my neck. "Harper is the fucking bomb."

I roll my eyes at her mouth but Harper giggles. "That's ten dollars in the swear jar, Aunt Kam."

Kam feigns shock. "I was singing your praises, you little shit."

Harper smiles while shaking her head. "Now it's twenty."

I grind my teeth. "Kam! Children. National television."

She shrugs. "Whatever."

The reporter looks at Harper, still in my arms. "What position do you play?"

She proudly announces, "Second base, just like Bails."

The reporter then jokes, "Do your sisters play?"

Harper answers in a dead serious tone, "They both will. Just like Kam and Bailey. I'll be training them."

TANNER

I'm in Fallon's suite helping to get the little ones to sleep. Of course, Rory is being difficult tonight when I'm dying to get alone time with my wife. Fallon told me ten times to just leave, but I feel bad. She's doing us such a huge favor.

She didn't want to, but I forced Bailey to go out for at least an hour with her teammates. She deserved to be celebrated and to enjoy the limelight. I can't begin to explain how proud I am of her. Getting back into elite

shape after both her accident and the twins was no small feat.

It took nearly a year and a lot of therapy for her grip strength to return. The doctors all told her it was unlikely that she would play again, and yet she was more determined than ever. I hope they were all watching today. Worthless fuckers.

After Rory mercifully drifts off to sleep, I kiss Fallon's cheek. "Thanks for doing this."

She smiles. "My pleasure."

I can see her starting to get emotional. "Are you okay?"

She visibly swallows and nods as tears fill her eyes. "I am. Today was pretty incredible."

Tears begin to stream down her cheeks. That's unusual except for when...

"Fallon, are you pregnant?"

She bites her lip and then nods. "No one knows except Bailey and Kam."

"Not even—"

"No. I want to tell him in person. I just found out. It was a bit of a surprise."

"I understand. Are you happy about it?"

She smiles. "Exceedingly. I didn't think I would ever get my second chance."

I hug her. "I'm thrilled for you. Our kids will be the same age."

"I know. Bailey and I are excited about it."

"I bet you are. I wonder what you're having."

"It feels a little different. I'm thinking boy. But you're definitely having a girl." She smiles. "Or girls."

My eyes widen. "Please, only one this time."

She lets out a laugh.

"Why do you think it's a girl?"

"Because you're meant to be a girl dad, Tan."

I nod. "I suppose I am. I can live with that."

"There's no one better at it." She opens the door. "Go celebrate. Have fun. The girls will be fine."

"Thanks, Fallon. For everything." She knows I mean more than this. We couldn't have made it through Bailey's training without Fallon helping with the girls.

She smiles. "Always."

I head back to our suite. Bailey should be back any minute. I want to draw a bath for her so she can finally relax after a crazy time period that saw her away from home a lot. She struggled with it, often questioning what she was doing, but it all paid off for her. Today was the culmination of everything she worked toward, and I couldn't have imagined a more fitting finale for her. She deserves every bit of the attention being thrown her way. I'm already fielding about a thousand offers of sponsorship for her, but I doubt she'll consider any.

In the elevator, I think about this journey. The ups and downs.

I chuckle to myself as I realize what today was. It was the payoff pitch.

I'm anticipating a sweet evening reuniting and celebrating with her when I walk into my hotel suite. There's nothing sweet about what's waiting for me.

Bailey is sitting at the table, completely naked except for my Team USA hat and her gold medal around her neck. Her legs are up on the table, spread open for me. I notice her closed laptop next to her. I think I know what it means.

I nod at her. "I like your hat."

She gives me a sexy smile and nods toward the large bulge now tenting my pants. "I can see that."

I nod at the medal. "I like your jewelry."

"I've got plans for that."

"Hmm." I motion toward the laptop. "Does that mean what I think it does?"

She smiles. "It does."

Bailey published a book a year ago with tremendous success. It was a child-appropriate book about blended families.

She shifted course on the sports one she had been working on for years. She wanted it to include this last part of her journey. She held off on the last chapter until the Olympics were over.

Publishers have been clamoring for it. I've been fielding offers, but she wanted to wait to see how the story concluded. Oh, what an ending it is. Her heroics of today will cause a bidding war.

She removes her gold medal and winks at me. "I gave my gold-medal performance, now it's your turn."

I'm a little confused as I take it from her, until she places her wrists together and holds them out for me. "Why don't you make use of that?"

I smile in realization as I use the ribbon of the medal to tie her wrists together. I then slowly run my fingertip up her bare leg. Goosebumps immediately spread across her skin and her pink nipples pebble. I love the effect I still have on her.

My finger continues its upward trajectory on her body until I reach the hat and flick it off. "I want to see your eyes. Keep them on me."

She nods. She knows what her intimate eye contact does to me.

"I thought you'd want it slow and sweet tonight. It's been an emotional day."

She shakes her head and runs her tongue along her lower lip. "I want you to do me in a manner in which you're questioning the whole time whether or not I'll use my safe words."

"Is that so? Well, then get on the bed on all fours. I want your ass in the air. Now."

Her eyes shade over with lust. "Whatever you want, Daddy."

THE END

Thank you for reading Payoff Pitch. Scan the below to enjoy the extended epilogue, which takes place during Harper's senior year of high school.

ACKNOWLEDGMENTS

To Bailey and Tanner: Tanner, you allowed me to return to my roots of writing older characters. Man, are you sexy. Bails, I love your inner strength and the balance you bring to life. I miss you two already.

To the Queen, TL Swan: This amazing journey would never have begun if not for you and your selfless decision to help hundreds of women. This crazy and unexpected new path in my life has brought me so much happiness. I owe it all to you. Please know that I try every single day to pay it forward. Getting to meet you in person was the icing on top. It's amazing when your mentor is even better in person.

To Lakshmi, Thorunn, Mindy, and Brittany: Thank you for being the best beta bitches a girl could ever hope for. You're there for me in both my good and bad moments, always cheering me on. I appreciate each of you so damn much. More than I could ever express in mere words.

To Jade Dollston, Carolina Jax, and L.A. Ferro: I love you crazy bitches. You're stuck with me for life.

To My OG Beta Readers Stacey and Fun Sherry: Thank you for being there for me since day one. You've been my biggest and hottest cheerleaders every single step of the way.

To The B!tch Squad Members: I remain in awe that you all continue to support my books. I love that so many of you have been with me for a long time, yet our group continues to grow and welcome new members with open arms. I appreciate all of you!

To Chrisandra and K.B. Designs: **Chrisandra**: Thank you for making me feel illiterate. That's what makes you such a great editor. **Kristin**: Thank you for helping this artistically challenged woman. Thank you for your innate ability to read my mind.

To My Family: I truly feel bad for you. An immature mother and wife can't be easy. To my daughters, thank you for tolerating me (ish). Thank you for telling everyone you know that your mom writes sex books. I appreciate that by the time you were each six, you were more mature than me. To my handsome husband, thank you for your blind support. You never question my sanity, which can't be easy. But let's face it, you do reap the benefits of the fact that I write sex scenes all day long. Every single male main character has a little of you in him (only the good stuff - wink wink).

ABOUT THE AUTHOR

AK Landow lives in the USA with her husband, three daughters, one dog, and one cat (who was chosen because his name is Trevor). She enjoys reading, now writing, drinking copious amounts of vodka, and laughing. She's thrilled to have this new avenue to channel her perverted sense of humor. She is also of the belief that Beth Dutton is the greatest fictional character ever created.

AKLandowAuthor.com

ALSO BY AK LANDOW

City of Sisterly Love Series
Knight: Book 1 Darian and Jackson
Dr. Harley: Book 2 Harley and Brody
Cass: Book 3 Cassandra and Trevor
Daulton: Book 4 Reagan and Carter
About Last Knight: Book 5 Melissa and Declan
Love Always, Scott: Prequel Novella Darian and Scott
Quiet Knight: Novella Jess and Hayden

Belles of Broad Street Series
Conflicting Ventures: Book 1 Skylar and Lance
Indecent Ventures: Book 2 Jade and Collin
Unexpected Ventures: Book 3 Beth and Dominic
Enchanted Ventures: Book 4 Amanda and Beckett

Extra Innings Series
Double Play: Arizona and Layton
CurveBall: Ripley and Quincy
Payoff Pitch: Bailey and Tanner
Off Season: Kamryn and Cheetah
Faking the Book Boyfriend: Gemma and Trey (Being published as part of the Book Boyfriend Builders collaboration)

Signed Books: aklandowauthor.com